PRAISE FOR MORE THAN ONE...

"*More Than One* stands on the shoulders of 1970s ecological science fiction greats but advances and extends the genre in a fresh, visionary, heart-felt, and richly imagined future. The best of sci-fi based restorative story-telling that broke me open and reminded me of the deep connection between living beings. It pulled me in, broke me open, and gave me hope for the future."

— Carrie Christopher

"This is not a good book. It's an incredible fantastic unbelievably real down to earth everyone needs in their life book. I have communed with trees since very early childhood. This book is a homecoming."

— Magnolia Bushnell-Alexander

"I really enjoyed this. It's a sci-fi story that's really different from what I've read before, ...really creative with the trees."

— Wayland Smith

MORE THAN ONE

CL FORS

EPITOME PRESS

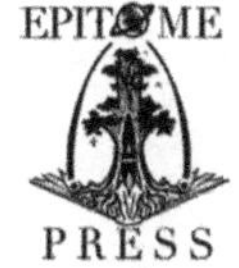

Epitome Press Publishing

An Epitome Press Book

Cover Art and Design by CL Fors

Paperback: 978-1-943212-44-6

Kickstarter Paperback: 978-1-943212-39-2

Kickstarter Hardback: 978-1-943212-40-8

Epub: 978-1-943212-41-5

Hardcase: 978-1-943212-43-9

Library of Congress Control Number: 2025917200

For the trees and the children who grow under them.

CONTENTS

CHAPTER 1

CHASING SECRETS

ERF HEADQUARTERS-ORCHARD A16

YEAR 3216

Quin couldn't bear to see the full expanse of the orchard, so she ducked down and crouched at the base of the nearest sapling. The decline was creeping in here as it did everywhere, despite her greatest efforts. This orchard, like the last she'd tended to, was a sea of sickly yellow with shocks of brown and bare branch where dead saplings stood out amongst the rest.

The scent of resinous pine and moldering leaf-litter filled her senses here on the ground where her green canvas-clad knees were pricked by fallen needles and the damp seeped through to her skin.

A16 was an attempt to mimic natural woodland: balsam fir with its dense evergreen needles, white-barked birch, pale-faced aspens with leaves like mis-hammered coins. Each of them showed signs of distress in their own unique colors, their suffering as clear as if they had faces. She reached out to caress a cheek of cool bark—hesitated, hand hovering over a fir that was weeping needles into a copper-hued carpet.

Shameful, this reticence to feel what her saplings felt, to sink herself into it with them. What good was it to be the only expert in arboreal linguistics if every forest, orchard, and solitary tree, from the great sequoias of Earth history to the shrublike remainders of today, died out? The thought hollowed out her stomach like a well-thrown fist.

That end wasn't far off. Only orchards and tame city trees were left on the planet; the giants were long dead. Planet-wide oxygen farms were a costly and inefficient replacement with Earth's organic lungs all but wiped out, and those were being shut down as well. Bureaucracy stifled larger solutions and she was the last stopgap, the last gasp of a program that could have fixed things. Just another miscarriage of scientific advancement and effort squashed by fear, funding, and functional ineptitude. . . .

It had been too long since she'd spoken with the ancient trees on Ross-128b. She was falling prey to short-sightedness. And Chase hadn't answered for so long. Silence from Chase made the doubts seep back in.

She shook her head, puffed air at the multicolored

braids that tickled her face in shades of autumn. A bitter smile pulled at her lips. The rest of her hair was its natural black, the tight curls cropped short in the back so it wouldn't tangle on the implant stage at the base of her skull, a hairstyle all in service of her symbiotic translator.

The creature that grew from Quin's biotech implant —aptly named Synesis for the wisdom she gave— reached soft nubby appendages towards the sapling in front of them, all eagerness and impatience. The Mushroom Symbiont's voice spoke in Quin's mind, chemical signals manifested in words.

Go in . . . Under, inside, burrow in . . . a taste? A taste?!

"Tabban—alright, Fitiry—My little mushroom . . . Allons-ee!–let's go!" Quin's words came in the many tongues she spoke, blended together with the arboreal language.

She set her mind back on task. Too many errant thoughts slowing her down today. She wasn't seeing the saplings for the orchard. . . . She'd blame the headache percolating just behind her eyes, and she'd blame that on the angle of the sun. All of her real problems were too big to look at just now, at least if she wanted to keep going.

On the ground in front of her, was a carpet of wilted orchard grass and Taraxacum Officinale, common dandelions gone to seed with their downy silver heads nodding around the base of a birch sapling among many. She had to focus in, one need at a time. She put a hand on the closest birch and began the upload. The first strains spread from her fingertips into the bark of the tree, then she froze—There were thudding footsteps coming closer, and she felt the whole orchard's questioning. They didn't have a grasp of history to give them fear of axes or a life long enough to have known non-human animals large enough to shake the ground. The orchard's saplings may as well have been fresh from their seeds.

"My apprentices . . . young ones like me. Here to learn from you. And they are late."

"Sergeant Fleury?" It was the soft southern lilt of Jordan's voice.

Quin turned, still crouching with a hand on the side of the tree. One of her quickest apprentices was standing there.

"Oui, Jordan?" She pulled her hand away from the tree, the papery bark tickling her withdrawing fingertips even as Synesis cried out in her mind.

Regret burned in her temples. These young ones were a distraction, another need to fill when her focus belonged on the saplings. The voice of her mushroom symbiont tugged at her attention—*treeee*—and she clenched her fists against the urgency pulsing in her head.

Sweat broke out along the lines in her mahoghany-brown forehead under the front locks of her hair. Jordan was talking again.

"Ithaca and Ronin and I, we think we could give some of the uploads to the orchard, as much as we've learned . . . so you aren't doing all of it. And for practice."

Quin scowled at the copse of saplings instead of Jordan. She brushed her knuckles across the papery bark of another birch. No answer. This one was dead already when it had been thriving just days ago.

"Sergeant Fleury . . . ?"

She forced her attention back on the waiting child. "Jordan, as the team leader you will tell them no. Listening to, communicating with each of the trees that I have reeducated, that you may do. Speak to them, go slowly. Wa, Intebihu illehum—pay attention."

Jordan tipped her head, ponytail flopping to the side along with her flailing mushroom. "But I feel like I can do more than that and—"

"You cannot. Not after last time."

"But–Yes, Sergeant." Jordan ducked her head, cheeks flaming. Her stride thumped harder than it had on the way over as she walked away.

At least she had restrained herself, ceased her arguments before Quin had to give a formal reprimand. Not a thing she enjoyed, but there was work to do here, more dire than she had expected.

Synesis strained towards the lifeless tree again and Quin reached one hand back to pet her, to comfort. There wasn't much room on the creature's back with the many large fruiting bodies that grew there, large open-capped mushrooms showing gills in a crown that framed Quin's face.

She tucked her hand between the mushrooms to reach the small, soft body and scratched gently like one would a cat, a cat with the wrinkled, naked body of an echidna with many stubby legs. Synesis was more fungus than mammal, but both were in her genetic cocktail.

All but the top two sets of appendages grew from the coppery implant stage that ran the length of Quin's cervical vertebrae. A jointed leather sling attachment like an inverse saddle supported the creature's body, ensuring its pseudopods wouldn't be pulled away from the implant stage by its own weight.

Quin pressed the curling brown leaf ends between her long sepia fingers, her close-cut nails stained with loamy soil.

She forced a smile. Pulled in a steadying breath and closed her eyes. "Your leaves, they're crisp like out of an oven, eh? Quel dommage. We will fix this for you . . . "

She didn't have to fake the concern in her voice, but she added optimism and hoped Synesis would take the hint and assist her with the proper chemical messengers to make it feel real, something to slow her heart, stop the racing thoughts of oncoming cataclysm.

She delved one hand into root-populated soil and rested her other palm on the tree's bark. She could taste the slow response to her words, a weakened mewling sort of gratitude for her presence, a muddled questioning as if this were an old and ailing mind . . . and underneath, the musty decay of languishing.

Flexing her fingers in the earth, she tamped down the fear boiling up in her belly for a second time. What this sapling needed was for Quin to speak back the arboreal truths as she'd learned them, to remind this young one who had forgotten and would keep forgetting until they could remember.

If these saplings grew large enough—she knew better than to think size or age was the issue—No, these tame trees might never be able to hold what a wild tree could. A twinge of unease teased her. She pushed it aside. No more time for doubt.

"Shhh . . . tais-toi Chér. Quiet and listen now . . ." She felt the tree's struggle through her fingertips, understood it through Synesis. The sapling was trying to remember, but it had lost the beginning of the All-Question completely. The middle was muddied, and the end was devoid of meaning without the thread that bound beginning, middle, end in a continuous loop like the growth rings of a tree.

Quin started the upload from her mind slowly, gently. Synesis translated what Quin delivered as imagery, words, and ideas—into chemical signals and blueprints for growth, for protection from disease, and for expanding the underground network for communication between this birch sapling and all of the others in A16.

Quin broke into a sweat, a sharp, throbbing pain in her skull and an ache in her chest. Linking herself into the muddled, aching confusion of this young mind hurt. The tree struggled to grasp and keep even a fraction of what she was imparting.

The words slipped away. The meaning with it. She

repeated each refrain of the message again and again until that bit seemed to take hold. She added more of the All-question, linking the parts in hopes of forming a web of knowledge interconnected enough that it would hold.

The drift of knowledge began as soon as Quin stopped repeating and added something new. The tree's despair crept back in.

No! Still young—You keep going. . . . That's the message. If you hear it all at once, you'll see it! You'll remember.

She pushed harder. She sped the flow from a drip to a gush and flooded the tree's awareness with the All-Question, willing it to fit, willing it to stick.

She conjured it first from memories, the same memories it had linked to as it settled into her own mind when she'd heard it sixteen years ago.

Her daughter Lumina, tiny—the size and shape of a tadpole, growing, then grown to child-size, no longer staring up at her through the membranes of the AUC she'd grown in.

Chase. There was always Chase—from the before times when they'd met, saplings themselves, young, giddy, that spark in her eyes that meant she'd never sit still. Their hands pressed into the same ruddy tree bark, fingers linked, and then after, on Genti-6 with little Lumina between them, looking up through Chase's green eyes, their own seedling, then grown to sapling, strong but still so young.

The memories bubbled freely into the link between Quin and Synesis. Synesis translated into the same cycle that the Tree song would be delivered, *soil—seed—sapling—growth—rest—recede*—in an endless loop that grew in size and complexity until it built from single note to full orchestra of knowledge.

Lights flashed in Quin's mind like strobes of red and purple—a warning—and when she took note of her body state she found she was dizzy, lightheaded. Synesis pulled her back, stopped her from further recklessness, cut off her desperation.

She sucked in greedy gulps of air to ease the dizziness and sat back, only one hand in contact with the tree.

The sapling needed a pause as well. She eased back in, gentle—slower like before, but the small tree couldn't fit much more. The birch began repeating the All-Question through her roots to herself and to all the trees in the orchard, just the beginning, but it spread through the orchard's shared roots and the sparse mycelial network in the ground.

Quin sat back on her heels, brushed the clammy feeling from her palms onto her uniform. She pulled a handheld computer from her pocket and searched the schedule. Twenty more orchards were showing signs of imminent decline, and she'd need to upload for them today. There would be more tomorrow.

Fatigue settled heavily on her shoulders, but it couldn't smother the relief of a successful upload.

She sunk to the ground and found it warm against her back. The sun heated her mahogany skin in a way that stilled her. Lassitude made her muscles loose and heavy, her mind slow—slow like the trickle of an upload these trees could take.

There was a light breeze stirring the orchard's leaves, making the tiny quaking aspens sing with a loud but musical rustling. The fir saplings gave off the scent of warm, golden sap. Peaceful, but once she stood, Quin stared at the small trees with a growing heaviness like dry rot in her limbs. She'd be back here in a month, unless something changed.

It isn't going to change on its own.

The wind kicked up just enough to push at her back as she left the orchard, threads of sharp, acrid fear running along her neurons. Synesis would be soothing it away if the fear was unjustified, but it wasn't. The ecological team was the next step. Their proposals were the only way to stop treading water until the decline overtook them and Tree became a dead language, a part of history, and Quin with it.

"Allons-y saplings!" She placed a hand on the nearest little fir tree and repeated the message directed at her apprentices. She felt them through the mycelium, linked to other trees across the orchard. The unique flavor of their minds greeted her, Jordan's independence and strong sense of self in bold blues and golds, a taste of saffron and cayenne. Ithaca, mild, patient like the flow of sun-warmed honey in the hive, and Ronin, solid, kind. She pictured long-standing edifices when she felt him in the link.

It was time to go back, before fatigue from the

uploads made a waste of what day was left, so she urged them faster.

Break the link.

She tried to temper her growing impatience, but they felt it through the mycelium and one by one disconnected from the trees. They followed behind as her feet picked up the speed and rhythm to keep taking the next step, and the next, a microcosm of what she was doing with these trees, just taking each step until she could get someone with more power and resources to listen.

GENTI-6

Lichen couldn't talk, at least not in a way that she should understand, not without a mushroom symbiont to translate, and Lumina wasn't an Arboreal linguist. She didn't even live on a planet with trees. . . . Nope, lichen couldn't talk to her. The reminder bore repeating. Because the whispers in her head were different now, louder, more like words but not, and she wasn't as sure as she ought to be that the lichen wasn't—*couldn't* be speaking to her.

Lumina scrunched her nose at the tufts of crusty plant-life on the newest addition to her rock collection. She leaned in, scowled at it like a cat stung on the nose by a scorpion, still irresistibly curious—and then touched it with the tip of her tongue.

Blech—Bitter!

And tingly, and did it just thank her . . . ?!

With a shiver, she dropped the slate-grey rock from her hand and brushed fragments of yellow, scabrous, lichen off on her green overalls. She spit into the trashcan under her desk even though the taste was already gone—She hadn't eaten it after all. If any was left on her skin, she might keep hearing it, and she needed it to stop, for now at least. She smooshed the sides of her face between her hands, fingers digging into the yellow-brown of her skin enough to blanch the knuckles, as if she could rub away that odd, tickling feeling in her mind.

"Ugh . . . okay, just wait a minute."

There were still residual tastes of what she'd heard, little echoes flitting through her head like ghost-lights in the dark. Maybe she was losing it. First that tingling in her fingers as far back as she could remember, as soon as she was big enough to toddle and pick up bits of lichen and moss, or Genti-6 brambles. Later, the tingling became a sense of connection, of wordless communication with the growing things she touched. Now it was so much louder, almost words. . . .

This wasn't the first time she'd thought that something was wrong with her. It was the second or third time, at least. This was just the first time she was certain of it. And the urge to keep testing it wouldn't go away.

She hesitated, reached, and then brushed her fingers across the lichen again, cringing in anticipation as she did so.

No words, no language . . . She just felt that bubbling, tingling feeling across her nerves, the same that she'd always felt. She could almost believe she'd imagined the words, but then it came again.

Not clear words at first but a sense of pleasure, encouragement, and other things she couldn't understand but was certain were actual words. All she knew was that the lichen appreciated being pet by her tentative fingers, and it particularly liked the salty taste of them. But that was too much of a leap without questioning it. It was pure fantasy. She was sixteen, not five.

No, this was something that would have to be explained—even if it meant she was sick, an illness of the mind maybe. But there were other possibilities first and she knew where to look. Somewhere she shouldn't.

The papery yellow lichen seemed to stare back up at her from the otherwise smooth back of the grey-blue rock in her hand. The Genti-6 colony site was covered in rocks like these, and she had many of them in her collection. She put this one down gingerly, careful not to brush it with her fingers again. Then her eyes strayed to the computer tucked into her mother's bookshelf in the family library.

She felt her armpits get sweaty—guilt-sweat, an easy hint that she was doing something she shouldn't. Better to just wait, just ask for permission. But Chase was in the birthing caves for the season and, while her mother would answer her call eventually, Lumina didn't *want* to wait, and she didn't want to ask her. It would hurt

Chase's feelings that she didn't want to ask her these things. No doubt.

Her cheeks flushed hot with shame, but it didn't change facts. She would rather ask Quin. Quin was the one who might know—It was a stupid thing to want. Good luck with an answer from the Tree-Whisperer. Earth was a long way off from Genti-6 and the Tree-Whisperer was in high demand. She wasn't allowed to forget that. Chase made sure of it.

But if Quin knew what was wrong with her, that meant she'd always known and had a reason not to have told her already.

Again Lumina's eyes were drawn to the metallic glint of that computer, thinner than any of the books next to it, with a single power light like one drowsy eye blinking in slow motion. Sleep mode.

It winked at her.

Your mother isn't here . . . Wink.

They're just old letters . . . Wink.

Lumina stepped over the collection of rocks spread out on the floor and reached for the thin body of the computer. It was right there. She could access all of her mother's files and her letters from Quin—Chase wasn't big on passcodes. She could find out more about her own history.

Taking the thin, pliable device, Lumina folded it in fourths and shoved it under her arm. She climbed into her favorite chair, tucked herself into the worn green-velvet cushions. She loved the curved arms and claw feet, polished by age and admiring hands, and she loved that the antique was solid enough to have had a hover function added on.

She tapped the little panel installed under the right arm and it rose, with smooth bobbing motions, like a ship on a mellow sea. Anticipation fluttered in her stomach. She knew so little about her origins, just what Chase had told her when she was little. Every night the story of the baby-gift . . . Now that she was older, she didn't know how to feel about being a gift—spliced together, grown and carried just so that Chase could have her.

When she was small it seemed like a special thing, the way her mother told the story as she brushed and braided Lumina's soft, dark umber curls, weaving words the way she wove her hair.

Lumina sat on Chase's lap listening with rapt attention as she told her how she'd been grown in a capsule, an AUC— artificial uterine chamber—strapped to the body of a dear friend, nourished by her bloodstream and grown, then brought here to Genti-6 for Chase to raise.

It wasn't a completely novel way to come into existence. AUCs weren't unheard of if someone didn't have a womb, or else didn't want to use theirs, but they weren't common. The AUC itself wouldn't explain what was wrong with her. There were three children her age in the colony that she knew were AUC born and they weren't out of the ordinary.

Lumina opened the computer, a tight scowl of determination pulling her brows together in a little V above her green eyes. She had Chase's eye color, the shape too. What did she have of Quin, her other mother, the Tree-Whisperer? Her skin tone, some of it anyway, more melanin than Chase but not as much as Quin, and her hair that defied gravity all around her face in a fluffy crown of springy curls. Maybe other things. Like ingredients in a soup, she was a mix of them. . . . There had to be something in those old letters. She could read just enough to find it, and then ask questions. She just needed to know the right questions to ask first.

Chase's old files and messages weren't hard to find on the hard drive; the file was called "Quin Letters".

She laughed, covered her mouth, and then stared at the door as if anyone was there to hear it.

She could search for keywords but then she might miss something. Instead, she set them to sort by file date and opened the first.

She held small screen cradled in her hands, cheeks normally the color of sunlit ochre sand flushed pink through a peppering of ruddy freckles. The same burnt umber flecks appeared in her green irises as if spices had been sprinkled across her face without care for where they'd land. Sprinkles—That's what Chase called them. The memory made her want to close the screen out and confess.

Would her mother—the woman called Chase in the letters—be angry if she knew Lumina was reading them, and was it fair for her to be angry when she kept so tight a lock on her stories, even the ones that should have been Lumina's as well? She read the words on the screen, searching for any mention of her name at first, but as the letter pulled her in it became a story and it swept her along.

LUMINA TRACED the patterns on the tile of the library floor with one finger, spiraling green fern fronds, and then shrugged at Chase. Her mother appeared on the screen in three dimensions, splashing in water, being nudged by the sea-creatures she was working with, something large, and grey, and mammalian-looking.

"No, I'm okay. You just surprised me because I know you're busy." She glanced at the open letter on the screen behind Chase's image and her chagrin stabbed at her. She'd been caught stealing—figuratively. She'd scrambled to arrange her face and answer as if she hadn't been reading the forbidden words.

"Well, it's not too late to join me at the caves this season. You could put it in as work-study with the school." Chase's tone was casual, too casual, which meant she wanted Lumina to come.

"I don't know. . . ." Lumina couldn't find a solid yes or no quick enough.

"Ooh! Come tonight and we can camp out on top of the caves, a real fire, peanut-butter s'mores—perk of the job—first dibs on snack imports!" Chase's excitement was normally contagious, but not this time.

Lumina bit both lips, brows creasing in the middle. A no would hurt Chase's feelings, but the caves felt far away, and wet, like work. The last time she was promised s'mores at the caves there was a rash of whale calves stillborn and several more in distress. They'd spent the whole night and the next morning resuscitating and stabilizing the ones they could. Tired or not, that was what Chase did, rescued things, brought them back from the edge, and then gave them reasons to stay on this side. And it had been good, exhausting but good.

Not tonight.

Something heavy was lodged in her thoughts. She needed to curl up in blankets and let it work itself out. Chase could work stuff out with her hands deep in some sort of task. Not Lumina, she needed space. She needed to keep reading those letters.

Still no answers, but maybe if she kept reading . . .

"I think . . . I think I'm too tired." Lumina's yawn was a real one.

"You okay? You need me back? You look like you need to talk."

"No, no—But thanks for calling me."

If she went to the caves, she might talk. She might admit to reading Chase's letters, and if she did that she couldn't finish them.

Chase pushed a newborn whale calf away from her, off camera towards another handler with gentle coaxing hands. "Invite Laila over maybe? And the offer for s'mores stands, okay? Maybe when I get back, dark chocolate, peanut butter, toasty melted goodness—"

"Deal." Lumina closed the chat, rolled over on the chilled tile and shivered. *No, no Laila.* Laila would talk her ear off about all things that didn't matter, and she'd avoid answering Lumina's questions if it meant deepening the conversation past school and future plans.

No Laila.

Instead, Lumina dragged herself up and asked the fire to light with its warm electric glow and requested hot cider from the wall unit, more imported perks. No apples here, but the taste could be mimicked and there were herbs grown on Genti-6 that gave it a rich, spicy taste, different from anywhere else in all the colonized planets. It made her taste-buds tingle almost like licking Lichen. Ha, ha, ha. There was lichen in the mix— Maybe, it was saying don't

eat me.

She curled up with Chase's olive-green flannel blanket in front of the fire—*everything should be green*— the computer next to her with its tempting secrets. But Chase's face echoed in her head, inviting her to come have s'mores with her. She shouldn't keep reading them.

There were other things she could do to figure out what was happening to her—Chase would take her seriously if she told her what was happening, now that she was older and could explain, and now that it was changing, becoming words and not just that little tickling sensation in her mind. Or she could ask Proctor Vetrano at school, or a doctor . . . or Quin. She could write a letter to Quin.

But with each thought of a person she could tell, she recoiled and tucked the secrets deeper. No. It was too personal, it was *hers*. Figuring herself out had to be like that too. Like when she was seven and she'd learned to climb the stone statues of trees out in the garden, no help up, and she'd felt so much bigger than she ever had before. She'd sat at the top for hours watching the sky change colors from midday to sunset, to full dark, savoring being so high up. She never wanted to come down.

Or there was the first time she remembered meeting Quin, so tall she could have been a tree herself, with the sun haloing her hair like fire at the edges, and when she'd crouched down to pick her up it was like something new sprouted up inside Lumina, something that was supposed to be there.

The fire was making her drowsy, her thoughts drifting, until they became little conversations, the echo of words, not quite dream, not quite thought, but somewhere in the liminal space between. There were patterns when she closed her eyes, the weaving trail of branching

threads. Figuring out the mystery of herself could be something like climbing a high precipice, or finding something you'd misplaced for a long time. That thought settled her mind enough for her to sleep. She pulled the edges of the age-softened blanket over her cheek and leaned back. It smelled like her mother, like herbal teas and soft skin, and rosemary oil. The fire sent flickering shadows across face.

There were great shapes in the dark behind her eyelids as she drifted in and out. Craggy pillars of living bark soared high into the sky with their needled branches creaking in a rushing wind, giants she'd never seen in such vibrant reality. It was as if she waited beneath them now, and as she stood barefoot, her toes sank into the ground, growing and stretching, weaving with the roots of the forest.

She descended deeper, through layers of consciousness to a place full of whispers, voices speaking incomprehensible language in counterpoint to her thoughts. She listened, tried to decipher them as she had the lichen words while waking, but drifting became dream, dream became a dark stillness, then the oblivion of sleep.

"ANOTHER'S OUT!" Chase rubbed one freckled forearm across her forehead, and only managed to spread the algae-tinged sea foam across her face instead of wiping it off. Her hands were so covered in foam and the sticky protein filled fluids from the over-sized birthing capsules beneath the surface of the water that they'd be no help. Salt-water and green foam dropped into her eyes and she squinted, laughing as she tried to shake the water off.

She leaned over the water's edge, closer to the seal-sized sea mammal being born until she fell in with a messy splash. The head was still easing out of the capsule's opening, the umbilical cord pulsing and blood-filled—still attached. It wriggled as it slipped free, and its fins splashed in the water, ready to swim from the moment of birth. Chase grabbed hold, wrapping her arms around the large whale calf. The eyes were clear and bright, well-formed, and the mouth and throat patent—open. The water was warm enough, perfect for the calves to grow in until they developed thick enough blubber for deeper ocean temperatures.

She stroked the orca's nose and released him to join the others. Two-hundred-eighty-six of them filled the sea caves, swimming and bobbing along the sun dappled surface of the water.

The gaps in the ceiling let in warmth and light, and narrow tunnels allowed exchange of water from open ocean to clean the caves. It was a refuge to keep the calves from growing cold or escaping into open water before they were ready for independence.

The calf nudged Chase as she pulled herself from the water onto the stoney ledge. She gripped the metal rails so she couldn't slip back in, but she turned and dangled her feet, nudging the calf back.

"There's no milk on the birthing wall, cub. It's over there." She gestured to the curve of cave wall where the older calves were nuzzling and bumping the milk synthesizers to release their meal into the water. "Do I need to swim you over?"

A hand slapped her shoulder and feet splashed into the water next to hers. She looked over at Manalou with her freshly algae-drenched nose crinkled. She wiped more salt from her eyes. It didn't sting anymore. She'd opened her eyes underwater before they even started, and it would be a while on dry land before the sting would come back. She was a water creature now, three weeks into the biggest spawning on Genti-6, drenched head to toe daily so that Manalou's playful splash was nothing.

"You coming to the blue's cave or is your shift over?"

Chase grinned, and pulled herself up with the rails. "Shift? What shift?"

Manalou chuckled, electric-blue hair falling over their eyes and covering a half-smile. "You know sleep is a thing right? Food?"

"Psh . . . I eat underwater."

"Right, right. Eat, sleep, breathe water. What are you going to do when the trees get here and they have us working on land?"

Chase stopped on the stairs, gripping the rail harder and wetting her lips, tasting ocean brine. All she could see was trees and sudden panic turned corporeal, rough mahogany red bark peeling in long soft strips and thick green needles smelling of that acidic orange peel tang of conifer leaves. She was also picturing Quin. "Trees?"

Manalou looked askance at her. "Yeah, trees. Because as soon as this spawning is over, the trees are arriving. Coming in with the Tree-Whisperer herself. Do you read emails yearly?"

"Trees . . . after spawning . . . Mmm . . . " Chase shrugged to cover the way her brain was glitching. She didn't want to explain that, yes, she had entirely missed all the news about something as high profile as trees coming to Genti-6, and she really didn't want Manalou's laser-focus on her past with Quin. "So, I guess I'll have to grow roots then." She shrugged and kept walking.

They were across from the magnetic rail station that would run them inland and then back out to the coast further south to the blue whale spawning caves.

The train car was warm and dry. Still, Chase shivered at the temperature change as her damp clothes began to dry out. She wished that she was wet, well not *wet* so much as submerged. That in-between place where one is neither dry nor fully wet was the only part of spawning that was hard to bear. The weight of the water was comforting, and the buoyancy helped her breathe, helped her think. Land felt heavy after so many weeks in and out of the water.

She leaned her head back and tucked a hand over the scars on the back of her neck. The hardware left there was small, the more cumbersome implant stage and harness for a mushroom long gone. They'd only left the port there when she was discharged from the project.

Just in case.

She fingered the circular prosthetic, fidgeting idly as her thoughts darted. While spawning was happening there was no sense of time, no tracking of days or room to plan what would come after. Now the forward motion of the train trapping her body in place, along with Manalou's concerned stare, brought back the uncomfortable sensation that she'd forgotten something, or delayed it—and time was up. It was an itch that she couldn't scratch because it was somewhere within the spongy tissues of her brain.

Anxiety churned in her gut like those calves in the water stirring their milk until the cave became a murky soup. Trees . . . and Quin . . . And she'd told Quin she had things to show her next time she came. She wanted to bring her to the spawning caves, and to the city with all of the new diversions being built there. But also, "things to show you" meant she'd tell her that Lumina wanted more of her, and that *she* did too.

It wasn't supposed to be so soon, Quin coming back to Genti-6, maybe not for years. She wasn't sure she could tell her. It would sound like a demand on Quin's so very limited time, or an accusation, that what she already did wasn't enough—letters, visits so infrequent from a child's perspective, and from her own. But holding back wasn't telling lies. Honesty could be selfishness in disguise. Quin was doing what she needed to do, and she was doing the same—

Manalou scooted closer, turned Chase's face with a warm, dry hand on her cheek. "You okay?"

She nodded, gave them a quick kiss on the cheek. "There's blue whales at the next stop aren't there? I'm perfect."

Manalou dropped their hand and bumped Chase's shoulder with their own. "When you do that . . . " They mimicked Chase's hand at the back of her neck. "I know it's hurting. And who you're thinking about."

Chase didn't move her hand but instead pressed it firmer; the pressure was comforting.

"It's not painful. Just weird, like I left something somewhere and I can't remember what it was or where it was—but physical—sort of."

Manalou raised a hand to her shoulder with a quizzical brow, then hesitated for Chase to nod or lean into the offer. And Chase did. Was it reinforcing a lie to let Manilou smooth and knead the scar tissue, pressing away the knots of tension and distracting her from that internal ache?

It was a physical feeling even if it wasn't just that, but she didn't feel it so much in the muscles of her neck and shoulders. It was deeper than that, internal, like nerve pain, a jumpy tingling feeling that extended into her thoughts, and yes, Quin was always a part of those thoughts when it got bad.

Manalou's hands were just rough enough, just gentle enough to soothe until the ache faded and was replaced again by the promise of the next spawning cave, and the warm salt waters of Genti-6.

CHAPTER 2

THE SAP THAT SEEPS SLOWLY

"No, no, se pas pwoblem nan."

"But isn't it Quin? The problem . . . it's at least partially that you need a break—yes, I understood your creole. I listen and I learn." General Waters nodded to punctuate his sentence. He looked less grizzled and worn than the last time she'd seen him, at his retirement from the service. Rest was suiting him, along with those longevity treatments he'd finally earned. His hair once auburn, was still showing patches of snow, with silvery streaks in the top-knot he was letting grow out, but the lines on his weathered face weren't cut as deep and his blue eyes were clearer, sharper, when they looked at her.

He reclined his stocky bulk in an old-fashioned fabric hammock under the shaded garden dome. The artificial oasis overlooked a deep gorge on the edge of base housing. Heat radiated over the canyon outside the glass in disorienting waves, and the last rays of light painted their faces in hues of pink and gold. Overhead misters came on, and Waters stretched and grinned. Arm muscles built from decades of hard labor, softened with age, were tightening up again, increasing his look of strength and vitality. Quin shivered under the misters but was silently grateful on behalf of Synesis who stretched pale fleshy pseudopods into the chill mist just like Waters.

She shook her head and leaned close enough to Waters for the smell of mushroom to hit him. It wasn't unpleasant, but it was strong, earthy, and she knew it made the General's nose itch. "It's bigger than that. I'm going into orchards monthly. Just like before. It's as bad as if I'd never gotten the All-Question to teach them. We thought we were teaching them a little at a time. We're teaching nothing. Just prolonging the end."

"Got to a year in between for a while . . . " General Waters was frowning down at his drink now, something blue and smelling of mint and bourbon. He stirred the ice with his straw. Took another drink.

"Oui, C'est ça—That's right. Now we're back to monthly and they're sicker each time. I feel like I'm patching up holes in a rotting carcass. None of my requests or proposals are going through."

"Bet they'd approve you taking some leave if you've been putting in that many requests."

She laughed with him, the tight, impatient sort of laughter that meant she had more to say. "They aren't just my requests, Waters; it's the team of ecologists, and I'm backing them, so why are we getting ignored?"

He groaned and set down the empty glass. "I think you know why you're getting that reaction and I don't like it any more than you do, but people are tired. Hope's gone out of 'em since you came back with the download and only scattered orchards have survived, nothing new growing, or spreading. No miracles. It wasn't the fix the ERF expected."

Quin threw up her hands and Synesis mirrored the motion with her pseudopods. "I'm doing everything I can. Uploading, training their latest batch of recruits with their fresh baby mushrooms, but the researchers need more resources, approval to work with other strains of mushroom."

"They're pulling out, Quin. Slowly—slowly, little bit every day but you see it. People have options, they can shift to any colony site, that's what gets people excited now—"

She couldn't hold back the bitterness in her voice. "Not trees."

Waters looked about to speak and then shrugged. His eyes were shadowed. "Yeah, I guess that's right. It's hard for people to keep trying to save something that seems hell-bent on dying."

"Difficile?! Hell-bent on dying? How can you say that to my face? Knowing people caused this . . . and what I do with these hands every day? How can it be hard for the ones doing nothing if it isn't hard for me?

Because it isn't. It is the easiest thing in the world." She held up her soil-stained hands for emphasis.

But he was right about one thing. She could see the side-stepping happen the more she pushed for bigger investment in solutions, solutions for what used to be the cause and was now looking more like a forgotten fad. People didn't want to make a third push for rejuvenating Earth and its most valuable inhabitants, the trees and plant-life that had once made up the bulk of the planet's biomass.

They couldn't see what she saw, that this was just one more step, a series of obstacles she could picture humanity stepping over like giants, inconsequential once it was solved and they looked back at it. Would they see it if they hadn't had their heads turned by the wider universe, or was humanity fatally short-sighted, unable to hold onto a single goal for longer than a lifespan?

It sounded like Tree in her head, that question, and she winced at the connections she was making. The people stepping away, giving up, finding other more exciting places to throw their energy and resources were very much like the orchards full of saplings that she fought to educate—fatally short-sighted, giving up each time she withdrew her hands.

She groaned, shoved her face into her palms, bent over her knees. The mushroom on her neck tilted itself towards Waters until he scratched under its muzzle with one finger. Synesis shivered and the reaction spread into Quin through the mycelial network in their shared nervous system. She shook off the warm tendrils of pleasure that were not her own. She didn't want to feel comforted, distracted, least of all aroused.

"What about you?" Her voice came out muffled until she moved her hands and faced him. "I know you're retired, but are you still on my side—still a part of this thing that you dragged me back into?"

He cleared his throat, shifted in the hammock that accommodated his heavily muscled frame. "I am retired, Quin. Lots of—um—lots of places to do that now. Same for you when you're done." His eyes shifted away from hers before coming back to settle on her face with a more solid resolve and a large helping of shame.

She stood and did a full spin to show off the large crown of mushroom fruits that grew from the back of her implant like an ever-expanding crown, a halo of fungus that mirrored the internal changes, the spread of mycelium throughout her nervous system and maybe elsewhere. They didn't know for certain how far the implant would spread over time, and hers was the longest successful symbiosis. It was all through her brain, her spinal cord, and laced with her nerve fibers. There were spores in her bloodstream. She knew that much.

She looked Waters in front of her and saw him as he'd been the day he asked her back into the program, desperate, with the fire of idealism sparking in those sharp blue eyes. He'd spent the better part of an hour convincing her that the ERF needed her back, that she was the answer to the decline, and if she would just accept a new mushroom she could be the savior of arboreal kind. She'd said no . . . until she'd finally said yes with a silent apology to the child she was growing in an artificial womb under her civilian clothes. Synesis hadn't put her into a second coma; she'd made her whole again, for a steep price. She crushed out the old voices of self-judgement for the choice she'd made and the many things she'd given up.

If the fungus in her bloodstream was of any other type it would have killed her, but this one was genetically engineered. It formed a mutually beneficial partnership with her nervous system and lulled her immune system into acceptance. In exchange, it gave defense against any other fungal infections that could threaten her. This was a mammalian fungus, rather, something in-between animal, plant, and fungus, and therefore able to interface between all three. But it was temperamental, vulnerable, especially in the first few years, susceptible to rejection from a host if that host proved a hostile environment.

Quin's environment was anything but hostile. She had welcomed a second mushroom into her head, into her thoughts, and into her decision-making, and her second symbiont had filled all those spaces left gaping and bleeding when the first implant was lost. Maybe that was why Synesis had taken so well for so long. A long term mycelial interface hadn't seemed possible before or since.

Sixteen years.

Growing, thriving—and becoming more and more

intertwined with Quin and Quin with her. Synesis, the unification of reason and insight, understanding.

Quin lifted her chin, gesturing now to that crown around her face. "When I'm done? If I'm done because the trees are all gone, I don't expect there to be a retirement for me. You've seen what happens to a mushroom without the trees. You saw it with Chase and the other trainees when you froze their access."

"You were in a coma, Quin—"

"Arifu—I know. You were protecting them from the same. But their mushrooms declined, shriveled up on their necks, and then separation sickness. Their mushrooms died off. Do you think on this scale—" She made an arc with her arms encompassing her head and the antler sized projections. "That it won't kill me?"

He'd gone silent. He pulled his eyes off Synesis and stared at the sky over her shoulder, then he heaved a sigh. "No, I don't suppose it won't. There's the mother trees though, the forest on Ross 128-b—"

"Oui, the mother trees, access forbidden, because we don't know the forest there won't decline if we go back. We don't know if they could sicken from some contagion we bring. If I can't go there, what of the other colonies where I bring these 'educated trees'? When do you think I'll have to start topping them up, re-uploading every six months, then every two—every week. How long can I do it? How many orchards? And who after me if this mushroom dies off? If the ERF quits, what happens to my apprentices, eh?" Noticing for the first time how her voice had risen, she lifted a comforting hand to Synesis and said prayers into the mind link. *Le ismah Allah—bondye padon* . . . More a comfort to herself than the mushroom.

"Those proposals you're trying to get through . . . "

Quin smiled and sat back down, pouring him another drink from the cold metal pitcher propped in ice between them. She pushed it over to him, didn't take one herself—hadn't since she'd taken on a second implant. She'd grown used to abstaining. It wasn't worth intoxicating Synesis when the implant could do the same with a little psilocin through their connection, psychedelic compounds that the mushroom used on her at times. They were small doses, sometimes larger to convey deeper messages and to facilitate the upload to saplings when she was too tired for it. Everything she took into her body needed to be for a purpose and beneficial to both of them. She ignored criticism of her near religiosity on the matter; Synesis's longevity was too important to risk with frivolity.

She pulled out a small computer screen and unfolded it for Waters to take in the other hand. "Daeni arik, shuf hna. There are three of them. Sorry—Here." The prayers had put Arabic at the forefront of her tongue, and she had to shift to something he'd understand more of. "The first two things the ecologists want to try and then my idea. All of them need a fair shot before we let the decline happen. Our mycorrhizal networks need diversified again, more strains of fungus—"

"I still think a vacation would clear your head, make

the uploads easier." His eyes had taken on that protective look she'd noticed after her first coma, all soft and full of worry.

"You know the only place I'd take a vacation, and you know why I can't go there."

He pressed his lips together the way he always did when battling acute frustration with her. "An idea . . . Have you thought about sharing these proposals with our local homeworlder leadership?"

"What, Inaya?"

"I think she'd be interested in comparing notes."

"Oui, probablement, but I don't think collaborating with anti-ERF radicals would make the chain of command more amenable to any proposals I am pushing."

Waters shrugged.

He could not be serious. "And do you think Inaya would trust it coming from the ERF?"

"You aren't the ERF—you're something else, people see you differently."

"Inaya sees me as a sell-out and a pawn. She told me that herself once. After showing me what they could do. Citizen scientists, grass-roots researchers, minds that should be working with the ERF and she is poaching them for her protests."

"And I'm sure you told her she was rigid and unyielding, too radical to know what was good for her?"

"I might have."

Waters frowned and leaned closer to the screen and

then backed away as if he'd forgotten his vision was clearer now.

Quin watched him read, a small measure of hope rekindling. He might have been retired but he had friends who would listen if he pulled in favors—giving up wasn't an option.

THE DICTATION FLOWED from Quin's lips in a rush of unfiltered expression. It was almost stream of consciousness and she spoke in any and every language she knew. The words that fell from her lips trembled with vehemence and exhaustion. The program transcribed and then translated her letter into a language Chase would understand, mostly English, but the French and several words and phrases she had taught Chase would remain as Quin spoke them.

Chase,

I won't be there long. It can't be a vacation for me. If I'm gone too long the trees begin to die off again and I'm butting my head against wall after wall here on Earth. Nothing is as simple as it seems when it's all tied up in the bureaucracy of a fading government. Fading because they'd rather be in the Kepler system, or Gliese, and Earth is old to them, pulled back from the brink too many times and trees non-essential so long as we can grow and synthesize food some other way. Even though the oxygen will not last. It is like the early years of the decline when species died off one at a time, slowly enough for them to ignore.

It's impatience. They are impatient and they are bored. They think they've tried three times but they've never pushed long enough or hard enough to cross that threshold where it won't spring back like a—like a damn rubber band with no anchor on the other side. Does that make sense? It feels like I'm the only one here seeing it. General Waters I think sees it but doesn't want to. I think he's still old in his head— brain tired—but he's trying.

And then there are the homeworlders, fighting what we do instead of joining the cause of the ERF. Protests, influencing investors and scaring them off . . . We have the same goals, stop the decline, rebuild Earth ecosystems and they are doing it, on some scale, not trees but gardens, food production the old ways with better results than could be expected. There is value there, knowledge we need. They make me angry, the choosing sides, harsh stances, such waste.

I have a secret thing that I wonder. But it's a thing I would only tell you. It is this: sometimes I wonder if we would all be fighting the decline together still if our training hadn't ended as it did. Inaya, and Mara, yourself, and I. Would we still be friends, instead of scattered and at cross-purposes, at odds, or devoted to other things as you are (and rightly so)? We had such hope for our place in the scheme of things. When I went under, it all fell apart. It's just a thing I think sometimes. What if my weakness and the consequences (I know I was young and should not be blamed), what if it could all be rewritten? Alors . . .

And here I am rambling about how I can't stay before I even arrive as if you've ever tried to hold me there. I'm excited somewhere underneath this fatigue. I'm excited to see you and to see Lumina. I'll stay for anything you want to show me. Genti-6 is a miracle because of what you do there, that's the truth. But these trees I'm bringing. Your colony wants them, but I can't promise they'll last, survive, grow tall like your ecologists picture. I'm bringing them because the request was made and it was approved. I'm not the one making these decisions.

Yours,

Quin

If it bothered Chase that the letters were so raw, like the gushing flow from a broken pipe, she had never said so. She'd never asked her to write less often, to slow down, to stay on topic, and why would she? There was a time when Quin had worried that Chase didn't want her letters and that she was only writing them for herself, during the dark time after she'd woken up in the infirmary. After she'd woken with Chase gone to Genti-6 and both their mushrooms dead and extracted from their implant stages. The separation sickness was so acute, the grief so sharp and all-consuming that she couldn't find where she ended and the pain began. Once she'd reclaimed her sense of self, she'd begun to remember what was between them, and she'd decided that entertaining the smallest doubt diminished them both.

Did she still need the reminder? She couldn't help but smile at the seeds of insecurity that still cropped up. It was just a rule. It didn't mean that doubts never came, or that she didn't worry when months passed without any word, but it *did* mean she didn't feed the doubts and she didn't put them on Chase. She would simply nod at them when they came up and then turn them away from her door.

She sent the message and tossed the device onto the bed, where it slipped down the terracotta-hued sheets onto the floor with a light thump. She left it there and walked out onto the balcony. Twinkling lights lit the night in the shape of a stone forest of high-rise buildings. They were massive tributes to what old Earth had missed the most, the deep forest, trees as big as these and bigger. Most had never seen the real thing, and never would unless something significant changed.

Quin leaned her bare arms on the cool metal rail, exhaled warm breath into the equally warm night air. She wanted to see these monuments as an effort in the right direction, as a sign that people still valued the natural world, but they'd been built before her time. They were just memorials when she looked at them now, tombstones. Beautiful? Yes, they were both beautiful and functional, housing hundreds in relative comfort, filtering water, producing food in the upper canopies. Still, people were leaving them for other planets.

The ERF reserved the ground below for reseeded plant-life and animals to reclaim—what animals there were—most couldn't be reintroduced with such barren ecosystems, holes in their food webs as pervasive as a Swiss cheese.

It was better now than it had been before their predecessors came back from Mars to rebuild, after the plagues of Massospora had burnt themselves out and it was once again possible to repopulate and continue the process of cleaning up old Earth's mistakes.

But looking across the expanse of Earth's largest city-center, Quin felt only grief. They were teetering on the edge of a precipice, and on one side, she saw the forest grown back, tall, sturdy, and finally able to provide the protection and stability that smaller growths needed, that animals and people needed, something to cut the glare of open sky and root the soil in place. But on the other side of that ledge everything rebuilt here crumbled, dried up and blew away like death that is too dry to rot and instead withers into dust.

A heavy sigh escaped her, and she gripped the smooth metal railing with both hands before pulling herself over and finding the access ladder to the higher canopy. There were trees there, small, tame ones that she could check on. She could soothe their doubts before they started to suffer physically. A visit tonight might carry them through her absence while she brought trees to Genti-6. She felt a thrill of excitement from Synesis, a little taste of dopamine like candy, encouraging her choice of action, moving her faster, and she chuckled into the empty dark of the high garden.

Oui, Fitiry. I'm going.

"Can I help you?"

"Oui, There is an urgent matter I need to bring to the commander in chief." Quin considered forcing a smile but kept her serious mien.

"Excuse me?" The woman in front of Quin was frowning, shifting in her hover-seat. It was only a few inches off the ground, but it gave her the appearance of floating behind the desk. The young woman's black and yellow mottled jumpsuit, black halo of hair around soft cheeks, and the friendly smile she wore made Quin think of a bee trying to get off the ground with its tiny buzzing wings. But the way her eyes widened and then shifted away from Quin as if looking to pass responsibility was not encouraging, not at all bee-like. She had to be a civilian contractor, by the lack of uniform, her position an intersection between the military structure of the Earth Rehabilitation Force, and the main governing body of Earth. What were the chances she would be cooperative or at least helpful? Functionaries like this were not known for entertaining personal crusades.

Quin's eyes fell on a bedraggled ficus tree by the desk and she scowled. The soil was wet enough to breed tadpoles, with a slick of algae along the sides of the ceramic pot. This woman was sitting in the ERF headquarters at an antique wooden desk made from the bodies of long-dead trees, completely oblivious to the distress of the potted ficus in the corner.

Quin clicked her teeth and gave the ficus a look of sympathy; the cracked and bubbling white paint on the wall, negligently layered without regard for the flaws beneath, was enough to make anyone wilt. But this was a case of clear neglect. Certainly a tame tree was hard to keep alive past a certain age, but the least they could do was keep her comfortable and nourished. Quin opened her mouth to demand as to why she hadn't been called to see to the tree's health, but instead pressed her lips tight and refocused.

"Min Fudliqi, can you please get me in touch with the commander in chief?"

The woman at the desk made another face. Quin rubbed a hand across her forehead and willed herself to find patience. As a branch of the ERF, the Interface project should have had further points up the chain of command to the ERF commander in Chief and then all the way up to Earth's governing body. On paper that's how it was, but somewhere along the line the chain broke and dangled off of nothing. Or at least that was what Quin was beginning to believe. She eyed the struggling ficus and steepled her hands on the desk, before she could be further distracted. Synesis was already perking up.

"Sgt. Fleury. I'm sorry, but the commander of your project will need to make that request or it would be breaking protocol, and I don't actually have the right procedures to even do that on my end."

Quin pressed the edge of her steepled hands against her lips and then leaned closer to the desk, Synesis leaned with her. The woman's brows raised, a subtle flinching away from the biological implant. It was something Quin was used to. They were in awe of her, of the mushrooms, but also repulsed, maybe a little afraid, as if somehow the condition for which Quin had signed multiple consents and safety releases could somehow be catching, spores maybe. If a mycelial interface was that easy to achieve, there would be far more of them.

Most people weren't compatible. They had to have their genetic profile checked. An interface could fail even after desensitizing the immune system and priming the candidate's nervous system for a symbiotic graft. But this woman didn't know that. Quin leaned in a bit closer and glanced at her name tag.

"The problem, Madeleine, is that my commander is currently in the Gliese system, and not only does she not have an ETA for her return, she claims not to have privileges for scheduling a meeting with the Commander in Chief. I was told to contact your office."

Madeleine allowed her chair to drift back from the front of the desk, the thin metallic frame the newest looking item in the over-sized office. She didn't hide her discomfort well, but she tried.

"What I can do, is forward you the forms to request a formal breach of command chain protocol for addressing serious complaints, abuse of power etc." The transparent computer screen in front of the woman was pulling up forms that flashed for confirmation.

Madeleine tapped the screen. "Yes . . . That one, 32C and these other three as well 46C and 72B."

"No, no, no. Le aridu dahlik, Chéri. I don't want that. What I'm trying to do is follow chain of command, not breach it—" Quin felt her mushroom's increasing presence, the tell-tale taste of soothing psychoactives as Synesis stamped out her fires of panic, but the mushroom could only do so much without compromising her mental faculties.

Quin pressed her hands into the desk, thumping her fingers there as the woman worked. Madeleine was oblivious to Quin's expression, or her attempts to stop her, and the frustration was making Quin angry, heating her body with adrenaline.

A barely perceptible hissing sound came from the implant stage. The cooling system switched on to counteract her rising body-temperature. She welcomed it as a reminder to check her temper as well. The implant sent a flood of cooling gel onto the mushroom's pedicels and the limb-like projections where fungal hyphae grew into Quin's nervous system swelled with moisture. Mushrooms needed to stay cool.

Another mental nudge from Synesis adjusted her thinking. This woman wasn't responsible for the command chain problems happening here, she was just one small link in the tangled mess. Anger and frustration wouldn't help.

She felt Synesis agreeing with her, pulling her back from the sharp words and heated arguments that wanted to erupt from her mouth. "D'accord, thank you so much. . . . Can I get you to pull up some other documents for me?"

Madeleine's pale young face was lit by the glow of words, numbers, and file icons through the transparent screen she sat behind and the relief on her face was clear. "Of course, that is something I can do."

Quin almost felt bad for what she had to do, and

Synesis was questioning her reticence to speak—*Do what?*—Duplicity didn't come across easily through their mind link, she would have to explain carefully, for now she had to set this in motion and hope it would work.

"Merci—separation documents. I am up for reenlistment in three months time and I've made my decision."

"Oh." Madeleine's lips pulled down in concern even as the computer offered her the forms and waited for her to authorize and send. She no longer looked relieved. She looked like she had just realized something else was happening here than she'd expected.

Quin felt the stirrings of anxiety rise and then gently fall, smooth over into something that was instead the heaviness of gravity. It was a serious gambit. There would only be one other point to pull back and ensure the worst didn't happen. She couldn't lose her position in the Interface Project.

All the same, she couldn't keep doing nothing, treading water and letting them ignore proposal after proposal as the decline rushed ahead like an oncoming train. The years invested resolved into her awareness, years that she knew were just the very beginnings of what she needed to do to complete the task entrusted to her, not by the ERF, no, the commitment ran so much deeper than the shallow roots of any Earth organization.

The commitment she was risking dated back to the

carboniferous era, maybe as far back as the Cambrian if she considered when fungus first started affiliating with plants and facilitating the development of roots. She would have laughed if not for Madeleine's presence. Her real chain of command was much older than any of these people standing in the way; she couldn't pin down whether they were fungus or tree or where to start counting—somewhere between 1.5 billion years ago and 400 million. Madeleine wouldn't see the humor in it, and neither would the ERF chain of command. Maybe Waters would have . . . but he was retired, and he would be pissed at this play she was making. He would accuse her again of needing a vacation and acting in desperation. Perhaps she was. He'd looked at the proposals, agreed to bring them higher up and pull in favors. But he'd said to be patient, and time wasn't on their side. This was something she could try now.

"Yes, that's the right form, Chéri." Quin gestured at the flashing separation papers on the screen displayed in miniature. "You've been most helpful." She reached an idle hand over to the yellowing ficus and ran her fingers down the smooth bark. A rain of yellow leaves fell to the waxy marble floor, the age of the room showing in the layers of residue from decades of drone mop and wax cycles.

A stream of stilted Tree dialect rushed through the neural link to Quin's mushroom, almost unintelligible at first, but Quin listened, furrowing her brow and nodding as the essence of the babblings became clear. A potted ficus was a tree, but a very small, simple sort when you accounted for youth and the isolation of the pot—like raising a child in sensory deprivation. Even more stunted than the little orchard trees.

She caught Madeleine's attention with a raised finger. "Your little companion here needs less water."

"Less?" The young woman tilted her head, blinking in confusion at the sudden change of subject.

"And a repotting. Her roots are soggy—attend to drainage this time, Chér."

"Ah . . . um, okay? So she uh, said all that?"

Quin chuckled and waved her free hand. "Something like that. It all comes through as she speaks. There is also the recounting of her story, you feature quite a lot." Quin gave her a wink and then closed her eyes focusing back into the link with the stunted plant, she shouldn't try to teach the tiny thing what the larger trees could know but the urge was there, her own and Synesis's.

Just a little . . .

She sent the simplest phrases, the lightest translation of the all-question into the link and felt the tree go quiet, listening, and then felt an upwelling of excitement, a questing for more.

Quin hesitated, and then continued.

Not too much . . .

She had to hold back, or else the inevitable forgetting that would come in a month or a week would kill such a small one.

She withdrew her hand, rubbing fingers against her palms as a deep frown creased her brow. A wave of guilt and shame welled up as she pulled away. To deny a child with the thirst for knowledge was a crime. She was criminal in her complicity. She wanted to give the whole message, give this child her heritage back and restore to her the grandeur of her ancestral knowledge. But she didn't know why they forgot every time—she needed to know—but whatever the cause, they *did* forget, and the forgetting was eventual death. Quin hoped this one wouldn't die of forgetting, but she might still perish of root-rot and neglect first. At least she had a taste of what mattered first.

Madeleine was staring at Quin when she looked up, waiting. Her face had that look of veiled disbelief and judgement that Quin was used to seeing on the faces of most that witnessed her Tree communications. She covered it with a nervous smile.

"I'll send these forms, but your commander or the next in your chain of command will be contacting you to discuss reenlistment options before any completed forms can be signed and finalized."

There was a growing awareness in the woman's eyes, awareness and suspicion as she spoke and then she nodded and hit send. "But I see you were expecting that, Sgt. Fleury . . . with your position in the interface project, you might need to speak to the Chief of Command and get his signature on these forms to begin separation procedures.

"J'espere—I hope so, Madeleine. But I'll be off planet for a while. Making deliveries to other systems. They'll have to convince me to reenlist when I get back."

CHAPTER 3

TWO ROADS

Winged insects of excitement bounced and scuttled along Lumina's nerves as she watched the elevator come down from the upper atmosphere. The shining structure stretched all the way to the space station in orbit and disappeared from view high above, obscured by dust, distance, and atmospheric gases in that order. Genti-6 wasn't ordinarily a dusty planet; there was natural ground cover, a resilient brush-like vegetation that swelled like fat colorful frogs and turned vibrant greens, yellows, and oranges in the rainy season then shriveled in the dry season into skeletal fingers draping the landscape. It was more rock than dirt, but the high winds on days like today could pick up enough of the planet's slate-colored dust to obscure the horizon.

The elevator craft disappeared into the domed station built around the frame of the tower, a glint of morning sunlight marking its passage. Lumina squinted in the harsh light and stood up from her portable workstation. It was all jointed lightweight aluminum framework and transparent surfaces to block the wind for an outdoor learning experience.

Her screen displayed a living specimen in 2500x microscopic detail, but Lumina stared at the elevator car rising back up through the atmosphere instead. It would take multiple trips to bring the cargo down. Space elevators were slow but safe compared to the catastrophe of engaging a shift drive inside a planet's atmosphere.

She pulled her eyes away and opened a micro-file on her screen, embedded in the window that held her lesson so her proctor would be unaware that she was off task. With flushed cheeks and furtive looks around her, she read Quin's first letter to Chase for a second time.

Chase,

I searched the room for your face, expecting to see you there still, the same as you were before I started that last download, next to me, your miraculous grin and one hand squeezing mine, the other hovering over the tree bark a step behind me in starting … then all dark, stuck in there and now that's all I am able to feel—stuck—and this pulling sharpness like I've been pierced through with metal cords, one from me to you and the other me to the mushroom implant they took off of me—dead now and gone so the cords bleed and weep at the broken ends. I know that you've gone to Genti-6 like you said you'd do someday—but I know nothing else. They won't tell me anything. I don't know if you have your mushroom still or if you know how this feels. It's as if whole sections of me are gone, ripped out with her. . . .

Lumina flicked her eyes towards the front of the assembled class. The proctor could come over any second and rap on the desk with his knobby knuckles, or the dismissal chime would sound and the screen close out automatically, taking her assignment and her letter with it.

But she couldn't stop reading. The larger-than-life figure of Quin that Lumina knew, someone distant and warm at the same time, far away, known by all, here and then gone—that Quin, the living contradiction that was her other mother had been young in these letters, young and different.

She let the words draw her on; she couldn't stop reading now that she'd started, couldn't seem to make herself. She'd started reading to find answers about herself and now, still without any answers, these characters kept calling her back. Even as her head warned her that it wasn't for her to know, her eyes devoured the words, and her heart ached for the girl-Quin's pining.

. . . . Sometimes I picture all of us like we were, new, hopeful, naive, thinking we could stop the Decline—I try to remake the bits in my head that are missing. The doctors insist the only cause for this 'lost' feeling is the separation sickness, from the mushroom being gone, that it will pass. But Chéri mwen, how do I know it?

Lumina sat up taller, gripped the arms of the chair as

the letter reached its end. She felt the heat in her cheeks and ears, her pulse fast as if she'd been running on the ground instead of through stories, but the thrum of secret revelations kept her frozen. Then with a sudden keystroke, she closed out the hidden file to conceal its secrets.

No one could see that she read the letters. No one would know she had unless she tried to ask questions. Her mother was still away, in the spawning caves, and she'd be there for at least another week. Spawnings this size took time and couldn't be left to chance or nature. That's what Chase would insist if asked. But Lumina knew it was her passion for the work that kept her gone so long. Still, it was better to read the letters here than at home.

She pressed her teeth into her bottom lip, leaving just the exaggerated points of her upper lip visible. A little twinge of self-doubt and guilt pulled at her again. But weren't these letters about her as well? Many of them had to be, the later ones at least. These first ones were about the time before she was made. They read like confessions or some sort of diary and, to Lumina at sixteen Earth years, they read like love letters.

She reopened the file.

Chéri mwen . . . beloved. Lumina had had known those words of Haitian Creole before she'd ever studied it. She knew more of the language now, but this bit had always been in her head. It was there with a great many other things that had come from Quin, and here it was in the letters referring to Chase.

Lumina could count on one hand the times that Quin had set foot on Genti-6. She could count it with fingers left over, and she could do the same with the number of words she'd heard spoken between Quin and her mother, and yet, these letters were telling a different story than she knew.

Years, decades of correspondence, and the tone of them was strange to Lumina. It was as if they knew each other better than Lumina could ever know either of them, better than Lumina thought she could know anyone.

Were they lovers? Friends that were so close they spoke like lovers? Was it just that they'd made Lumina and *she* was the bond? That didn't seem enough. But she hadn't even gotten to that part of the story yet. The letters began when Quin woke after months in a coma, and Chase's written response was immediate, ecstatic. It made Lumina's heart sing for a reunion she knew never came.

Quin!

I was losing hope. I was sick with seeing you like that. My screen is wet from crying as I write this! How are you back? How did it happen? Sgt. Waters got me transferred to Genti-6. He said you could follow if you woke but he didn't think you would.

That's what he said to us to try and make us move on, but I don't think he believed it himself. You should have seen him, always there with you when I came in to see you, and he'd scrub at his eyes and think the pink wouldn't show around them and give him away.

But you've asked me questions! No, I don't have my mushy. They wouldn't let us near the trees again after what happened and it killed her. Sgt. Waters should be telling you all of this. . . . It's hard to put into words but I don't like to think about how it happened, so slow I could feel her slipping out of my mind bit by bit and I had a sense she was begging me for what she needed. I could do nothing.

Are you coming here? Say you will. I'll get you over this sickness. It's hard but I'm better now and I know you can recover from it too. You're stronger than I am, remember?

Please come!

Yours,

Chase

But Quin didn't come.

The letters didn't stop after that. There were fewer from Chase, but that was her way, long periods of introversion, absorption in her work, the same Chase as she was still. But Quin wrote so frequently that most days in the first year after she woke were marked with a letter. Lumina skimmed these, searching for a mention of herself. There were none.

Quin spoke of her work as a civilian contractor for the ERF, translating what she could of recordings of Tree contact. Even without a mushroom she could use her training for rudimentary tasks. In this way she helped develop a new training program for arboreal linguists, working behind the scenes. Lumina could sense her discontent in the letters she wrote, even while she claimed the position was what best suited her.

Then, several years after Quin's resurrection, the letters shifted. Quin was growing a child that would be hers and Chase's. *"Did you mean it when you said we should make her?"* Chase said yes. And Quin said she would come to Genti-6. The letters from this time were alight with a growing warmth. They were familiar and full of hope.

But as she kept reading, the character of the correspondence changed again.

Chase,

I said yes to something and I don't know if I should have. I've already signed the orders to lead a search for trees on other planets and make contact. I'll be the one to speak to them. It could break me again, for good this time.

If the new implant doesn't take, I might lose myself in the implant rejection. But I don't care. I thought of you all the way out there on Genti-6 and myself with Tadpole still growing and dependent on me, attached like a mushroom implant. I thought of our plans. But then I thought of us, practically infants, trying to make sense of our first downloads. The oaths we swore and the reasons we swore them. We didn't have a choice before, but I do now.

I don't know if it was arrogant to believe I'm their best hope or to go along with it as if I believe it. But it's important enough to go backwards for. It feels more than important. It feels like I need it and I'm angry at myself for being excited, for wanting it. I've been lying to myself that what I do is enough. If the Decline is advancing as fast as Waters says and I can stop it then I had to say yes. It could be a final cure!

Would you have said yes? I think I would have said yes even without the open wound in my psyche, but I'm having trouble being objective. You won't see this before it's over. The mission starts immediately. I'm not expecting a solution so don't feel burdened to solve this for me. It is already decided.

All my love. Sending pictures of Tadpole.

Quinlan

Lumina had seen these pictures before. Her own face, tiny and barely formed, blunt-nosed, with her eyes closed like a kitten's. Her features were blurred by the amniotic fluid, membranes, and outer wall of the capsule she was being grown in.

Tadpole?

They called her Tadpole. A smile pulled at her lips, but her eyes felt tight and there was a growing tension in her throat and chest, a constricted feeling as the letters drew closer to her birth. She shifted in her chair, tucked a foot under her and kept reading, her surroundings otherwise forgotten.

Chase,

I have a new mushroom! It's feels like being real again, and awake. I'm really conscious for the first time in so long. You remember how you can taste them in your mind? And there's a fresh smell like being dipped in a salad. It's like the weather has changed in my whole body. She feels like it felt having you in my head, like a whole forest of cedar trees, that warm smell, sun and rain on the same day.

But I haven't tried to download yet. I feel sick when I think of it because I could freeze up again, get stuck in it and they're jumpy. Sergeant Waters is jumpy, carrying all that guilt from before and he'll rip this mushroom out like the last—he said that, and I can't survive that again. I can't feel that again. I think I'd fight him off even if I were unconscious.

Yours,

Quinlan

Lumina put a hand to her chest. Her heart beat fast and hard, not with her own fear but Quin's. There were no replies from Chase. Where was her mother then, and how could she not answer letters like these? She wanted to call her now and demand an answer, to accuse her of not loving Quin back. . . .

Chase,

I didn't think what we were doing was strange, but I'm having doubts. Not doubts, maybe just . . . I'm confused, disappointed in myself? I don't feel the same as I did when I started Tadpole, and I'm frightened. Sergeant Waters assumed we were lovers. He always has, and he asked questions I couldn't answer so easily. Why am I not on Genti-6 with you? Why did I choose to stay in the ERF working at a desk? But we aren't a partnership are we, not lovers. We aren't anything people would understand.

I don't care about that, really, but it feels like I'm misleading people. I look at Tadpole and I wonder why I need a better reason to make magic out of flesh than the joy of feeling it happen? Did I make her for myself? For you? I worry that I've made a promise I can't keep, to put Tadpole first. I've already broken it once in getting a second mushroom. I risked my life doing it and in doing so hers. That isn't what a mother is meant to do and while it's a quiet worry I've tucked away until now, because it isn't fair to you, I'm afraid that you won't want her. You did before. We made that promise, but it's been so long since then. And now she's coming and I feel . . . guilty because I am not enough for her on my own.

Quinlan

It was hard for Lumina to breathe.

Not want her?

Her chest moved as it should, air came in, but her body didn't seem to want it. Chase not want her? Of course she wanted her. But how could Quin not have known? The idea ricocheted in her head like a marble shot and trapped there, leaving tracks of bruised tissue in its wake. But how *could* Quin have known when Chase hadn't answered her letters in so long. Not since before Quin had said yes to the ERF's mission.

There was a gap in the letters after that and then they were different. Chase sent Quin pictures of Lumina in her arms. Quin sent reports of the decline, the trials of arboreals and her struggle to save them. These letters were from the Quin Lumina knew and no longer the girl who wrote to her mother: SGT. Quinlan Fleury holding the Decline at bay with the oldest living mycelial implant still translating, a living historical figure, the Tree-Whisperer. Quin made no more mention of coming to Genti-6, except for the rare visits, and neither did Chase ask her to.

Lumina's stomach twisted and dropped as if she were riding in one of those shining space elevator cars down through the dusty atmosphere. The story of her birth wasn't here, and neither was the reason Quin had brought her and left her on Genti-6 and not stayed herself. Were there letters missing? Did they just not talk about it?

Lumina opened the most recent letter. This one only three weeks old from her mother to Quin and sent before the spawning had started this season.

Quin,

Yes! I'm glad you are coming. I have things to show you and the spawning will be nearly done by then. I know you're busy with the trees but stay just a little to see what we're building here. I'll come home to meet you if you give me warning.

All my love,

Chase

The last letter was from Quin, more talk of the Decline worsening but the last part caught her attention. She was bringing trees to Genti-6. . . . Chase hadn't told her Quin was coming at all. Three years gap this time. And the dates brought her here today. Lumina's eyes widened and she turned to face the elevator on the horizon. Quin was on that glinting speck of an elevator, or in the station right now. And Chase was coming home early.

"Lumina . . ." The proctor was calling her name, deep creases and folds of age crinkling around his mouth and eyes with an impatient frown. Lumina turned slowly, unwilling to pull her eyes away from those ant-sized elevator cars moving up and down the tower.

She answered rapid-fire before looking away, before he could say her name again, or check her screen more closely. "I labeled the specimen . . . spores, hyphae, gills, all that." She kicked her feet to dispel nervous energy. The movement tipped her chair back, almost destabilizing it despite the motors whirring to right it.

"Lumina, if you can't keep from tipping over I'll have to deactivate your hover function. You need to keep something grounded until your lesson is over, if not your brain then your body."

She opened her mouth to answer, embarrassment burning at her cheeks and making her freckles stand out. The other students were silent, watching the exchange. The only one among them that she would call a friend was trying hard to cover her smirk and keep her eyes on her own specimen.

Another car of cargo was glinting down the track. She jumped from the base of the hover chair that she'd neglected to lower. "I'm finished!"

Proctor Vetrano frowned and glanced at the time on his own screen. Lumina knew her work was there with a cheerful icon showing that it was complete in its entirety. An 87%, the minimum required to move on. The Proctor pressed his lips together and hesitated, but his faded blue eyes were warm, relenting. "Dismissed. But I expect you to have questions on the next tasks when you come in tomorrow."

She was out of the study space and exiting the school grounds before any of the other students could catch up. Blessed silence. Her head was too full already. Fragments of conversations between her mother and Quin replayed and lit up in her mind like a string of lights. She needed to be there when Chase and Quin saw each other, when they spoke—she'd see it in their eyes if they were in love.

The path home from the only research and youth education center on Genti-6 was a small magnetic tram and then a scrolling sidewalk unless she wanted to take a steep two hour hike up the cliffs to their villa on the hill. Sometimes she would sprint along the scrolling sidewalks with the wind at her back, and it felt like flying.

She stopped in front of the tram just as it pulled up, nearly silent and smelling of well-oiled steel. The metallic, bullet-shaped surface of it and the tinted one-way poly-carbonate glass of the windows was coated in the same dust that choked the horizon line.

This one would take her home where she and Quin and Chase would meet up, and they would talk, and play family for a few nights until Quin moved on to the next colony delivery. But she didn't want to wait anymore, not with Quin already at the station.

In a split second decision, she passed the loading dock for the tram. She wasn't going home. Instead, she climbed on the larger, faster tram that would take her to the elevator station. Her mother wouldn't be back until tonight. She could see Quin first and maybe see what she'd been too young to see before. All those secrets, buried in letters . . . She had more questions than answers.

THE CHANGE inside of the elevator station was almost immediate. Once brought down from the ship, the full orchard of trees filled the enclosed space with their humidity and a fresh, green scent mixed with the loamy smell of damp soil. Quin's older apprentices were here. Ithaca and Jordan she kept busy with cataloguing and check-ins with each tree. Ronin was on record-keeping. Apprentices were good for the things she hated to do herself. The space bustled with people, the colony's ecological team coming and going with soil samples for her to examine. Tasting them, that was how she thought of it as she dipped her fingers into the jars of dark, crumbly soil.

With a purring sensation in their shared mind space, Synesis confirmed her thoughts. The colony had outdone itself, embellishing their mineral rich land with years worth of composted organic material. These fungal species had a light, fruity taste that she wasn't experienced with, similar to the ones the ERF had provided to Genti-6, but distinct. Synesis hummed with approval and nuzzled into the back of her ear with a cool damp snout. Quin's spirit lifted with the barest stirrings of hope. This orchard might fare better than the others; it was wanted, well prepared for, and Genti-6 was getting funding from *somewhere* if it could afford such lavish care. She gave the mushroom a pat and reached for the next sample.

But as the doors leading out of the elevator station opened, voices carried through with them, not the excited greeting that Quin expected for a mission that was bringing trees to Genti-6 but instead sounds of protest, voices raised in disagreement and aggression.

She moved closer to the exit doors. She tried to pick out words coming from the mash of bodies just visible through the frosted glass of the domed walls. There was something familiar about the voices, the phrases they were chanting. She could ignore them; that was the official stance of the ERF regarding protests, but curiosity drew her. Genti-6 had requested these trees, a yearlong process of approvals, funding collection, paperwork, and they'd clearly been preparing for decades to have such rich, tree-ready soil. A protest was counterintuitive here.

The air was dry outside, the voices louder, and Quin was struck as always by the foreign smells on the wind, the pungent herbal reek of Genti-6 plant life that was strong even in the dry season. It made her eyes water and her nose twitch to sneeze as she surveyed the crowd.

But the protestors were only a fraction of the crowd, a small but vocal fraction, six individuals, many-colored braids trailing down their backs and clothing in layers of re-tailored, pieced together antiques, the reuse of old resources. Tattoos of Earth flora and fauna covered much of their visible skin, and they were holding signs, some moving holograms projected over thin foldable screens that served as multipurpose computers, others weighty objects in wood or scrap metal, hand-painted with care.

Earth resources belong on Earth . . . SGT. Fleury, Ally or Traitor? Tree-speak or lies?

An older man, with short, greying braids and shaved sides, held *Tree-speak or lies?* He met her eyes, nodded. She knew him, knew *of* him at least: Roan Stanis, early researcher of mycelial interface strains, but never a part of ERF. He'd refused to join, and remained an independent, a radical.

These weren't Genti-6ers opposing the new orchard; no, these were homeworlders. Quin frowned, resisting the pull of anger, homeworlders following her ... Each planet she brought trees to had a few, brought in on colony planet tours under the guise of tourism, staying with friends, vacationing. They were wasting resources to follow her, for what reason? Their goals were the same as hers, but those signs didn't make it seem that way.

The woman in front couldn't be missed, her long black braid and colorful sari instantly recognizable, dark brown eyes bright with fervor. Their leader or one of them anyway. Inaya nodded to her as she approached and stopped at the railing that kept the protestors away from the station's entryway.

"Vas ist das? Yah kya hai? Inaya . . . Are there not better ways to use your resources?"

Inaya laughed, indicated her sign that asserted how Earth resources should be used. "We travel with ships already leaving, we spread the message, return. The only finite resource we use here is our time."

"Isn't that as important as the others, more so even? I know that I'm short of it. Stopping the decline takes all I have; is it not the same for you?"

Inaya shook her head. "The world needs to know there are other ways to set our priorities, that the choices of the ERF are not the only ones. Taking our trees, spreading your tiny orchards, spreading yourself across galaxies when our one home needs all we have is a mistake."

Inaya's conviction put a fire behind her words. It was more than Quin had to offer back. Her own fire was dampened, spread thin, but there was an answering echo, a distant ache. "You think I am not doing everything I can on Earth? It is all I do, Inaya. I don't have children, lovers, hobbies, none of those things have my time."

"And here you are." The woman stood firm, crossed her arms.

"And here you are." Quin couldn't help but throw the words back at her but the question in her breast wanted to be voiced. "What am I supposed to be doing then, eh? What would you approve of, you have a solution to the decline that I do not? It is criminal not to share it then."

"We have solutions, many of them, and you have the resources."

It was Quin's turn to laugh. "No, no Inaya, we do not have them, not enough and not–" She lowered her voice. "Not for the new things we need to try, not resources, not support. We are treading water. I am treading water." It was an admission of things the homeworlders didn't need to hear, fuel for their protest signs. *The ERF is just treading water!*

But Inaya appeared to be listening closer now, and her voice came out strong and vehement. "You shouldn't be spreading our trees out like this then! Limiting what we can access instead of supporting us on the home planet."

"Inaya, the ERF has had meetings with homeworld leaders, requests to collaborate, share resources."

"Mm . . . no, they have made a show of it, Fleury, thrown their refusals in our face. Denied our requests to keep Earth seeds on Earth! Earth resources on Earth, not in these far-flung colonies when we already have a planet to tend to."

Quin sighed, rubbed her forehead, the sun was hot and the air dry outside of the station. Better to be back inside with the trees for all the good this was doing. Fatiguing or not, saplings were easier to reason with than people. "Inaya, it takes both parties to bend, to negotiate, and your people are known for this stubbornness."

If Inaya wasn't truly angry, before she was now, eyes flashing, her body language tight and restless. She held her sign up higher before whispering a parting shot. "The same is said of you. Unbending like an old oak, unable to see the forest for the trees, for all your talk of speaking to them."

Quin nodded, refusing to let the insults motivate her words. "I am—doing everything I can. And these trees? They are a hope for Genti-6, they are also a promise of funding for the ERF, the only organization fighting for the survival of arboreals, on Earth or elsewhere. They are part of the continuation of the project, but this was not my decision." Quin paused, looked at the crowd in front of her, the ones closest listening to her outburst, mostly homeworlders, and the ones craning their necks to see what they could see of the trees inside, excited Genti-6ers. She shrugged and met Inaya's eyes. "See you on the next world, oui?"

Inaya held her sign up higher and began a chant, but Quin had stopped listening. She was striding inside. Her irritation faded just enough when she saw the trees there waiting, the many crates ready and organized for drone pick-up and transport to the new orchard site. It was true, she would not have brought them here, spread herself even thinner, but it would increase funding, give time for her proposals to go through. It was a compromise, a bending, something the homeworlders would have to learn if they wanted ERF support.

STUMBLING over the guardrail and cracking her head on the storage case holding cartons of saplings was not the reunion Lumina had intended, but slowing down and watching for the exit to the scrolling sidewalk just wasn't possible. She was too busy staring. Quin was there ahead of her, the prominent figure that held so much mystique flashing in and out of view between the trees as the moving walkway brought Lumina closer.

The woman was tall and long-limbed as ever, her skin a sun-warmed mahogany, the same as the soil at the base of the aspen saplings she'd brought with her, and she was walking between them, pressing her hands against them in what looked like a caress. Her hair was different than Lumina remembered it, no longer the well-groomed afro she was used to but instead a shock of short copper, pine-green, carmine, and sunset-orange braids in front. The mushroom crown that sprouted from the back of her neck framed her face like an enormous upturned collar, a cliff made of fungal growths that dwarfed her skull. The uniform she wore, in fitted lines of green, copper, and white, marked her as a member of the ERF.

The complete picture that was the Tree-Whisperer made most people stare, but what held Lumina's attention and moved her to complete distraction was Quin's face, the crease between her brows and the way her eyes grew distant then fluttered and rolled back in their sockets before they closed. It happened with each tree that she touched, and Lumina was transfixed.

The end of the walkway came suddenly, tangling Lumina's legs and sending her sprawling over the railing into the crate of trees.

The right side of her forehead hit a freshly-pruned sapling. The sharp edge of one branch made a deep gash in her forehead, spilling her blood on the smooth grey bark of the tree. Pain lanced through her skin, but the cut, with its sharp sting, wasn't what dropped Lumina to the ground at the base of the tree.

Blurred images flashed through her mind with a speed and force that paralyzed all other thought. She swam past the pictures invading her mind, searched for meaning even while she couldn't form a single thought or question of her own. They were images she was unable to place, dreamlike and foggy as if seen through smoke.

She tried harder, and a single question formed in her mind, a concept she couldn't give words to at first. She didn't even recognize the language and yet she knew it originated from her and not the same place as the invading images.

I should understand. I should know this—

But it felt like old secrets she'd been told to forget, steeped in the ringing gong of deja vu. Then there was pain, sharper than the cut in her skin, flashing like a network of spiderweb set fire in her skull.

What did she say . . . ?

"Lumi?" Quin's face hovered over Lumina's, the large, wide-set brown eyes, a vibrant shade of sepia, searched her own green ones. She was kneeling over her, one hand on Lumina's bleeding forehead, the other on the aspen tree. She slipped her hand off of the offending tree and now used it to snap in front of Lumina's eyes. There were other faces hovering, a girl with blue eyes, a starburst of ivory in their centers, leaves tattooed along her right jawline, and another with honey brown eyes and hair the same, darker skin. "Merde—Lumi, ou anfòm? Are you here?"

The words Quin spoke, even the ones in English didn't make much sense. Of course she was here—It was just a scrape wasn't it? She couldn't help but berate herself. Because she was distractible and clumsy and because she'd come here on impulse without anyone knowing.

Quin was checking her head again—for further injuries, Lumina assumed, pressing the bones of her skull gently, assessing her in the same way she seemed to assess the trees, and then with less alarm she was gesturing with one hand over her shoulder, waving for someone to come.

She still hadn't answered Quin, hadn't thought to answer or even realized that she hadn't. She stared back at her, silent. She wanted to laugh at her own stupidity, and to apologize, but it felt like laughter would take more effort than speaking. There was something she wanted to say but there were no words for it. There were people crowding in now and she winced away, closed her eyes tight and curled in on herself. When she opened them again, she found that she could say something, not what she had wanted to say—that she could no longer remember—but something.

"I'm okay . . . mwen Byen."

Quin let out a breath and pulled Lumina in close, squeezing her. She smelled just like Lumina remembered, sun-warmed earth and growing things and faintly sweet like the juice of fresh cut cucumbers. It was an old memory without words, just that smell and knowing it was Quin, a place more than a person.

Lumina's eyes welled up, and she hugged back, catching her breath before she could cry. That was when the missing hit. But it was more than missing, and Lumina searched for the better word . . . nostalgie if you wanted French, hireath in Welsh, the sort of missing that's deeper than one person or one thing. That's what this was, and it was too big to cry out all at once, so she squeezed her eyes against it. "I'm sorry. I didn't see the stop."

Quin hugged her tighter and then pulled away, too soon. She helped Lumina to her feet gradually and made room for the medic, a young man with black hair, the ends of it transitioning to bright green, and the patch of an apprentice on his front jacket, a name just beneath, Lwen, Ronin. He spread wound-heal on Lumina's forehead and a light layer of skin graft to hold the cut closed. She gave him a silent apology, a smile of gratitude.

"Where is Chase?" Quin was searching the walkway and surrounding area with her eyes. There was no accusation there, only gentle questioning, and it made Lumina feel safe to answer.

"She's not back until tonight. I came without her. I'm sorry."

"Lumina, there isn't anything that needs apology, except to the little birch perhaps, pauvre-bébé; she was quite startled."

"Oh." Lumina extended a hand to the tree, hesitated, and then as Quin watched, she placed her palm against the surface that was as smooth and cool as marble but softer against her skin, and alive, so much more alive than she expected. "Sorry . . ." The word came out as a whisper and before she could find more to say, there was that electric pain in her head again, spreading out first from the hand that touched the tree. She swayed from a sudden wave of vertigo then pulled away and clutched her hand to her chest.

Quin touched the same place on the tree and her eyelids fluttered closed. Then as Lumina watched, she too withdrew her hand and raised both brows. "She forgives you."

Quin gave her a soft smile and brushed her cheek, then turned and spoke to the Genti-6 colonists loading the trees into a transport drone.

Lumina was on her feet again staring at the tree, tall but spindly with nearly round leaves that came to small points. They were like nothing she had seen before, nothing she had ever touched certainly, and she found herself reaching out. She wanted to feel the smooth bark beneath her fingertips again. These were the first trees on Genti-6, the first plant life taller than the succulent bushes that only grew up to her chest.

But why was there pain when she touched them? The ones loading the trees into the cargo portion of a magnetic railcar didn't seem bothered by grabbing the trunks of the small trees and hauling them up. But they wore gloves.

Maybe it was like stinging nettles; plant defenses were not an uncommon thing.

She hovered her hand again. If she touched it longer, would she see images again, and maybe understand them this time? Quin seemed to be watching her, that quizzical expression pulling her brows together and before she could lower her hand, the last group of trees were carted away and the space in front of her was empty, leaving herself and Quin. Synesis was waving its free appendages, reaching in the direction of the departing trees but Quin didn't move.

"I think you should come with me Lumina—with the trees."

A silly grin split her face, the disastrous stumble all but forgotten. "Go with you?"

Time with just Quin . . . She could ask questions if her own nerves didn't silence her. "Can I help plant them?" The thought of being the one to plant these trees, placing their roots in the ground and seeing if she'd see those same pictures in her head, maybe clearer than before, made her hands shake and it made her words tumble out with sudden urgency.

Quin laughed and guided her with a gesture towards the magnetic railcar, one of the big ones with the bullet-shaped noses. "Not today, we aren't planting today, but we're bringing them to the site to acclimate slowly. And I need to check the mycelium beds your terraformers have prepared—besser vorbereitet als leid—better prepared than sorry, Chéri."

THE HEAVY WINDS that had kicked up so much dust on the horizon and dropped a thick mass of grey and black clouds over the whole of the Eastern coastline, finally settled. Only small gusts remained to rustle the aspen leaves like tiny paper cymbals.

A batch of saplings, still in their pots, stood in a semicircle around Quin and Lumina where they were all gathered under a large outdoor structure with a shade cloth above and three walls to provide windbreak while the young trees acclimated to the climate. Through the open wall Lumina could see a vast field of lumpy tilled soil, rich and dark and full of bright green weed sprouts taking advantage of the water. More water than anywhere else on the planet this time of year. A damp, fertile smell came up from the field and threatened to overwhelm her senses.

Lumina sat back on her heels and tucked her hands between her knees. Quin reached for one tree and then the next for several minutes at a time, and in between, she appeared to rest, a light smile curling her lips. She sat back from the seventh tree and dropped her hand with a soft sigh and then that smile appeared again.

"So you talk to them."

"Wi, it is a dialogue, not just a lecture, they ask questions and I answer—it helps them absorb it if we go slow like this. Some today, more tomorrow when they are connected by the mycelial beds and can hold more. These ones are very small and new, and they are healthier. They haven't begun to forget so teaching them is—more pleasant."

Lumina frowned. "I think I just don't really understand why. Like, I get that you can speak to them and you're teaching them, but I don't know why? What's the point? Why would they need a person to do that?"

"Because—" Quin opened her eyes, and they looked distant, meditative. "These little ones are tame trees, descended from generations of tame trees—so far removed from forests and wild trees that they are missing the knowledge they need to grow strong and to have the stamina for seasons, for years, and then for centuries . . . to grow into the giants that Earth used to have."

Quin sat up and placed her hands on the next sapling. She dug gently around the roots, then patted the small silvery trunk before leaning her forehead against the tree and going still. Lumina watched, questions crowding in for her to ask next, but there were too many and some of the ones she wanted to know the most would have sounded out of the blue. Others would make it obvious that she had read Quin's private messages to Chase, like why did Chase leave the interface project and not go back? Why did Quin stay on Earth after she recovered and not come to Genti-6?

"She misses you when you leave." The words tumbled out before she could think them through.

Quin opened her eyes again and they were distant,

like dreaming. Lumina looked anywhere but her face, but then the spark returned, her eyes brightening and sharpening into focus as if a heavy bank of fog had cleared. "You are talking about Chase, wi? I miss her too."

Lumina nodded, suddenly nervous now that she had blurted it out. "I know she does because I know her."

A playful smirk rounded Quin's cheeks and lit her eyes. "And you think I do not?"

"Um…No? I mean you're really close right?"

"Yes." Quin's brow furrowed and then smoothed but Lumina saw the shift. "Your mother is dear to me. And sometimes we are close—sometimes we are very distant, but always precious—Perhaps you should ask me what you are wanting to ask."

Lumina froze under the realization that she was apparently so transparent, but she didn't want to miss the opportunity presented to her now that she'd fumbled her way into it. Quin was sitting back with her legs out in front of her, waiting instead of moving on to the next tree. The Mushroom's fruiting bodies towered over the top of Quin's head casting shade over her face and giving her shadow on the ground the look of some antlered creature.

"I just wonder why you never stayed here." She looked down, biting at her lips as the uncomfortable heat of embarrassment filled her face and slowed the flow of her words. "Why if you both miss each other— why not—just stay. Or stay longer or . . ."

Quin blinked and the smile dropped from her lips. "What does your mother say when you ask her this?"

The wind kicked up again rustling the thin branches and small leafy canopies into their faces, as if the trees were demanding Quin's attention.

"I haven't really asked since I was little, I guess. But she always said something about you doing your job and she doing hers."

"Oui, that is just so." Quin looked relieved as if Lumina had let her off the hook.

"But that's too simple to be the whole answer."

Quin shrugged. "Do you think if I were here that your mother would not be in her caves and her laboratories and her gardens . . . for weeks at a time?"

"I don't know?"

"Ah well, I do know, because I know your mother. And I also know she would not ask me to stop doing this thing I am trying to do. If I were here, I would not be stopping the decline, trying to anyway—these little trees would not be here, ready to start a forest someday if I can make them learn and then remember, if I chose selfish hypotheticals. Chase feels the same about what she does, so that is your answer."

Lumina's brow furrowed and she looked down at the brown leather gloves on her hands, Quin's work gloves. She traced their pitted surfaces with her eyes. "Okay."

"But I think you are trying to ask something else . . . yes?"

"I dunno." Lumina tucked her hands under her legs again.

"What I think is that you are asking about feelings and you have gotten caught up in the expected—If Chase and I love each other enough to have a child together, to have you, then why do we not live in the expected way of lovers?"

Lumina opened her mouth to object but found that she didn't really want to let any such words fall out, not if it would stop Quin from answering the question she'd just posed to herself. Now that it had been voiced out loud, she found she wanted the answer.

But it was several moments before Quin spoke again, stretching Lumina's underdeveloped stores of patience.

"That is not something . . . I can make you understand—or anyone else—für diese Angelegenheit. Is it not enough to know there's love between us?"

"But I didn't ask—" Lumina felt her embarrassment returning as Quin pressed her.

"Mm . . . You were asking with these other questions. Ask yourself Chéri, were you not?"

Lumina's heart was pounding. Terms of endearment, secret confidences shared, all of them read with a sense that she was stealing, and they were surfacing in her head again now. She didn't know what she would say until she said it, or she might have thought better of it. "But there are all those messages."

Quin's eyes widened and then she seemed to be considering something. "There are very many by now, if she has kept them all. What did you learn from them?"

"Enough to have a lot of questions and ideas about

how you were before, back on Earth together." She fidgeted under the sharp stare that Quin fixed her with. She couldn't tell for sure if she was angry; Quin kept her face arranged in careful neutrality, but it felt like she might be.

"Curiosity is like that. It will give you information that is not yours to understand if you let it move your hands. A natural consequence of snooping."

"I was looking for things about me." It was barely above a whisper.

Quin paused, opened her eyes, understanding dawning there and filling Lumina with hope. "I see. What are you looking for, Lumi?"

"I just–anything different about me. Things I know but don't remember learning. Places . . . words, and sometimes I—feel things, hear things like a tingling in my head, like bubbles." She cleared her throat and pushed on. "Almost words. And when I touched the tree it was like—"

"Fell on her, you mean?"

"Yeah."

Quin's eyes brightened, lips pursed with words collecting and she started to speak, but then stopped, damning up whatever revelations she might have revealed. "You are—Lumina, perfect, and also growing up. That is a lot of change all at once, and I think Chase would like you to bring your questions to her."

Lumina brushed her gloved hand across the papery bark of a sapling. Her cheeks burned and her stomach felt all tight and heavy. Was that even an answer? Or a way to avoid the question? "Yeah, sure, probably right." It was a throw-away response but Quin wasn't listening.

Quin had already turned away to greet the next sapling with a gentle caress before going still and silent as she communed with it. The apprentices Quin had brought with her were doing similar things farther off, but they let go faster and recovered slower. The one with the leaves adorning her jawline as if they had grown there in her sleep instead of being tattooed by an artist, was taking soil samples and loading them into a machine. She brought the machine closer and showed Quin a set of numbers on a screen, bright blue eyes alight with some joke they shared. Lumina couldn't hear the quiet exchange but it was warm, familiar.

Lumina picked at the edge of the gloves that Quin had insisted she wear. She wanted to rip them off and throw them. Those apprentices worked with her every day, traveled here with her, and they couldn't be much older than she was. She scowled. They were already apprentices, traveling to colony planets, training on Earth, but more than that. They were with Quin.

"SEE how they strike the walls, just gentle nudges, it releases the milk. When I get into the water they do the same to me, especially the ones I birthed from their AUC's. Second generation is when we'll see if we've managed to preserve the instincts they need to nurture young." Chase was breathless with enthusiasm, those green eyes shimmering in the dim light of evening that made it into the caves from high up in the ceiling.

She was already wet from the whale's splashing before she lowered herself into the water but she didn't seem to be bothered, to the contrary she was grinning as the blue-green depths soaked into her clothes and pulled her ebony hair down into water-made spirals. The whale calves surrounded her, their blunt noses bumping and prodding at her as she'd said they would.

Quin watched as Chase stroked the calves' faces and chirped at them, and they talked back to her with little clicks and squeals.

"You have to get in with me, Quin. When else are you going to swim with baby whales?" She was laughing and pushing them gently towards the walls where the milk was released, the water turning opaque and creamy as if a barrel of flour had been dumped into it.

"In my uniform?"

Chase grinned.

"In whale milk?"

That goading look on Chase's face wasn't budging. Quin took off her boots and removed the jacket and pants of the uniform leaving a green undershirt and then climbed down the ladder into the warm frothing salt-water. "Better?"

"Well, isn't it?"

Quin tread water away from the splashing, but Chase lunged for her and pulled her into the swirls of milk water then guided her hand onto the back of a blue whale calf.

"Yes, Chéri mwen, much better to pet whales with you than stand and watch, even if my mushroom gets all soggy. She takes hours to dry, you know."

"I remember."

Quin smiled at the intrusion of a memory, feeling certain it was the same in Chase's mind, a sudden downpour after training, the rain droplets making rainbows on their skin and hair in the light. The lamps lit just moments before as the sun set over the horizon. Both of them with young, smooth backed mushroom symbionts, no fruiting bodies like the ones her Synesis had now. The mushroom's delicate skin was slick with the rain and boggy as if the water was soaking in as well as coating them. They were an oil-slick of iridescence and the rain coming down all around them refracted the light like diamonds.

She interrupted the course of the memory, but she couldn't interrupt the warm, nostalgic thoughts that came with it and filled her with a feeling of being back in that time, just the two of them.

Chase was silent, treading water with a light smile on her lips. So many of her features she'd given to Lumina, and it was easier to see now that Lumina had grown.

Especially the eyes. So full of light . . .

A thought occurred to Quin and she latched onto it, a raft to lift her out of the feeling of intimacy before she sank too deep. "Lumina's grown more inquisitive with every inch of height, I think."

Chase laughed, fracturing the silence as Quin had hoped she would. It was a musical sound and Quin loved startling it out of her. "Oh, is that why she went and collected you at the station. To interrogate you?"

"So it would seem. But she questions more with her eyes and what she witnesses. Question after question about the mycelial fields for planting an orchard, about my implant and then—She asked me if I missed you—have you not told her how excessively I say those same words as if they had the power to fold time and space? Tu me manques . . . Ishtac-tu ale-ki . . . mwen manke-ou . . . Ich vermisse dich?"

Chase blushed beneath her olive skin and climbed out of the water, allowing Quin to give her a hand up. Her eyes darted and then dropped to the towels and dry clothes on the bank. "She asked that?"

"She did, and did you notice how she watched you and I both when you came into the room. I think . . . I think she's looking for something, and we make a good focal point for her. But it's just a feeling; you know her better."

She watched Chase's face for signs that she knew already, that the things she wrote about showing her were one and the same as what Quin knew now without a shadow of a doubt. Before she even placed a hand on the aspen sapling to ask, she'd known. But then it was undeniable, the residues of a recent conversation, a connection that shouldn't have been possible.

Chase was drying her hair, squeezing the excess water out of her hair and then busying herself with drying off as much of the water as she could from her clothes before stripping and changing.

"Lumina doesn't know what she wants from life. Right now, it's everything if it's anything, but she looks up to you—probably wants advice. And she is sixteen—making up stories in her head about love, and loss, and longing. You remember doing that, don't you?"

Quin snorted an uneasy laugh and shrugged. "I still do those things . . . when I have my own thoughts in my head at all."

It was the sort of explanation given to minimize problems and comfort the self in the face of a fear, or a challenge to the status quo. It wasn't like Chase. But it sounded true, and Chase didn't lie to her. She never had. She'd have felt it if Chase had done that, and the gap between them would have filled up with more than just the distance between solar systems. But this answer didn't give any sign that Chase knew what was happening to Lumina. Better if she already knew. At least suspected. Telling her would bring worry and it would feel like overstepping.

Chase was watching her tread water at the side of the pool a warm smile playing at the corners of her lips. "Come to dinner with us? We'll get Lumina and eat in the city.

"Mm, oui, Chér." Quin nodded, climbed out. The

wet undershirt had to go. The clinging fabric held on and she pulled at it in little jerks when it caught on her muscled shoulders and then eased it over Synesis's mushroom crown with greater care. She had to stretch the neckline to lift it over her head without catching it on the growths and prematurely dislodging them. It would be easier once the mushrooms released, at least until more grew in. The thought turned into worry. Each batch marked the progression of time and aging; Synesis was already ancient by symbiont standards.

The shirt caught anyway, on her forearms and head. She felt Chase's breath on her neck, her hands working to help her, deft and gentle. The drenched shirt fell free on the floor of the cave.

She flushed and shivered, heat within, the chill of the caves stippling her still damp skin. She dropped her arms and faced Chase. "Dinner will be nice. Tomorrow is planting day and departure. Tonight is ours for anything you want to share with me."

Chase was dressed now, her cheeks flushed from the same chill that Quin felt. A small smile curled on her lips. Was she sharing the thought that had hold of Quin? If they moved, time would restart again and dinner would be over, the saplings planted, the ship boarded . . . But for now, standing in the same space, not words on the screen, or a hologram, or a recording, was like time travel. It was as if the Chases from every time were overlayed atop this one, sharpening the outlines of her until she existed in all dimensions. Chase didn't move away, so Quin didn't move. She memorized her—tomorrow she would be at the next colony planet and the space between would spread out again like an accordion stretched taut but never released.

Chase would be here whether Quin was or not. Chase the universal constant.

Synesis was whispering in her mind, nudging her as she did when there were trees to commune with. Dim flashes of tree species, cypress, oak, sequoia, surfaced in her mind as if Synesis were riffling through her memories and throwing them at her.

Her melancholy was confusing her mushroom brain. And much as she wanted to hold still and pretend time wouldn't flow past her, it would.

"Chase is not a tree, Chér . . . what do you want with her?"

Still Synesis leaned and peaked around Quin's face.

Chase gave a brilliant smile. "Did you miss me too, Seni?" She reached, her wrist brushing Quin's cheek on the way, then she stroked Synesis's downy skin. Quin sighed, closed her eyes, fought to cordon herself off in her own mind, to separate herself from the waves of sensation, heat, and light, and aching need.

Chase was looking her in the eye when she did it. She knew from when she had her own symbiont, the intensity of a touch like that, magnified through the creature. But it had been years for her, over a decade to forget the intimacy between host and mushroom. Whether Chase remembered or not, whether she'd meant the touch how it felt, that path could only lead to wanting things and disappointment.

She drew a fortifying breath and laughed at herself, then stepped towards the paved trail, breaking the contact between Synesis and Chase. The waves of loss that Synesis felt and so generously shared with her were the natural consequence.

"Allons-y, Chéri?" She put on a smile, took Chase's hand, then pulled her towards the sunlit corridor that would lead out and back to the villa to collect Lumina. "And at dinner . . . You said there were secrets to share?"

There was a hesitation in Chase. Quin felt her hand stiffen in her grip, worry in her eyes, but the smile didn't waver.

"After dinner. I promise."

Quin shrugged. "D'accord, Chéri Mwen. Whenever you say."

CHAPTER 4
ENTANGLED

The sky-scraping luxury building rose above the city's other buildings like a UFO mounted on a high tower. Big money had taken an interest in Genti-6, and buildings like this were new to the colony.

All of Genti-6 was on display for them in an arc around their table. The curved walls, more window glass than solid structure, revealed the lights of the colony far below, the full expanse of a jagged coastline, and the ocean in a dizzying display of midnight blues, and greens, all of it framed by the darkening star-studded sky. The view from this height was so complete and expansive it could have been a virtual reality world. Even the lights of the space elevator were visible far in the distance, magnetic rail tracks winding their way across the sunset darkened landscape in tracks of light.

Quin stood by the window, facing west, still in the uniform she'd arrived in.

She paced along the curve of glass wall, brow furrowed, as if some worry ran back and forth in her thoughts. Lumina tracked her every movement, staring hard so she might catch some tell-tale sign of what was in Quin's head. Was it the awkward and disastrous head-on crash with the sapling, her blurting out about the letters and essentially telling on herself? Or Chase . . . Maybe Quin was thinking about what she had said about Chase missing her, or having anxious thoughts of moving on, back to Earth and the trees there? Whatever Quin was thinking, it didn't seem a good time to interrupt her thoughts with questions. Especially ones like the one pacing in her own head and looking for an opportunity to tumble free. Her opportunity to ask them seemed to be passing. They had already ordered, but nothing had arrived. Her throat tightened at the thought of missing the chance, but it tightened more at the thought of taking the leap. Soft music played just loud enough to cut the silence without stifling conversation.

As Lumina watched, Chase stood and joined Quin at the window. She whispered something that loosened Quin's features, softened the look of concentration.

A wry smile pulled at Quin's lips. "Perhaps I need to ask Genti-6 for research grants. She seems to be growing up and putting on her fancy clothes."

"Is that a saying or did you just make it up?"

"Je pense—I—think I made it up."

Chase shrugged, the look on her face amused and

apologetic. "I'm not involved with funding. But I'm sure there are people we could ask."

Quin snorted. "I'm better at speaking to trees."

Chase raised a hand, gesturing for the volume until Genti-6 electro-strings filled the room with soaring notes and vibrations Lumina could feel through her whole body.

Well, she couldn't strike up a conversation over that, now could she?

Chase loved to dance, head thrown back, more hips than foot-work. She reached for Quin with a smile that said "dance with me", eyes flashing under the overhead lights. Seeing Chase dance, it made Lumina remember being lifted onto her mother's hips and bounced to music like this. Memories of being always together. Wherever there was Chase, there was Lumina. It was like she was Chase's mushroom symbiont, a perfect pair.

The thought opened up an ache in her chest, and with it worry, confusion. Chase hadn't died, hadn't gone anywhere.

But it wasn't the same.

Was it something she had done or something that just happened to people. She shoved the feeling away. She didn't even want to go everywhere Chase went anymore, tag along to the caves, or the geological surveys. So why did it feel like a branch had broken off from her canopy and fallen in front of her with a hollow thump?

Chase caught her eye from where she was dancing

and reached a hand towards the table, towards her. *Oh no . . .* Lumina shook her head. She couldn't move like that, especially not lately. She barely knew where her feet were in comparison to her head. She'd somehow manage to fall into a tree even in here. And besides, Quin was here, that would just be awkward.

But Quin indulged Chase and allowed herself to be pulled into the dance. She broke into a smile mirroring Chase's and they moved in sync, spinning each other as if they danced like this every day.

The two circled, passed close enough to the table for Chase to grab Lumina's hand. She tugged and laughed, the mischief in her eyes goading. It *was* infectious. Before she could put up any resistance, Quin took Lumina's other hand, as if dancing had been her idea from the beginning. "Come Lumi, you need to get your sap flowing. Li Narkas maen!—Dance with us!"

Chase bumped her with a hip. "It's just for fun, you know."

She resisted their pulling hands, made her body heavy like a cat being lifted from a chair. It was futile. Her own grin threatened to split her face as the hover stabilizers of her chair engaged and she slipped from the wobbling seat. No one was here to judge, so who cared if they had fun?

"Okay, okay . . . " Lumina stood back and did a twirl. She followed it with a series of hip bumps even as she folded over and broke into laughter. Her face was hot with embarrassment, but it was the fun kind that left her feeling victorious. She'd risen to the challenge.

"Yeees!" Chase clapped for her and took her hands back so that they were all linked, laughing and moving with the music.

"Well, I better have learned *something* from you."

"Oui, you don't just get gifted with a mother who knows how to move and not pick up skills."

It was the perfect opening to broach the subject. *I could learn from Quin too . . . You don't just have the Tree-Whisperer for a mother and not pick up some skills.* But the words didn't make it to her mouth, and the moment passed.

The space was too warm and the sky fully blackened by the time they'd circled the room several times. The music slowed and Lumina sat. She rested her face on her arms and watched them sink into quiet conversation still swaying together.

They danced like old friends, like companions, like something more, and the longer they danced the less Lumina recognized them. The woman with dark waves falling around her face, a flirtatious smile pulling at her lips, worry lines gone under the lights, she couldn't have been her mother, and what of the mahogany-skinned stranger that danced with her, movements tender, familiar? These were the women from the letters—not the Quin and Chase she knew.

Another song ended, doors opened, and the whirring bustle of bots on track-wheels and smaller hovering drones came in with the salad course. Quin and Chase stepped apart—Was that surprise in both flushed faces as if they'd forgotten this was a restaurant?

Lumina pretended to study the multicolored, fragrant greens on her salad plate and buried a smirk under one hand; to do otherwise felt like a breach of privacy, her very observation an intrusion. She speared a greenhouse tomato and wrapped it in a leaf of purple arugula to pop in her mouth together.

Oops.

She cleared her throat and leaned in towards the bot's speakers. "Thanks bot-head and chefs. It's delish!" The kitchen staff could hear through the bot, and she was feeling more buoyant now, playful even.

The thought recurred. It wasn't too late. There was a real chance, now that they were having a good time together. The dance had given their cheeks a warm blush, with smiles lingering even as they sat at the table. She could ask now while they all settled into some good food.

Lumina shifted her eyes from Chase, across from her at the table, to Quin in the seat next to her.

She pushed her plate away and sat up straighter.

Now or never . . .

"I want to go with Quin when she leaves tomorrow." She said each word as if it were a study in maturity, cultivating a tone she hoped would sound calm and well-reasoned—an opening for discussion. Silence followed. It felt like the breath had been sucked out of the room and all of the warmth of their dance with it.

Quin leaned forward and Chase's eyes widened but

neither spoke. She could either wait or explain herself. It was harder to slow the words now and they tumbled out. "I want to study the trees on Earth and I—want more time with you. I want to be your apprentice."

Quin steepled her hands on the table, but she was still silent. Lumina pleaded with her eyes. But Quin wasn't looking at her, she was watching Chase, which meant what it always did. She'd defer to what Chase wanted.

Her hope deflated. Quin wasn't even looking at her, she was looking at Chase. Chase's skin had blanched, and the smile disappeared with no trace left behind. Lumina's heart beat fast and loud in her own ears and then her breath went out of her.

"I don't think so, Lumina. Not this time at least. It's—"

Quin joined the conversation weaving her words between Chase's. "—Short notice. With no time to think this through."

Chase's voice softened and her cheeks flushed. "We can consider it in the future."

"With more time to plan. How long would you stay with me? What would the character of our time be? Vacation, shadowing like an apprentice if that is truly what you want? And right now I am—overtaxed."

"I could help!"

"Mmmm . . . li pas posib, Lumi. Not even the little apprentices can help yet. The All-Question drowns them, and the answer more so. You are not a linguist at this time, if that were even what you wanted."

Chase's voice was brittle now, pressed. "Which you haven't said before. Biological sciences, ecology—That's what you've been studying most."

"And isn't that what I'd be doing, but there in person with real trees! Quin does all of that, doesn't she?"

"Quin—brought us trees. Right here where we live. And they'll need tending to. You can work with my team."

Lumina stopped trying to sound reasonable, adult, and her voice pitched high with emotion. "Those are babies—"

"Which are you asking for? Trees or time with Quin, because I can't tell." Chase threw up her hands.

"Both!? Can't it be both?"

"The trees are young, Lumi, like yourself. There is time for this. But not now. Sispann—stop. Arret. Qef." Quin's voice was calm, measured, but there was no space for argument as she cycled through the many words for stop, one language after another in quick succession. This was her angry, something Lumina had seen only once before but couldn't forget. Not the reason, it was too long ago for that. She just remembered how it made her feel. Like she'd ruined everything.

Lumina stood up from the table with a jerk, her chair, still set on hover, nodding out of her path. "If you don't want me with you, then fine! You're already leaving tomorrow."

"Lumina." There was hurt in Chase's voice, and censure.

How dare she say out loud what they all knew was true.

She had to get out of there.

The door at the back of the room opened as she approached. Her footsteps were like explosions on the polished steel floors, her stomach heavy, nauseated. Her cheeks burned—If Quin didn't want her, she didn't want to want *her* either. She shouldn't have asked. She should have stopped the words before they fell out, but the idea had grown up so vividly in her mind—an invasive species in an already established ecosystem— that she was convinced it could work.

"Lumi, Chér, you cannot just—"

She could hear their voices calling after her. The elevator wound its way through the stalk of the building in a spiral, the black-curtain sky and night-lit city glimmering at her through the glass. She knew they would follow, and they would talk about her. Her cheeks flushed again with heat. She wanted to be somewhere else, anywhere else, not back home with them.

The visit was over. Time was up, and the last of it she'd ruined. She stared out past the city lights to the sky full of stars. There were dozens of colonies and planets in other star-systems, aside from Genti-6, and so many people out there. Quin was supposed to be a gateway to that world and to some ineffable thing she couldn't name.

In which case, Chase was a door shutting her in. She couldn't even get her fingers past the door-jam. They thought she didn't know what she was asking for or what she wanted. But how could she, if she was stuck here? Quin gone again and she hadn't gotten the chance to figure out what was happening to her.

"IF IT'S what she wants so badly—and it's your decision, Mwen Chéri . . . What are you going to do?"

The dim, simulated firelight of the villa cast an orange glow across the side of Chase's face and shoulder and left the other side in shadow. It reminded Quin to keep her voice low lest she wake Lumina down the hall.

Chase didn't answer immediately. Best to be patient. *Give her space to think.*

The pungent, herbal scent of dew-damp plant-life in the garden came in through the open window, along with the indeterminate sounds of native insects and rodents scuffling in the dark. The night was coming to an end, the window to sleep before the day's work ahead, shrinking the longer they sat up in the waning dark.

This was their ritual, each possible moment squeezed out of a visit, sharing a year or two or three worth of experiences, hopes, longings, until the sun rose and Quin's departure time came. There were the old stories, reliving their time together in the ERF.

Talking through, explaining, and reframing the events that led to Chase on Genti-6 and Quin on Earth, and then Lumina, growing and changing every year. Sometimes there were tears. This time the conversation shifted and flowed back to Lumina's request again and again. Each time dissecting a different aspect without settling the matter.

"I'm going to teach her that jumping on impulse almost never gets you anything you feel proud of later."

Quin stuck her lips out, pressed them together and shrugged. "And if that doesn't work for her? Some of us need to jump and fall again and again, oui? You told me that, Chase . . . Your first apprenticeship in Earth's ocean rehab project, and then the ERF where we met—Genti-6, but you are happy here, no?"

"You want me to let her do that?—to run around, colony after colony because she's restless, because she's growing up?!"

Quin raised her hands palms up and sat down next to Chase. "I wouldn't say that. Wouldn't tell you what to do with Lumina. Anti al-Oom—You are her mother, the one caring for her. I trust you."

Chase's shoulders lowered from where they'd pulled up tight around her and her face softened. Her voice came in a low whisper. "I'm sorry, I was projecting on you, because—"

"Because you are scared."

A nod.

She reached for one of Chase's hands and traced the short, sun-kissed fingers idly. She memorized the shapes with her eyes and with her fingertips, the new wrinkles and roughness from time and hard work, a little pink scar running down the pad of her thumb. The words they shared were important, but so was this act of memorizing. She could conjure the texture of each species of tree she had ever felt, and she could conjure Chase. She spoke slowly, gently. "You should never be afraid of me. That I would take her. Don't you know this?"

Chase opened her mouth to object but Quin watched her face fall into self-doubt instead. "I'm not afraid of you." She reached up a hand and brushed the pads of her fingers along Synesis's exposed back.

Again, the touch lit up every neuron in her body, more than a brush against her own skin. It spread from Synesis into the link, the sensation fuller, more nuanced, than the simple gesture that it was. She didn't pull away—This intimacy was earned with hours of close conversation and shared struggle and she welcomed the warmth that flooded her. It was the beginning of goodbyes.

She measured her words with even more care. "But you are afraid she'll leave too soon. Jump into something and get hurt."

"Yes."

Synesis reached for Chase each time she went to pull away. Quin laughed and claimed her hand from the greedy creature, taking it for herself. "That is very distracting . . . and I think there was something you said you were going to tell me, or show me—not that I want to rush this moment, on the contrary, but the sun doesn't plan to wait for us to sleep before it rises."

Chase hesitated, looked away, collected her hands in her own lap.

"Chér, you say you aren't afraid I would take her, but then you are keeping this secret."

"I didn't expect her to want to go with you and that makes it feel like I'm being conspired against."

"By me?"

"No." Agitation was clear in Chase's eyes, the way the words collided and forced their way out reminiscent of Lumina's passion-driven pleas. "By circumstance, or past providence grown to fruition. Like I won't have a choice." She smelled like fear, a damp, feral scent that Synesis picked up and analyzed, naming the chemical compounds and delivering the knowledge to Quin like language. The many flavors of fear, doubt, mistrust, loss.

Quin nodded, her own ache for Chase's pain blossoming. Was it better to tell Chase what she already knew, easier maybe? "Lumina has a reaction to the plant-life on Genti-6. She hears things."

Chase met her eyes, resigned as if Quin's knowing had been inevitable. "It's only a small thing. She feels . . . bubbles, that contact feeling, like an interface just starting but fizzling out."

"It's more than that, Chase-love. Those are smaller order plants, not trees. She—fell today."

"What?"

"She fell into the crate of trees. And I saw her eyes

go distant—saw her drop and black out, Chéri. It was only for a moment, but the tree felt the contact—spoke to her—and Lumina answered without knowing she did. She wore gloves with me after that, and she'll wear them tomorrow."

Chase was on her feet, the color drained from her cheeks. "Why would she black out, she doesn't have an implant."

"She doesn't. But she was attached to me in the AUC, sharing my bloodstream when I took on Synesis."

"Oh . . . oh—" Chase's eyes widened, the green of them darkening when her pupils dilated.

"I think she was inoculated then. I expected it would die off by now if that happened. It should have—it isn't hurting her—this sort of fungus can't, but I am not a mycologist."

"You knew this when?" Chase was trembling, her eyes shadowed. Quin took her arms, guided her back down to sit and Chase let her.

"You have to take her with you then. I don't get a choice. And that's what I was afraid of."

"No. We already decided—I'm not taking her from you. This can wait. She is well."

"I don't want what happened to you—"

"To happen to our Lumi? It will not. Je te promets —Unless you want her to take an interface, an implant —to try and learn. Then I can make no such promises."

"I want to know when you knew!"

"Today, Chéri. I knew today. I wondered before if

there were any traces in her. But I knew nothing, had no basis to think it would do anything."

Chase closed her eyes, fell silent. The sun was threatening to rise, the gradual shift from dark to grey dawn just beginning and Quin knew she had to stop this lingering—to disconnect. There was a guest room holding the minimal things she'd traveled with and more importantly a bed.

She took Chase's hand in her own, laced their fingers together and brought the place where they connected to her lips before pulling away. "And after I leave Genti-6, you'll think and decide and I'll speak to the symbiont mycologists in the ERF, specialists in Mycotremata, to see if we can remove it, kill it off maybe. If that is what you want …"

Chase looked like she had recovered some of herself. But she was pressing a hand over the dormant implant port on the back of her neck, massaging the old loss as she followed her down the hall. "Separation sickness, like we had. She would feel that, wouldn't she?"

"You still feel it, don't you, Chéri mwen?"

A sigh. Chase let the silence bleed into them both before she followed the soft exhale with an answer that wasn't really necessary. They both knew she felt it still, the smallest fraction of what it had been just after her implant had died off, that creeping, aching, tingling feeling like all of her nerves were looking for something. The absence of it sent pulses of alarm up her spine into her skull. Quin knew the feeling. She knew it intimately because she had lived it for sixteen years before she took on another mushroom. It was agony; the barest fraction of the feeling a torture.

They paused at the first room where thin sunbeams filtered through gaps between the drapes.

"Quin?"

"Oui, Chéri?"

"Does she want this because of that? Because she has it in her, calling out?"

Quin opened her mouth to speak and found the answer hard to put into words. So much of language was insufficient, even with all of them to choose from. "We both were called to the cause before we had our symbionts, and she is a little of both of us. Is it so hard to believe she wants to help the trees like she says? She is us and however much of the fungus is in her, if I am right to think it."

"Would she be—Lumina without it? If we took it out?" Chase's answer was stilted, and Quin heard the words catch on the choices that Chase doubtless felt hovering just ahead of them.

She nodded with a pained smile, glanced at the empty bed in the guest room. It was time to go, to sleep however long she could before she oversaw the planting and spoke to the saplings one last time. But the thought of being the one to finally break away, and leave Chase with her troubled thoughts, it felt like betrayal. And maybe didn't want to be alone.

She gestured to the bed, squeezed Chase's hand and then released it. "If you don't want to be alone …"

Chase shook her head. "I can't sleep. Lumina could wake up and I want to be there. If she needs to talk."

Quin nodded, climbed into the bed and listened for Chase's footsteps to fade before she let out her breath. She would be tired when she woke, her apprentices would be waiting at the new orchard, and she would do what needed done. She would give the saplings as much as they would hold, try to spread the knowledge as deep as she could into the infantile mycelial network the colonists had grown. That might buy this orchard some time before it needed her back.

Another thought occurred to her, one she felt guilty to anticipate; they might need her to return frequently and there would be more time on Genti-6 with Chase and Lumi. A selfish thought and one she couldn't want, not while there were trees on Earth. Inaya's admonishments rang in her head. This project would take her time and her energy, time and energy that Earth needed from her.

What was done was done, and the ERF had been paid for these trees. She'd return only as needed and each time she did they would have to revisit this thing with Lumina.

FOOTSTEPS, in the guest room down the hall—Lumina perked up in the claw-footed chair in the foyer. Her legs complained as she shifted her crooked, curled up position. Three hours. She'd been waiting three hours for Quin, ears straining for sounds of waking while the sun crept higher and dust motes streamed in the sunbeams that peaked through pine green drapes.

A flutter of excitement had woken her early and as she showered, dressed, and waited the excitement grew into a bright spark of anticipation. Quin was leaving today, but first they'd plant the orchard together and she'd slip her glove off so that she could feel the bark of the tree. Then she'd see if anything else happened. Even if she couldn't go to Earth with Quin, there were trees on Genti-6 now, and that meant a chance to convince Chase that she should apprentice with Quin.

Her face warmed and her nerves flared up. She couldn't sit still so she paced, peered out the drapes at the stone garden full of low water plants, lichen, succulents, the dry little ferns designed for Genti-6. She was waiting at the door when Quin got there with cold buttered bread in one hand, a placeholder for breakfast —Quin must be anxious to reach the trees now that she was up.

"Time to go?" Lumina's voice chirped in sharp contrast to the way she'd sounded last night, she almost judged herself, mocked her own swift turn of mood. But time was too short for grudges. She moved to disarm the security system on the door; the sensors would identify her and that was authorization enough.

Quin's eyes traced over her with a look of concern. She was slow to smile and Lumina's heart did a flip-flop of anxiety. Something had gone wrong–changed overnight. "What?"

"You're staying home, Lumi." Chase's voice reached Lumina from the hallway where she leaned against the wall. Her clothes were rumpled as if she'd fallen asleep in them, and her hair was a mass of dark tangles.

Lumina shot wide eyes at Quin and saw no objections, no questioning of Chase's edict. She was instead looking away, out the window where the position of the sun showed it to be well past sunrise.

Then Quin's posture softened and she reached a hand out for Lumina's. "Trees are something you'll have to adjust to carefully. There are risks for you. Je suis desole."

"What? What risks?" Disappointment choked her voice, made it pitch higher and break. She didn't take the offered hand.

Chase stayed where she was and crossed her arms. "Quin's work takes her full attention, she needs all of her energy for educating the trees and settling them in."

"Fine—I can be extra hands. I'll be silent, no questions! I just want to be there." For some reason Chase flinched at what she'd said. How dare she take this personally? Chase's sudden decision didn't make sense and it didn't match up with her explanation. Quin didn't have energy for her now? That wasn't what she said when she got here. They were lying, keeping secrets or else they'd decided to go back to treating her like a literal infant. But Quin's invitation to plant with her was before she asked to be her apprentice and then stormed of.

"No, Lumi. You cannot argue through this and we

are not—we cannot explain better because I have to go. Your mother will explain it when she decides what to do."

Lumina's head filled with fire and the words came out before she could stop it. "And aren't you my mother too? You said I could help—now I can't go with you to the other colonies and I can't even go to the orchard here?! Do you just come back so I can remember you don't want me?!"

"Lumina!" Chase had crossed the room; now she reached for Lumina's shoulder, but Lumina shook it off and ran down the hall. Her heart pounded as she fled, but it couldn't drown out the voices in the foyer or the sound of the door hissing shut behind Quin. Angry voices, hurt bubbling into words like poison from a cauldron with the fire too hot beneath. Were they arguing now? They never argued, not in her memory.

She ran faster, shoved her face against the rumpled bed-sheets and crushed a pillow over her head.

The anger settled into a heavy sickness in the pit of her stomach. After the initial storm of tears she went through the motions. When evening came, Chase led her out of the villa but she only shook her head or nodded, no words for Chase's softly intoned questions. Was she hungry? Could she get her jacket?

She didn't know why she'd said what she said or if she meant any of it. Her own words replayed in her head and each time they did they left a residue of shame and a heaviness that made walking, or sitting, or holding up her head feel like too much work. Chase still hadn't tried to explain why she kept her home, and she didn't ask.

When they reached the station, the space elevator's door was open for Quin to step inside. The three apprentices were strapped into their seats waiting, too far from her for Lumina to hear their whispered conversation. She envied their uniforms, and their whispers. Most of all she envied their seats on the elevator. What were the chances they would believe her if she climbed in while Chase and Quin were distracted. She could say Quin was bringing her and sit on the far side of the back-to-back circle of seats and she might not notice quick enough. . . . But Quin would send her away.

The two of them stood off to the side, hands interlaced, foreheads together in ritual parting. They'd always done that, but this time the gesture was fleeting. She could feel their tension, as if the physical space between them itched to grow wider instead of longing to close up.

Quin stepped away and her eyes landed on Lumina. She must have felt the silent observation. All thoughts of trying to sneak into the elevator withered. It was absurd fantasy, a joke without humor. And the joke was on her. Quin didn't want her there, remember?

"Lumi, Chér . . . It's time for me to go."

She hadn't spoken a word to either of them. And she'd sworn she wouldn't. Now that Quin was really going, she wanted to hold on so tight that Quin wouldn't be able to leave yet. Part of her did.

What would she say? How would she explain?

Quin took a step toward her, offered a hug. She didn't resist. She even leaned into the embrace, but there were too many raw emotions that would spill out if she relaxed against Quin. So she stayed still and stiff, and she waited even as the ache grew into a throb of grief.

Quin touched her cheek, smiled. She didn't have a smile to answer with.

Then the elevator car swallowed Quin up. The door hissed shut revealing the smooth metallic surface with a sign warning her *"Caution when door is shut"* and *"Keep back."*

The car rose in the shining frame of the tower, out of the station and up through Genti-6's dry atmosphere. It made the squeal of a rocket taking off on bumpy metal tracks, much louder in the station than anywhere else in the colony, loud enough for her to cover her ears.

Quin was gone again, along with her chance to reach anything that mattered.

CHAPTER 5

DOWN THE PATH DARKLY

I t was not an argument.

The words between herself and Chase were only fear for Lumina. Chase trusted her, Oui? She had to know that Quin would never have caused such a thing on purpose.

Quin stared out at the star-studded blanket of space enfolding the cabin of the shift drive. It still smelled like soil and the respiration of trees. A scattering of leaves decorated the shining metal floors, vestiges of the saplings she had known since they'd sprouted seed, all of them likely to die on Genti-6.

She repeated the refrain to herself in Arabic, in Creole, in Tree, in hopes that it would stick—Lam yecun hujatan—It wasn't an argument . . . se pa sa . . . But Lumina hadn't spoken to either of them at the loading dock. She stood there like a wooden doll, if wood could seethe and suffer in her arms.

And why would she? Why would Lumina want to speak to either of them?

Gloves would have been enough to keep Lumina safe in the orchard. They weren't enough for Chase. She'd kept her home instead, cut short their time together with thin excuses and placations.

Quin had pushed the gloves. . . . She shouldn't have pushed.

She turned away from the memory and waited for the ache of it to pass.

The safety straps in the ship froze and refused to move as she tugged. She jerked harder, anger puppeteering her hands. The target of her ire made it worse. Could she be angry at Chase—was that even allowed? It felt like sacrilege, like being angry with Synesis—impossible. But the emotion kept welling up, and under it, thoughts.

Chase was wrong about this, and Lumina would feel the consequences.

She dropped the straps and willed her mind to follow a different path before trying to adjust them again. Chase was justifiably scared, Lumina longing, fighting for something she felt she needed. And she was caught between the two. She felt Synesis's thoughts flow with her own, little sparks of imagery breaking up her turmoil like points of conifers breaking up a horizon.

She tried the straps again and they settled into place with a click. The course was already plotted— but she hesitated.

Genti-6 had its trees. The other colony orchards in a handful of systems needed her attention. They could wait a day. Her apprentices were already on the way. They could rest, take inventory of any tree deaths, take soil samples, and the replacement trees could acclimate to their new planet until she arrived.

Jordan wasn't likely to attempt interfacing without her, not after the last time. Still, the thought—the *fear*—that the child would take risks crossed her mental landscape like a taunt. But it was too late to stop what she'd already set in motion. She was needed somewhere else.

Too long. It had been too long. She had to make time for this if no one else would and now that she'd decided to go, she wanted to, needed to for herself as much as for the Pain Trees.

There was time. Even if it wasn't on the itinerary. The ERF wasn't here to approve or disapprove, no General Waters or other supervisors to deny her an extra shift destination.

A trip that should take years only took hours—none of her mission, the colonies, the seeding of planets, the spread of Earth life to other systems would be possible without shift drive technology, technology that she engaged now with a single command to "Initiate Shift."

Lumina and Chase wouldn't get out of her head, the argument that wasn't but felt like it was. Chase was wrong. Lumina was floundering and Quin had caused this, then left them that way—left them when they needed her to—what?

Chase and Lumina were a unit, just like she and Synesis. They didn't need her interference.

They couldn't.

She closed her eyes against waves of rolling vertigo and her stomach flipped over itself as she came back into static space in a new location. She had to reorient her sense of direction, her place in time space once the shift was made. A slow breath in through her nose while the nausea receded. Another. Out slow and steady until the spinning in her senses stopped.

The planet below was uncolonized, one of the old seed planets, and it hung there like a misty red and olive-drab marble with swirls of darker pine. It orbited a red dwarf at a distance just far enough to avoid being tidally locked–the Pain Trees wouldn't have grown here at all if the planet had permanent light and dark sides, but with such a small sun it was cold and foggy where the Pain Trees grew.

It could have been a colony planet, but the whole of it was boggy and unstable, prone to sinkholes and shifting terrain that would be hard to get started on. Quin dropped into the atmosphere using only rockets and landed in water, then brought the ship to hover above the surface and the Pain Trees.

Her movements and mental processes were mechanical, perfunctory as she ran the small ship that was infinitely complex in its conception and construction but simple in its operation. It left more space than she wanted for her thoughts, what Lumina had said—shouted at her really.

Aren't you *my mother?*

A canopy of leaf-laden branches swaying, with sunlight streaming through and revealing blue sky flashed into her mind—Synesis directing her thoughts. She shuddered, pushed back instead of accepting the redirection. The chemical comfort she fought as well, turning ease to guilt with her vehemence.

No, the answer was no. She was not the child's mother, at least in the way Lumina was asking it. She had combined their gametes, grown Lumina in the AUC attached to her own body, fed her with her bloodstream, birthed her . . . but was she her mother? No. That was the decision she'd made when she took on a second mushroom during the pregnancy and become the carrier for the mother tree's knowledge. How many could she tend to with all of tree living in her?

Lumi needed more, deserved more. So she'd brought her to Chase.

To mother was a choice, not a biological imperative. A choice made in innumerable moments across a lifetime, to sacrifice, to nurture. And she had made the choice to give Lumina up.

Chase had chosen to accept full responsibility for the child. To contradict her decisions for Lumina now would be a betrayal. But to tell herself it wasn't what she *wanted* to do would be a lie.

The implant stage on Quin's neck set off cooling features and she felt her whole body sigh along with Synesis. Indulging this anger, blocking out their mind-link with the intensity of her grief was heating their shared neurons.

A thick fog surrounded the ship. There were shapes resolving from the grey, twisted, jagged shapes that she needed to reach. She opened the hatch and the reek of boggy decay and sodden plant-life hit her on the way down. Volatile organic compounds, ethylene and tannin heavy, set her nerves on edge—these trees were in a constant state of alarm even after the reparations she'd made.

Her boots sunk deep but she held on to the ladder long enough to test the ground. The mud was thick here but more solid deeper down, and if she moved quickly she wouldn't sink into the mire.

The shapes solidified as she drew closer, the mud making sucking sounds against her boots. Twisted trees that were meant to be cypress stood with their spreading bases deep in the wet ground and their peeling bark blackened and sap-stained. They weren't as they'd been when she first saw them, limbs bent at sharp angles and trunks crushed together, fragmented and confined by broken oblong delivery capsules. Those capsules had become shrapnel as they descended through the atmosphere and landed without opening properly to distribute their seed.

The shrapnel was gone, cleared away, the largest sections of it at least. Some had to be left, so deeply was it embedded in the trees. At Quin's insistence, the broken branches and fissures in their trunks had been repaired by a team of arboriculturists from the ERF.

They needed more care, but when it became clear that these trees held no further answer to solving the decline and were only a drain on resources, the chain of command had drawn the line.

Quin raised her hands over the bark of the largest of the trees. Its presence was like a current of ice water bubbling and chuckling deep underground. She felt it before touching, the tree's life-force, like hovering a hand over a child and feeling warmth and breath. She braced her knees against the shredded, red bark and sap seeped into her clothes. It was better than submerging them into several inches of water and sinking knees into the mud along with her boots.

Synesis urged her forward. She promised escape, pleasure, release if she communed with these trees. None of those things would come. She knew it even as she obeyed, lowered her hands and pressed them into the damp bark. These trees were tortured, trauma filled and holding centuries of suffering. Their minds couldn't hold the answers to the All-Question, no longer than the forgetful saplings, but Quin searched for any traces of it as the discordant screaming of the Pain Trees filled her head.

They screamed in her mind just as they screamed into the air with their volatile compounds—scent-based warnings to other trees that weren't there and calls for help that wouldn't come.

Nothing. There was nothing of the All-Question there, nothing she could grasp onto. It had been too long since she'd comforted and reminded them. The demands of fighting the decline had kept her away and she ached now for their years of suffering—lost, empty, without direction. They had no tether to the trees that had born their seeds on Earth—long dead—or to the other seeded planets. Their mycelial networks sustained their physical existence but couldn't spread far enough to link them to the remaining trees in the galaxy—ones that might soothe and balance them and hold more complete memory of the answers they needed. This planet had nothing at all to offer them, too foreign for them to integrate into its alien ecology. They shouldn't have survived at all, but here they were, clinging to existence.

They were alone—so Quin would teach them, replay the call-response song of the All-Question and answer for them as you would tell a bedtime story to a child, the words repeating and repeating and repeating until they managed to soothe.

She began the story with seeds—tiny pods with infinite potential to create, buried deep and nourished. It was as she told it before—

A lance of pain in her mind shoved back at her—pushed—instead of listening this time, the Pain Trees answered back, the visceral imagery of cramped, trapped seeds: most of them moldering and decaying back into the soil, others sprouting and struggling. It wasn't a song but a scream and before Quin could assert more of the story she'd been repeating for years, teaching and reteaching the meaning and history of what it meant to be Tree, the scream filled her mind.

Pain—the story of trees grown mangled, damaged and struggling, saplings sprouted, dying off until only this small cluster remained, cut-off, alone. The trees asserted their truth and it seeped into Quin until she felt herself answering.

She was alone, separate, without a single tether to bind her—she *was* the Pain Tree. Aching, calling out, her whole body spasming in the silent stillness of a tree.

She slid against the tree's rough bark and sank into the mud up to her waist. Or was it deeper? How long had she been here with the trees? So long—many hundred letters to Chase of time, all of them unread and unanswered. A voice whispered in her ear, small and fragile like a child's—Lumi wasn't wanted. There was no bond between them. Lumi was a void and Quin had made her so by not loving her.

Synesis should have denied the voice, given her pictures of beauty and hope. Her mushroom should be silencing that voice. Quin reached for Synesis but the mushroom was silent, dead on her body and slowly shriveling.

Panic moved her, filled her mind and body—that wasn't right, was it? Synesis dead?

She couldn't be certain.

A sudden impulse forced Quin away from the tree. She shoved against the sticky bark, splashed into the water, rolled onto hands and knees to crawl on all fours, sucked in air. Her stomach clenched and she vomited, spitting to remove as much of the sour taste as possible. There wasn't much to throw-up—the toast from breakfast was already digested and she'd had nothing else.

She sat back shaking and raised one cautious hand to the mushroom. Her whole body flushed with warmth and relief, numbing lassitude, and the ripples in the bog water took on fractal shapes, the scraggly leaves of the cypress were outlined in bands of rainbow light. It had the taste of high-dose endorphins with a touch of psilocin. Synesis was fine. The surge of adrenaline must have been her as well.

Merci. You pulled me back . . .

Synesis wasn't dead, wasn't shriveled. Euphoria, gratitude, relief flooded her, and then

faded, replaced by a slick current of unease. It wasn't supposed to happen that way, she was supposed to give them the All-Question, to soothe and heal them, but instead she'd joined them where they were.

She sighed as the endorphins worked on the cramps in her muscles, leaving her limp and breathless but pain-free on the wet ground. *Enough ...*

The thought was her mushroom's—*Enough. Go home.*

Quin sat up. Her hands were still shaking but she reached for the tree. *Just a bit more. I can be careful.*

She collected the next section of the healing message she'd meant to upload, ready at the forefront of her mind before touching the tree. When she started the upload, she pushed the message past anything the Pain Tree screamed at her. It was like shoving a boulder upstream. A wave of nausea hit her hard and fast. *STOP!*

I can do this, Syny. Quin pressed her mud-smeared forehead to the tree along with both hands and forced more of the message into the link; still, some of their pain seeped past what she was giving them.

She had to stop. Her vision greyed out in gnat-swarms of black and white and she slumped over. It was like drinking poison, worse than it had been the first time she'd come here.

Why weren't they in less pain, or at least a little healed from the efforts she'd made? The removal of the confining metal capsules that bound them and limited their growth, the broken limbs and weeping gashes shored up and healed?

It should have helped. It should but it—didn't.

She groaned, fought the urge to keep trying. She needed to make them better, to assert the truth to them, to prove that it *was* the truth and that it mattered.

But she didn't reach for the tree again. Her hands were too heavy, tingling. Her arms and legs were heavier. She laughed, one escaped sound that felt more like a cry and was too loud in the isolated landscape. She pressed the backs of her shaking hands against her eyes and fought to keep them open. Synesis was sedating her, whispering soothing words into the back of her mind, urging her toward the ship.

THERE WERE messages for her when she returned to the ship. The Liaison for the Gliese system wanted to know if she would be arriving later that day as planned and the ERF commander wanted confirmation of her current location. Nothing from Chase.

None of this matters. It was a thought bubbling up from somewhere deeper in her subconscious. She shook it off. Of course it mattered. All of it mattered. She entered the next destination in the ship's computer. It was the next step. And that was what she needed, planned, predictable steps to keep moving until she could shake off the bone-deep fatigue from her contact with the Pain Trees.

Her mushroom was pushing her along, but the adrenaline it took made her shaky and a little nauseous. Maybe that was hunger too but the idea of putting anything in her system made her stomach turn.

Another shift travel would make the nausea worse, but she'd be planet-side soon enough.

She opened the message screen, the ever-ready channel to message Chase. Openings ran through her head, testing themselves out, but she pushed each aside, settling finally on a simple string of questions that would likely go unanswered until the questions no longer mattered. *Is Lumina speaking to you? Have you explained the medical problem we were protecting her from? Does she understand her options?*

There was a moment of choice between closing out the message and sending or continuing on, spilling out her own thoughts, detailing the nightmare-scape of fear driven insecurities that had taken hold of her with the Pain Trees: that Chase and Lumina were separate, distant, and they wanted it that way, would be better off that way. But Chase didn't need her to project that mess onto them when she could process it herself and then put it in its place. Better to send it this way.

She engaged the shift drive, and then closed her eyes, waited for the shaky feeling of existing outside of reality to pass while the ship made the much slower approach to the geosynchronous space station above Gliese.

A hand shook her, and she startled. There wasn't supposed to be anyone there in the ship with her and this hand felt more like a branch, rough and sap-covered where it squeezed her shoulder too tight, the grip biting and abrasive even through her uniform.

Quin's eyes snapped open but her mental processing was three steps behind—she wasn't with the Pain Trees, *click*—this was the inside of the space elevator car and it was stopped, that spinning was in her head, *click*—the hand belonged to her Gliese liaison and it was firm but gentle, respectful, shaking her awake when she hadn't answered, *click*–The rest of the information came together and she adjusted her posture, checked her straps and her facial expressions, put on a self-deprecating smile as she focused in on the older gentleman that was staring at her with concern.

She cleared her throat. "Commissioner Elkan."

"Sleeping deeply there, Sgt. Fleury." His leathery skin creased in a warm smile surrounding sepia-brown eyes that were watery from natural aging.

She disengaged the safety harness and stood up, looked around the elevator car as she took the hand he offered her. Everything seemed in place, expected but she didn't have any memory of getting into the elevator. The interior of the space was spare and compact but padded and built to withstand impact should the cables break and result in free-fall. Everything was normal, but it didn't feel that way.

The support beams of the elevator overhead and the smiling faces of the ecological team, the commissioner who'd woken her, she fought to see them as they were.

There was a dreamlike quality to everything, a buffering feeling to her processing and to each of her senses. Her hand in Elkan's felt almost numb as if she was only feeling it on one level—with a minute portion of her sensory processing. The tree branch on her shoulder, on the other hand, had been hyper-real, and the sense of dream persisted making her shaky and more nauseous than she'd been on the Pain Tree's planet.

"I think—" She took another few steps and then placed a hand on a young woman in a lab coat's shoulder. "I think I need to eat before seeing your orchard."

"Your apprentices are there already. They can wait a little longer. Hold your place while you eat." The assemblage laughed, some of it nervous laughter. *She'd really been hard to wake*, their faces said. *She'd looked like she was dead.* Some of their faces said that too. The laughter was a release, and they moved together as a unit, unwilling to separate or slow down lest the loss of momentum leave their Tree-Whisperer behind on the platform passed out from exhaustion or hunger or whatever was bothering her.

Quin felt a measure of chagrin as they placed hands on her, walked with her—tense enough to catch her if she stumbled. They seated her in front of food, but found she could only take in a few bites before the nausea welled up. A heavily-spiced grain and legume delicacy felt wooden in her mouth and there seemed to be compounds missing from its profile of scents and flavors. Her disorientation lingered and buffered her from the greater part of how she must have seemed to them.

There were protestors outside of this station just as there had been on Genti-6, but Commissioner Elkan seemed to take no notice. The protestors were so completely ignored by the party surrounding her and tending to her that it could have been a hallucination when she saw Inaya's silhouette pass outside of the windows, either a hallucination of the woman or of a return to Genti-6 where they had last argued.

She toyed with the idea that she was coming down sick, something near-impossible with a mushroom symbiont buffering her immune system—stress sick maybe—Commissioner Elkan, the warm man that she'd exchanged messages with between visits to the colony's orchard, offered up that it was exhaustion coupled with the frequent shift travel that could be a strain on the mind and body.

He offered her hot tea after the meal that she'd forced down so little of and suggested she meet with the trees tomorrow; they were losing leaves again, but not so fast that a day would matter, not if it refreshed her. The trees would have no recourse if she collapsed. But the way he said it, he was more concerned for her health than the orchard. That made her decision.

The trees *were* dropping leaves, and some had fallen prey to black rot and would need to be burned. She could smell the faint musty perfume of it. She hovered a hand over the strongest tree in the orchard and then paused. There were several ecologists present, lingering in case she needed anything. Her apprentices hovered to watch, some placing their hands on the tree Quin had chosen to passively shadow the interface.

She looked at the assembled ecologists and her apprentices. "Si vous plait, bitte—Can you please—leave us? I'll need to do this without any distraction. It takes more focus when I'm tired."

Jordan was closest, her face pinched with concern. Quin gave her a look that she hoped said *don't argue this time,* and the young woman withdrew her hands from the sapling. She heard Ithaca mumble something contrary, Ronin was silent.

They accepted the lie so quickly, but a certain amount of reverence came with her position, the mature mushroom she wore, and by virtue of being the only Tree linguist capable of an upload on this scale.

Why lie to them? Was it Synesis's question, or her own?

They were already worried and seeing her struggle—she couldn't bear any more of that attention.

With everyone gone, exhaustion settled over her. It didn't matter. This was no more than she'd done before. Her hands pressed against the silver-white bark of the young aspen. The tree's consciousness, like a band of chill air, hovered around the bark, against her palms and then in her mind. They were confused—talking in circles and interspersing fragments of what she'd taught them the time before, with plaintive questions.

She closed her eyes and began the upload, slowly at first and then with more force. She cycled through everything she had for them again and again. It needed to stick this time. It needed to last longer. She began again, circling back in hopes that this tree would make the ever-elusive connection that she'd felt when first linked to the mother tree.

It was elusive, not only because none of the saplings ever seemed to fully grasp it, but because she'd had trouble with the full scope of it herself after that first moment of insight and understanding. She had replayed it so many times that it had begun to lose meaning, like a word rewritten or said aloud until it is nothing but a collection of letters and meaningless sounds. As she pressed on, there was a sense of numbness as she played the story of Tree for the umpteenth time.

It was the same cycle, the same story that had enlivened the young trees before, but that feeling of profundity didn't come, it didn't bring tears to her eyes as it had for the first thousand replays, and in the absence of that feeling she found darker thoughts surfacing, a replay of the Pain Tree's alternate story. It was only in flashes, and she turned away from it and renewed her attempts to replay, repeat, and feel the message the orchard needed. But it was insidious, insistent, and it returned each time she pushed it away.

The sun was setting somewhere outside of her awareness. Hours must have passed in the orchard. It felt like hours, weeks even, but an upload didn't take that long.

She opened her eyes to the orchard in twilight—cold, she could see her breath and her hands still pressed against the base of the tree were stiff and aching with the chill. It was a good thing she'd told them to leave under the pretense that their small sounds of pacing, or fidgeting, or whispering, could distract her.

The possibility that she'd black out and frighten them had been real enough that bending the truth was necessary. She'd lost time somehow, but there was no one here to be concerned. She could collect herself without their worrying and the protective, doting behavior that made her feel so exposed.

When she collected herself, brushed off the leaves and made her way to the ecological headquarters the team's concern was palpable. It had taken her so long, well past sunset, but they were comforted by her reports of success and happy to take her instructions for handling the black rot, and then let her move on to the next planet waiting for her.

Several more planets. The same pleasantries and behaviors pasted over different faces, each of them some percentage reverent, some percentage afraid or repulsed by Synesis, anxious, protective. And Quin went through the motions, shaking hands, laughing appropriately, accepting hospitality before she could do the work she came for.

With complete commitment, she poured everything she had into the trees until she collapsed at their roots only to begin again, there or in another orchard on another planet until they all blurred together and she still saw their outlines in her mind's eye and felt the smooth, rumpled, or roughened bark under her hands once back on the ship.

The apprentices hovered around the outskirts of her awareness, and she could feel a coming storm through them. Jordan's face grew sharper, those quick eyes looked closer to discern the reason behind Quin's behavior. There wasn't time for teaching. There wasn't energy for it or patience. It would have to wait until Earth. After she had rested, licked her wounds. No letters from Chase . . . no word about Lumi.

She was only grateful that her apprentices kept their questions to themselves and if they were thinking of cornering her, demanding answers, she didn't give them a chance. Her duty to the trees didn't give them a chance. All of her waking moments were spent with hands on bark or fingers delving down to the mycelium around their roots.

Quin was on course for Earth before she finally slept well and deeply without the sudden blackouts of upload exhaustion. It took that long for the messages from the colonies she'd visited to begin reaching her, and much longer for her to ever see them.

QUIN WAS sicker than she could remember being since taking on Synesis. Sixteen years with nothing more than that allergic reaction to wildflowers on Gliese-7 and a bout of food poisoning. Neither of those could compare to this. Chills, fever, nausea—a taste of decaying compost in the back of her throat. A burning sensation in all of her mucus membranes. She wasn't the only one affected. Black mold infestation had started in Synesis and spread through the implant stage, making the mental effects worse than the physical.

Because of the differences in their bodies the mushroom struggled against Quin's heat, the implant stage cooled itself and Synesis to keep her from overheating, but Quin needed her fever. The perpetual cold at the back of her neck, normally a comfort or a minor inconvenience, made her tremble violently as her body fought to burn away the illness. She could feel

Synesis's delirium. Her mind on fire, a landscape of wavering smoke and shadows.

Upon waking, she reached for Synesis to soothe her and found to her horror, her hands were strapped down. She couldn't even roll onto her side. Hours later or just moments, she couldn't tell which, hands were moving her, bathing her heated skin and changing her clothes, pulling at the tangled sheets beneath her.

There were voices in the room, there and then gone, and she didn't want them there. Something about their whispers felt like loss, phantasms of voices she would have wanted to hear. There was a sickly-sweet scent of fear for which she couldn't find an origin.

Were they afraid of her implant or the sickness it might spread? But when the attendants were gone the smell remained. It was coming from her. Sounds in the room came and went along with the rising and setting of the sun through the windows—more whispers, the rush of fans and the low beeps of machinery.

Synesis was dying, the voices said, and she knew that decaying sweetness was the mushroom's smell, her normally buoyant, crisp scent of life turned sweet then sour then musty. Was it real this time or was it in her head like when she interfaced with the Pain Trees?

Her eyes opened on Sgt. Waters—retired General, he was a general now not a sergeant. There were attendants carrying in potted trees, pushing them close to the bed. The attendants, people she recognized from the ERF implant laboratories, pressed her hands against the trees. She couldn't lift them herself, but she could feel something, whispers, not human voices but Tree.

They didn't make any sense at first until—something stirred in her mind. Synesis could hear the tree whispers. *Not dead . . . not rotting.*

She woke for the first time without a fever. Events seemed to flow more slowly, more linear each time she opened her eyes, until time reasserted itself at the pace she was used to, and she found herself able to sit up and think without getting carried away in the rushing river flow of delirium.

Her hands were free again and she reached back to find the edges of her implant stage, her mushroom still there and alive. There were healing caverns and valleys in the mushroom's back. The fruiting bodies had shed during the illness but smaller bumps that would replace them were already beginning to form.

Trees circled the bed, small citrus in pots, orange and lemon, brought in to keep her mushroom from suffering withdrawal and dying off before she could respond to the antifungals used to combat the black rot. She would have to thank Waters for that, at least. Black rot . . . they'd contracted it somewhere in their travels, or maybe already had it. For how long?

Synesis was resistant to black rot, exposed many times without effect. She looked back on the weeks of exhaustion and compromised judgement during her trip. She could have been infected the whole time, slowly growing worse until she'd finally given out on the trip home or it could have come from the colony on Gliese where some of the trees had black rot.

"Hey, Waters?"

He was sitting on the edge of her bed reading something from a screen that he then folded and tucked in a pocket of his jacket, cleared his throat. "Are you ready to talk then?"

"Ahh . . . am I?

"Maybe I should call your nurse in?"

She rubbed a hand across her mouth, and squeezed her eyes shut tight before opening them again. "Le, Laisa min alduroor. The proposals though. Have you shared them? Any progress? Was General Élysée sympathetic?"

There was something in his manner that made her stop. He was restless in his seat, shifting his posture and his eyes evaded her searching until he pulled the screen out of his pocket and handed it to her. "About that . . . Seems you've gotten yourself into some trouble."

A yellow leaf fell from the nearest orange tree. The screen was full of messages, her messages.

The first several were marked urgent, all of them from officials on the colony planets she had visited. One from Inaya of all people.

"They're all cc'd to the ERF—your chain of command has them. I—pried into your business as friends do. What the hell happened out there?"

She sat up straighter and skimmed the topics and keywords of the messages. The air in the room became oppressive, heavy around her and her guts clenched as the meaning of written words sank in.

"The trees I contacted with, all but Genti-6 looks like. They're all sick, declining fast. Mwen oblije tounen —I have to get back there."

"I don't think you're gonna be going anywhere anytime soon."

"If they want their trees to live, I will." She looked back over the emails more slowly searching for a cause to the sickness and finding none. "They all must have black rot. We were sick with it—I felt sick the whole time. I thought it was lack of sleep."

Waters was shaking his head, his eyes begging her to stop.

"What?"

"That's not what happened Quin. They don't have black rot. They don't have infestations. Mineral imbalance . . . nothing. They have decline symptoms, and they've been hit hard since right after your uploads, so I'm going to ask you again, what happened?" His voice was gentler than his words, but his brows furrowed and there was a twitch in his jaw.

"I was—I was sick, so maybe the uploads didn't work when I thought they did." She searched her mind for details, for signs that the uploads hadn't worked at all. But it had never happened that way before, no matter how tired she had been, even blacking out by the end of an interface didn't mean anything for the trees, just for her.

"Well, whatever you said to your commander she's

come back early from leave and she's waiting to see you in her office when you've been cleared medically."

Quin's heart-beat flipped-flopped and her eyes widened. "Oh."

"Oh? You want to tell me what it's about?"

"Weh. I put in my separation papers before leaving for Genti-6. It's probably about that."

Quin's voice trailed off. She was reading Inaya's letter now, avoiding his eyes.

Sgt. Fleury,

Sometimes the taste of being right is a bitter fare. Word travels fast. Your little tame orchards are all but dead. You are sewing the decline deeper instead of unraveling it. Are you beginning to see from our perspective? Come to my home when you are ready for true collaboration.

Inaya

Earth Is Home

Waters' patience wore out and he leaned into her line of sight. "What?"

"The letter from Inaya, curious … I think she must have a fungus in her brain—"

"No Quin, what you said. Separation papers? Are you out of your mind?"

Quin waved a hand and leaned back in the bed. Her head was throbbing again. "It was . . . It seemed like the thing to do at the time. I will straighten it out."

CHAPTER 6
GIFT OR CURSE

Lumina's eyes moved over the printed words in the hard cover book, *Fundamentals in Molecular Mycology*, the pages brittle and musty smelling. She didn't look down from where she hovered by the tops of the bookshelves, but the words on the page gave no meaning, not with Chase standing in the doorway pleading for her to talk, to stop "brooding". She closed the book and used her most steady voice. "I never see her and now she's gone. I needed . . . time with her, to figure out some of this stuff in my head."

Chase ducked her head but then righted herself and crossed her arms. "What stuff can't we figure out?"

Lumina sighed and searched that earnest face, those eyes that said her mother wanted to be her everything, and if she wasn't it meant she wasn't enough. It was hard to draw out the words meeting those eyes so she looked away, at the curling fern patterns on the tile floor. She traced them with her toes in the air, little spirals. "Just, things about her and about us. Things that I shouldn't remember but do. And things you don't tell me."

The hurt in her mother's eyes blossomed. "What things? I tell you things."

"No. You don't, and neither does she and now you're both saying I can't go to the orchard and I have to wait for you to explain to me why? Well, when is that happening?"

Chase stared back at her, wordless, holding herself and leaning against the bookshelf by the open doorway.

"Exactly."

"That's not fair. You act like this is the way it has been, the way it always is."

Lumina dropped the faded, antique tome on the top of the bookshelf, and then she lowered her chair with a soft whir, dropping out of it before it reached the ground. "You want me to have things that interest me, outside of this room, these books, the garden—and then you shut me down when I do want something, force me to wear gloves, why? And you won't answer."

"No, I won't answer anything when you're yelling."

Lumina froze and listened to herself, the mental echo of her words. *Yelling?* She wasn't trying to yell but her volume had slowly crept up and all of the hurt and anger since Quin had left had seeped into her voice. She collected those raw feelings and tried again, to lower her voice and her intensity. "Okay, what's the reason?"

"Quin told me what happened in the elevator

station. You hit your head, blacked out. And the things you feel when you touch the garden plants here. It got me worried that you could get sick like Quin did once."

Her heart was thudding in her ears, and her pulse racing. If they thought it too, she wasn't imagining it. *Like Quin.*

"But you don't have an implant, and it doesn't make a lot of sense, so Quin and I wanted to find some answers first."

The explanation should have made her feel better but instead it was worse, so much worse. Quin wouldn't be back any time soon. She never was.

"I could have worn the gloves. Or you could have let her decide if I could handle it." She didn't yell this time, but Chase flinched as if she had.

"I'm sorry, Lum. Could we just—start this all over?" She reached out with a beckoning hand, the sort a child makes begging to be lifted up.

Lumina held back, suspended for a moment between her hurt and the urge to forgive. They always forgave each other. She fell into the offered hug, rested her head on Chase's shoulder, felt her shuddering breaths and relief heavy sighs "So start over how? Cuz Quin left already and—"

"Can't fix that but—s'mores tonight? Because you know we didn't s'more yet and the prescribed amount of s'moring is—well, a lot more than none."

Lumina wiped her eyes and couldn't stop the laugh. "Oh, is that the message I'm supposed to learn— s'mores for all problems?"

Chase shrugged and tweaked one of Lumina's tight curls. "At least s'more s'mores.

"Fine so, s'mores and talk—and you answer all my questions about you and Quin and the ERF and your mushroom . . . "

"Ah, if I can, yes. But you too. I have questions too."

"Oh sure, as long as the s'mores loosen your tongue —chocolate and peanut-butter and marshmallow should make you talk." Lumina grinned at her. Even if the smile was fragile, it was better like this. On the same side, even if it didn't bring Quin back faster.

THE AIR WAS hot and oppressive, thick and humid like a coming storm, and Lumina hoped it would break while they were still outside on the path to the transport station, anything to cool the heat in her throbbing temples and drown the recurring thoughts. A deluge of water should douse her properly and wet her roots—toes. It was in her dreams last night and popping up in her thoughts all day at school, the things she had seen and felt when she'd knocked her head against the sapling. Describing it to Chase had brought it to the fore—or maybe it was a peanut-butter s'more-fueled nightmare.

"You know, if you don't know what you want there's the shadow program. Follow the colony provost for a few days or someone else . . . a systems analyst, or an ecologist like your mom." Laila walked along the moving sidewalk with Lumina, her long dark ponytail whipping in the wind.

"Do you have any idea how much I've shadowed Chase?" Lumina's feet were too restless to stand and wait while the sidewalk moved them; more than restless, they were driven to get somewhere.

She walked faster, tempted to run to get away from Laila. Instead, she let the girl's voice blur out with the wind.

The railcar home was waiting for them when they stepped off the sidewalk onto the platform, its shimmering silver surface reflecting the slate-grey clouds with bursts of sunset red between them. So was the one that headed out to the Asimov research station right next to the orchard. Lumina pulled at the fingers of the soft leather gloves Chase had given her last night. She remembered the warning—*wear them, please, at least till I get back?*—Then she'd left to check on the spawning caves, a short trip not the marathon of spawning season.

"Lumina . . . "

She stood in front of the train locked in indecision, the static electricity from the doors tingling on her skin, bathed in the conflicting smell of track lubricants, and heated metal, all mixed up with rain and wet lichen on the wind.

"Lumina? Hey . . . Lumina? The door is open." Laila pulled at her arm and then gave up when she didn't answer.

Lumina bolted for the other railcar, the one that led

away from civilization instead of towards it. Laila stood, mouth hanging open a moment longer, but she didn't see it. She was getting on the other car. Laila's footsteps followed her through the doors of the railcar and into a seat next to her. The girl was out of breath and bubbling with questions.

"Where are we going? This car doesn't pass your place or mine."

Lumina sat up taller with a welling up of excitement now that she'd made a decision for herself. She turned shining eyes on Laila. "I'm going to show you what I want to do—what I can do, so you'll stop asking me. It's better than following around politicians and analysts."

"Sure, okay. What is it?" Laila was clearly concerned, a little irritated, but also interested.

"I'm gonna show you, not just say it like that. I don't need you acting like I'm just being weird or something."

The ride didn't take that long, but it was too long when she considered how many times she had to redirect Laila and how many she almost told her to just go home because she wanted to be alone anyway. She did want to be alone, but Laila was a witness. Someone who could attest that it was real.

She reminded herself of the same as they climbed down from the platform and again when she turned her ankle on a rock at the entry to the orchard.

There weren't guards on duty but the sign at the gate stated there would be a Wild-Spaces Shepherd there to answer questions or put a stop to any bad behavior. Any needs that required consultation with the orchard's ecology team would have to go to the headquarters or the Asimov center.

Lumina sighed as she approached the young guardian and then put on a broad grin that stretched her freckles across her cheekbones. "Hey, I saw you at the elevator station. Picking up the trees. Quin wants me to check in on them." The words weren't completely untrue, but Lumina still felt a twist of guilt at the lie.

The Shepard's eyes widened. People liked to be remembered. Then he stood up taller, smiled down at her and leaned in with a wink. "How's your head?"

"Oh." She blushed and reached up to where the cut was mostly healed and half forgotten, just a thin pink scar remaining. "It wasn't a big deal."

He was flirting and it was a bit too obvious. He was older, though not by much, and his smile had that Peter Pan charm of mischief held scarcely in check. But there was something about his eyes, a dull gleam that made the flirtation feel empty, fizzling where it started. Laila was fidgeting next to her. Lumina smiled back at him and then gestured toward the trees with a nod. "Gonna go check the trees."

"Oh right. Sure . . . There's a curfew for the orchard!" He called the rest after them as Lumina picked up a jog. "Thirty minutes and I have to clear you out."

"What was that about? He wasn't even cute." Laila whispered into her ear, puffing and turning sharply to keep up with what must have seemed like a random maze-run to her.

"I was being nice. Don't need the curfew changing because of some guy's hurt feelings."

What may have seemed random was actually a rapid search and attempt at pattern recognition. She was looking for something in the growing dark, a certain shape, branches pruned just so. She held the image in her head, scanning each tree and looking from all angles until she found it. She dropped down at the foot of the tall sapling, unbothered by the damp cold seeping through her clothes.

"What are you doing?"

"Shh . . . I'm going to talk to it."

"What?"

"Shhh!"

She yanked at the gloves, pulled at the fingers and then growing impatient let them turn inside out. She threw them onto the ground next to her and flexed her fingers. Chase had warned her...

"Quin thinks it's a kind of communication—an interface without a symbiont—it could make you sick."

She had asked her questions, with the taste of melted dark chocolate to sweeten the difficult answers, and they'd left a maze of more questions because as much as Chase tried, she didn't know any of it for sure. Lumina had had to push aside the resentment that bubbled back up—*Quin probably knew.*

Now that her hand was so close to the bark of this sapling that maze of questioning resurfaced. If she could be stuck in an interface like Quin had been, could she also learn how to get out? How much of this fungus was in her? Keeping her away from the orchard, away from trying this felt like an overprotection. The moss and ferns didn't make her feel sick. Communication with them, if that was what it was, felt like the tickling of a bubble bath. Hitting her head on this little tree had given her pictures, words—touching it now could be more of that, and she could always pull her hand away.

She flexed her fingers again and moved her hand closer. Caution presented Chase's face and the concern in her eyes—*wear them, please*—but something deeper in her mind, something that felt new—no, not new, newly *awake* and urgent moved her hand to the smooth skin of the tree. She found the pruned branch where she'd cut herself and she felt the sharp edge of it with her fingers.

The contact was almost immediate, less sharp than spilling her blood against the pruned branch had been but deeper, more probing. Lumina's eyes opened wide and she pressed both palms against the bark. Her head tipped back and her mouth fell open. She was aware of her physical body locking up, pressing the whole of herself closer to the being that was speaking directly into her mind and then her hands, arms, the whole of her body separate from the tree, seemed to dissolve from her awareness.

The flow of words was fast, so fast, bubbling through her with the tree's exuberant youth and inability to control the flow of its speech. It was beautiful, like a song, only this song was sung in some other language, but not completely foreign to her, no. It was a language she'd heard in her dreams, or had whispered in her ear while drifting to sleep. She'd learned the root of it before language as a concept existed to her.

She listened harder. She grasped for what she thought might be words but could have been whole phrases, sentences, concepts. Maybe they were both—either way she reached for them, pulling them deeper into herself as if collecting every drop would bring understanding, clarity. She took all that the tree offered and then asked for more. *Please. I want to know . . .*

It didn't come across as words at first. It was a feeling of joyful acquiescence, but her mind gave it words. And then the flow of the message came faster, and faster again with a force that locked Lumina's muscles, and made her mind cry out in sudden panic. The communication didn't stop or slow as her mind beat against the linked communication, a trapped bird beating against a cage of roots. She couldn't breathe—didn't know she needed to breathe and then something snapped. She felt herself falling but she never hit because darkness swallowed her.

CHAPTER 7

NETWORK

Quin stood with her hands behind her back, feet apart in the military posture of parade rest intended for respectful listening. Synesis couldn't be held to that standard. Instead, she waved her upper appendages and swayed on the implant stage. Her naked back resembled a hillside of fresh turned soil after a rain, the rumpled brown flesh erupting in new mushrooms. Scales and larger fragments of the fruiting bodies' fleshy veils dotted the surfaces of the new caps.

The commander, Mara Lariat, sat behind an antique wooden desk. Better those relics be used instead of burned or recycled but it was like using corpses for furniture.

Mara hadn't spoken yet despite the way she stared Quin down, hard-eyed—then she broke that silence. "I've approved your separation papers."

Quin cleared her throat and regretted it

immediately. There was a raw ache that still lingered from her protracted illness. But this pain was better than the thick, swollen glands and mold growth from before. "I didn't expect you to approve it so quickly. There's a process—I thought we'd discuss re-enlistment options first."

Mara leaned forward, canting her head just a little and narrowing her eyes. Her hair was pulled back tight from her face and twisted into a low bun at the back of her neck, in a way that made her face look more severe. It was hard to see the same woman she'd known before Mara had taken the command in that narrow face—the eyes closed off and full of sharpness. But she remembered the girl she had been well, the whispered confidences and shared hopes between she and Chase and Mara.

"Sgt. Fleury, if I thought you were using threat of separation to improve your reenlistment options, that would be a serious problem for you. It would be a crime."

"No. I didn't say that. I wouldn't do that—but that's the process."

The commander sat up straighter. "That was the process—*was*. I don't need to be reminded how to do my job."

Quin didn't speak any of the words that came up in her mind. This wasn't the way the conversation was meant to go, not at all what she had expected. This woman that she'd known more than two decades prior was throwing up walls and ego barriers and she would not play off them. Instead she remained silent, waited for Mara to look up. She lowered her voice and tried to catch her eyes.

"How are you, Commander Lariat?" The question stopped Mara short. She looked to have been searching for the next barb to toss out in response to her competence being somehow challenged.

"I—I'm tired." Her own response seemed to surprise her.

"Desolet—I'm sorry to hear that." Quin continued to speak softly as if soothing an animal to coax it back into a cage. Her voice was pitched so low the words could have been missed entirely, but she could see by the subtle flinch that the commander heard her.

Commander Lariat continued with renewed venom. "I was less tired before I got your repeated insistence that the ERF isn't doing enough to stop the decline, your collection of proposals and signatures from our previously satisfied researchers, and I was tired before I got your resignation papers while on a much needed leave to see my mother."

"How is your mother?"

"She's dying, thanks. It's taking too long and it's a painful process—so yes, I was even more tired when reports started coming in that our only linguist with a mature implant was somehow killing colony orchards with her recent uploads."

Quin reached a hand up to pet Synesis into a calmer state and hopefully still the distracting waving of her pseudopods. Her heart was beating too fast and there was a heaviness in her stomach. Recovered was a relative term. "Je sais pas—I don't know what to say—"

"I do. Because I was angry when I got your separation papers and surprised—yes, surprised at first even more than angry—could the great Sgt. Quinlan Fleury finally be tired as well and finished with the ERF? But now that I see it's some sort of manipulation tactic or sabotage—killing the colony trees so they don't have to be maintained, discrediting the ERF just before resigning—I see that you've provided me with a solution. Because, Quin—I am that damn tired."

"I haven't sabotaged them—I was sick—and I can reverse whatever happened. Those proposals, if you'd read them, have several good options for stopping the decline instead of just myself holding it at bay."

"You see that?—I'm not the only one tired here and ready to move on, am I? Earth recolonists are moving on, picking other systems; only the diehards will stay. The ERF holds no purpose without you, Quin. None of those apprentices will hold an implant past a year. You know that. But you've made shutting down the ERF easier for me."

"Don't do that. Read the proposals."

Mara's face contorted with, what seemed to Quin, uncharacteristic rage. "You think I haven't read them, Sergeant? You want a full initiative to dig up the whole surface of the planet—grow new mycelial networks using inoculate from another planet—accelerate the growth with technology we don't actually have yet, move the orchards we have growing into these hypothetical 'old' beds. That's just the first initiative, requiring resources that we don't have—maybe when the ERF was young, but now? Not even close; resources come from interested parties. Human and material labor doesn't just materialize."

Quin couldn't hold back any longer, couldn't filter out the urgency in her voice. "If it works on Earth, it will work on the colonies. We can get backing with that."

Mara shook her head and blinked, squinting at Quin as if she didn't believe what she was seeing.

"Have you forgotten the part of the last few weeks where you killed off orchards on seven colony planets? And then didn't answer the urgent requests for help?"

"I was—"

"Sick, yes, you were sick because you—like myself—are only one woman. And you're trying to hold up a failing system that we can work around and do without. Humanity won't die off without trees like we once thought—"

"That's not why the ERF was started. We're preserving something, Mara, we're stopping an extinction and I know, I know it's been a long process, thankless maybe but that's because we have to see it through just a step more, je te promets—maybe two more. I can see the edge we need to push ourselves up to, drag the project over to see it through. If you could just—"

"Whatever you've been doing all these years—sixteen long years—hasn't made a scratch on the decline. The forests are gone, last gasps turning into dry compost. A fire hazard on a dying rock. Not the glorious revival that you sold us coming back from Ross 128b, was it? Drunk on power and hallucinations. You sold us a sham solution, and what do I see now, the woman behind the curtain playing smoke and mirrors with people's hopes and the ERF's budget."

The commander placed a portable screen with a contract on it in the middle of her desk. "I've already signed your request—Sign it, Sgt. Fleury, or I'll have you brought up on charges of perjury for submitting this without actual intent to separate."

Quin froze. She searched Mara's face. Her expression had only hardened further and any opportunity for understanding, for connection had passed, if it had been there at all.

"You can't prove that I submitted this for any other reason than to discuss separation. We've discussed it and Allah hsnaan—bene allora—you changed my mind. The ERF needs me to stay if leaving would allow you to shut down the interface project."

Mara stared directly at her face, doubtless searching for some chink in Quin's armor, some doubt that would make compliance easier. But Quin didn't flinch or turn away, even as a headache brewed and her throat burned from speaking. There were messages coming in on the device in her pocket, but she ignored them.

"You're wasting your time then. I don't have to cancel the project myself, because the resources you need aren't coming. If the decline isn't stopping—which it isn't—and it won't then the project will die off with the trees, or maybe you'll wear out first . . . or you could sign this and take what remains of your reputation to a well-developed colony." Mara's hand hovered over the contract then snatched it up, shoving it into a desk. "Suit yourself. You're dismissed. Travel restricted until you present logs showing you only shifted to approved locations."

Quin walked out of the office. Another message came and reminded her of the others. The vibration buzzed through the fabric of her uniform pocket into the muscle of her thigh. Her hand shook holding it—it was too soon to be up and arguing for the survival of forests. She was lightheaded, nauseous, Synesis urging her to sleep. She should sleep. The interface project would be facing the same problems when she woke up and maybe she'd be able to think more clearly.

"Read messages please." She continued past the front desk and outside, breathing deeply of the fresher air. It was better than the recirculated environment inside but too dry, too barren and devoid of plant perfumes. Instead, she picked up the cooked-tar smell of asphalt and the flat mineral scent of chalky topsoil whipped up by wind over dead fields.

The device complied in its almost human-sounding French accent. "From Chase on Genti-6: Quin, Lumina's unconscious and she isn't waking. It's been at least an hour. She went into the orchard herself, with a friend I guess, and she blacked out like you said happened when she hit her head but she isn't getting better. Please Quin, help. Can you come? I need you here."

QUIN'S THROAT burned as she forced the words out. "She restricted my travel—is planning to strangle the project out until I give up or all the trees are dead, and I need to get to Genti-6—now—Lumi is unconscious." Her voice broke on the last words, and she searched the room for the drink dispenser, for water, tea, anything to cut the burn and keep her voice working.

Waters shook his head as if to shake away the excess words that hadn't landed right. He reached in his pocket, handed her a lozenge.

"Keep that in your mouth—Now, I'm going to need you to slow down and explain in a way that makes sense. One cataclysm at a time, please, sergeant."

She didn't slow down or back-track, but she did take the lozenge with a look of gratitude and tuck it into her cheek. *Lemon and honey.*

She had control of her hands, mostly; they were laced together, then tucked in her pockets, then stroking her mycelial implant. But she doubted that she was coming off as calm and controlled as she was trying to project. "It's a processing overload, like happened to me before the coma—too much too fast and not enough experience to translate. The mushroom could have helped me through it, except you took mine off of me and I got stuck—Lumina, she has no mushroom to translate, so it's just like that. She isn't going to wake up on her own for a very long time, if at all, unless we do something. Please—"

Waters lowered his chair to the ground and leaned forward, scrubbing his hands in his hair. "Quin, you're giving me a damn headache—Your kid doesn't have an implant, so how the hell are you saying she's in a—in a processing coma."

"Are we friends still, Waters? All those years, and then I bought back in with you—took a second implant when it could have killed me, and now you're asking *me* for details?"

He opened his mouth and then closed it again. "I don't have a ship." He threw up his hands and then paced closer.

"And if I don't get there, they will use antifungals on her before we have a chance to try something else."

"That's a bad thing?"

He wasn't following. She wanted to reach out and shake him. It was one of the many moments when she wished he could follow at her pace. But it was *her* pace and that wasn't fair. Instead she took in a breath—slow, deep and exhaled just as slow. She followed it with another, willing herself to settle. Her heart slowed and her mind cleared more than breathing could account for —Synesis had joined her efforts to ease the racing of their shared mindscape.

"Oui—yes. Because Lumina has a vestigial mycelial network. From me—from this implant's inoculate."

"Oh." His eyes widened as the realization dawned.

"I already knew. Chase and I were discussing it—"

He made a face. "Was it a discussion or a monologue?"

"Please—I was going to bring it up with the implant specialists in the Interface project. This vestigial mycelial network lets her make contact with trees—"

"And you just brought them trees on Genti-6—She had a heart to heart with her woody siblings and now she's out."

"Merci—Yes! And now I need you to get me there along with someone from the implant labs."

Waters was nodding now as if it all made sense and he would go along with it. "Right—who else are we bringing in this shift drive that I don't have?"

"I don't know yet. I have to convince one of them."

"Oh."

QUIN HELD the tattoo on her wrist under the scanner for a third time. She winced at the machine's ear-splitting buzz of denial. "I'm supposed to have access."

Waters pushed in front of her. "And I'm not but I made a phone call." He scanned his own tattoo. "People like phone calls. It's why you brought me in on this. Old commander gave me access for today—I pulled a favor."

She shook her head and the mushroom swayed with her. "Merci."

He shrugged. "Thank me if I get a shift drive."

The Mycology Laboratory was half-dark and low-staffed. It was always low-staffed, with only the bare minimum of fresh inoculates kept ready for replacement implants should one fail. But Quin's apprentices were few, five at any one time. Only 1.6 percent of enlistees were both suitable and willing to take on a mycelial implant, and a smaller percentage of the implants actually took. Enlistments were low, so the need for implants was even lower.

Their footsteps echoed along the halls, and she shook off a chill. This echoing emptiness was in sharp contrast to the bright welcome she'd had as a new recruit and even as a re-enlistee when she'd taken on her second implant. It wasn't the cathedral quality of a forest. It was a cemetery.

"Ahlan wa—sahallan? Hello?" She raised her voice to be heard.

There was a light in the far right corner, a smaller room adjoining the larger laboratory with its many unused implant stations and inoculate production cubicles. She zig-zagged through the confused laboratory, ducking and weaving around research cubicles stacked with crates and piles of equipment to be sorted. It looked like it was being repurposed as a warehouse.

The door to the well-lit room was wide open, the single inhabitant unaware of their presence until she waved a hand in front of his face, then he startled and a bright grin broke out on his narrow, youthful visage. He was an over-sized child, somewhere in his teens—an apprentice—couldn't be much older than Lumina but he was wearing the green lab-coat of the Interface project with official patches and name tag on shoulder and front breast-pocket: a mushroom that transitioned into a tree, both of them superimposed over the blue and green orb of planet Earth. The breast pocket held the simpler ERF patch and his name: Drinian Cope. She had never seen this apprentice before. How long since she'd been in the lab? Months? At least that.

He reached for her hand and shook it, large, near black eyes sparking with unrestrained excitement. "Sgt. Fleury—Wow—I'm so glad to meet you—" He craned a look over her shoulder at Synesis, and his grin broadened before he dropped her hand. "Just wow."

Waters chuckled under his breath. "At ease, son."

"He's a civilian contractor, Waters." She cleared her throat. "I need one of your preceptors—someone experienced for a—a medical check-up for my implant."

"Oh right! Because of the black rot—a check-up. She looks good—"

She looked at his tag again. "Your preceptors, Drinian . . . where are they?"

"Oh . . . yeah, sorry, they've all gone home for the day. I'm just reviewing old research—you know, can't get enough of it and they aren't really pushing ahead with implants—phasing it all out they're saying—but if you ask me—" He gestured at the workstation behind him.

His words and competing trains of thought were rushing out like water—like an exuberant sapling spitting back the All-Answer in response to Quin's utterance of the All-Question and she had to restrain herself from taking him by the shoulders and making him focus in. The screen at his desk was covered with documents, all of it old research as he'd said, many of them featuring her implant.

She turned to leave. There had to be addresses on record, contact numbers for the scientists in this department—she could see if Waters could pull another favor, call one in. But that would take longer, draw more attention.

"I could do it! I do physicals—I do implants, too. I bet she needs a nitrogen boost by the color of her. The apprenticeship process in here is slooooow—I'm beginning to think they don't plan to move me up—"

She turned around and narrowed her focus on Drinian. He was young, yes, but his eyes had a sharp intelligence and while his speech was stumbling, the words he used were confident. He might be able to tend to her mushroom—maybe—but was he well-trained enough to help with Lumina?

He ran a thumb across his throat and winked at her. "Not before they kill the project."

He likely expected a laugh at the bit of dark humor. A half a smile had to be enough.

"How old are you, Mesye Cope?"

"Ah—seventeen—But I . . . I started young, fourteen, special dispensation and all that."

She raised both brows. "Not a child then; a prodigy."

She wet her lips, met General Waters' speculative squint. "Do the basic physical and then we'll see— Waters—why don't you see about the next step?"

He mimicked her, wetting his lips and then turned that same cautious look to Drinian before stepping out of the room. His footsteps echoed, receding from their hearing.

"Alors?"

Drinian's eyes widened again in a way that made her question her decision to give him a chance. "Right! Okay, exam table—This way to station two because it's my favorite. One of the recruits etched a mushroom into the headrest while waiting—unprofessional but also cute in its crudeness—Right, prone please, with the opening there for your face—you know that—you know that."

He was falling into a rhythm of speech that showed he was used to this but then questioning himself as if she was above the routine instructions he gave new recruits. She wished she could strip away her fame as the most prominent linguist of the interface project and regain anonymity, put him at ease.

"Take a breath. Do what you know." She laid down on the table face down for him to see and access Synesis.

Drinian mumbled under his breath between quick verbal reports to his handheld computer, then he attached the calibration and implantation equipment to the side of Quin's implant stage to run diagnostics while he continued his physical assessments.

Synesis purred into her mind at the attention, a sort of mental humming. Drinian's hands were deft but gentle and she could feel him relax into a process that he was indeed good at. She gripped the undersides of the headrest that cradled her face and traced the etchings on the bottom of the otherwise smooth acrylic surface. It was a rudimentary mushroom with stalk and cap and a human face. "I see why this is your favorite station."

He gave a short laugh. "Yes, yes. It's the little human bits that make it ah—special. I think. Same as the mushrooms—not human, but the mammalian genome making them compatible with us."

"Hmm. Lien, le rapport . . . connection . . . tarab is close. All the languages I know and a single word with the full meaning evades me—each leaves something out. That's why they like to use so many synonyms in Arabic."

"The same for Hebrew."

She almost sat up, restraining herself when the resistance of the machinery hooked up to her neck stopped her. But the words bubbled out in Hebrew. "Ata medaber ivrit?"

Drinian laughed, nerves in his voice again but also excitement. He answered her in a competent Hebrew dialect that she recognized. "Yes-yes, but don't go too fast. I'm a slow processor with words when I'm rusty."

He unhooked the calibration machine and Quin peeked at him. He'd turned his attention to the screen that was filling with data on her mushroom's status.

She righted herself and continued in a slower less exuberant Hebrew. "You learned it as a child. Your accent is colloquial."

He smiled and tapped his teeth with a stylus, attention still on the screen. "Mm—yes. The Tree-Whisperer—Sgt. Quin Fleury does not disappoint—you can hear that in a few words?—But! You and your mycelial implant are malnourished, and I'm sending extra nutrients with you. Some for you and some for her because I suspect you don't take enough in for a high enough excess—it is a symbiosis, one that errs on the side of the human counterpart not the fungus—it's one reason they're fragile." He spoke the pronouncement with an odd cadence and flourish. The little smile and the spark in his eyes meant he was growing comfortable and pleased with himself.

"Then we'll need to bring extra with us. I don't know how long we'll be gone, and we'll need other equipment, a few strains of inoculate—"

"With—with us?" His eyes widened again, not in fear or nervousness this time but curiosity and he put out a hand as if catching her words mid-air.

"I need a technician, a specialist that knows the physiology of mycelial implants and their hosts, one that can do what you just did, maybe put in an implant, maybe kill on. And I need them—*you* to come with me to Genti-6. Now."

"Oh—wow. I'm . . . I'm in."

"I don't have any authorization for this, and the project commander is out for my head. It won't be good for you." She was still speaking Hebrew, any security cameras picking it up would take longer with that than more common languages.

He paused, mouth falling open and then a smile curled on his lips bringing out dimples. He hesitated as if tasting the idea and then started making a list. "We'll also need a portable station—I assume, yes?"

QUIN COMPOSED the letter as she walked, extending her long legs into a full, rapid stride without running. Running would draw more attention. Maybe it didn't matter and she wasn't being monitored but maybe she was. She only had a few minutes while Drinian gathered all of the equipment they would need. Waters was better than expected. He'd procured a shift drive during her and Synesis's examination with a few calls. She should have expected it with his history and his number of friends, but time was hard to judge when stakes were so high. What would the doctors on Genti-6 do, thinking they were helping, if she didn't get there soon enough?

The message wasn't long, but it had to go out now.

Chase,

I'm coming. I've had my travel restricted and my access to the mycelial interface laboratories cut off. I was sick for weeks or I'd have written. There is too much to say in too little time, but I regret our last interactions—I feel like we weren't in harmony as I've come to expect. I am writing you simply to say that I need you to wait before making decisions we can't go back on. I know that I suggested anti-fungal treatments, but that was before, when we presumed Lumina would be able to make the choice with us. I believe there is more going on than I thought and I'm afraid anything the doctors there could do might make her worse. Please wait for me. I'm bringing help.

Yours,

Quinlan

She sent the message and then leaned her face against the door in front of her. It was her infirmary room, unoccupied now but she needed to see for certain before she left, that drooping look, the yellow leaves falling and dropping to the tile of the floor. She had noticed but didn't see the significance or process it until now, not while she was so ill.

The door slid open, unlocked. The small space was empty, no sign of the trees they'd brought in for Synesis. She made an about-face and searched the halls, the empty rooms. They weren't there. But why would they be? They'd served their purpose. It didn't mean they were dead.

She moved faster, checking small office spaces, exam rooms, behind curtains.

"Sgt. Fleury?" One of the nurses stood between her and the next stretch of hallway, her eyes questioning.

"Ah . . . weh, I have found you, it seems."

"Oh, are you unwell?" The nurse's face was lined, her eyes gentle but tired.

"No, no. But a question if you can answer it. The

little orange trees that were in my room. Where have they gotten to?"

The nurse blushed and fidgeted in place as she searched for words and then put on a sad smile. "Well, I'm not sure where they've been taken."

Quin saw the confirmation of her suspicion in the nurse's eyes. But she needed to hear it.

"And were they well? Healthy when you saw them last?"

The nurse's brows tipped up and she worked to smooth her features, to project comfort without falling into the grief of her message as if she were delivering tragic news to a patient's next of kin. "They were–I'm sorry, Sgt. Fleury. They were all dead when they were taken from the room."

GENERAL WATERS EYED the apprentice as he strapped himself into the third seat in the front of the elevator car.

"You sure about this one?" He jutted a thumb behind him at Drinian and then worked on his own straps. "We could still wake up one of the old guns, someone with more experience. I have the ship until Monday."

Quin glanced over at Drinian and they exchanged raised eyebrows. It had a familial feel, as if they'd known each other much longer than the hour and thirty minutes that had passed between them, with years to build up shared expressions. "Well, he speaks Hebrew so . . ."

Drinian raised a hand to Waters. "Shalom."

"You're funny, Quin. Sometimes you are very funny."

She gave Waters' shoulder a squeeze. "I'm not being funny. He's bright and he knows his mushrooms—There are masters, sure but I don't need a master for what we're doing—I need a Drinian."

"Fine." He shook his head, giving up control of the situation. "Is he going to throw-up or pass out when we make the shift though?" He shoved a long suction tube with a funnel on the end towards Drinian. "Here, here's the vacuum before we take the elevator up. Just don't vomit in the Ambassador's shift drive."

"You thought that about me once, I remember. And you were right, but I was otherwise compromised." Those memories weren't the sweet kind. They made her think of hard choices and hopes that never panned out.

"I remember—you had the tadpole strapped to your chest all unfinished and making you seasick."

Tadpole—That was the nickname she'd given Lumina in her AUC capsule, first a little embryo and then a growing fetus swimming in a world of water.

Drinian raised a finger. "Drinian—the first Drinian—was a sailor you know, so seasickness, similar to shift travel, is not likely."

Quin ignored Drinian's monologue, instead looking at Waters. "How much did you have to tell them?"

"I've shifted—a vacation when I was six but—" His

interjections were quieter as if he was speaking to himself but Quin still heard them and shook her head with a half-smile as she waited on Waters.

"I am surprised at your underestimation. I am meting out a favor for an old friend on Genti-6, the Governor herself—who will be quite demonstrably grateful to our Ambassador for loaning me the ship. I have friends, Quin and it's in large part because I don't spill my friend's secrets—even to other friends."

Relief flooded her and a flush of chagrin heated her skin. "Oh."

"It's fine." Waters leaned back in the seat with his fingers laced behind his head. The elevator lifted them at a steady pace and the view through the windows changed slowly. The cloud coverage faded into mist and then what looked like a blue film coated their vision. "I hear trees don't call in favors."

"Not from me, no."

Drinian's voice, deadpan serious inserted itself between theirs. "And she spends all of her time talking to trees—interesting conversation, if it can be compared to mushrooms."

He pushed his wiry black curls aside revealing a long thin neck and when he turned his head, an empty implant stage, sealed off like Chase's.

Quin blinked several times and glanced at Waters. She reached a hand towards the implant stage but didn't touch. "You had an implant?"

He gave a small, wistful smile and nodded.

"Sometimes—ah, sometimes that's the best way to learn."

CHAPTER 8

GRAFTED

Lumina appeared to be dreaming, not a peaceful dreaming but one that she had to fight through. Chase pressed a hand against the freckled skin of Lumina's forehead. Her skin was damp and flushed, heated up to fever temperatures when she was tossing like this and then suddenly cool and sweat-drenched again when she settled.

The small glowing transmitters on her forehead and scalp sent data to the AI run electroencephalogram in the corner alive with beeping and lights. More on her chest tracked her heart rate, temperature, BP, and respirations. All of the data was being collected into the same program. A translated image of her brainwaves combined with her body's responses to those thoughts played out on a large screen. In front of that screen, a physician stood consulting with the AI.

"I can't give it a single diagnosis yet." Doctor Reyn shook her head, tapped a stylus on the screen.

Chase pressed her teeth into her lips and came closer to that screen where a jumble of rapidly forming shapes built themselves and then shifted, growing into something else and then changing again without ever finishing a single construction. It was moving too fast to pick out singular images or coherent thought patterns. It was a second-by-second Rorschach test. Was it shadow and light through branches? Were those waves or melting wax? Unsettling . . . It was unsettling. "It's been ten hours."

"Ten hours and one moment it resembles a psychotic episode and then I think—no, stroke, this is textbook stroke regardless of her age." The doctor shoved a hand through her short-cropped blonde hair. "It looks like both of those things with some points of comparison to a psychedelic experience—or even a schizophrenic episode. Toxicology shows nothing and the only other symptoms she has are a low-grade fever and high bp, tachycardia, but those are likely caused by whatever is going on in her head."

"I told you she put her hand on a tree in the orchard and seized up. Her friend called for help."

Chase turned her back to reveal the implant port in the back of her neck. "It's like what can happen with an implant, if the download is too heavy—"

The physician put up her hands. "I don't—have any experience with that technology, but your daughter doesn't have one, so I don't see how—"

"She has her own mycelium. It's inside her. We were discussing anti-fungal treatments but—"

The door opened and a physician's assistant stood in the gap. Quin pushed past him followed by a boy Lumina's age.

Irritation suffused the doctor's face. "Antifungals? There is no sign of fungal infection in her bloodstream, but we could—who is this?" She turned a confused frown to the door.

The physician's assistant glared at Quin. "She says she is the patient's mother, and I've informed them that—"

Doctor Reyn turned a questioning look to her and Chase nodded, tears stinging her raw eyelids. Quin took her hand in her own gloved one and locked their fingers together. "No antifungals, Mwen Chéri. This means she has a full mycelial interface inside of her, grown there itself. If we kill it, she suffers a loss of self—like we suffered through the mushroom death and separation sickness. We wake her up and then she chooses, oui?"

Quin, who had never asserted any demand or even request with her before, especially not about Lumina, had her eye's locked on hers, not demanding but willing. Her grip was firm with conviction, fierce as her eyes.

"Okay, if you can wake her up then yes, she decides."

Quin squeezed her hand once then turned to the display and Doctor Reyn.

She gestured for the young man to join her with a

frantic wave of her hand as she locked onto the imagery in the center of the screen, traced the flow of it with slides and dips of her head. Then she pointed at it, trailing a finger along a shape that was gone before she could finish, then another. She turned back to Chase with a pained smile on her lips. "She is replaying the All-Question." She gestured at the screen again. "Only a piece of it in a loop, with no way to translate—no knowledge, no experience."

Pain pulled her features into sharper angles. And there was something else, exhaustion. She looked terrible, thinner, tired.

"It is a place I've been. She needs help to come out of it. A translator." She kept her eyes on the screen.

"Am I missing something?" Her young friend furrowed his brow, and he looked from one to the next in the room. "You're a translator. You're *the* translator."

"Yes." There was something in Quin's voice that caused the boy to pause before pushing forward.

Chase watched the interplay between them trying to read Quin's hesitation.

He continued. "Then I can set up an interface chain between your Quinlet—"

"Her name is Lumina."

His cheeks colored and he gave an apologetic smile. "Right, right—Lumina. An interface chain between you—"

Chase spoke quietly, but loud enough for the room to hear. "She can't do it."

"Of course she can. I can set it up."

She shook her head. "All those colony orchards dying off. After you uploaded . . . News travels between colonies. Especially news like that."

Quin turned to her young companion. "She is right. I can't."

"You had a full physical, your mushroom—er, name? —is healthy, fed. You're maybe underfed but we're working on that—"

Quin raised gloved hands. "I call her Synesis. I was sick—and I was struggling with something that I couldn't keep out of the upload. But I won't touch Lumina's mind unless I know I can't hurt her. I can't—I don't know where I can test it."

Chase's voice came out a whisper. "Not the orchard. Or you'd risk killing what you just planted."

Quin nodded. "Someone else will have to do it. Two others here have a port."

"But no implant." He seemed to grow more animated, he tapped his lips with his fingers. "Right, I would try—my mushroom died the slow and natural way—three years—the usual span but—" He gestured at the screen. "I don't know this All-Question. How do I—ah—help her without knowing what you know?"

Chase frowned at the young man standing next to Quin. He was tall, with arms that seemed too long, hands too big, evidence of growth that hadn't evened out yet. His features were large on his face, with eyes wide and quick moving as his thoughts. It was clear why Quin had brought him but not why he had come. She cleared her throat and faced him.

"I don't even know what to call you, and you're offering to take on a second mycelial implant and undergo everything that means, symbiosis, psychological pairing, dependance on Tree contact, and then eventually separation sickness when it dies off." His eyes were like window-glass as he listened to her, his thoughts and emotions clear in his answering expressions.

"Well, it's Drinian and ah—you're welcome?"

"Why do this? Are you a friend of Quin's?" She turned a look of skepticism onto Quin who was smiling in half distress, half pleased surprise.

"Well, sure, friends, very new friends, but I'd say close." He looked a little embarrassed as he glanced at Quin for back-up or confirmation.

He seemed harmless but he was a stranger. That could go very wrong. But was it worse than her doing it? "I could take a new implant for Lumina. I don't know how well I can help her. It's been so long, and we argued when you left. It's a little better now but—"

Quin's face softened and she took her hand again. "I know it's not something you wanted to do again. You made your choice a long time ago. She ducked her head close to touch foreheads for the barest fraction of a second. "Let him do it, Chéri." *A second request in one night.* Chase opened her mouth and felt the words tremble there just at the back of her throat.

Drinian filled the silence. "It's something I can do. It's what I do—I study them, learn, so I can help. Now I can help."

"How old are you, Drinian?"

"Ahhh . . ."

"The truth please."

"Seventeen. Last month."

"Because she doesn't know you. We don't know you. And the—the intimacy of an interface is—" She glanced at Quin. "It's lasting. How do I know you won't take advantage of that?"

His eyes widened and he sat down hard on the small, cushioned bench against the wall. "Right, right. I guess you don't." He raked both hands into messy black curls and pulled in a way that distorted his features. "So, something else. Not me, not Quin . . . Lumina can't accept her own implant, and too young, definitely too young . . . " The monologue of brainstorming continued under his breath.

"Chase? There are worse things." Quin gestured with her eyes and her own gaze followed, to Lumina flushed and restless on the bed, locked in her own mind.

Quin was right. Chase's reluctance gave way when she met Quin's eyes. "Yes. There are worse things than having someone else in your head."

"We could wait longer, a few days, see if she comes out on her own and then . . ."

"No." Chase shook her head. "You told me what it's like. And I see it in her face, like when you were—"

Quin reclaimed her hand and placed a kiss on her palm. "D'accord ... We will get her out now. Drinian—are you still willing to take an implant?"

"Ah—" He hesitated as if pulled from distant thoughts.

"I wouldn't ask . . ."

"I wouldn't if it was just a whim, or ah, ah—casual research, but yes, I will."

Once his decision was made, he moved quickly, his hands shaking but deft in their manipulation of the materials brought from Earth, an implant stage, coppery but pliable. These things he attached to himself with extra hands from Quin, just below his cervical vertebrae, then he stretched his arms and his slender neck, with several pops and a nervous smile.

"Right well, now we see if it takes and ah, get this going." He produced an inoculation syringe from another package and, without further hesitation, inserted it through the stage port, punctured through the skin into his subdural space with a sharp, hissing wince and a blanching of his cheeks. He lowered his head onto his knees and let his arms hang down.

It was something to watch. The overconfidence and arrogance of youth maybe, or all bravado and show, to inject himself like that? Not with those shaking hands. She caught Quin's equally impressed look and then watched as the skin of Drinian's neck flushed and mottled, sweat beading around the implant stage. Several minutes passed, several more.

He groaned, stirred, then laughed.

When he sat up, there were tears streaming from the corners of his eyes, triumph in his shaky smile. "Well it ah . . . I think it worked this time." He laughed again and reached his hand back to feel the small fleshy creature growing from his neck into the implant stage. The streamlined organism wiggled tiny stubs of appendages, three extra from the usual making ten to brush his hand as he stroked the smooth little back. Patchy indigo blue and sepia splotches marked it as if it had been splashed in colored inks. Drinian's face transformed with delight, a broad smile, relief and gratitude lighting his eyes.

Chase found her own hand on the aching, tingling space at back of her neck where the old hardware sat like a placeholder in her skin. She was almost envious of him.

Almost.

To go through that again . . . She'd have to make certain he felt appreciated.

Drinian sighed again, relief softening his features as he sat back against the wall. "So yes, or no? Now that it's done."

"Yes, Yes, if you're willing. And can be—careful."

He nodded several times, his face sobering. "The most careful."

"Okay."

The doctor was still in the room, listening, watching the display and watching Lumina each time her tossing on the bed increased and her heart rate went up then subsided just enough not to set off alarms.

Chase came up next to her. "We need to have some equipment brought in." And then she inclined her head to Drinian. "So that he can get started. Can you do that?"

THE FEEL of a hidden conversation rushed into Lumina until it was ALL. The not-words she heard became concepts, concepts that soared above her ability to understand, then turned to face her down and flood into her. They *were* her.

Her mind fought to process, some part of her racing to catch up and keep up with the wordless flow of story. Tastes and smells arose like notes in a song, the scent of burning wood, falling ash, sap hot and running until it popped and sparked. They were replaced by other notes, ones that burned and froze her nerves with sharp sensation.

At first, conscious thoughts wouldn't come, there was no space. *Someone here . . . where is here?*

An answer arose for the question. She was in a landscape of fire, a burning forest, her leaves scorching from the heat well before the flames licked high enough to reach them. *Are you the forest?*

Yes! No . . .

She wasn't sure which answer was her own. But answering pulled her into herself just enough. The forest on fire wasn't her, it was in her.

Colors flashed behind her eyelids in the shape of the small blood vessels there; she was aware that she had eyelids again and that they were shut, that she could open them and there would be something different. But she didn't open her eyes.

No . . .

Someone told her no, asked her to stay and it wasn't Drinian—Drin—*who?* Who was Drinian? Someone she'd met in the fire? That felt right. But it was so long ago; the fire lasted eons. It was still burning now and would flare up again if she watched it. Just thinking fire brought it swirling around her, catching her tenderest branches ablaze.

The someone saying no felt like herself but new, different.

Even as she became more aware of self and the possibility of other places than this, she saw the fire in her mind in a way that felt like being there, not imagining or dreaming. It wasn't a good place to be, that darkness lit only by smoldering coals, flaming branches falling and breaking apart on top of her as her whole body split into a million fragments and yet, she was still there, only the shell gone.

But it wasn't a bad place either. It just was.

She needed to stay, to see it again and again in that constant loop of sensation where she was being, seeing, and witnessing all at once. She sighed and her body moved in the bed, tried to roll, to cover herself better from the chill in the room. She was on a firm surface, the sheets falling off of her, straps holding her on her back. Where her body pressed into that surface she ached. But as much as she felt herself move and breathe she couldn't choose to. It was out of her control.

There was someone near to her, someone in the physical world outside of the fire, the sound of breathing. She wanted none of it. She dropped deeper into her mind. Didn't open her eyes. Instead, she willed the fire to flare up again. But there was a voice, not in the room speaking out loud. It was in this place, under the fire with her.

Er . . . Lumi—Lumina. It's pretty hot in here.

No, it's cold, Drinian—she knew his name.

Right—the room is cold because you're waking up.

She searched for the one she was speaking to, but she could either see the light behind her eyelids or the fiery darkness but not the source of the voice. *Where are you?*

Ah, I'm right next to you.

Who are you?

Well, ah, Drinian, a mycologist—er apprentice, a friend of—

Show me. She made herself small. She couldn't see him. Why should he see her? And her fear became a force around them.

But this space was shared. Drinian felt what she felt, saw the effects of that fear manifest into wind and smoke and then transform into a screen of burning leaves. Of course she was afraid. He was an unknown, and too close. This could backfire, push her further into the forest's broken message.

Okay, so I know you don't want me here. We can leave— open your eyes in three, two, one—

No. I'm not leaving.

She pulled in a slow shuddering breath and then tried to forget that her body was there on a bed, that this Drinian was somewhere nearby. He claimed she could just open her eyes and wake up but it didn't feel like that. She couldn't move, couldn't wake up, and now somehow he was here, a dream figment or whatever he was—*I want to see you in here.*

In your head because—that's where we are—pretty um, unexpected ask.

He felt her waiting and she felt that in turn, a feedback loop of awareness forming between them the longer they were there.

Okay so . . .

A thought recurred to him, a promise—*the most careful*—He had promised to be careful in forging any connection. But she had to know him enough to trust him and she was asking. In their shared mind space saying no felt wrong. She could feel even the flavor of these thoughts of his, witness the replay of the memory, feel his reticence.

You don't want to? The flaming forest flared up around them and become more real the longer he hesitated. They both felt it, the smoke in the air thickening, sparks and ash coming down between them.

I do . . . just, don't want to be reckless. He reached out towards her as if taking her hands in his, guided her back towards him, away from the falling branches, the ash laden air.

She felt him relax. The membranous mental barriers between them dissolved, and an impression of him, a conglomeration of images coming too fast to separate formed between them in place of the fire, something shifting and growing.

A child's hands were out in front of her as if her own, a dying songbird cradled there, the wing splinted. They were not her own hands, but his. A broken leg, grossly misshapen at a sharp angle and then healing, bruised, long running legs and hands larger than they were before and a face that was always the same, the features shifting and becoming larger, more purely themselves but never quite coming together into a harmonious image, nose too large and eyes so big in his face they took up too much real-estate, lips the same between gaunt cheeks, all of his features excessive.

A laboratory loomed large, the image of a mushroom and a tree intertwined, endless combinations of genetics unraveled before her eyes, and then he wasn't alone, not just one mind—two. The memory faded, darkened and then he was covered in mud, dripping in rain, sunburned once, then contorting in pain, hands holding the back of long limber neck, weeping, then standing again as the body of a shriveled mushroom symbiont fell from his hands and saplings sprouted up around him.

The stream of shared story thinned, tapered until it was like a mist around them, his thoughts clearer to her now than they'd been before he started. The mental distance was truncated as if they'd stepped closer.

Wow . . . Lumina took a mental pause, what would

have been a breath outside of this place. She had to step back from what he'd given her. *Can I–can I do that?*

Oh—probably, probably yes—if you feel comfortable.

Was it uncomfortable for you? It hadn't occurred to her before she'd asked, not the full extent of what she was asking. To see him.

Yes. But—ah, that's part of the point isn't it? Of communication—to both get uncomfortable until you're . . . not anymore.

A sudden thought occurred to Lumina: could she even tell lies in a place like this?

Okay here goes . . .

She tried to do as he had—project a sense of self, a history, a face, but it wasn't her own, it was Laila's.

So this is you? There was a question in his thought, but his tone said he already knew the answer.

She stepped back toward the darker spaces, those glowing coals in the corner, and she felt the current of thought moving her there. She turned back to where she felt Drinian's presence.

No, it was a joke, a lie.

Why lie? I know that's not you.

It was a gentle sort of questioning, not an accusation. She stepped away from the fire, away from the repeating loop that some part of her wanted to return to. There was no judgement or anger coming from him, just curiosity and what felt like the bright buoyancy of amusement—then something else, another presence tied to him that was of him but not him.

You don't have to show me anything, but you do have to

wake up. Once you wake up, we'll break the connection. Open your eyes.

Wait . . . I want to.

This time she collected all of herself, as if rolling up a tapestry, and unraveled it in the shared mind space, from earliest thoughts, her own infant hands—fetal hands in milky fluid, swimming inside a membrane. Quin's face, giant red-barked trees touching the sky, falling, fire again, seeds unfurling . . .

She was pulled along with the flow of narrative. This was her. It was in her, but was it her *really?* She pulled away from the rushing flow that went on and on, like water, like wind, a high-pitched keening, and then she tried to have shape, a body, a face. Does the physical form hold the meaning, does the face—the curls that gradually tightened over the years until she and Chase had to learn how to care for them, the green of her eyes that were Chase's, and skin that was only a fraction of Quin's depth of color but with its own glow, and the way that the plants tickled her senses when she touched them, a body and mind grown so restless on Genti-6 that sometimes she had to run until she couldn't feel her legs anymore or catch her breath.

Does form hold the meaning or is it the places the mind goes?

Is this what I should show you, Drinian, so you know me—if seeing is knowing?

More memories, ones that she couldn't give order or name to, came with words and phrases in so many languages that she didn't know, not herself, at least until she had looked up each phrase and made herself a dictionary of seemingly random linguistic sound bites as if she had learned them from herself, both pupil and teacher. Chéri mwen, ti-progebébé

When she stopped she was out of breath—or out of meaning to convey, she wasn't sure which, but it was so still and silent in the dark that heat built up in her ears, a flush of embarrassment. She'd shared too much—way too much without realizing she would when she'd started.

I'm sorry, That was—a lot.

No. No–I'm—thank you.

Sure.

The awkwardness between them had faded, replaced by familiarity. The mind link was warm, close, like sitting in front of a fire on pillows and blankets.

She blushed or maybe that was her real body warming up. The room wasn't cold anymore wherever it was and if she woke up Drinian would be there with her —if he was real.

So, how do we do this?

Right, like I ah—mentioned before—just open your eyes. Your actual ones.

She was staring at the ceiling and she couldn't get up, could only turn her head a fraction and every part of her body that touched the mattress hurt.

"Hey."

She startled and then looked for the source of the voice. It was familiar but it felt—lighter. There on a medical cot next to her, green lights flashing in the display above a graph of vital signs, he was lying prone, arms on the headrest cradling his face.

He waved to her.

She mimicked him, with effort. It seemed the connection between her brain and her muscles was still tenuous, her hand slow to respond. Her attention was all on seeing the one next to her and it took a minute to realize she was still trying to move in the mindscape they shared, to think the greeting.

She stared at him. His eyes *were* overly large and also a deep brown, shining even in the dimly lit hospital room. They were so bright they seemed to pick up all of the light and reflect it back in twinkles. This face wasn't what he'd shown her in her mind, not really, the face he'd shown her was similar but distorted, all the little imperfections magnified, the parts less harmonious.

She was staring. Could she switch over from thinking to talking? There was a many-layered running monologue in her head. Maybe he couldn't hear it anymore but she wanted him to.

He wet his lips and tried to suppress a smile. It came out as a smirk. He was staring just as she was and hadn't flinched away from her observation. "Mm, not as clearly, the other stimulus is distracting from it. But the general tone. Maybe we can ah—disconnect now. Wake up your people."

Heat rose to her cheeks and she opened her mouth to speak, but her throat was too dry and constricted around the words.

"Here. Drink water. Drink water." He held out a

tube that came from the side of her bed. "Slowly—you've been in there longer than I have."

She started slow but once the water hit her throat she drank in long, greedy slurps. She wiped the water from her face and then drank more. She was fully aware that Drinian was watching with that same amused smile she'd heard in his voice, but it didn't bother her. He was there in her head a moment before, was still there just distant.

She formed the words again and this time they came out, but she needed more water to finish. "This is kinda weird—could you tell me what this is? And also—you don't look like you think you do."

The last part tumbled out and she shrugged then reached to examine the straps and caging holding her head in place and blocking her hands from her neck. Her hands shook as she traced the cords. There were tubes extending from it over to a similar housing on the back of Drinian's neck, restricting his movement as well.

"I gathered that from the way you stared. Well, you know human perception is subjective, and I am not immune—" He put up a hand turning it midair as if to shift the train of his monologue. "Sooo . . . a neural interface patch linking my mycelial implant to your brain—not just your mycelial network—now, translation—it's a mind link where my mushroom can help your mushroom-brain translate whatever that tree told you when you touched it."

She breathed out a shaky breath. "So I have an implant? Like Quin's?"

"No. You have mycelium from her inoculation—I'll explain inoculations later—we wouldn't give you an implant while you couldn't consent but yes, back here —" He gestured towards his own neck to demonstrate. "Mycelium from my implant, travels through that tube and a thinner tube into your neck where a port would normally go so our mycelium could ah—connect."

Lumina scrunched her nose. "Not making it less weird."

Drinian shrugged. "I'm kinda used to this sort of thing. Well not the uh—connection with you. That's very weird—new weird not bad weird, but the implants, sharing my headspace with a mushroom, all that. And it's made me feel very light. This new one is a cheerful fellow and mushies like to share." He sighed and adjusted his face against his arms. "Oh inoculations . . ." He spoke the words but let the new topic hang there and just looked at her instead.

She could feel the buoyancy of Drinian's mushroom symbiont in her mind, a sort of warm contented feeling. It was making her drowsy. "Maybe we just stay this way for a while longer and let them sleep?"

He smiled and gave a little nod. "Sure. Let them sleep and we sleep, I think it's okay now. I think we'll wake back up."

THE SUN LIT the hospital room a soft golden hue through the lightly tinted windows. Lumina pushed her toes across the sheets of the hospital bed into the warmth of the sunbeams where dust motes floated down and then back up in little whorls and eddies of imperceptible airflow.

"Lumina?"

"Maybe just after breakfast? We could do it after breakfast."

Drinian laughed next to her from his cot, but he didn't speak aloud. *It'll be weird to have the link gone but it gets easier and for you it won't be so bad—for me—once my implant dies off it'll be—ah uncomfortable, very uncomfortable.*

I'm sorry.

No, no, I've done it before, it's worth it every time. Especially this time. You're more interesting conversation than a mushroom.

She felt the sincerity under his teasing and her face grew warm. The mushroom mediating their link accepted his statement with a mental shrug as it wiggled its pseudopods around his face. She wanted to hide the heat of her blush in the sunbeams at the foot of the bed, but she was still strapped in place. Moving freely wouldn't work so well with them physically connected by tubes and mycelium. There was that at least in favor of moving ahead and breaking their connection.

Well, it's definitely weird, the whole thing, but especially feeling like I don't want it to stop.

"Weird." She tried the word out loud for extra emphasis.

"Yep, but not bad weird." He was smiling and shifting his arms under his face. "And yet—a full stretch will be good."

Chase and Quin were both watching them, tracking their expressions, and it made her feel like some things she should say out loud, but others felt like they should be mind speak between her and Drinian.

Drinian, who you'd never met before yesterday.

He laughed at that and shifted again.

Chase looked restless, uncomfortable as if she wanted to say something, a lot of somethings that she wasn't saying. And then Quin came and sat at the foot of Lumina's bed. "Lumi, Chér. It will take longer to settle back in your own mind the longer they are connected to you. Perhaps."

An automated attendant carried in a tray with steaming dishes and deposited it on the bed, wheeled back out and then returned three more times with three more trays.

"—So perhaps right after the food."

Lumina's eyes widened and her brows pulled together and rose. "Okay, yeah. Right after."

But after breakfast didn't feel any easier. The food was gone too fast even though she tried to savor it— they were both ravenous, and bots cleared the trays away. There was nothing left to wait for.

The doctor released the straps and rolled Lumina onto her side. "At the count of three I'll remove the connection. You'll feel a pulling sensation."

She closed her eyes. *Hey Drinian?*

Hm?

Just checking . . . He was still in her head, that warm humor that seemed to come with colors, bronze and deep royal blue and earthy brown like cinnamon bark submerged in hot tea, the combination of Drinian and the mushroom he carried. It was a full feeling, comfortable.

It's going to feel—

Weird, I know.

The doctor's hand were on the back of her neck and she flinched at the cold touch, dry and papery against her skin. There were alarms going off along all of her nerves, pain when those hands brushed the attachment site with an icy disinfectant.

"Okay, about ready to start Lumina, nod if you hear me."

She nodded.

"Three . . ."

Drinian was bracing himself too, she felt it.

No, Lum you don't know, not just weird. That was me being careful—not to scare you. But it's going to hurt.

"Two . . ."

Like physically? She squeezed her eyes shut tighter and clenched her fists in anticipation.

Relax or it will—But no—it's like being sucker punched and having the breath knocked out of you. It feels like someone just died.

"One . . .okay, I'm removing the tubing now. You'll feel some tugging—maybe a little sting."

Better to open your eyes, Lum. And breathe.

The doctor's hands braced against the nape of her neck, warmer hands now but still foreign. She wanted to shove them away, but it wasn't a logical thing to want. She clenched her fists as the pulling started. Her fingernails pressed crescent moons into her palms. The pulling she was warned of was deep inside and then there was a sharp tearing release that sent needles of pain down her spine. More tugging, more pulling as the tube slid out, a clanking sound as the doctor dropped the end of the tubing into a pan at the bedside. Cold wet cotton was scrubbed against the pinprick wound and then pressure, a bandage.

Lumina covered her mouth and opened her eyes. She held back sobs as her gut clenched and a searching panic sent her onto her hands and knees then curled her in half like waking from a nightmare. In the dark. Alone.

"Count your breaths, Lum." Drinian's voice sounded thinner and more distant when it wasn't in her head.

Then Chase was holding her, wrapping her arms around her and Quin was there too on her other side, a hand rubbing her back. Her muscles were locked and shaking until she started to breathe and count.

"That's it—see? Getting better?"

"No it—it's the worst!" It was hard to talk, but

worse to be silent, worse for *him* to be silent. Her muscles relaxed with each breath, leaving her drained, but she turned in Chase's arms and found Drinian sitting up, removing the tubing from the base of his implant stage with shaking hands and one eye squeezed shut, a half grimace. "There—phew." He breathed out and then back in syncing up with her. "Better, right?"

"A little."

"Now multiply that times a hundred—take off a full mushroom of your own or have one die on you? Times a hundred." He shook his head, handing his end of the severed connection to the doctor. His eyes were too bright, a film of moisture on them as tears slid down around his shaky smile and then he took another breath. "Just saying all that so you know. For later."

CHAPTER 9
FRIENDS OF MY FRIENDS

"You brought her here?!" The governor of Genti-6 leaned forward with the force of her voice, a forelock of greying waves playing contrast to her smooth freckled skin, and the sharpness of ice blue eyes.

"Right, and I thought you were more reasonable." Waters set his drink down hard sloshing amber liquid onto the triangular, orange table, then feeling chagrined, picked it up again and took another long draught before setting it down more carefully. "I'm only telling you any of this because she agreed to it."

"Reasonable?" She sat back and adjusted the hover height of her seat once more before resuming her meal. The moons around Genti-6 were high over the horizon, an innumerable display of stars visible through the glass walls of the private suite of the mile-high restaurant. She took a bite of the cultured meat, cooked rare and seasoned with local herbs and spices. Imports needed to be kept low if they were to build self-sufficiency. At least Genti-6 was salt rich.

"Paul, you telling me this means I'm going to have to ask her to leave or lie if anyone else of consequence finds out that she's here—or that I knew it—It looks reckless, foolhardy."

"Gwen—"

"No, it *is* foolhardy. Seven dead orchards. Do you know what an orchard costs on a colony in a distant star system? It costs influential backers who want a stake in the colonies they back; they want to carve out land and resources for their children and their children's children and they want a hand in the politics. Seven dead orchards, and you brought her back here."

"Look, she'd be up here telling you this herself except that I told her you were a friend—now is that true or not? And does it mean something different out here on Genti-6?"

She shook her head and took a sip of the pale golden wine in her glass. It rippled with viscosity, sweetness. There was a stubborn glint in her eye. "You know it doesn't. Or I'd have already escorted her back up that elevator. You see the lights blinking on it?" She pointed out the window to the west. "It runs all night. Now convince me before I get tired."

"Whatever happened to those other orchards, she's solving it. She was sick, bone tired, but she refuses to go near an orchard until she can guarantee it won't happen again."

"She doesn't need to be here when her willpower runs out. It could be an accident, and I'd still have dead sticks in the ground like the other colonies."

"Okay, sure, but the ERF commander isn't playing nice, and she wants to shut down the program instead of solving the problem."

"The decline is almost past history. There's little left to protect. Leaders have to cut their losses somewhere."

"You too, huh?"

She took another sip.

Paul Waters watched the face that he knew so well, the lack of concern for whatever was happening on Earth. He resisted the urge to say something harsh, to shake her up. "I get it. Genti-6 is your concern. So, what I'm telling you is that those trees you put so much effort into getting here are not going to last more than the first year without monthly reeducation by our pariah Tree-Whisperer. There's a flaw in the solution, and what we're trying to do is buy time and support for more research, for a real, permanent solution—"

"What makes you think it isn't a losing investment?" Her eyes were still hard, but she was looking at him now. She was listening and he saw interest in her face.

"I know Quin and I know the team she's working with. And I know those trees on Earth would have all been dead sixteen years ago if she hadn't agreed to come back on the project—and, well, I can say that because I'm coming out of retirement. That's what I'm doing, because I'm convinced it can be done."

The governor of Genti-6 sat up straighter, leaned forward with intention instead of ire. "I want her kept indoors unless I'm warned. She has a week, unless my people can quell the rumors and replace them with something more palatable before then—unlikely. Minds change slowly all the way out here. The impermanence of a colony around a foreign star breeds stubbornness. But once they begin to turn, they turn on a dime and it will be hard to go back again. Keep her in."

"And a shift drive?"

She tilted her head and poured them both another glass of wine. "You got here, didn't you?"

"That was borrowed. I only have it another day. We're going to need something more permanent."

"I'll consider it. Until then, keep her inside."

It was dark except for the screens, Earth's single crescent moon hanging above the horizon. Commander Mara Lariat grimaced back at its yellowed Cheshire Cat's teeth. The thing was taunting her. Back again after a full cycle of moon phases with her still here, on Earth, when time and the things she had to do with it had grown so onerous.

Once she'd considered the moon a friend, imagined it rising over a renewed Earthscape, with trees, forests, life-filled glades. That was young Mara, the girl that thought she'd join the interface project but couldn't tamp down her fears on the implant table. She'd have to hope someone else could save the planet.

She'd imagined a lot of things before all that youthful hope had petered out with each failed attempt to push back the decline and each friend relocated on other planets, around other stars.

The earbud that was delivering words she didn't want to hear was crooked and giving her a headache, but she'd have to tolerate it long enough to get answers. She grit her teeth.

"No, I didn't know she was gone until just now. Look I'm—dealing with something. Can you just find out who authorized them to go up the elevator in the first place?"

The voice on the other end of the line was cautious, aware of her rising irritation. "Well—there's no record of them going up an ERF operated elevator, so it would have had to have been civilian owned."

She gripped her short-cropped brown hair and squeezed her eyes shut. They stung from lack of sleep and the needle-sharp intensity of it when her eyes watered made her consider seeing a doctor, there were things they could do for insomnia but each of them required her to acknowledge it was a real problem. She couldn't see that rising to the top of her list any time soon.

On the other half of the screen were messages from twelve distant relatives and six assorted others with questions about her mother's remains, messages collecting like proverbial flies on a corpse. The comparison made her want to laugh but it would have come out sounding wrong, that hollow but much too loud sort of laugh when something isn't actually funny. She couldn't be certain the tears she was keeping bottled wouldn't flow out on the tails of an outburst like that.

She sat back in her chair and let it rock on the cushion of air underneath it before she lifted it higher, making a buffer between herself and the conversation she no longer wanted any part of. The sooner she could shut down the project and leave this posting the better she would feel. Earth was too far from her family, too far from everything, it was just another corpse she'd been guarding for too long.

"Commander Lariat?"

She opened her stinging eyes and lowered the chair. "Yes?"

"The governor of Genti-6 is offering asylum to Sgt. Fleury and General Waters. She would like to discuss terms for their transfer to Genti-6 or safe return to Earth without repercussions."

"What?!"

"She wants—"

"I heard you. I have—funeral arrangements to make. But if Sgt. Fleury sets foot back on Earth, I will be making good on my promise to file suit to complete her separation documents and have her implant—property of the ERF—repossessed. You tell the people protecting her that."

She closed out the communication and tucked her

tablet away in the drawer of the desk. She knew what she would see if she looked at her reflection in the screen, her face pale with swollen pouches under her eyes, another sign of the nightmares. The whites of her eyes had red tracings in them but not from crying. She hadn't cried.

Her mother would have cheerfully reminded her that it was good for her to let it all out, but there never did seem to be a time or place where it wasn't a liability to do that, just drop her guard, split herself open like that when someone could walk in and see all of her grief spilling out.

There would be someone at the door or another call, another question she had to answer with a clear head. Because her mother was dead. Dead at sixty-five, a week before longevity treatments would have been approved for her. A week sooner and maybe she would have been alive. A year sooner and there was no question that she would be. Tell that to the people who kept control of the when and the how and the who of the human lifespan, people with old money, the only meaning of it coming from stockpiled resources and generations of connections.

She stared back at the screen and answered several messages about time and place for burial. Her mother wanted her body back on Earth, like most people from her generation. That wasn't unexpected. The place was becoming one big funeral destination. Once the generations that clung to Earth, as if it was their actual mother and they suckling children, were all in the ground it would be little more than a graveyard.

The younger generations were finally moving on; only fanatical homeworlders and the Earth Rehabilitation Forces remained, aside from a few politicians that liked the idea of being ruling elite on the old planet.

They could have it. But she was certain that once the ERF was disbanded at least the politicians would move on.

Her mind was wandering. She dragged it back for the umpteenth time. Funeral arrangements. And after that she would have to deal with the persistently problematic Sgt. Fleury and General Waters, because they were forcing her to.

Her hand hovered over the next file but she hesitated, couldn't remember where it was supposed to go.

She could ignore whatever was happening on Genti-6 with Sgt. Fleury, but as long as there were any arboreal linguists remaining—especially Fleury—someone could be convinced to petition for the ERF to stay on Earth and keep fighting to revive the twice dead ecosystems. They'd cite progress and show the remaining wetlands, and deserts, the orchards until those died off, but if the trees were finally gone she could convince any outliers of the futility and they could focus on new systems, new planets. Even Mars was faring better than Earth despite the decline of *their* trees.

She submitted the file—it was for the coroner—and then paused again. There were more tasks roiling in her head and competing for attention than the funeral and the position her mother's absence put her in—the doer, the leader, the matriarch when she wanted no part of that. It was a different problem with the same oppressive flavor but it was a simple one. Her mother was dead but at least she'd had the courtesy to do it quickly once it was inevitable instead of drawing it out for long painful years full of treatments, sick beds, and failed attempts to hold on.

Earth was dying and she hadn't given that same courtesy of doing it fast and sudden. Instead she was clawing onto the jackets of anyone who would listen, dragging it out for centuries, with extinction events, erratic temperatures, and broken ecosystems. She grew inhospitable and unstable, like an aged relative whose breath stank of death but refused to let go and instead tainted the good years of life for her younger friends and relations.

Mara had paid her respects with visits and even encouraged treatments for years. She was one of many who'd cried with relief when Sgt. Fleury came back from the seeded forest on Ross 128-B. She'd championed her as hero and savior of Earth, but that was sixteen years ago, and it was time to let the dying die off. Time to make funeral arrangements.

THE VILLA WAS TOO large and spread out to feel full, but it was so much less empty than it had been in a long time. Quin and Chase were under one roof with her, and now Drinian and General Waters. They took Waters to find a room, talking as they trailed down the sunlit hall that circled the garden atrium with guest rooms. They were still watching her like she might break or pass out again or, more realistically, curl up in a ball of tears like she had in the hospital, but they were letting her find Drinian a room. Quin was being weird. She'd hesitated at the threshold, Chase and Waters waiting just behind her.

" Itha torideen ay shai—We'll be just this way if you —need anything, Lumi."

"Like? What?"

Quin shrugged and turned down the hall, pulling Chase and her worried eyes with her. "Shai'en ma— anything."

She scrunched her face at Quin. Did she not trust her anymore or was it Drinian? They didn't seem to trust Drinian. They *liked* him. She could see that, but there was something else. Back at the hospital room where she and Drinian had been disconnected, when she'd reached out for him there was fear in Chase's eyes, Quin's too.

That was it. They didn't trust him with her.

The hall-lights lit as they walked down the wide

corridor. She was just ahead and looked back to be sure he still followed. He was. And he was looking too. She wanted to look away and also didn't, couldn't, so she smiled instead, blushing again, her guts doing a flip-flop of nerves. She walked backwards until she clipped a hall table and almost toppled a lamp then faced front and sped up. Now she was being weird.

"This is ah—ah long hallway. Does it end?" His voice was playful, a little nervous.

She had to stop, not because the hall ended but because there was something else there. . . .

"Oh, it does end? No—I see the light around the bend—and then more hall." His voice trailed off, concern replacing humor.

Lumina ducked and covered her head. Fire all around, falling debris, smoke, growing things grasping at her skin as they shriveled and turned to cinders and sparks.

She opened her eyes, blinked, stared with wide eyes —where was the hall?

"Lum?" He was close, his breath against her ear.

"Um, yeah?" She was breathing too fast so she held it, blinked, breathed out more slowly this time. Drinian's face was there close to hers, the hall light haloing him.

"A flashback, right?"

"Is that what it was?" Relief flooded her, and warmth, tingling in her skin. Drinian was holding her up, an arm around her waist. She leaned her face closer to his, the space between them wasn't much.

"Mm-hm, probably." He turned his face, searching the hall, the motion deflecting her attempted kiss, if that's what it was, so that the end result was leaning her forehead against his temple.

"I see a door, just there, right side of the hall. Is that a room with a bed? That's all I need. Maybe a table?"

She let out a shaky laugh and stepped back, widening the gap between them. "Yeah, that's a guest room. Most of them are guest rooms actually."

He opened the door and let out an approving whistle. "There is a bed and a desk, and a window—no, no, two windows."

He went in, reaching for her hand. She pretended not to notice the hand but followed. Her heart was still beating too fast, and she was suddenly lightheaded.

"There is a bed, and two chairs, I see." He pulled an ornately carved mahogany wood chair from the desk and set it next to her. "I see your mother likes antiques —You are very pale for you, maybe ah—a rest—a seat?"

She sat. Pride would be stupid if it meant he'd be picking her up off the floor in another moment. "Is that why they were so worried about me going with you?"

"Ah—maybe, partially. Also they don't trust, well— not us but the um, the mycelial interface bond." He cleared his throat and his face reddened. "They don't know me well yet."

"You just say everything, don't you?"

A nod. He was unpacking his bag in rapid movements laying things out on the desk in no particular order until he found something, a small tube that he lifted to his lips and ripped the sealed top with his teeth. He handed it to her and gestured for her to drink.

"Well? Slurp it. It's viscous . . . nutrients, electrolytes, fast sugars, protein. All the good stuff."

She lifted it to her lips with caution and then squeezed some into her mouth. It was sweet, but full-flavored, the taste shifting from fruity to nutty as she swallowed it.

"Yum." She took another eager slurp.

He smiled, a twinkle of mischief lighting his eyes. "It's for mushrooms, or mushroom wearers. Concentrated nutrients for quick feeding."

"What?" Her laughter bubbled up between sips from the little packet. "Welp. Guess I'm a mushroom."

He winked at her. "Little bit. Feel any better?"

She kicked her legs in the chair wishing it had a hover function. "Yeah but—is that going to keep happening? And this . . ." She gestured from herself to Drinian, hoping he got it without more explanation.

"Well, well . . . the flashbacks will fade, yes, and it'll feel like memory after you process it more, but you'll need—"

There was a knock at the half open door and then Chase was there assessing the distance between Lumina's chair and the desk Drinian leaned against. "Found a good room?"

"Yes—and a very good room. Two windows, this beautiful desk of yours. Thank you."

"What happened?"

"Mom, I'm fine."

Drinian gave Lumina a look of advance apology, clear enough she felt she could hear it. "She had a flashback in the hallway, very quick. I gave her snacks."

Lumina stood up too quickly and had to place a steadying hand on the back of the chair. "See, all better."

Chase laughed at her bravado, her look for Drinian softening. "I see that. Now—maybe we get you to your own room, dinner, sleep … there's time for socializing tomorrow."

Lumina crossed to the door, glancing over her shoulder to catch his expression as he watched her go. He was watching, and she was certain that look held disappointment along with acceptance. She felt a little surge of warmth, of victory—then worry.

"I probably need more than mushroom food, I guess."

Chase scrunched her face but didn't ask as she directed Lumina out the door then paused, turned back to Drinian. "And thank you—for before, and now."

He looked like he didn't know what to say but the thoughts were visible on his face. Lumina watched over Chase's shoulder. She needed to see his answer, not just hear it.

He looked up from his hands not to Chase, but past her, meeting Lumina's eyes instead. "Yes well—I'd do it again so—you're very welcome."

GOVERNOR GWEN COLLORAN'S space seemed too large for an office; it was more like an art museum. The open space was all geometric shapes, smooth lines and sharp angles achieved in metallic surfaces and transparent colored glass made from the abundant sand on Genti-6. The floor was unusual in construction with stairs leading down three steps to a carpeted space, a conversation pit and instead of hover chairs for seating there were antique couches in bright colored fabrics like something out of a retro history catalogue.

Lumina rubbed at the goosebumps on her arms and curled her legs under her on the orange cushioned couch. It even smelled orange, like cinnamon and citrus incense.

Drinks were brought in by a robotic assistant, water, alcohol, coffee, grape juice. The bot repeated the menu for each of them and filled their glasses with their drinks of choice.

Waters took his glass filled with the golden wine Genti-6 was becoming known for—not from Earth-grapes, but a native shrub that grew sweet yellow berries—while the others took coffee. The governor, Lumina knew her face from broadcasts, took the same as Waters—Paul, the governor called him Paul. They all appeared to know him better than she did, but he'd come with Quin and he seemed alright.

They were all there, Chase, Quin, Drinian, Waters,

and the governor, but the reason still wasn't apparent and no one had explained. If Drinian knew anything, he'd have told her. She glanced over at him. The bot was handing him a glass of water, and his attention was on that.

Better than on her. It was beginning to feel strange, difficult, especially if anyone else noticed how often they looked at the same time and how long they looked.

It kept happening. And she kept expecting to hear him in her head when it did, to feel the color of his thoughts, and when she couldn't there would be a wave of disappointment and a restless nagging feeling in the back of her mind. It spread along her nerves like scuttling worries about forgotten obligations.

She rubbed at the back of her neck and stretched it left and right to alleviate some of the stiffness that was still there. It had been a day and a half since the mind-link was disconnected. How many hours? She wished she knew if this was a social call or some sort of reprimand for what had happened in the orchard—if anything worth a reprimand had happened. What would she even apologize for?

I 'm sorry for touching a tree and blacking out. I am sincerely remorseful for inconveniencing the tree steward or whatever. But she had heard something in whispers. Chase and Quin when they thought she was still sleeping. There were colony trees dying on other planets and Quin wasn't welcome there. The thought made her nervousness tick up even higher and she squeezed her arms, blanching the skin around her fingers a paler yellow.

He was looking her way again, mouthing words. "You okay?" And then he sipped his water, tasting it as if it were something with more flavor.

She shrugged and then pulled at her lips with her teeth. She wanted to switch couches, scooch over and grab his hand, not for comfort but so he would . . . what? Hear what she was thinking without her saying it out loud? Yeah, that was it. Her lips cracked into a smile, and she made a face mocking herself. They said it could take a few days for that connected-disconnected feeling to go away. He smiled back, quirking his brows up in question, but the governor was finally beginning to say something.

"So you've gotten yourselves into quite a spot. And Waters here is trying to convince me that it's actually an opportunity. I'm not easy to convince."

Waters cleared his throat and shifted. He pinned Quin with a stare. "The ERF Commander isn't budging, and there's more than that. She's doubling down. She's taken off all of the apprentice's implants and has orders filed to enforce your separation for submitting paperwork under false pretenses and stealing ERF property."

Lumina remembered their faces from the orchard with Quin, the blue-eyed blonde Jordan, and two others, all with the small mammalian bodies of mushroom symbionts curled on their necks and reaching into their hair, a tall boy—Ronin. She pictured their faces as they worked with the saplings, smiles of reverence for what they did.

"Que diable—What in hell?!" Quin's face was a mask of growing disgust, incredulity—horror. "Took them off? Juste comme ca—like that? Hard won apprentices? With so few available … and they might not take new implants after this. They'll reject if the gap is too long. Even if it isn't long, sometimes—"

"Did you hear the rest of what I said? Those apprentices were half-done anyway. You've got a bigger problem—your implant, which she's planning to use to get you back on Earth—because whatever you said or did in that meeting, she has it out for you."

Lumina felt sick. The gap between herself and Drinian suddenly too large. She got up slowly, squeezing her own arms, watching to see that no one was looking at her.

The others had their attention on Quin, so she crossed the gap between the couches, abandoning her orange one for Drinian's purple and sitting next to him. She scooted close, careful not to brush his shoulder or leg with her own. She didn't look over until she felt him take her hand in his much warmer one.

Better?

Was that a thought or a whisper, maybe both, either way, she answered with a quick hand squeeze.

Quin leaned forward in the chair and reached back to pet Synesis. Whether it was Quin's agitation or the mushroom's Lumina wasn't sure, but the creature flailed her appendages around Quin's face. "She's done with the ERF and she is punishing me for pushing to see it through. C'est tout pwoblem sa. Because that is all I did. I sat for hours with our ecologists and I put in those proposals. I told her it could still be done. But she —has given up."

Her voice had risen in volume and her eyes were flashing. Lumina watched her, transfixed. Quin was never angry, or emotional, not anything like this—but it didn't last long. Synesis settled against her neck and they both visibly calmed, sat back and sighed.

The governor called the bot over for a refill and then tapped her lips with the glass. "I've already contacted your commander at the ERF and told her you are under my protection—"

"Shukran. Merci. I hope she cannot afford to cross you or the other colonies, the ERF is—was, funded by colony leaders."

The governor continued. "But my first and only concern is Genti-6, and right now you are accused of being a threat to our newest investments—if you can't show me that's not the case I won't be able to keep you here, regardless of what I told your commander."

Lumina startled, a sharp surge of anxiety rushing through her, Drinian's hand the only anchor. "What? But you can't turn her in!"

Chase shot her a look, a reminder more than a warning, to be patient, to calm herself, to let the adults handle it.

Quin sat up straighter. "I cannot show you that I am —untainted, not a threat, until I know that for myself. But I would never endanger an orchard—"

"But you did—" The governor's eyes were hard.

"Not knowingly. I was not well." Quin held up her gloved hands, eyes flaring again like a sun out of the dark. "You forget who planted those saplings, educated them, and you forget—or you do not know who brought them up from seed. That was me; they are my children. The ones that live and the ones that die."

The governor pressed her drink-cooled glass against her cheek, the condensation dripping down her face. She looked uncomfortable, startled by Quin's unexpected outburst of passion.

There was a shift in the room as tangible as the bodies of her friends shifting in their seats. Adjusting perspectives were somehow as loud as throats being cleared. Lumina wondered if Drinian felt it the same way, then squeezed his hand tighter and wished for the shared mind space for the third time in one day. It was less than yesterday and still too much.

The silence persisted a moment longer and then the governor took out a digital form for Quin and Drinian to sign, accepting asylum on Genti-6. Drinks were refilled.

"I'm taking this as your word and backing it up with as much legal consequence as I have at my disposal."

Quin nodded, passed the form to Drinian.

They would be staying, whatever else those forms detailed, that much was clear. This was better. Even with the circumstances that brought them and held them here: exile, a threat to Quin's safety.

They were locked here together.

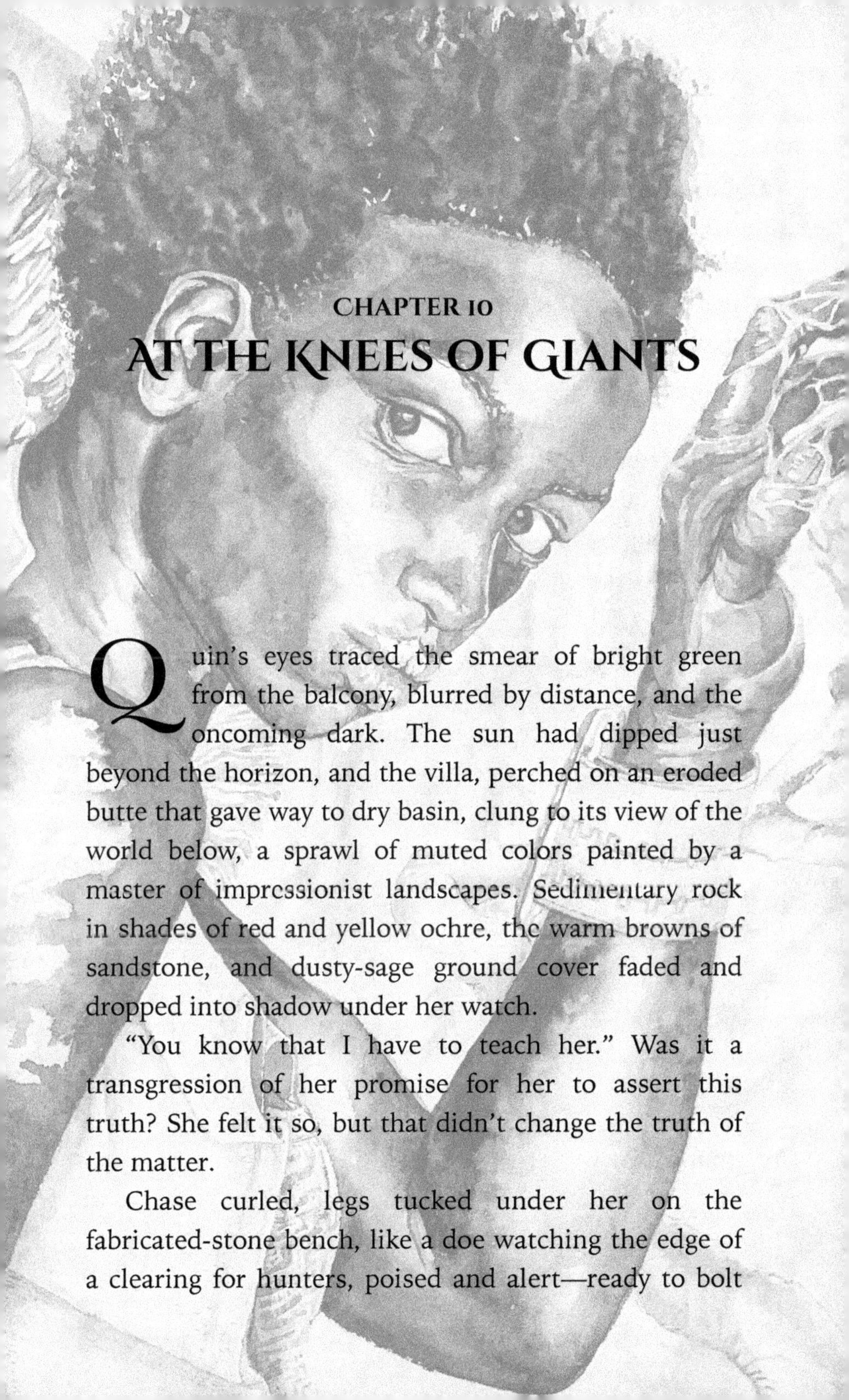

CHAPTER 10

AT THE KNEES OF GIANTS

Quin's eyes traced the smear of bright green from the balcony, blurred by distance, and the oncoming dark. The sun had dipped just beyond the horizon, and the villa, perched on an eroded butte that gave way to dry basin, clung to its view of the world below, a sprawl of muted colors painted by a master of impressionist landscapes. Sedimentary rock in shades of red and yellow ochre, the warm browns of sandstone, and dusty-sage ground cover faded and dropped into shadow under her watch.

"You know that I have to teach her." Was it a transgression of her promise for her to assert this truth? She felt it so, but that didn't change the truth of the matter.

Chase curled, legs tucked under her on the fabricated-stone bench, like a doe watching the edge of a clearing for hunters, poised and alert—ready to bolt or fight as needed. The picture she cut caught and held Quin even as she waited for an answer, a denial of what they both knew or an acquiescence. How could she be so exquisitely invested in everything that mattered to her without being crippled by it? *Incomprehensible.* She was still able to move, to breathe, to make decisions under duress despite the stakes. It would be so easy to submit to paralysis with such responsibility.

The answer, Chase parceled out word by word as if each could stand alone. "To . . . protect her. Yes. If you can teach her so she isn't so vulnerable. Can you do that?"

The moons, long since risen, competed with the last strains of sunset to paint Chase's face, a soft blue cast mixing with horizon pink. She tilted a questioning look at Quin where she stood leaning against the wrought-iron balcony.

"I can. But Chéri, what if she wants more? Un peu de connaissances est une chose dangereuse. . . ."

"Knowledge is a dangerous thing?"

"A little of it, oui."

But Chase was already shaking her head, brows creased in refusal. It was too much, too fast to push her boundary for Lumina. Better to leave it except—the problem would come again if *Lumina* were to push this boundary.

"Chér . . . I am only saying that we are treading in dangerous waters. She wants this so much, she went behind your back."

"She was angry at both of us. And—she's impulsive." Her tone was defensive, a warning.

"Alright. I hear you. I teach her until she is safe enough, should she have any more contact with the trees."

"Just enough—I just, I don't want her path written for her so young." Her walls had dropped again. This was the soft Chase, the one who needed Quin to understand and not feel hurt over the boundaries she was setting.

Quin crossed the balcony to sit beside her and brushed a stray lock of hair from her face with her gloved hand. Chase's face flushed with warmth. She directed her eyes to the moon instead of Quin's. Perhaps it was too intimate for the moment, the years of distance too numerous for the simple gesture of comfort—or the gloves too stark a reminder of Quin's sickness.

Quin withdrew the hand and tucked it in the pocket of her uniform, curled her fingers as self-consciousness coiled and slithered in her thoughts. "You do not want what happened to us to happen to Lumina." It came out a whisper that could have been lost in a light wind but in the still night air settled and wrapped around them both as a somber cloak.

"No—Yes, I don't want that for her."

"Then we won't let it. I will be careful what I teach her. I will be slow. Even if I have to wrap her ankles with ship's anchors." This was the right track—Chase exuded certainty again, ease with her. "And I will have her bring the question to you herself. For permission, so that you can have your say, D'accord?"

"Okay." Chase's laugh cut through the chill creeping over the balcony with the twilight, a bright buoyant sound like birdsong on a battlefield. Making her laugh was better than everything else Quin did. Even if Chase would wish away their time in the ERF together, the consummation of all of the risks they'd consented to when they'd signed waivers and took their implants. What happened after was beyond the risks they'd signed up for, but it was also what joined them together.

"WHAT ARE YOU READING?"

Lumina startled and gripped the sides of the chair as it stabilized. The aged green velvet felt prickly beneath her palms, with bare patches worn smooth and soft again. The wood had long since lost its original finish, instead polished by the natural oils of many hands. The hover function, added long after the chair was crafted, made sitting there like sailing in an old ship on a sea made of water instead of stars. She had been lost in that sea when Quin's voice reached her.

Quin's barefoot step was light and didn't make the echoing clicks that her feet would have normally made on the tile floors of the library if she was wearing shoes, if she was leaving. She had always seemed to be leaving. Now here she was, and Lumina couldn't remember seeing her barefoot and out of her uniform before. She was wearing only the soft green t-shirt she wore under the uniform and coppery silk pants, borrowed from Chase.

"Just—*The Wonderful World of Mushrooms and Other Fungus.*" She tipped the cover for Quin to see as she lowered her chair to the floor. Colorful mushroom caps decorated the surface of the worn book, the fabric covered hardback shredding along the edges and devolving into threads. She had to hold it in both hands to keep it together.

Quin quirked her brows at the old book. "A good book, but there are newer resources."

"I know, but I like starting with the old ones and working my way to the new ones, like I'm learning how people did."

Quin wet her lips, an odd look coming into her eyes. "How are you feeling now?"

Lumina set the book down on a shelf still open lest she lose her place. She put one hand over her stomach and the other, a fist against her forehead. "Like I'm all emptied out and there are bits missing. Maybe like I was sick and threw up some extra parts?" She scrunched her nose at her own words. "That sounds so gross out loud."

"As much as before?"

"No—yes, um I guess no. It's more distant but just —you know that feeling of being separate from everyone else and like they see and understand each other and you aren't a part of that?"

Quin nodded and she had a shadowed look in her eyes. With that look she did know the feeling and wasn't just agreeing.

"Well so, it's like that except it's like it went away and came back a lot bigger."

They both sighed at the same time and then smiled at the accidental synchrony.

Lumina looked down at the tiles under her feet and traced the spiral of a fern with her toes, an old habit. "Is it really a hundred times worse with a mushroom?"

"We call it separation sickness, and yes it is. You seem to … have your own mycelial network and that is buffering this feeling for you. When a fungal implant dies like the first I had— though it was premature, they disconnected her—the mycelial network they build to link to your nervous system dies off with them, all of those connections die and you feel it—and even after you recover you might keep feeling it like pain in a phantom limb."

"Like Chase does?"

"Nam, kdalik—just like that."

"But if I have one—mycelium anyway, why doesn't it just die off like people's mushroom's and what does that mean? I'll keep getting stuck like that if I try to hear Tree-speak?"

Quin sat down in front of the electric fire that warmed the night-chill from the room, her eyes reflecting those flickering flames. She gestured for Lumina to join her.

She knelt like she imagined an apprentice might.

"You have this thing because of me. I can only guess. You were growing in the AUC, attached to me when I took a new implant, so all I can think is that while you are my child and Chase's, you are also hers—Synesis's." Quin reached back and placed a hand on her symbiont. "I do not know if you can learn to process Tree or if it will always be too much, but I think there is a chance if we do it right."

Lumina wet her lips and tried to wait but the question came out anyway. "Do what right?"

"Teach you, everything I can teach you without an implant, and then we'll see. But we don't have any others like you to know how this will work."

"Wait, you're going to let me try again?"

Quin shook her head. "Not so fast like that but, oui. We teach you first and then you can decide what to do with it. If we have any trees left to work with by then."

Worry, a sharp but fleeting twist of near panic made her stomach somersault, but then her hopes rebounded like soil turning over. It couldn't be so dire, could it? "There's the new orchard though, right?"

Quin stared into the flames and then met Lumina's bright, hopeful gaze. "Those trees won't last here unless I can make sure it is safe to reeducate them. They are not immune to the decline—the gradual death of all trees, on all planets. They are more susceptible. Your colony is less stable than Earth ever was when the problem started."

"That's what you're doing, isn't it? Fixing it?"

"I am holding it back but now—losing ground."

"That's what I want to do then. To help you, to learn Tree and stop the decline with you." The upwelling of purpose felt like a fire kindling along her nerves and setting her mind alight. She jumped up, pulled books from the library shelves, anything on trees, forests, ecosystems, the one on mushrooms she was already reading, several others. Then she dropped next to Quin and surrounded them in books, her smile echoing the one that warmed the Tree-Whisperer's face.

"I will teach you everything I can with these gloves on—Chase will caution you and she is right to—but it will ultimately be your choice, not ours."

THE PINK GLOW at the horizon softened the frown that pulled Quin's features into tight angles of disapproval. "You are going to have to talk to her. We agreed. I cannot go behind her back, but it is for you to tell."

Lumina glanced away, sidestepped a large fern, yellow and brown crisping on its outermost fronds, and then crouched at the base of the black, marble tree in the center of the garden. "She was—going to work."

She *was* going to work. It wasn't a lie. But there was that one moment between good morning and farewell when she'd felt the opening to stop her, to say more and then she hadn't, and the door had closed with a click. She hesitated then settled her fingers into the bed of moss.

It was cool this early in the morning and the garden's recycled moisture had collected in small beads of iridescent condensation in all of the dips and crevices of the tiny plants. When she touched them there was nothing more than the bubbling, effervescent whispers she'd always felt. "It feels—the same."

"Mm . . . First, mosses are bryophytes—no mycorrhizal networks. But they do host fungus, endophytic kinds, and that is enough for an interface, a tiny conversation. "

Quin lifted Lumina's hand out of the moss and placed it back on the cool black marble of the stone tree that stood in the center of the garden. Lumina frowned, confusion and irritation pulling her attention from Quin and whatever she wanted her to do and back to the mosses.

Her thoughts were rapid, chaotic, a tumult of desires, to plunge her hand back into those minute plants, a compulsion more than a want, and stronger still, the orchard came into her mind, little aspens and firs shivering in the heavy Genti-6 winds. She could go there again. She could bring Drinian there and . . .

Quin was waiting for her attention, one gloved hand resting atop her own bare ones. Lumina pulled her mind back to the courtyard and turned startled eyes on her.

"Lumi, your mother going to work is not a reason to be keeping this secret. If you want a thing, you have to be transparent with her. She is not an obstacle to you. She loves you."

She looked up at Quin, resentment shadowing her eyes, but it wasn't for Quin this time, not most of it.

"That's easy to say."

"Oui, of course, but you need to be grown up enough to do difficult things for this, because it only gets harder, Chéri. What you felt with Drinian, when the separation came, that was a taste, and learning the difference, learning to survive without the connections and not crave it like you are, fixated on the orchard, fixated on him . . ."

Fixated? She couldn't deny it, not in so many words. She reached for the moss again but Quin stopped her with another question. "Was she right or wrong to try and protect you before?"

Lumina's brow furrowed and she scowled. "She didn't tell me everything—and you said you want to teach me this, so why not just tell her you're going to?" It didn't sound right to Lumina's ears once the words were out. They were her words, her feelings, yes, but with crucial pieces missing. Chase *was* trying harder, sharing more.

Quin ducked down to catch Lumina's eyes. "You want me to speak for you? I am not your translator, and I won't step between you and your mother."

"But you—"

"I am your blood, your family, but not your mother. I have said this before. That is not the role I claimed. That is Chase's."

Quin's words hit like an impact and sat back on the gravel path hard. Not your mother. No, maybe not, but something more than this. She could be more than this. "I don't want her to say no like before. Can you please —please just tell her for me?"

Quin crouched down to her level and sat back in the bed of mossy ground cover, curling and unfurling the frond of a fern with the fingertip of her glove. "Being a linguist is at the core an act of humility first, then bravery, then connection. We meet the speaker where they are, we share, we exchange. If you cannot do that with your family, can you do it with anyone else? If I tell her it will be like taking from her. If *you* tell her, she will see you."

Lumina's ears burned with embarrassment and she felt certain she was being told she wasn't ready, that she wasn't old enough, or brave enough and yet paradoxically she had to do it herself because Quin wouldn't. The little orchard trees shimmered in the sunlight of her memory. She'd only seen them in moonlight, but light was light. She needed to get away, to think. She stood up and jumped over the cluster of ferns in front of her.

"Where are you going?"

"If I can't do this yet, then—"

"Who said you can't?" Quin's head tilted up and she blinked at her, a gloved hand shading her eyes from the risen sun, then gestured at the spot next to her. "Stay and learn. Just tell your mother what you want when she is home. Piachere—please . . . Sit."

She hesitated. Looked across the courtyard to the arched gateway that would lead out of their villa. Her heart was thumping hard in her chest, resounding in her ears, and then it wasn't. Her thoughts slowed, cooled. She would do as she was asked. There was still the urge to leave, to run.

What is wrong with me? Emotions flaring and fading. This urge to run. Fixations . . . She sighed.

That would be spiting herself, wouldn't it? Quin was here, teaching her, not-mother or whatever she was to her. She pressed her lips together and knelt back on the path. "So just touch them, like before?"

"Just so. But then you listen. It felt the same because you weren't listening. That is what today is for, for you to learn how to listen and what to listen for."

She looked up at Quin, a grin stretching her face, excitement bubbled up in place of doubt. "And then what? Will I be able to have an implant? A real one like the one you have, and Drinian has?"

Quin opened her mouth to answer but then hesitated, working her thoughts into words. "That depends on how well you learn these things. You are young, so the risk is high for you like it was when your mother and I took implants and it made me sick. Apprentices to the interface project—the ones who take implants are trained and tested young and still they have to be a bit older for an implant. For now, you learn like this."

Lumina nodded, pushed down her disappointment, impatience that made her want to argue. Instead, she pressed her hand into the moss at their feet.

"Close your eyes. It takes away distractions. It will

be less than what you heard from the sapling in the orchard, but it will have a similar feeling if you listen long enough."

She felt that strange tickling sensation in her head. "It's there, the bubbles."

"Listen closer."

She lowered her face until her breath, warm and moist disturbed the surface of the moss and warmed the top of her hand. And she listened. It was like small voices arising somewhere in her mind, bouncing around and through her usual train of thoughts. It rose and fell in volume and cadence like the natural progression of a conversation. Her eyes flew open. "I hear it!"

"Good. Just listen and follow wherever it is going. If you listen long enough you will start to hear pieces that repeat or almost do, with subtle variation. That is how long you are going to listen. That is how you start. And it is how you will build your vocabulary."

"And then?" It was no more than a whisper. All of her focus was on that rise and fall of voices that was beginning to sound like language, like listening to the sound of waves or echos in Chase's birthing caves and hallucinating meaning in the sounds.

"Then we will see what you can do with it, Lumi Chér."

ONCE THE SUN SET, the sound of crickets became a background music to her study. The moons rose, while she listened. She couldn't call it Tree, maybe Plant. Plant streamed through her fingertips, into her mind, filled all of her senses. The whole of her experiencing, processing, understanding the signals passed through the ferns she sat in, fingers unfurling the little fronds and then releasing them to watch them curl again.

Somewhere a door opened. Light brighter than Genti-6's small moon's spilled across the crushed pumice path into the ferns. She pressed the fern fronds against her face, all of her skin tingling with what she now knew was a message, like a stream bubbling directions to the sea, not the All-Question with the all-consuming flow that Quin had described to her but continual, cyclical in the same way.

Footsteps, a light crunching on the path behind her.

"Lumina?"

Someone crouching, a hand on her shoulder.

She dropped the leaves and looked up, not seeing at first, still hearing. "Oh . . . hi."

Chase crouched next to her, brushed her hand across the ruffles of a fern frond and shivered.

"Do you hear anything anymore?"

Chase shook her head, one hand absently reaching for the scars on the back of her neck. "No, just remembering when I did—you didn't come in for dinner."

"Oh yeah, I wasn't really hungry I guess."

"Not hungry or not ready to talk?"

Lumina scrunched her nose. "Maybe both. It's hard to stop."

"It gets harder. How far are you thinking you can take this?"

"Mom."

"It's something you have to think about."

"I have, and I want to do this. Everything Quin does, I want to help."

Chase sighed, turned her face up to the small, rocky moon and its odd-shaped twin. Lumina couldn't see the look in her eyes, but her voice was strained. "We're in a place where there's a lot to help with, colonies like Genti-6 . . . I just—"

She felt the ache in Chase's voice, the vulnerable curve of her shoulders, she felt that pain as her own. "I don't—I don't have to do any of this if you don't want me to."

"Don't do that. Don't self-sacrifice."

"No, I mean, maybe I'm being selfish or just—" The strings she felt pulling her to keep learning, keep listening, were stretched taut. There were other strings, the ones tying her to Chase, to home.

Chase stood up straighter, shifted to sit on the ground. "That's not what I'm saying, Lumina. I just want you to be sure, and not go so far so fast. There's time for all this."

She was rubbing the back of her neck more than normal, massaging it with a grimace, shivers, and flinching at things that weren't there.

"Do you regret leaving the project, not just getting another—um mushroom, when the first died?"

Chase sighed. "No, not usually, but—sometimes, very much."

"You think I will?"

"No, no. You aren't me. But I don't want you to think you have to do this to have more of Quin in your life."

"Oh." Lumina almost choked on the word, on the feeling it brought up. "You think that's what I'm doing?"

"No, I just, I know what that feels like. And you need to make your choices for you, Even if you need more from her."

"I might be, a little, at first at least. But not mostly, I don't think."

"I thought so. Maybe just slow down a little, okay? Make sure."

"Okay." Lumina's hand's fidgeted back to the fern fronds, tracing the veins in them and hearing the whispers of language. It wasn't enough. They both wanted her to slow down—Even this felt like crawling, like grasping for more when the threshold is just above. "Slow down, so maybe, dinner and then we talk about my mushroom?"

"Ah no." Chase was brushing herself off, standing, and the laughter meant she'd taken it as a joke. Lumina let go of the fern fronds and followed Chase in, palming a fresh lichen covered stone to take with her.

Lumina reached a hand through the open doorway as footsteps approached, that distinctive gait that was almost a swagger but she knew was just energy mixed with the casual step of someone very flat-footed. Drinian's face appeared in the doorway, eyes alert and curious, and then that smile appeared, a smile she knew the motivating thoughts and history of at its very root. "Hey—someone's in here in the dark?"

Her heart raced and she froze like some nocturnal animal, a rabbit caught under the beam of a flashlight. She wished for a moment that she hadn't followed through, but then she pulled at the white cotton sleeve of his shirt, bringing him into the room with her and forgetting that she needed to back up, to make room. She stared up at him—and then stepped back.

He smiled and wet his lips and then looked into the firelit darkness at the bookshelves towering around the walls of the room and the spiral of shelves that jutted from one wall, making a secluded labyrinth of books. "What's this?—what's this? Actual paper?"

His eyes fell on the pile of books on the ground, some open and draped over others. She had left them ready to read in front of the electric fire. The pile had grown since the first night to include books on linguistics, and symbiotic relationships as they occurred in nature, others on genetic engineering and the history of the Interface project on Earth. Drinian crouched down and lifted a book from the top of the pile, read the first few sentences and gestured up at her with the open book.

Her pulse beat in her head, louder than it should have been, but it didn't drown out the soft sounds of conversation that drifted in from the dining room where the others were still talking over the last course. Quin's warm treble, Waters's deeper bass, and Chase's light husky tones interwove in a way that sounded like the moss-speak she'd spent more hours listening to than not from morning until evening and again with the rise of each day's sun. Some nights she would wake and come back to it, fingers delving into the moss, black in the moonlight. Everything sounded like plant speech and her dreams were filled with it. She watched Drinian's lips moving in that curious way they did between words, as if everything were exciting or clever, the smallest thing worthy of deep scrutiny and interest. The undertones of his voice too, sounded like fern-speech.

He was reading the first paragraph of the book aloud while she stood there, reciting it to her like poetry. "The act of isolating DNA fragments—these ah, acquired from a donor organism; then what follows being the insertion of a chosen donor DNA fragment directly into a vector genome and then by great perseverance and the miracle of some great mystery accomplish—the growth of a recombinant vector not in isolation but instead in the body of an appropriate host!—The author waxes, ah nearly religious in his enthusiasm—and I guess, why not. Sorry—you already read all that though. Getting serious about this, I see."

The flow of words was distracting—distracting her from what?

But she didn't want him to stop. She blinked but couldn't move, couldn't take the next step. She'd pulled him in here and now wondered why she had—if it was the same reason she gave herself. The firelight on his face made the color of his eyes, a deep red-brown, visible in a way that they weren't in any other light.

She didn't want to see him so clearly when it wasn't clear enough. That didn't make sense. Her thoughts and feelings were in conflict, a back and forth argument that neither was winning. She closed her eyes, then realized after several more seconds that she was trying to hear his thoughts, expecting to and feeling that acute frustration and loss that she'd felt the first few days each time she looked at him.

But if she was hearing him, he would be hearing this chaos in her head, and he'd know what was distracting her, silencing her. Maybe that wasn't such a good thing. Or maybe she wouldn't mind that, if she could hear him in her head and could have this gap of space and confusion removed.

He was still talking, listing mushroom species from the sound of it. "Ophiocordyceps unilateralis, glomeromycota, Ambispora, Amanita Muscaria, various ascomycetous varieties, basidiomycetous as well, many of these went into the engineering of the first mycorrhizal neuronal symbionts."

"Mycorrhizal neuronal symbionts?"

"Right, but MNS is a dull name, so we just call them mushrooms. Quin's strain is dubbed mycotremata longaevitas."

She closed her eyes again, kept them shut, and listened to the small sounds in the room.

Pages ruffled, a book thumped. Shuffling steps and he was closer, holding her hand. She opened them. "I want an implant, Drinian. Like you have."

"Oh?"

"Yes, a mushroom." It was somehow easier to find words with him right there, as long as she let them come out just the way she thought them, as if he was in her head. "I want to talk to trees for real. My head is full of what moss whispers and what ferns mumble, but I have the voice of that tree from the orchard branded inside my skull." She paused to catch her breath and looked up at him. He felt closer with her eyes open. "I wish you hadn't helped me out of where I was, not taken an implant, and then maybe they'd have had to give me one of my own. Quin says I'm too young and I'm just—so sick of feeling like more than they think I am."

Drinian pressed his lips together and adjusted his hand on hers. "Mm . . . your mother would have done it then. No one was going to give you an implant while you were unconscious—But why are you telling me?"

"Because it's what you do. You could tell them I'm ready."

"Oh." He lifted her hand to inspect in the firelight and She let him. He traced the lines on her palm as he spoke, his words pausing and restarting every time he stopped tracing and started again. "You feel like that's a place you want to go back to so soon? And ah—you'll come back out okay if you have one of, one of these." He raised his hand and hers up to the smooth body of the fungal creature mounted on the back of his neck, half hidden by his hair. It was smaller than Quin's was, with no fruiting bodies adorning its speckled back.

She felt a flash of hurtling through space and time, inundated—bombarded by the message of Tree. It filled her senses, then it faded back into the recesses of her mind.

She pulled in a shaky breath, trembled as the residual taste of it lingered. "Go back there?"

Drinian nodded. "Sure. What we worked through together was only the smallest fraction of what Quin says there is when you speak to wild trees. You got a single phrase, a fractal refrain of the All-Question. I had this mushroom here and I almost got stuck on loop."

She shook her head. Anger pulled her lips back into a scowl even as her eyes became deep wells of hurt. He thought the same as Quin and Chase—but she didn't pull her hand away, that would be like slamming a door in his face. "You're saying I can't do it."

"No, no. I'm saying you have to prove it to yourself, and to them that you *can*—and you haven't, yet. That's how being an apprentice works. I know because I'm, well I'm still trying to prove that to my preceptors on Earth. I'm still learning. But I do know better than to give you an implant without their agreement. It would be very, very bad for me if I did that, maybe for you too." He delivered the words with that same half smile, like a balm to soothe the wound as he caused it.

"I didn't ask you to do that."

"But I knew you wanted to." He released her hand and brushed his fingers against her forehead. "I know a little of what's in here." She sighed, expecting him to drop his hand, to turn and go, but he didn't.

He brushed a wispy spiral of her hair out of her eyes and then rested his hand on the side of her face.

The voices were still coming from the other room, no closer and no farther away. They might come down the hall any moment the longer he stood so close, her pulse beating bird wings in her chest.

"Drin, I just want to feel like it did while we were connected?"

She winced at the way her words sounded, recoiling from inevitable rejection before any came. She had to look away. "I mean—but, not because of this." She lifted their linked hands. "Not because of this—this us thing. Because I feel more and more like I did before that happened, just—separate. It's the same but worse. Like it's bigger now. Right in my face, you know?"

"Yes, ah, I do, yes—but the thing is, if you approach Sgt. Fleury—Quin to you, your Quin or your Chase, I think they'll see it as a symptom of your age. So maybe just read your books and—maybe, wait until it levels out some before you ask?"

"Ugh!"

"You think I'm wrong? Maybe that I'm trying to look bigger, older and use that to, I don't know—"

"Tell me what to do?"

"Yes! But, no I'm not trying to do that. And if I tell them you're ready—sure, right now they see me as more an equal because of my ah, expertise and the dynamic, they sought me out—but they maybe, they see this—" He gestured with their joined hands and instead of letting go he lifted her knuckles to his face, brushed them with his lips as he finished speaking. "They see this and maybe they'll see it as my judgement is compromised."

"Is it?"

"Compromised? Well, I think so."

She was stuck, a bee caught in a viscous golden sap of her own making and unable to move closer or move away, caught and being drawn towards him. Warm all over, flushed from head to toe. But closer would be an admittance, a conscious choice and the foot of space between them was a holding place for the question that beat in the back of her mind in time with her pulse. *Is it a side-effect?*

"Maybe in a few days that'll be more sure." He whispered a response to what she had only thought.

Her breath caught and her eyes darted between his face and their touching hands. She pulled hers away then reached back, interlacing their fingers again and squeezing.

Did you hear me?! She thought it with as much force as she could and stared hard into his eyes but he just stared back, startled, mouth grasping for words.

"Drin, did you hear in my head?" The shortening of his name came out naturally as if they'd been childhood friends for a decade and not just met days prior. She wondered at it, questioned it, and then said it again without the heat of embarrassment she felt at first.

"Drin?"

"No I—I don't think so."

"You sure?" She frowned, shook her head once, not certain whether she wanted to shake away his denial or the possibility that it was true.

"I think it was just the question I was thinking, have been thinking—so I answered it?'

The footsteps came up on them suddenly not giving time for them to step farther apart or decide if they wanted to. She turned wide eyes on the doorway. She ignored their clasped hands and hoped whoever was in the doorway would do the same.

It was Quin, standing there in the dim, flickering light, her voice low and casual. "Your mother wants to discuss a thing with us, Chéri, kite ale, allons-y . . . Let's go."

THE SITTING ROOM WHERE QUIN, Chase, and Waters had migrated after dinner was lit brighter than the library. Lumina had to rub her eyes and blink away the excess illumination, all the while willing the heat of her body and the flush of her cheeks to fade. She could feel Drinian close to her, but he wasn't. He was farther than they'd stood in the dark, but it felt the same, connected.

The general stood when she came in and gave a quick salute and a smile. "Heading out to the city for a bit."

She smiled back, returned the nod to be polite, all while hyper-aware of a feeling of strangeness in her own body, a preoccupation with how much could be seen on her face. But the general left quickly, just a glance and another nod.

Quin saluted back and then he was gone, leaving only family in the room—and Drinian. She glanced over her shoulder at him. She was still holding his hand; they had come in that way. She cleared her throat and slipped her hand out of his, wrapped her arms around her chest to replace the lost warmth. "Hi."

Chase looked at them, a subtle frown crossing her face before she smoothed it away. "I don't want to say anything that'll embarrass you in mixed company."

Lumina bristled at what sounded like an implication. What embarrassing things were there to say about her? "Well, he was in my head a couple days ago, so I guess it's fine."

"Lum, I can go." He mumbled at her back.

"No—Ugh. It's fine." She gave him a pleading look, then turned back to her mother. The words caught at first and then they came easier. Better to say anything her mother could be planning to bring up before someone else said it for her. "I said some really awful things before the orchard, to you and to Quin—I'm sorry. And you were half right about the trees, so I'm half sorry for that part."

Quin was stifling a laugh and Chase's face contorted with questioning amusement. "Half right? Then half wrong too I guess?"

Lumina flipped her legs over the back of the couch and slid down onto it next to Chase. "Sure, half wrong half right. Right—It was dangerous. Wrong—If I'd gone with Quin she could have seen me through it like Drinian did." She wet her lips and looked up at him behind the couch, wondering how much they could see in that quick glance but unable not to. "Probably better because she understands Tree and Drin—Drinian doesn't really yet."

He held up his thumb and pointer fingers an inch apart. "Little bit."

"Okay, you're right, Lumina. I was scared. You know I was in the interface project. I was there when Quin—

blacked out and it wasn't for a day, Lumina. It was for months."

"I know."

"Do you though, Chér? Tu l'arif?"

"I know they took your mushroom off and you got stuck. I know if I had you to help, I could come back out. If it happened to me like it just did, you could help —or if I had my own mushroom, I could learn how myself."

"No." It was Quin and Chase speaking in near unison. She could feel the upwelling of fear from them both, her own answering anger.

"Lumina . . ." Drinian came around the couch to sit a few feet away from her.

"They brought it up. Sort of."

Chase scooted closer and took her hand. "I don't want you to feel like I'm just saying no to all of these things. But you heard Quin say no too. There are reasons they don't put implants on sixteen-year-olds."

Lumina's pulse ticked up as she fought the wave of disappointment and worked to control her voice. "Then I want to know the reasons. All of them."

Quin nodded and then raised her brows. She looked over Lumina's head at Drinian. "Well, you know them better than anyone else in the room, tell her all of them."

She turned and looked at him, all eyes on him, and she saw his face flush under their stares. He was mumbling under his breath a moment before he let the words cross his lips. "Well, well—The younger the recruit, the higher the rate of implant success but the rate of serious side effects and duration of separation sickness at removal is um—inversely proportional. So what that means—"

"I know what it means."

"Right." He was nodding, cutting off his own words while they continued to play in his own head.

Lumina explained for him. "Because I'm younger the separation sickness will be worse and take longer. Well, maybe I'll just keep mine like Quin has."

"That is not a choice." Quin was leaning forward from the edge of an adjoining couch, arms braced on her knees. "It is a fluke or an exception, this one will die off eventually and I don't know if I'll come through the sickness again when that happens. It isn't a simple choice to take an implant."

"It's a lifetime choice." Chase was rubbing the back of her neck again. "And I think, I think we don't know everything Drinian knows about having an implant young, do we, Drinian? If you'll keep sharing . . . ?" Her smile was gentle, almost pleading.

"Well ah . . ." He looked away and it was a long time before he continued. "First thing is . . . I lied about my age. Changed it. I'm ah, twenty in the records. Height helped." He gave a half smile but his eyes were serious, pain-filled "It's hard to be taken seriously. Hard not to hurry when you can run laps around other people's thinking, you know? So I changed my records and that made me eligible for an implant. Not for being a linguist, no, no, I wanted to be a mycologist and to do that I wanted the ah, the experience." He looked down at his over-large hands, tacked onto long slender arms.

"What happened?" Lumina's voice came out a whisper. Her heart was thumping in her ears, aching as if she was there in the past with him again. She saw him burying the shriveled mushroom, wracked with pain himself—memories he'd given her in the link.

"Ahhh . . . It made me a little crazy for awhile. Couldn't tell what was me and what was Mush and I just, well I had leaky borders, couldn't focus. Left the lab at every whim to find trees that weren't there." He laughed swiping at the corners of his eyes. "Like looking for the moon on another planet, blinded by the light of it and waking up hours later staring at an empty sky with leaves and dirt sticking to my face. I'd sneak in with the study trees, learned some Tree that way. But then, I couldn't ah, access human language for a while, just Tree, just Mush talking in my head."

She reached for his hand and found it clammy, trembling.

"I hid it, like a drug habit. And ah—well, I could still study, research, but all the while I thought–I thought I was lost in there, stuck in my head."

"How did you come out of it?" Quin's voice was low, compassion gleaming in her eyes in the low light.

"Well, I had a psych eval, someone worried. Failure to integrate. Chsssh!" He mimed a stamp against paper. "I had to grow out of it—er grow into it, the implant, and it was hard. Three years, then she declined, and it was worse for a while. So much worse. Poster boy for a new type of failure to integrate. Delayed integration, age based, that came out too. I was lucky to keep my position—mostly so they could study it. And now, well I know a lot about integration errors and ah . . . caution." He met Lumina's eyes with what looked liked apology, sympathy for the urgency roiling in her gut that he seemed to understand, maybe even felt.

"Does it, does it happen like that a lot?" She tried not to show the fear and conflict in her face, or in her voice.

"Integration errors? Sure, but not that one because we don't put implants on kids—I was fourteen. Even six months ah, a year, two makes a difference. With this new implant I figured probably wouldn't happen to me again. Three years, so this time is ah, better."

She stood up and then sat back down harder, took a breath and smoothed her brow with effort. "I don't know how to explain that I'm not just being reckless and not listening to all these warnings. Wanting something, not knowing what it means . . . "

"Try."

"I have a mycelial network in me. I've apparently been hearing these things my whole life but now it's more. It's like I can't not hear, can't not listen, but I'm listening through a wall and you won't let me through. I'm just stuck here with my head against the plaster feeling like I'm going crazy!"

Chase had gone silent now and was looking at her hands. But as Quin's voice broke the silence she began nodding.

"You might be certain this is for you, but we are not. And if it goes wrong for you in some way, it will be our blame to sleep with at night. There is time still. Maybe six months, a year, like Drinian said. Let us think. And let yourself think."

Chase looked up then. "But for now the answer is no, okay. For now."

"Okay." The word took all of her self-control to say. Self-control. It was something they thought she didn't have, something they needed to see from her to believe she was ready.

She climbed over the back of the couch in one fluid movement and reached for Drinian's hand before heading for the door.

"Drinian?" It was Quin's voice, and it stopped him taking Lumina's hand. "Perhaps you can stay longer to look over possible new strains of mushroom with me? We need to continue trying to extend the longevity of the strains, and you and I are what we have for that. Your preceptors are cut off from us."

He looked at Lumina then nodded. There was a wrenching feeling in her gut, a tearing away, but she smiled anyway, acknowledged the apology in his eyes. It seemed purposeful, their needing him now, but maybe that was more of the psychological clinging that was taking so much longer to go away than it should—separation sickness—the training-wheel version.

She turned and walked down the hall towards the warm, flickering light of the library, where their voices would carry but muted, and she could think.

CHAPTER 12

THE FOREST FOR THE TREES

Quin cried out in the still of the garden, pulled her bare hands from the bark of a potted tree. She covered her face with them instead, leaving indents in her cheeks and the skin of her forehead with the pressure of her fingertips. A stone tree to her right held her up as she slumped against it. The real one next to her was raining glossy ovoid leaves. It was a small tame thing. Before she would have given it as much of the mother tree's message as it could hold, like she did for the young ones cultivated on Earth, not much but enough to cheer it.

This one was an orange tree, a dwarf species of four years—its whole short life spent in a pot. Chase had procured it for this purpose, and now it was dying. Two days speaking to her and giving Synesis the tree interface she needed to survive, and already it was sick. How did it get so far as this? The illness should have healed itself, if it was a lingering symptom of the black-rot that had infested Synesis. If not that, then surely she could unravel it here on Genti-6. But there was no sign of healing. Each time she interfaced with the orange tree it drained her more and the tree suffered the same.

It wasn't black rot, mineral imbalance, parasites or anything else physical they could test for, because she'd tested for them. Nothing. With shaking hands, she collected the scattered arboreal test kits and medical equipment and packed it all back into the travel case. The materials were from the Genti-6 orchard, delivered with the trees she'd planted and now borrowed back.

She wet her lips and stared at the small tree in front of her. It was gnarled and long-limbed, some of its branches competing for space and rubbing each other's bark off. Regular pruning schedules had clearly been skipped but it was overall healthy, vigorous until she'd touched it. She scowled and crawled forward, scooting across the damp soil oblivious to the mess it made on her uniform. She pulled in a breath and then let it out slowly, hovering her hands and then wrapping them around the thin trunk again.

The voice of this tree was imprinted in her memory, bright and effusive, eager when she'd first introduced herself, now it was faint, timid, retreating from her contact as if it had been drained and she was the parasite, the vampire, only taking and walking away, never giving equal, or enough.

Never enough.

She pressed her face into the tree and felt it recoil

further. *No listen . . . There is brightness with the dark, Never Enough–give with the take, a cycle, a circle, interlinked, interlacing and the sprouting, seeding, sunlight—dormant—sap to seed circling—take, take, TAKE! Never Enough . . .*

The tree cried out in her mind, choking, she was choking it with the flow of her language. Synesis translated and fed it the chemical signals to convey everything she offered.

She jerked away, fell back on her hands and knees out of breath, a steady, pulsing ache inside her head. It was like at the other colony orchards after her time on Genti-6, painful, disorienting, draining. But she wasn't sick now! The black rot was gone. Synesis—and herself as well now that she thought of it, they were being nourished better than any other time because of Drinian.

This shouldn't be happening. The thought was nonsensical, something she thought she was past. Shouldn't, should . . . should was a linguistic bludgeon used by the masochistic to hold themselves in line using fear and shame instead of love and acceptance. She knew that. She thought she did and yet here it was staring her in the face.

A mountain of judgements, a mountain of should-haves falling on her in a proverbial avalanche and making her question the past sixteen years of her life. *Should have been more present for Lumina. Should have known how much presence a child would need and the gaps she'd grow up harboring without that.*

Should have . . . Chase. Should have what with Chase?

Found clarity, looked her in the eye and made certain she knew what she wanted from her instead of now, sixteen years later, finding that look in her eyes that said maybe one of them was lying to themselves. Should have asked and waited for the answer. But just as loud, just as urgent, another should reared up and twisted like a knife embedded inside her. It was in direct conflict to the should haves of her personal life, she should have solved the decline by now—she had the whole of the knowledge of Tree in her head, didn't she?

Didn't she?!

She sat up, still out of breath from the cadence of the thoughts she had allowed to assault her. She brushed fragments of moss and damp loam from her face. Maybe it isn't there anymore. She was supposed to have it all there, had spent years pouring that repeating loop of overwhelmingly complex information into the woody, inflexible minds of tame and infant trees and now, now she wasn't sure if it was all there. Maybe there were gaps, things she was forgetting, and she was filling them in with herself, imperfect, poisonous even, and she was killing them all.

She sat back on her heels, closed her eyes and looked within. The chaos was her own. Where was the mushroom? She reached out for Synesis's presence until it wrapped its buoyant embrace around her mind. It wasn't until that moment, that she realized there had been a long absence. Synesis had been almost quiet, holding back, reticent.

She sighed with relief at the mental embrace, then

started slowly, softly, conjuring up the All-Question and its answers. Wind in leaves, light flickers, autumn's breath, rising sun to full 4000 lumens, breath of air and night fall, again, again, a rising crescendo, the subtle changes only noticeable by steady accretion over time that could play backwards or forwards or both at once. But as the intensity of the refrain rose, Quin felt herself in dissonance with it, breaking away, shivering, that thought—She could hear it interwoven in the message —never enough, never giving equal, reaching but never touching—it was invasive, occurring and recurring at random and each time it pulled her out of touch with the rhythm of the message.

She opened her eyes, searched the garden of stone trees and ferns, frantic for something solid to ground and hold her, to stop the spinning away into dark that came when her eyes were closed. She needed to cry out again, to scream, but walls were only so thick and she wanted less to explain to anyone inside the villa what was happening to her, to admit to anyone but herself that she knew what had happened to the colony trees and it was her fault. It *was* a poisoning and she'd done it with her mind, her doubts, made them sick—because she was sick and she didn't know how to fix it.

She pulled her gloves out from under her knees, damp and chilled from the ground and forced them onto shaking hands. The orange tree would die in a few days, that was certain. There was no way to stop it from happening any more than she could stop the eventual death of the last trees on Earth. Genti-6 would lose their orchard once they forgot the message that she could no longer remind them of.

She couldn't even remember where along the way she had forgotten it. Had it been a gradual thing? Little pieces eroding away detail by detail, the trees receiving less and less of it as time went on, and her gaps gradually filled in with this poison? Or had it come on suddenly, after the Genti-6 orchard, brought on by her illness? Had she damaged the Pain Trees with it and prevented their healing?

A deep fatigue settled into her mind like a fog. The orange tree next to her became salt in an open wound and she turned her back to the shower of yellow leaves drifting down from its boughs. The garden was no place for her.

THE ROOM WAS SO garish and bright that Quin wanted to close her eyes and block it out. The geometric shapes lacked the harmony of controlled chaos that could be seen in all areas of the natural world, trees, oceanscapes, even deserts in their austere beauty. Perhaps that was why humanity so thoroughly snuffed out, covered over, and adulterated all of those harmonious spaces in the world, because they couldn't perceive of beauty and color and order if it wasn't standing out in sharp relief making a grand assault on their senses. They needed the world to be as this room was, a dancing clown shoving itself into her line of sight no matter how much she tried to block it out.

They were bitter thoughts, but couldn't shut it off. The colors were too much, too numerous and varied for a single room, and it felt like she'd be able to think more clearly, to take the calming breaths she needed if she were somewhere else. But she wasn't forced to be here. She had come herself.

The governor was lounging on a backless settee upholstered in interlocking pyramids and squares that shifted in color at the points where they touched. Her sleeveless suit was equally vibrant—to Quin's eyes overdone like everything else in this space. She realized it was a blessing that the woman couldn't see her furrowed brows as she took in the room; the governor's eyes were covered with a delicate visor that made the VR meeting she was attending possible.

Quin placed a hand on her own forehead, a headache coming on. She hunched a little to make a physical shield of her own body so long as she had to sit here and wait for this politician to listen to things she didn't want to say. It would be like stripping down in front of the woman and extracting needles embedded in her abdomen, but it was what she expected of others and so expected of herself tenfold.

The woman was laughing, overly loud, then a click as she switched off the visor and removed it. She fixed Quin with a stare that was still laced with amusement even as her eyes narrowed down into the same shrewd regard that she remembered from the night they met.

"Now that's done. Drink?" The attendant was already coming closer with a cart, its wheel tracks smooth and soundless on the carpeted floors.

Quin shook her head and then waited while the governor accepted a glass of sparkling water from the bot.

"Too early for anything else." She shrugged and sipped at it, making exaggerated sounds of relief as she tasted it. "But you look like you could use something stronger—you wanted to discuss the problem with your uploads—is that what you call them?—to the other colony-planets' orchards. I'm all ears."

Quin blinked and sat up straighter, her accent coming through more than she meant it to, somewhere between French and Haitian creole with enough notes and flavors to confuse a close listener as to her origins. "I 'ave determined the nature of the problem, and it is myself."

The governor tilted her head and leaned forward on the settee. "Are you saying that the rumors from the other colonies are true? You caused it? Accidental . . . purposeful? Sabotage?"

"No, I am saying that it came from me, from a sickness."

The governor was listening, her fingers drumming the colorful shapes on the upholstery as she looked down and nodded.

Quin watched her body language, listened for the things she wasn't saying aloud. There were always thoughts that you could see arising while people posed to listen. People did not fully listen. Trees did, but not people. This woman was judging the content of Quin's admission as she gave it, turning it in her mind to the one purpose that she had already admitted would form the framework for her every decision—was Quin a threat to Genti-6, physically, politically …

"What I'm telling you is that I have a sickness. Not of the body, al akl—the mind."

She let the silence draw out in the room around them and she waited. The governor had questions. Better to let her ask than to fill the air with more answers that perhaps she wouldn't understand or even listen to.

"Sickness of the mind? The way you say that worries me—I'm going to need more." She sat up and handed her glass to the serving bot and collected the refill, but turned the glass in her hands instead of drinking. "We have psychologists, we have neurologists. Which is it?"

"I—" She found herself reaching for words but they were coming in tree, not words but feelings, concepts, causal relationships. Synesis was subdued, almost still on her neck and in her mind, not sleeping but listening. She closed her eyes and then took a breath before trying again. "It is of the mind, not the grey matter—except in that they are one and the same—but not of physical cause or my mushroom would make it known, a tumor, or a stroke, those things she would know and tell me. This . . . this is a defect in myself." She stood and moved to go, dipping her head in farewell and then heading for the door. "I thought it important you know. The gloves will stay on."

"Wait—Sgt. Fleury. Hang on, I gave Paul my word I'd help if I could, and you're walking out before telling me what you need. We aren't without medical resources on Genti-6 you know."

Quin paused by the door and turned to face her. "Do they, any of them, speak Tree? Because I can't seem to unravel my thoughts from the message—what is true and what I've corrupted. That is what I need help with."

The governor opened her mouth and then shook her head. "No, no, we don't have anyone like that."

"Then I will have to unravel it myself. And I don't know if I can."

LUMINA KICKED AT THE BLACK, porous, pea-gravel that made up the paths and borders of the garden, concentric circles a foot wide creating a bullseye pattern with rays cutting across them to form the little paths into the center of the space.

The little orange tree rooted in a large clay pot, stood in the shadow of one of the stone trees and Quin was crouched next to it, her head in her hands. The mushroom was easier to see that way, appearing to sit on the back of Quin's skull. The fruiting bodies erupting from her back were larger again, beginning to frame Quin's head, still a much smaller collar than the ones that had fallen off.

"You could just let me try."

Quin's head snapped up and Lumina knew before she spoke that she had said the wrong thing.

"Or Chéri, you could stop being reckless with yourself! This little one next to me is dying because I have poisoned her. Would you like to take that poison into yourself and maybe die with her before you have even learned to speak?!"

"Would it kill me, same as her?"

Quin's eyes flashed. "I don't know, Lumi! But I am not going to watch you try and then see you in a coma withering away like a poisoned orchard. You are too important!"

Lumina put her hands up in surrender. "Okay, I'm sorry—I didn't mean to make you angry."

Quin sat back against the stone tree and deflated, the energy of her sudden storm leaving her.

"Lumina, you didn't make me angry. The apology is mine. I have tried more times than I can count to fix what I have done to her, to the rest of them. I could fix her if I could remember what I've apparently forgotten."

Lumina shrugged. "So read it again."

"What?" Quin's face was a study of perplexed angles.

"Like a book. You read it again when you forget. So just read it again."

"It is not in a book Chér, it is in the trees—the ancient ones that told me in the first place—when you were born. We cannot go back there or I could spread the decline to them, or whatever this sickness is that acts one and the same."

Lumina's curiosity rose up despite the fatigue evident in Quin's voice. It was her birth story, the same Chase told but instead from the perspective of the one who was actually there. But Quin had fallen silent again. She would have to press.

"When I was born? But how could it be the same time?"

"Because, as you have experienced a fraction of now, a download of information from a tree can be overwhelming. The conversation was long and I was losing myself in it—I could not breathe or focus on your safety." Quin paused, collecting the breath that had caught in her throat with the next words. Her eyes shined as if the tears pooling in them might fall, but she blinked them away instead.

"I felt you kicking, panicking—you couldn't breathe because I wasn't—so I started the birth process on the AUC that I carried you in. You were born while I was still in communion with the ancient sequoia—She slowed down for us, or we'd have choked on it. You would have died. I wrapped you up and Waters held you while I finished learning what I teach the trees, the All-Question and its answer. Afterwards, I brought you to Chase."

Quin wrapped a hand around the orange tree's trunk and then recoiled, her face contorting. "Merde! Every time she is worse." She pulled back her hand and covered half of her face. "If there was a book for this, I would have read it a thousand times over and sent it to everyone who could read. But the apprentices I've had—none could follow the whole thing and so they couldn't pass it on to the trees. I had to do it myself and I'm just—tired. Waters was right.

"It wasn't working when I thought it was. All those years it wasn't working, and I lied to myself every day that it was or it would, that I could make it work. How arrogant. Now it isn't working at all, and I can't remember everything she told me—"

Quin shoved her hands back into a pair of black gloves and pressed fists to her mouth. "No, that is part wrong. I remember it—I cannot forget—but the feeling of it, *that* is gone and when I try harder to look for it— it's like digging for the dead and finding the ground is made of cardboard just before I fall through it."

Her words flowed out like black ink now, seeping into the ground and the air around them and into Lumina herself. It was a heavy aching miasma. Lumina felt it in her stomach, weighing her like stones, and in her head, shifting her thoughts so that each option or idea became pointless and impossible.

She was brought along with that flow of pain and she pulled back from it. That wasn't the right way to look at this situation, was it? Or any situation? She couldn't say exactly. Quin was Quin. But it felt wrong and it scared her, not the surface sort of fear that felt like butterflies and electricity but the sort that swallowed you up and convinced you that fear was all there was and outside of it was just more of the same. "Quin—I think you should stop."

Quin's eyes opened and she looked around her as if there was more here than ferns, stone statues, and their shadows stretched long over the ground. She closed them again, opened them, wet her lips. "Mwen regret. I am sorry, Chér."

Quin looked as though she might fall asleep where she sat, with her brow furrowed and her eyes distant, pain-filled; they kept turning to the struggling orange tree raining yellow for no determinable reason except that Quin had spoken to it.

"Leave me, Chér. I can't control my tongue just now."

Lumina turned on her heel to find Chase, or Drinian, someone else to help.

CHASE'S FOOTSTEPS roused Quin from her sleep in a pool of yellow leaves. Gravel clung to her cheek when she sat up. She searched the darkness like a prey-animal then reached for her mushroom, hands grasping at the small body and feeling for it until she was satisfied. She lowered her hands and slumped back against a black marble tree statue.

"Chase, you have found me."

Chase sat next to her and leaned against the same statue. She brushed gravel and leaves from Quin's face, frowning at the impressions in her skin. Quin flinched at her touch, just enough for Chase to see it. It hurt. It brought up an ache in her gut, and a stinging pain along her spine. Loss always brought up chords of the other losses encoded in her nerves. "Looks like I did."

"It's dark."

"And you're passed out in the garden. It scares me when you do that. Makes me remember."

"Desolet, Chéri. I will sleep in the house."

Her tone was uncharacteristic, laced with bitterness. It made Chase want to get up, to go back inside, back to work in the caves, anywhere but with her. But that wouldn't accomplish what she came for.

"Quin?"

"Oui?"

"What is it? What's going on inside you?"

Quin held out her gloved hands. "This is killing me —that I am suddenly venomous, a danger." She shrugged. "I tried to undo it. Instead, well look at her."

The orange tree's once glossy green leaves had turned yellow and brown and were falling as if autumn had come for her. Chase ran a hand down the smooth, unblemished bark of the sapling, a twinge of regret for the tree. The silence that greeted her touch silenced her. Arboreal voices were outside of her reach and had been since she'd lost her mushroom. She wouldn't hear anything from a well tree, but this one was clearly sick.

"You see, I poison them."

"Do you really think that's it? Because there has to be a reason. Something happening when you speak to them. This All-Question, it can make a linguist sick, so maybe it's—"

"No, no, that is because of weakness in the language, or in the mind maybe, not a flaw in the message—this flaw is in me."

She flinched from the words pouring out of Quin with a vehemence like small, sharp blades. They were meant only for Quin herself, but they cut Chase equally. "How can you think that? You're Quin, the Tree-Whisperer. You're hope personified—the only hope." She scrubbed at the tears that seeped from her eyes. It was hard to breathe under the weight of Quin's declarations, like the heavy blanket of an oncoming storm had dropped over them and was sucking all the air out of the garden.

But Quin didn't stop, she kept going. "Oh, weh, that's right, the Tree-Whisperer who whispers death, a sickening miasma from the hands that planted seeds and watered them, and from the mouth that spoke growing words—"

"Stop it! You don't do this. This isn't you. So *what happened,* Quin?"

"Ah well, you see it too then. I am . . . not myself. That is all I know."

The urge to take Quin's face in her hands, to move closer, was so strong it hurt, but the chance that Quin would pull away stayed the impulse. "Then talk to me. Let me help and—we can link, find what's wrong . . ."

Quin stood and brushed debris from her clothes, damp from leaning against the small, bushy ferns around them. "So that you can be sick with me? No, Chase. I will sleep in the house so that you don't worry. But you can't fix this any more than I can."

She was leaving, striding away, fleeing from Chase's offer. Alarm bells raced along Chase's nerves and settled in the pit of her stomach.

Chase went out through the back gate, down to the path towards the station. She needed to be somewhere she could breathe—the water of the caves. But the caves were far to go alone so she stopped at the empty station on the way. Manalou came quickly, warm and present on the bench next to her before she could even get cold. Yellow track lighting from the station gave their hair more a green cast than blue. Only the closest shapes were illuminated, leaving deep shadows beyond and, hemming them in. It felt private and secluded, even with the wind blowing gusts of chill night air into their faces, the smell of pungent desert flora inundating their senses, and the small sounds of night creatures stirring around them.

She leaned against Manalou, whose familiar body, both solid and soft under a hand-woven tunic, brought more tears. She glanced up and caught their worried smile, grey eyes that said she could take her time. So, she let the tears come until the words didn't want to wait anymore.

"She won't talk to me!"

"Okay, listening. Your Tree-Whisperer, yes?"

"Yes, and for all the letters she writes, all those— words—she pulls away. I know, acutely, how she feels but it's like I'm looking through glass. Like she can't hear me—won't take anything from me!"

"So family problems . . . relationship problems? And we have orchard problems, all the buzz at headquarters —a rush to plan for decline symptoms—fight it ourselves. I know the news . . . "

Chase nodded to all of this. They were planning for the decline, for Quin to fail. And she'd heard none of it. She'd been keeping her feet in water instead of land, avoiding the orchard and staying on whale duties while Manalou was shifted to orchard maintenance. The orchard was too close to home, the idea of working with trees again.

Manalou bumped her shoulder with their own. "So, what's actually happening with her?"

"She's unwell, so sick over—something, and just— beating her head against a dead tree instead of letting me help!" Manalou rubbed her shoulders in a gentle massage, nodding, mumbling okays and Mmhms as they listened. "I could interface with her, with my implant port and a mycelial graft, or take a full implant and we could fix this together maybe. I offered and she just–I don't know, changed the subject."

"You'd do that again, another implant?" Manalou's hands paused on Chase's shoulders so she could turn and see their expression—cautious, concerned, with no small measure of surprise.

"I—yes." The hesitation wasn't doubt but realization. Years on Genti-6, so many years. Another implant would hurt— oh, there would be pleasure, connection, that feeling of fullness—*not alone,* but there was always an end and then loss, separation sickness. And she would do it again anyway. It wasn't a question anymore. It was a certainty.

Manalou's brow was creased with pain for her, for the pain that was ahead. "Then I think, my friend, you have to do more than you've been doing about this. Make her see it too."

"It's been like this for so long. I don't know if we can change it—or if she wants that." She tried to still the shivering that came after a storm of tears. She'd have to go back, wake Quin and talk to her until they fell together instead of apart. She could picture it so vividly it made her shivering skin flush with the warmth. But there were other ways it could go that were just as real—Quin could push her further away, storming out or lashing out as she had earlier that night. So very unlike her.

She'd have to go back and push the situation in one direction or the other, but not yet.

Instead, she jumped up with false cheer. "I'm checking the whale calves, you coming with?"

Manalou raised a brow and gave a look but followed her off the bench towards the automated train. "Ahh . . . right, tonight? You know I am."

She thanked Manalou with her eyes as she stepped up to the train.

CHAPTER 13

MYCELIAL MESSAGES

Drinian's eyes narrowed, one hand out as if trying to grasp thin air and turn it into a shape that made more sense than what Lumina had just said. "You want to go there now? Try and do what Sgt. Fleury can't and you want me to go with you—not tell them?"

She winced at how her idea sounded when reframed that way and glanced out the window at the star-filled sky. The lights of the villa were all out and only the dim track lights leading to the rail station path could be seen weaving through the nighttime landscape.

The urge to move, to follow through with the impulse was so strong it filled her up. The path was right there, the whole house sleeping except for her and Drinian. Well, he had been sleeping, bent over one of her books in front of the library fireplace. Now he was wide awake, the bleariness he'd woken with erased by her words.

I want you to go to the orchard with me. . . . It wasn't going how she'd hoped, how she expected, yes.

He was still clear in her head, the pathways his mind would take, the feel of his thinking and his moods. She could predict his reactions with the clarity of imagining biting an object and knowing exactly how it would feel and taste because you'd done it as a child, before you'd learned better. She had a library of Drinian like that—a Drinian library. If she decided to go alone, he'd tell Quin or Chase but first he'd talk her out of it. She had to make him believe it was a good idea logically, or at least that it would be safe enough.

"Drin, I've been studying from the ferns and the mosses, talking to them—well listening— for hours, literal hours a day and studying arboriculture, dendrology, mycology. I can do better than before. But —what's the last step?"

He looked reluctant to answer. He rubbed his face, looked away and then turned back. "To learn from the trees, speak with them."

She plunged forward now that he had offered up what she needed. "Right! But Quin isn't herself. You should have seen her in the garden and I don't think she'll ever let me try it if she stays like this."

"Okay, granted, Sgt. Fleury is ah—different. But you don't have an implant."

"And I won't ever if the trees die off and the project is closed, but I just think, I have *something* right? The mycelial network which could be considered more of the organism than the rest—"

"Mmm . . . true with regular fungus not so with a fungal symbiont—It, has a central nervous system like a mammalian species, a brain for more processing power, higher order thinking. That's how it translates for us. And you don't have that."

"I can hear them." She blinked at him. Did it look like annoyed blinking like she meant it to? It took all of her willpower not to shout.

He reached for her hand. She no longer questioned the simple gesture; it was a physical comfort, a lifeline like the reaching of tree roots to intertwine, the joining of mycelium under loamy soil. The warmth of his touch had an immediate effect, slowing her heart-rate and smoothing over the resistance that was making a scowl on her face.

His voice was low, gentle like the touch. "But—you can't translate."

She frowned again, shifting her hand in his. "I think I can. And I think I need to because—"

She had to stop and take a breath. Now that she'd touched on the root of what drove her to pacing the halls at night, her chest tightened with unmet need, a need that would send her to the threshold of the villa with every intention of running the distance to the orchard if that was what it took. "I feel like I'm trying to breathe and I can't catch my breath, like I'm hungry but not for food. It's like I need to do this. Can't get it out of my head. Even when I remind myself that it's reckless, and dangerous, and it's going to look like I have no self-control—"

She scooted closer, leaning without realizing she was as the words tumbled out. His breath brushed her skin. His eyes widened. But he didn't move away.

"You could come with me, and I could do this and if it's hard you can help. Quin can't go to the orchard. She isn't allowed and she can't talk to the trees—but you could. And Chase isn't even here. I checked."

He wet his lips, a crease between his brows tugging his features into a frown. She realized how close he was, close enough to lean their foreheads together or their lips. She could taste his breath, intermingled in the space between them. The silence was so loud, thrumming with heartbeats.

She sat back on her heels and blinked back tears.

He cleared his throat and sat back himself, squeezed her hand and then let go. "I'm going to get Sgt. Fleury."

"What?"

"This isn't just an idea, a want—I thought at first— you were being impatient, even reckless. But that's not it. I think it's something else and I think we need her. Please, trust me."

His footsteps receded down the corridor, slapping the tiles lightly with the urgency of his pace.

She rolled over on the rug before the fire and stared up at the ceiling. The beams were patterned after woodgrain but printed here on Genti-6, a planet with no trees, like they all could be one day. They could be forests too, all of them. She could see it that way if she stared hard enough. It could all be forests.

LUMINA LOOKED to be sleeping at first, spread into the shape of a starfish on her back with electric firelight flickering across her body, deepening the shadows on one side, while illuminating the other. Her upturned face was the brightest; appropriate that she would burn so brightly in a dark room. Lumina—lumen—luminare, she was made of light after all.

Quin stepped closer, careful steps, and then she crouched down next to her, a gloved hand on her shoulder. Lumina's eyes darted back and forth under her eyelids, flinching, shuddering, a dream Quin imagined she could see. The same one Lumina described recurring since she'd woken from the tree-induced coma. A place full of shadow and fire, the crackling, shriveling of what was once green with miles of charcoal left and nothing coming after, no seedling pushing through ash to reclaim the cleansed space.

The vivid reality of the dream, come alive in Quin's own mind, made the firelight jarring, threat-filled. It was a part of the All-Question, a single note, but isolated like this it was a terror instead of a comfort. Quin closed her eyes tight, rubbed them, and when she opened them Lumina sat up.

Her eyes were wide, distant and full of flickering shadows before they cleared. She looked at Quin next to her, Drinian by the door. "Okay. So, what next?"

She sat down next to Lumina while Drinian hung

back leaning against the door frame. "Now you tell me more of what you're feeling. And then we see. D'accord?"

Lumina shrugged, but her eyes were showing anything but the resigned fatalism of that gesture. They looked like green and gold flame in the firelight and there was a fever to them that sent jarring waves of alarm through Quin's insides.

"Sure. I feel thirsty and sometimes dizzy. It's like I need something, and every time you turned your back in the garden I thought I should go to the orange tree and see if I could hear her. I knew she was sick, so I didn't—But I wanted to so bad. And there's the orchard —I think I hear them in my head, the wind shaking them, whoosh—whush . . . Please can we just go and try?"

Lumina's face contorted with the craving she described and she curled in on herself. Quin's eyes stung with tears. She had to look away. She wanted to take her gloves off, to cradle Lumina's face like a birch, a smooth grey aspen, a soft-needled pine—and listen, then speak what would solve this. But Lumina, her little sapling, was not a tree and if she were, her touch would make her sicker.

Quin caught Drinian's eye and nodded to his quizzical raise of brows.

But her answer she addressed to Lumina. "Yes, Chéri—we will go there now. I do not know if they will let us in, but what you are feeling . . . It means you will get sicker if we don't go."

THE SMALL OUTPOST, constructed in the style of a rustic woodland museum with printed logs showing through printed plaster, was well lit and surrounded by guards, the Shepard of the orchard was still present but he was sitting to the side with an air of resigned redundancy. At least twelve guards circled the few acres and Lumina could see them coming and going, jogging off through the dark in both directions from the central location where an individual drone vehicle had been landed to the right of the museum. Fences? When had they put up fences?

"We could hop it between their rounds, couldn't we?"

Drinian smiled at Lumina's whispered suggestion. Quin raised a brow. The look on her face wasn't encouraging. "No. We've been given asylum here, Drinian and I. We are not citizens. I'd rather not be extradited back to Earth just now."

"Okay. " It came out a reluctant whisper. She was watching the security force collect, break up and circle again. Climbing the fence would be fast while the guards were distracted. Quin was already moving, walking up to the central group of security guards towards the one that was wearing the triple moon rank of authority for Genti-6.

She called over her shoulder. "Attendez—Wait here, both of you."

Lumina opened her mouth to object then glanced back at the trees just a bit further down the path, fenced, guarded, but so close. Quin's look wasn't angry, or even sharp, but it was the sort not to argue with, it said argument would be a waste of time that they had so little of.

Lumina pressed her lips together and crouched on the path. Now that the trees were right there she could really hear them, not just the echo of that first conversation in her head. There was a gusting wind blowing in fits and starts through the shielded valley and the leaves were singing in the dark, calling for her to run through them with both hands out. But there were fences now, fences that weren't there when she came before. Had they been built because of Quin or was that always the plan—fences to protect a precious, now irreplaceable commodity.

How long had she been lost listening to the susurration of leaves speaking their arboreal secrets into the night air? Quin's voice weaved through the other sounds, her hushed tones directed to the head guard. She gestured towards his com-headset, nodded and stepped back, continuing to another guard and then stepping away. Her footsteps crunched on the crushed limestone gravel of the path back to Lumina and Drinian her voice coming ahead of her. "They won't allow anything based on their orders. They insist on clearing it with the governor. So we don't have much chance now—"

A sudden wave of tension gripped her, that tingling

ache built to a head. The trees were just there, almost in hands reach—and oh how her fingers burned as if she'd crawled hands and knees through Genti-6's nettle-like ground creepers. Making a run for those waving trees was more than just a temptation now. It was a distinct course of action with a ticking time clock and she wasn't sure how long she could fight it off. She needed to grab hold of something, but it wouldn't help if it didn't grab back. Drinian was watching her, concern widening his eyes as she met his.

Hold my hand. The thought took all the control she had and to say it aloud would have taken too much. Her look was enough. Drinian reached for her hand and laced their fingers. Relief. It soothed the ache, redirected the need. And it was enough, for the moment, to slow her if she broke into a run without meaning to.

Drinian cleared his throat. "What do we do then because—ah, she needs help."

"Right now, we wait for this answer. They are waking her, and I doubt that is going to put her in the mood to say yes to anything. If it is no, then we go back, we find another potted tree if there are any, they are better than nothing."

"Sgt. Fleury, I know that's what it is." He flicked a nervous glance at Lumina. "She has the mycelial network, and the use of it would encourage growth, development. She needs regular contact with the trees then, like someone with an implant."

Quin smiled and shook her head, but it wasn't a real

smile, it was pained, struggling. "I know what is happening. But I'll say again we don't know anything for sure because she—her situation is an anomaly. We are guessing in the dark based on our experience. If we removed our implants the mycelium left behind would die as it did before, but not so for Lumina. She was inoculated vicariously when I was, but with no implant stage. It should have died off in days and yet—here she is with it still, sixteen years later. So we can think but we can't know."

"If she does need regular contact, then she has the same problem that we have—"

Lumina couldn't focus on their words anymore, not with the trees so loud. Time seemed to be passing more slowly while they waited and the conversation about her with her standing right there made her more restless, more irritated. She could fix this herself if they hadn't locked up the trees like gold in a vault, a hoard to be guarded. It might not have been a fair comparison; the trees were precious and they were fragile, under threat because of whatever Quin was carrying inside of her.

She looked up at Quin. The face that usually projected a quiet strength and confidence was drawn. Sharp, angular lines pulled her brows and her lips into a tight frown. Even when she smiled there was a heaviness to it. Her hands, covered in long green-trimmed black gloves, a thick supple leather that molded to her skin, were shoved deep into the pockets of her uniform.

But she isn't a threat.

That idea was laughable, that she would do anything to harm what she'd spent her whole life trying to protect, to heal, to resurrect. The same urge pulsed inside of Lumina now, to connect and thereby protect what was a part of her.

She pulled her hand away from Drinian in one swift motion, strode to the cluster of guards before Quin or Drinian could stop her.

The head guard glanced through his visor, noting her presence. Even with the VR comm on-going she could see the governor through the visor.

"I want to talk to her."

The guard shifted his feet, cleared his throat. His face was red, and he had the look of a man who'd just received a strongly worded reprimand. He was still nodding, still murmuring affirmatives in response to whatever instructions he was being given through the comm.

She clenched and unclenched her hands. This person was standing in the way and every movement he made was slow, so damn slow. If she grabbed the headset, would he fight her for it?—But that felt off, not as if it wasn't her own but maybe Lumina plus, Lumina under the influence of this something else, this growing need.

Her hands shook with the realization and she stepped back, bumping into Drinian and Quin just behind her. They had followed her over and stood silent, waiting. Their proximity was a buoy of warmth, not heat-warm but comforting-warm like having back-up, a wall against whatever they were up against.

The guard put a hand up for her to wait, nervous eyes behind the visor shifting between the three of them and back to the governor on the comm. He cleared his throat again and slid the visor off. She ah—wants to speak to you—to you all." He leaned his face closer to the visor he'd removed for his voice command to be heard. "Project."

The governor's face appeared above the visor, distorted by the guard's nervous shifting from foot to foot behind the image.

"Well darlings, I'm awake now." The voice was slurred with sleep or too many night caps but she was indeed awake and looked as if she resented it. "Pietro has informed me that you have some sort of emergency and need access to the trees—and wouldn't you know I anticipated this, and my guards and fences are the result. Quin—didn't you just yesterday assure me that you were a danger to the trees, you personally, and would not be approaching them? Especially not in the middle of the night while I'm sleeping?"

Lumina turned to Quin, sudden anxiety at the governor's words twisting in her gut. Quin held up both gloved hands and raised her brows. "I am completely silenced madame—muzzled. I would not forgive an accident, and I wouldn't expect you to either."

The governor twisted her lips, seeming to consider the words and then she shook her head, She scrunched her face in groggy frustration. "Alright, what is this then? Emergency of what kind?"

Lumina stepped forward before the others could begin explaining what she needed again as if she were some sort of inpatient or science experiment.

"I have a mycelial network the same as Quin and Drinian have, their fungal implants—almost the same and that means I have to talk to the trees or the implant gets sick—er, in my case the mycelium. We think contact with the trees sort-of woke it up—so I need them to let me into the orchard—now. Please." She clenched and unclenched her fingers, gripped the sides of her pants and then rubbed at the back of her neck. Her whole body was aching, tingling now, but the feeling was deeper than what she could reach with her hands, it was in her nerves—hot like forest fire. It was in her bones.

The governor seemed to consider for several seconds. "And why do you need in, Fleury?"

"She needs a guide. She hasn't done this successfully yet. It could take awhile. She could get stuck. And this one . . ." She inclined her head towards Drinian. "He has an implant—no contact with me or the dying trees."

Lumina's toes clenched and unclenched in her shoes. Several more seconds passed and then the Governor leaned in close. "I'm letting you in. But Fleury—if anything happens to that orchard I'll hand you directly to your commander on Earth."

"You wouldn't have to. I would go myself."

LUMINA RAISED her hand in front of the closest tree, a young pine mixed in with the aspens. The slender fingers shook, an obvious tremor from where Quin sat. If the child moved too fast, started out wrong, or took too much in . . . The worries coursed through Quin's thoughts as a wave of doubt even Synesis couldn't temper. She put out a gloved hand, stopped Lumina's bare one. "It needs to be like what you've been practicing, to listen without letting the avoirdupois—the size, the scale of the message drown you. What you took in before was a fraction of the whole, don't expect to understand it—just let it be, breathe and then detach before it is too much."

"Okay." Lumina raised her hand again. It was clear in her eyes that she was in pain, struggling against the push to connect with the tree in front of her after too long a wait.

Quin knew the feeling in all of its nuance, the subtle, gentle encouragement to brush a hand across the trees in her path day to day, the tugging if she resisted and tried to walk on and go about her business, and eventually the aching, burning need when she was separated from even the smallest specimen of plant-life and could not make that crucial connection for an extended time.

How long could she go? Any longer than a week was too much and she knew Synesis would be at risk of dying off. First, she would drop any fruiting bodies she carried at the time and then she would go quiet, dormant. After that the shriveling would begin to progress until she eventually detached from the implant stage and there would be no going back.

She flinched away from the mental image and reached a gloved hand up to caress the small companion that was still there, quieter than normal but not dormant, not starving for contact even if it was less. The dying orange tree had been enough, but she wouldn't be any longer. Now, Lumina would be bound by the same need. Dependent on a type of connection that was a scarce commodity in a world of dying trees.

The girl was hesitating, her hand shaking over the rougher bark and bristles of the silvery lodge-pole pine. But she wasn't a little girl, not a seedling as Quin still saw her. She was sixteen years old, more of a sapling, growing rapidly towards maturity like these trees that were also her children. "Start with a breath, Lumina Chér, and if the flow is too fast then ask her to speak more slowly."

Lumina pressed her hand into the bark. She would quench her thirst with great gulps instead of sips; now that she had made contact, she leaned in closer, wrapped her arms around the trunk so that her forearms ran up the length of it and her cheek and forehead were in contact with the skin of the tree as well.

She held her breath for an eternity, then released a shuddering sigh. Quin sighed with her, an echo of need for the same that Lumina was immersed in. The urge to make contact with the trees tugged at her and then faded into a dull ache as she admonished herself and Synesis by extension. *Not these trees unless you want them dead.*

For several long moments all was well and Quin settled into this new status quo—Lumina a Tree-Whisperer, the long-term sacrifices of it not as imminent if she could do this part without being lost. Drinian hovered on Lumina's left, those wide brown eyes drinking in the whole scene and tracking what was happening, what could happen, what it meant for Lumina. Quin was grateful for his vigilance.

He sighed when Lumina sighed, flinched and adjusted when she did. They were entrained still, that much was obvious, and the bond was lasting longer than Quin expected. It was what she knew would happen, the heightened sense of connection, mirroring of thought and emotion that was almost like mind-reading. It had happened with Chase, an experiment when they were young and had their first implants, a simple connection between threads of mycelium to see what would happen that night under the trees. A light rain fell around them and the world seemed to be made of prisms. But it didn't last for so long as this Lumina-Drinian affair, the affection yes, but that was there before their little experiment. And they'd disconnected quickly, after mere moments of fleeting euphoria. How much more painful would Lumina's disappointment be when Drinian left Genti-6?

The sharp tang of fear pulled her back to the present. The sound of Lumina's breath had changed, rapid and shallow and her inbreath sounded tight, constricted with panic. Her forehead was a knot of tension and her arms gripped the tree hard enough for the bark to indent her flesh.

"Lumi, ask her to slow down. To be gentle . . ." Quin leaned closer to whisper it again but there was no change. She looked past Lumina to Drinian and nodded to the urgent question in his eyes.

"So I just . . . ?"

"You connect with the tree and you ask her to slow, to be gentle, and then you begin saying your goodbyes, sharing gratitude. It should make it easier for Lumina to disconnect without pain."

"Ah—okay, here goes!" Drinian placed both hands on the sides of the trunk above where Lumina touched and he closed his eyes. His face clenched, and he sucked in a breath, forcing it out slowly, slower—until Lumina's arms relaxed a little. Her face smoothed as his did.

Quin reached for her shoulders but she did not pull her away, instead she whispered close to her cheek. "You can let go. It is enough, d'accord?"

Drinian opened his eyes and released his hold on the tree. Lumina unwound her arms and let herself fall back against Quin. She opened her eyes, the shadowy green of yew trees in the dark, a shade greener even than Chase's olive ones.

"See Quin, I said I'd be fine." She closed her eyes, a smile curving her lips.

Quin smiled back but the sapling she held didn't see it. The trip back would be easier now, and Lumina would sleep through it with the cyclical, incomprehensible dreams of untranslated Tree-speak in her head. Tomorrow she would have to begin learning what it meant.

CHAPTER 14
GROWTH

The lights in Drinian's guest room were set to full brightness, the pristine curves of white arches, doorways, and windows fully illuminated. On the antique wooden desk, his cluttered disarray was equally visible. The heirloom came from Earth, and he couldn't make sense of it having been brought here, with its hardwood construction and ironic carvings of trees and fern-fronds like the ones clear-cut to make it. Vials, petri dishes, and preserved fungi samples covered the surface and to Drinian's right, a portable, self-loading centrifuge-bot used its four arms to collect the next samples for analysis, extracting and analyzing DNA. The soft, clicking of mechanical hands, the whir of gears, and the clinking of vials played counterpoint to his thoughts.

He waved a hand over the spreadsheet of data on the

screen. "Antifungals would have done ah—nothing, made her sick, maybe."

Quin stared at the screen unblinking, she had the look of a statue, frozen from staring too long and the signs of fatigue around her eyes were more deeply entrenched than the night before as if she hadn't slept at all. She continued for him. "Because it is a part of her genetics?"

"Ah, yes. I don't think we can separate Lumina from this fungus, or it from her—not really. They're—"

"Svicha—Entangled." She said it in Hebrew for both of their benefit.

His eyes widened. She had completed and reinforced the thought in his head. "Yes, completely. Fungal DNA inserted into Lumina's code. Lumina's—human DNA added into the fungal strain she carries."

"So, it is not the same as Synesis."

"No, not anymore."

Quin backed up and sat down on the edge of his rumpled bed, shock playing on her fatigued features. "And the danger to her? What it means for her?"

His pulse was thrumming fast and hard, panic kept away by the inky-blue and sepia speckled mushroom curled at the back of his neck. He needed to be just hyped up enough to keep working, driven to find the best new strain combinations, but not panicking, not horrified by the unknown he was chasing—fear for her. He pushed a hand into unkempt curls—tangles that would form mattes if he ignored them further—and rubbed at the sweat on his brow.

"That's what we don't know. Will it keep changing her? Entangling deeper? As in code-swapping, merging, borrowing? What will it be able to do? What will she be able to do with it?! Or—or—could it shorten her lifespan or lengthen it?"

"Could it?" Quin's tone was sharp, causing Drinian in his animated state to wince and stumble on his words.

"Ah—well, no, maybe . . . but that one I don't think. But I'm—it's a lot of code to unravel."

"Desolet—sorry Drinian, for my tone. I am—" She passed a gloved, shaking hand over her eyes. "Very tired."

"No it's—it's ah—expected. I have more nutrient gel for Synesis, another reason I asked for you—but actually to show you this." He pulled up another spreadsheet with Lumina's fungal mutation broken down into its genetic code and translated for traits. It wasn't complete yet, the data filling in as they looked on.

"Sec here?" He pointed to a line of code. "This is from Lumina—and I think, gives her fungus a human lifespan. Your Synesis is long-lived, but we don't know why—I thought maybe a more perfect symbiosis with you than has been achieved with others, but why? So, I looked and she has this same alteration. A different allele than Lumina's has, because Synesis borrowed it from you and I'm thinking that's what happened."

"When I became host to Synesis?"

"Yes—because why else is Synesis so much stronger

than the others? I think Synesis has ah—a mutation for more readily engaging in horizontal gene transfer, couple that with Lumina's vulnerable state when you joined with Synesis and exposed Lumi—still developing in artificial utero, and voila! We get Lumina—Lumi-fungus—Fungi-Luminous—this new strain." He shrugged, but the motion was full of energy—*excitement.*

"And you can use it?"

"Right! That was the long-awaited through-line—I think I can use it to make our new strain compatible with any host and last for a human lifespan."

Quin blinked, her eyes growing more alert than any moment since she'd arrived in his room. "Das ist eine grobe aufgabe— a tall-order."

"Right, right. Worth it though, isn't it? Unless there is something else I should be doing—"

"No Chér, do it if you can, and do it fast."

He didn't pause or hesitate. He grabbed up cultures of fungal strains he'd brought with him from Earth in vials of milky, mycelium-filled fluid. Quin looked on, lifting one gloved hand to his shoulder, hesitating and then dropping it when a panicked voice came over the villa's central AI speakers. "Quin?! Drinian?!"

He dropped a vial, and the thing shattered against the arm of the centrifuge-bot.

"Ah-ahhh . . . damn—Quin? Go, I'll scoop this into a new vial first?" She was already half out the door when he glanced up and didn't stop moving when he spoke.

He directed the mess into a petri-dish with the flat-edge of a glass slide. Panic moved him rapidly, efficient

—it was Lumina calling them, and she sounded terrified.

BEAMS OF MORNING light streamed through the window gap. She had opened it in the night hadn't she? Half awake, awake enough to feel the baking heat in her whole body and seek some relief. She'd asked the window to open and the AI had complied. Cool air like cool water, like salvation when it turned her sweat to ice on her skin. Sleep came again. She wasn't fully awake in the first place.

Her thoughts had been a tangle of brambles and growing things. She could still smell the orchard except it was also the smell of rotting wood, that pile of old decaying beams from demolished structures on other colonies, brought here to enrich the soil.

An old memory . . . She was sitting in it, picking apart the rain-softened fibers of wood pulp, fragments of lichen and soil sticking to her baby-soft skin, her hands so much smaller and rounder than they were now. Chase was tilling nearby with Manalou and a sea of other colonists, all of them sweat-slicked and glistening. The smell was damp, yeasty, rich, the smell of life and death intermingled.

She was there but she was also in her own garden, listening to the moss and ferns. She was in the orchard locked into conversation with the trees and she was hot, so hot that her own skin might burn her if she touched it.

It did burn when she scratched the tingling itch at the back of her neck.

The window was open and she was made of ice. A snow-melt river poured through her veins instead of body-heated blood, and she shivered with the winter of it. But she didn't wake up, there were too many layers of sleep pressed over her, too many tangled pathways into past and present and she couldn't understand what anyone was saying. Whispers and mumbles, quiet chattering conversations that held a rhythmic significance populated her mindscape. But their meanings were elusive. They shifted, changed and ultimately evaded her.

Open your eyes.

Drinian was in her head telling her to wake up, always telling her to wake up, to stop following that cycle of repeating cataclysm and rebirth that the tree had put into her head. There was more to the cycle now, so much more—but still foreign, ineffable. Behind her eyelids, the soaring bodies of bark-clothed giants grew until they touched the sky; branches and soft green needles crowded everything else out, a fever dream that lasted weeks, months, centuries longer than her conversation with the orchard sapling or the sleeping hours of a single night.

She struggled to hold it all in her head. It would fade if she opened her eyes, like wisps of dream, like disconnecting from deeper truth and turning her back.

She wouldn't be able to put any of it into words if she opened her eyes.

She was awake. The impulse kept occurring, rising up in her thoughts like earthworms coming up through soft soil.

Open your eyes.

It wasn't Drinian. He wasn't here anymore, not since they'd disconnected. This was different. There wasn't a voice to it really, more of a taste, a flavor like woodsmoke and rain, and crisp pine needles stinging the tongue. Had she ever tasted pine needles?

Ideas and feelings welled up—urges and realizations. Was this some other part of her mind, split off and thinking for itself? It was familiar, like family once met and buried in memory.

Thoughts from this distant relative pushed to the forefront of her mind with a wry quality that felt somehow older, not caustic but humorously sardonic— patiently mocking her questioning.

She opened her eyes and stared at the open window gap. Sunlight through the garden made false tree patterns on the drapes. The hotspots of light burned with such intensity that as she stared they became edged in rainbow, a prismatic splitting as her eyes shifted focus and began watering. She blinked. Blinked again then let the light split in her vision. Time was moving slower than normal, or she was, pausing in contemplation and getting lost in it.

She sat up, felt her body stretch and shift on the damp sheets. A wave of dizziness doubled her over.

Pain drove her hands up and she gripped the sides of her head; it was throbbing and her vision greyed into gnats of static.

The pounding receded, the one beating bass drums in her head backing away and fading into the landscape. In the absence of pain, a shivery tingling sensation traveled up and down her spine where the cool air of morning brushed her bare skin. It spread down her back from the base of her skull. There was a dull ache where the doctor had threaded the mycelial tube from Drinian's implant into her epidural space.

The tingling intensified with her attention to it until she couldn't keep her hands away. She scratched with a clawing urgency to still the itching, tingling, crawling. She couldn't see it but she was sure she left marks. There would be angry red welts—but the itch didn't recede. She scrubbed harder.

With a jarring sense of having gone too far, she felt her skin give way under the firm press of her fingers and the blunt tips of her nails. It was like peeling away dead skin or dead tree bark from a rotting log, and mostly painless, just a sting to accompany the hot ache from her scratching.

Her hands froze in place and she hunched her shoulders, held the shaking hands in front of her face. They were damp with fluid like that collected under a scab. Light stains of diluted blood mixed with the fluid. This was the point where she thought she was supposed to scream or black-out. But there wasn't any sound coming from her cotton dry mouth.

Blood pounded in her ears. She squeezed her eyes shut and opened them again. Nothing changed. This was not a dream or a momentary delusion. The blood and loose skin that had sloughed off on her hands was still there.

She took several breaths, shifted her legs under her to sit up higher as if that would help her see. She reached a tentative hand back to the stinging, exposed patch on the back of her neck. She felt for the edges of it then quested inward. Her fingers bumped something numb—bone maybe? But it was too soft, pliable even. She couldn't feel it as herself at first. The only feedback from the touch came from her fingers.

Instead, she heard it in her head, flutters, whispers, a presence. That taste again. Oh my god.

"Drinian!" Her voice was hoarse from sleep and too quiet. If the situation called for a scream then she was failing miserably. Panic froze her in place, but she found more of her voice. "Call Drinian. And Quin. Call Quin please. Now!"

The AI complied and the result was brisk footsteps, the door opening, Quin and then Drinian with a cup of Genti-6 cultivated coffee sloshing in his hand. Was it for her? He held it like an offering he now thought better of.

He hissed, licked coffee from his burned skin. Then his movements slowed as he took her in. His eyes widened and a hot flush of embarrassment crept into his face, then alarm at whatever he saw. He moved. Sat next to her.

Quin was silent, still, the same expression frozen on her face.

Lumina held out her hands as if they were ruined, soiled permanently by whatever was on them. "Um . . . there is something in my neck that isn't me." Her voice came in a near whisper, but she was grateful that the words came at all. Drinian cleared his throat and placed a careful hand on her shoulder, glancing up at Quin as she came up next to the bed.

His hand was warm against her skin, his touch tentative. He handed her the edges of her sheets, pulled it over the other shoulder and draped it there. She didn't have a shirt—it was the first time the thought occurred to her. There were blurred memories of her stripping down to her underwear in the night when she was burning up hot, before she'd thought to open the window. That same heat painted her face, her throat, her whole body as she realized her nakedness.

"Okay—okay, ah . . ." He was shifting to crouch behind her now, brushing the soft spirals of her honey-brown hair away from her neck. He cleared his throat, but she couldn't quite catch the mumbles that followed under his breath.

Quin sat in front of her and tied the sheet in place with a wrap across her chest and a knot at her shoulder. She examined Lumina's hands with her own gloved ones.

A sudden thought arose and Lumina turned wide eyes to the door. "Chase is going to freak. She's gonna just lose it—"

"No, Chér. She is going to catch her breath, and she is going to ache at not knowing what this is and then we are going to tell her, that is all."

Lumina felt her breath hitch and grow uneven. She was lightheaded, liquid fear racing through her bloodstream, the adrenaline of it turning her stomach. But then, just as quickly a response bubbled up in her mind, first feeling, then thought, then answering neurotransmitters—allopregnanolone, and serotonin. Without understanding or awareness of the chain reactions occurring she felt herself calming. Her thoughts cleared, slowed, and her eyes leaked a stream of tears that eased her with their passing. "So what is it then? I felt sick last night after the trees—well after I was asleep hot and then cold, like a fever."

She felt their shared silence and turned to see their faces. Drinian was smiling of all things, shaking his head with a hand on his face. Quin's look was more stoic, but her eyes were damp, full of some emotion Lumina couldn't discern for certain. "Guess I'm just rotting away . . . growing mushrooms that'll eat my walking corpse—could I at least drink your coffee first Drinian?"

He blinked at her and then was startled into a laugh. He handed her the cup, sloshing the dark sweet liquid on himself and the side of the bed, but it was cooler now and didn't burn her where it dripped.

"Well she is not far off from it is she, Drinian— haeynn zeh nakhonn?"

Lumina almost spit the warm drink, but held back,

swallowing it instead. It was a near miss and she had to hand the cup back to avoid spilling it while she coughed.

"You're kidding though, right?" A shadow of fear tried to drift back into the calm that had asserted itself a moment before.

"You've got—well it's mushroom I think—Seems you're ah, growing your own implant. It's just —"

Her eyes widened and she reached a hand up to her neck. She touched with tentative fingers with this new context. "It's just what?"

"Well, it looks a bit different than ours. Mushroom strains can mutate."

"So like, my mutation has a mutation?" It sounded like a joke but she didn't feel like laughing, not until the presence in her mind, that piney taste took up echoing her sentiment with heightened amusement.

She shifted on the bed, scooted back to observe Quin and Drinian face to face, then wet her lips. "So, contact with the trees, and then more contact. This is the result?"

"It's what you wanted." Quin's voice was low, sympathetic. Her tone belied the dry simplicity of the words and avoided any suggestion of how Lumina should feel about what was happening.

"And now you can't say no or wait . . . or you're not ready. But also, I can't say that anymore either and neither can Chase."

Lumina blinked and went silent. There was a

humming in her mind, not a sound but a current of presence.

"Lumina, you still can decide about this. You can have the growth removed and undergo treatments to eradicate the mycelium it is arising from—gene therapy, it would take that." Drinian's words were rushing out quickly the more he spoke, those long hands making tracks in the air, shaping the ideas he was putting forth. "An implant stage like we have, both limits and supports the location of growth and you don't have one of those, but I've done removals. I ah, I know the whole process. Yours is different but—we could try."

Quin gave Drinian a quizzical look but then she was nodding along with his words. Lumina watched her face, the guarded look in her eyes. Drinian's suggestion, to take it out of her, that wasn't what Quin would do.

Cut her out? It wasn't a question. Revulsion curdled in her gut. How could he even suggest it?

"No, I've already decided. She's part of me. Just bigger now, older—like me. That's it." She shook her head as she spoke, pressed both hands over the growth with a fierce protectiveness. Then she stood, taking the sheets that covered her along and shooing Drinian and Quin towards the door. "I'm getting dressed, and then I'm going to go and show Chase."

Quin raced the scrolling sidewalk of Genti-6's only large city—suburbs, outposts, and scattered homesteads didn't count. There was no pace the sidewalk could move her that was fast enough for what she needed to do.

It wasn't quick enough to tame her racing thoughts either. She was out of the villa before Lumina could cross the hall to her mother's room. Better Lumina tell Chase alone. It was what Quin had wanted from her, wasn't it? That chin tilted in defiant confidence as she met her challenge—and her mother—head on. Did the child know the extent of this trial? Did she have an inkling of how unknown these new developments made her path forward and how dire the threat of the known? Or had they protected her from too much of it?

Drinian's study of Lumina's genetic code loomed large in her mind. Lumina was so deeply entangled with her symbiont. How could the eventual decline of the trees not take her with it?

The nursery was small, tucked away in the district where scarce luxuries were peddled to the elite, imported antiques from Earth and spices that the climate here couldn't yet support. In other times a store for procuring plants and trees would be a staple of a community, especially on a frontier. Quin hadn't lived in those other times. In the memories of her childhood all things green were scarce and protected, not even for sale to a common buyer—here and now they were an oddity.

The space was too small for what it held, the plants crowded, shoved and stacked. A rank miasma of despair came from the living merchandise, a smell that she knew too well—the scent of rapid decline.

"Trees? Where do you keep your trees?" She raised her voice to reach the shop keep who could be heard puttering in one of the aisles not readily visible to her.

"Trees huh? Not many left. Not many and prices going up, what with current events . . ."

Her blood rose at the mention of price, the beginning of an attempt to extort and haggle over living beings. The air of the place, the suffering of the plants filling the tight space cut off her patience and sharpened her tone to the edge of a blade. If she could not cut through this man's attempts to be coy with her she might strangle him with the wilting vines of a pothos. Call it poetic justice.

He ambled into view, the sharp eyes of a salesman lighting on her.

Merde.

Did he recognize her? Stay inside—the governor had exhorted her to stay inside and Waters had insisted she would flay him alive if Quin didn't listen. But this was an extenuating circumstance. Lumina needed whatever she could get.

She tried to wilt like the stunted vines and sparse bushes and she kept herself front-facing in hopes that he would not notice Synesis.

The man squinted already-narrow eyes and cocked his shaved head. "You're one of those tree people."

She cleared her throat, pitched her voice higher and adjusted her accent as best she could. "I was. Most of us have given up. No point in it now, is there?" The lie tasted like sand in her throat but she tried to sell it. "Your trees please. I have a friend with a fondness for them. I'm not worried about price." That part was true. Chase's account would cover it and even discount the price and she wouldn't hesitate if she were here.

His eyes widened, feathered brows rising up his forehead. She kicked herself internally. Being inconspicuous wasn't working. The limp leaves of a bicolor pothos held her attention while she waited for his footsteps. Would it alert him if she chastised his poor care of these creatures? Or pelted him with the empty pots stacked along the walls?

Footsteps should have ended the train of her thoughts and turned them back to the task at hand but the two trees he brought out were equally neglected. How hard was it to learn basic care? To pay close enough attention to the well-being of your charges? Or was she being too harsh? Humanity was largely isolated from the arboreal language. They couldn't even taste the organic chemicals in the air that signaled danger and distress, not even when it was as thick as the fog of this shop.

She bit her tongue, paid quickly for the undersized saplings, and left with a certainty that he would tell stories about her and it would get back to the governor. The path back to the station and then to Chase's villa was sparsely populated as it was on the way to the city, but not enough to alleviate her worry.

Breaking promises wasn't part of the plan. If she

were evicted it would be worth the consequence. Lumina would have these saplings to play teacher and companion now that she had a true symbiont. They could travel with her.

But those purposes only scratched the surface of why she needed these trees. The root of that need was a raw and beating thing that she didn't want to examine too closely—they would stave off separation sickness when they had to leave this place. Another arc of anxiety made an erratic dance through her nerves.

Leave here with Lumina . . . As soon as possible to protect her from the fall of the trees whose fate she would now share. And Chase? What of Chase? She had promised to keep Lumina safe, and that is what she would do.

It wouldn't be enough to teach her here, to try and protect her here. Not anymore.

This place could only host them for so long if the young orchard died, if she couldn't heal herself first. There was little chance left of that. Her gloves separated her from the pots she held and so it would stay. But Lumina needed to be somewhere that she might have a future, the last bastion of Tree-kind. The forest of giants.

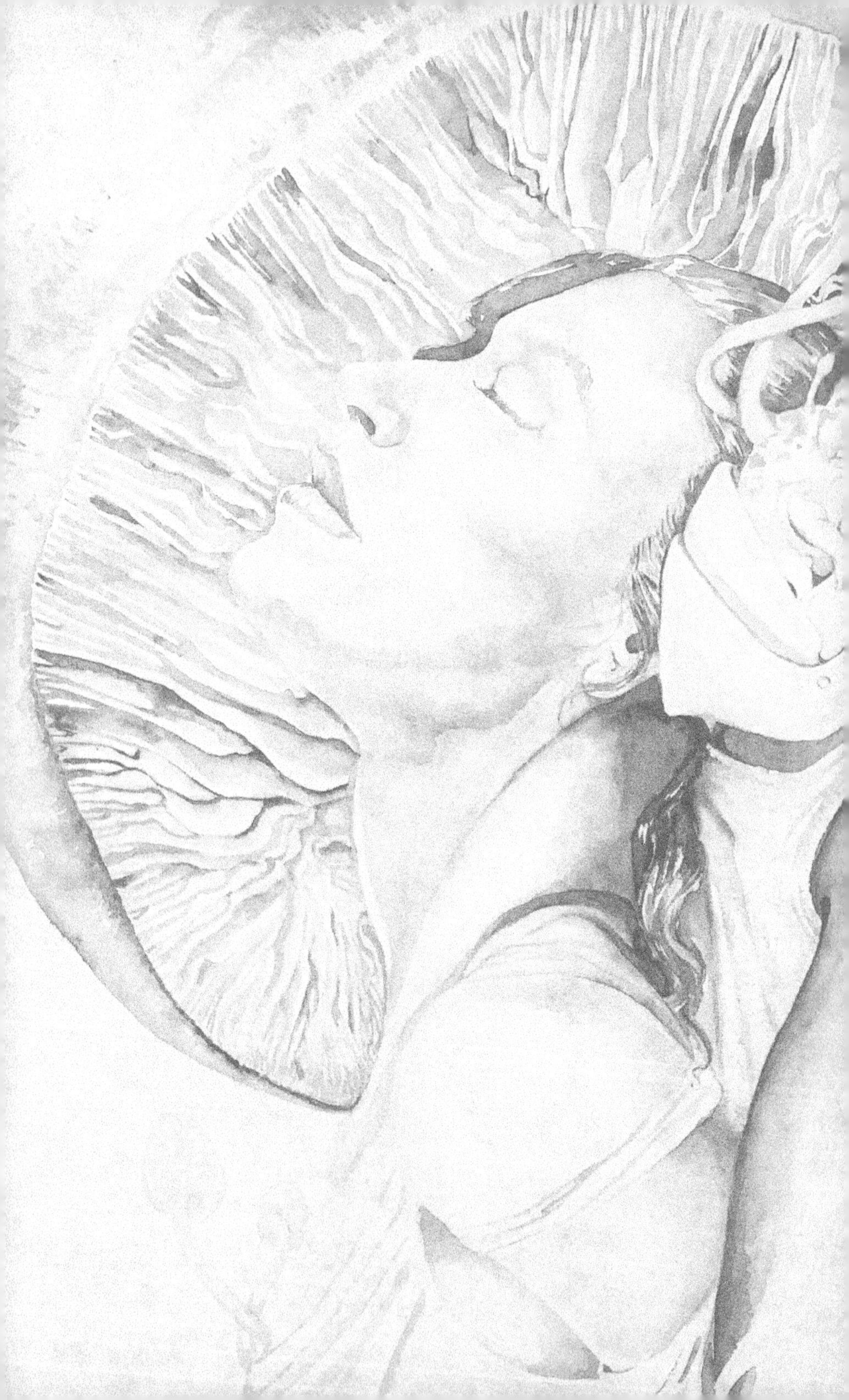

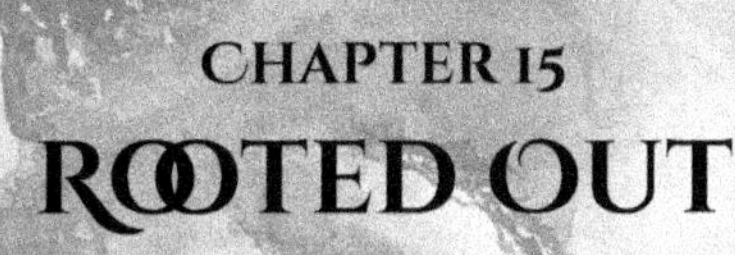

CHAPTER 15

ROOTED OUT

J ames Élysée sat silent with his hands folded, a crease pulling his brows together in the center just so. It would be taken as a sign of serious listening and not the problematic harboring of a dissenting opinion.

It was too warm for a meeting such as this one. The ERF headquarters insulation was multilayered and fail-proof enough to cool effectively, but resource usage was resource usage and shut-down protocols were in full effect, despite this meeting to announce that it would begin in the coming weeks. The walls were bare of the artwork that had adorned the space for decades—forests, desertscapes and wetlands framed like windows into another time. Motivational posters were gone as well. Nothing that could encourage dwelling on a dead project remained in view. Even crates had been drone-packed and removed to warehouses quickly—moving boxes brought up fears, doubts. It slowed the process, and this commander was taking no chances.

The imbalance of energy in the room was clear. The ERF commander was a pacing, raving force at the head of the room that none of the older officials could match. There were a few, Donohue, Lee, and O'Connell, generals all, who looked as if they would have jumped up to join the tirade if there was room for it, without stepping on the commander's figurative toes. Instead they gave sharp nods of agreement as she continued and mirrored the light of vehemence that shone from her flushed face.

"We have put in our years. We've put in our resources, and we have put our trust into a rehabilitation project that was never viable. The ERF is moving on—reallocating resources to successful colonization of planets that will accommodate a modern lifestyle, not this fanatic fundamentalism that's sprung up on Earth."

Donahue raised a finger to interject, making certain there was a long enough pause to keep his words from overlapping the commander's. "And she's encouraging them. Getting hopes back up. It's a disaster. I'll say it if no one else will. The interface project is a disaster."

James worked hard to control his face; it was taking all of his effort, but the direction this was going required finesse.

The commander's face had split into a broad smile and she was standing still now in a bubble of smug satisfaction. James watched her shifting features, the light in her eyes. A week ago those eyes had been dark and puffy with grief, and now they were shining too bright. It was the look of a fanatic, a mind pushed too far until the axis tipped and skewed.

He glanced around the circle of assembled generals and wondered if any of them were observant enough or honest enough to see what he had seen. None of them had called her fitness for duty into question as she systematically dismantled one ERF project after another in preparation for an unprecedented complete pull-out from the planet. She'd done it fast enough to cause far-reaching shock by the look on some of their faces. Too fast for objections.

"I didn't want to state it in such plain terms Donahue, but yes. Sgt. Fleury's breach of orders is an affront to the ERF and it's a misuse of power. She has, I admit it, a reputation as a sort of savior with the homeworlders and the romantics. I . . . yes, I was also taken in by her cure-all solution for the decline—"

The silence drew out long enough that James looked closer at her and what he saw startled him. The commander was floundering, confusion made her eyes flick around the room as if she had forgotten who or where she was, and then the light came back sharper. No one else in the room seemed to see the lapse for what it was. He almost stood up, almost raised his voice to try and call attention to the growing infirmity of the ERF's commander. But the moment had passed and she was gathering herself, continuing her tirade. Instead he watched her, listened closer.

"I was disappointed. What we got with Sgt. Fleury was a failed experiment, wasted resources. Wasted years. And now we need to pick up what's left and move on."

The commander's final words were delivered with a vehemence that could only have been backed by sincerity. She meant every damn word, the belief in Sgt. Fleury's ability to fix the whole planet for them, the disappointment when it grew more and more clear that it wouldn't happen. She meant it all and the other generals in the room were eating it up.

Two thirds of the room, no, closer to three fourths were nodding or outright cheering and General Lee began a round of applause that the others took up. James felt a wave of disappointment. Some of these generals were his friends. All of them had a history of serving the ERF with a high degree of selfless dedication, and now they were clapping for the end of the Earth's last preservation efforts, a thing that could only succeed through stamina. He didn't want to judge them too harshly. Each of them looked tired, worn, disillusioned in some way. Many were on longevity treatments, but the youthening effects had not touched the expression in their glassy eyes.

As the applause continued, he felt his heart-rate pacing up, thumping noisily in his ears like some unwanted harbinger of the consequences that would come if he didn't speak up now.

The applause died down and he cleared his throat, lifted a hand. "And Sgt. Fleury? It sounds from rumors like she's trying to continue the interface project from Genti-6. What is our position on that? With the ERF being dismantled, maybe it isn't something we need to handle?"

He looked around the room. It had gone silent, the uncomfortable silence of shifting bodies and shifting resentments.

The commander was nodding, building up to some response, but the smile at the corners of her lips didn't evoke confidence in him. It was a cold smile, and the nodding was not that of agreement. "Any equipment issued to Sgt. Fleury will need to be collected and her breach of orders means she'll be brought up on charges. She also put in for separation and I intend to see that she signs the appropriate documentation. The difference in pay for voluntary separation vs dishonorable discharge is significant. The same for her accomplices. We may be dismantling the ERF, but we'll tie up all the loose ends."

James broke out in a cold sweat. Uniforms were permanent issue not something that was returned at the end of an enlistment and weaponry was a thing of Earth past.

"Equipment?"

The commander nodded again and it made his stomach turn. Sweat collected at his hairline and he could feel all eyes on him, singling him out as the only one asking questions.

"Well, the implants used in the interface project are signed for, issued equipment. They are property of the

ERF and will need to be returned for storage or disposal." She shrugged instead of nodding again, but it was a facade. The meaning behind the words weren't the same as she was trying to project. It wasn't a matter of following a procedure. This was personal.

James looked around the room and saw what he expected, despite his hopes. Lee looked momentarily shocked, but his eyes flicked away from James's. Donahue's pressed lips and subtle head shake left no room for the protest James needed to push it any further. Instead he nodded. He put on a smile and he collected his things. There was nothing else he could do under observation, nothing he could do from this room, and he didn't know how much time he had to work with.

THERE WAS another message coming in that Paul Waters didn't want to open, not after the first. Quin wasn't any better at lying low than her daughter was. She was damn lucky people had poor pattern recognition, and the governor could trace and block communications off planet when keywords like 'the Tree-Whisperer' pinged her system.

It was useless to hold back the groan of exasperation each time he thought of her recent escapade. The message flashed on his screen. He knew he needed to see whatever it was about but damn if he couldn't have done without any and all messages from Earth, even from James, good fellow, but right in the middle of ERF leadership. James wasn't messaging him out on Genti-6 to come by for a drink. He didn't even have a return ride unless the Governor of Genti-6 really wanted to give him a loaner. That made him laugh. Gwen wasn't the type to loan anything out without a good trade. He was on borrowed hospitality already—And Quin wasn't helping.

Taking the ambassador's ship to Genti-6 with a promise to send it back had been a leap, a whole Grand Canyon sized leap past the peaceful retirement he'd now forfeited. The ship was back on Earth where it belonged, and he was here, on a rocky early-form colony for young and adventurous types—and big investors. It was not a place for retirees, and besides, any messages coming in from Earth weren't really for him. They were for Quin.

It was true wasn't it? He felt a twinge of guilt and he wasn't sure why at first. Because what was a message for Quin if not a message for the whole damn Interface project? That's what she was now. The last real linguist and the last holdout against giving up on something he had believed in. And he'd called her back into it once. Now he needed to stop dragging his ass and decide if he was all in or not. Retired General Paul Waters hovered a finger over the screen and then dropped his hand instead. "Alright, read it to me I guess."

"No, I don't think so. I don't feel sick anymore. Just last night. I'm kinda tingly now. And really, really calm."

Chase sat next to Lumina, the both of them curled up on the couch half under covers with the large central hearth lit to carry away the drafts of oncoming autumn. Quin watched the way they looked at each other, mother and child, with a sort of softness and intimacy that made her feel justified in giving them to each other. Lumina's nose crinkled in a laugh that was very much Chase's and Chase joined her. There was moisture in her eyes. A film of tears that had appeared when Lumina flopped onto the couch to show her the oddly shaped growths on the back of her neck.

None of those tears fell, but they kept appearing even as she laughed, even as Chase reassured Lumina that she wasn't angry or overly worried or blaming her for any of what was happening. Of course she wasn't, but Lumina couldn't not see those threatening tears, and the tumult throwing clouds and shadows across the open windows that were Chase's eyes.

"I really am okay."

"Of course you are. I guess it's just kind of a big deal." Chase rubbed a hand across her eyes. "I guess this is what was always going to happen."

Drinian took frequent sips of a new mug of coffee, gesturing with one hand cupping the rim so as not to spill it again. "Except . . . except without trees on Genti-6, maybe not. The trees catalyzed something that would possibly have remained dormant and never matured otherwise."

Quin almost laughed. He was caught up in the thrill of theorizing, oblivious to the fact that Chase likely knew that possibility and had said what she said to soothe her own feelings of responsibility for what was happening. "We have no idea that is the case, Drinian."

"Right, right."

Chase scrunched her face in the same way Lumina had. "It's okay." She turned a warm look on Drinian and then gestured to herself. "This is just processing—because none of what's happening is face value. This is where everything changes. Isn't that right?" She turned and caught Quin's eyes, the film of tears thinner now and beneath it that sharp practicality under pressure that Quin had always admired. Quin kept her gaze even as she wished for the safety of a screen, something less vulnerable, less intimate than that stare.

The discussion was intimate, too many quiet thoughts being forced out for group examination. Chase wasn't going to like the answer. It went against everything she had promised when Lumina was small. She hadn't been asked for the promise, but she had given it just the same, as a gift, but also a sacrifice. "C'est ca. She needs to learn to speak it now, for real. She needs hours of training—she is going to need my help. And I'm going to need hers or we'll both be—in a bad place before long. No trees to contact, or killing them if I do."

Chase blinked several times and Quin could see her thinking, one leap to the next from pain, acceptance, logic, plan, reworking. It was a thrill to watch when they were younger, with the same passions and priorities. Now it was a relief to have another adult mind, someone that could keep up in the same room and on the same side. Or close to it. Chase had given up on the ERF—maybe that wasn't fair. She had moved on. Lumina was Chase's priority and that made the trees her priority as well.

"You need somewhere with unrestricted access to the trees. Last night was a close call."

Quin gave a slow nod. "The other colonies have dead or dying trees and I am on a list, blocked from entry. And Earth—"

Paul Water's voice carried down the hallway ahead of the AI security announcement of his arrival. "Well Earth just isn't an option. Earth is less than an option. Earth is a threat, and it looks like you can't stay here either."

Quin let him cross the distance across the room and come up beside her. He put his hands over the fire, body language casual but eyes sharp. That spark in his gaze was more fire than she'd seen in years. It wasn't the look of a retired man but one who'd been reactivated in the midst of a crisis, catalyzed into action by something she couldn't guess. He didn't speak right away, but left a tension fraught silence hanging in the room while he warmed his hands.

"Well—well, a threat?" Drinian set down the mug he was still nursing.

Quin raised both brows. "You can't enter like that and then leave us to guess. Why a threat? We weren't planning to go back there. Not now at least."

"Mm-mm." He shook his head. "Not anytime as long as the ERF is still active. But staying away isn't good enough. She has it out for you, the commander."

Quin frowned. "I knew she was angry. She resents our—difference of opinion. She has made threats."

He was shaking his head, looking for a place to sit and then seemed to decide better of it. "She's taken it farther than that. You're being brought up on charges, submitting paperwork under false pretenses, breaking orders, absconding with ERF property. And she's going to hold you to all of it."

Confusion shifted to dawning realization and horror that was echoed in her shared mind-scape. There was only one thing she had taken from the ERF. It was the one thing they had begged her to take, Waters had begged her and spent hours convincing her until she consented for a second time. She needed to hear him say it out loud. "What property have I stolen? What do I have that is theirs?"

He looked her dead in the eye, and then gestured with a tilt of his chin. "Your mushroom. She took them off your apprentices and she's going to do the same with you and Drinian."

Quin blinked. She pulled in a slow breath. The air in her lungs became a filled life-raft on a rising wave. She couldn't think through the surging tides. Lumina stared wide-eyed, no-longer reclined under a blanket. She cupped both hands at the back of her neck where the new growth was still small enough to be covered. Drinian was pantomiming in the air in front of him and he had sloshed his retrieved coffee, this time on his clothes.

Chase watched her, followed her silent processing. It was clear that she had no intention of sitting through further conversation. Her narrowed eyes blazed a sharp green in the morning light. "They can't do that. The governor promised protection, asylum on Genti-6."

Waters took a seat across from Chase and laced his hands. "I already talked to the governor and she can't stand in the way of desertion charges, theft, any of that. James thinks they're going to send a security force to pick us up."

"They don't just do that. Not since they knew better —It'll make her sick." Chase's eyes pleaded with Drinian, as if his expert corroboration would change anything. He was uncharacteristically silent and she continued on her own. "Ask any of the implant technicians in the project. When it happened before I—I didn't think she would ever wake up. No one in the interface project would agree to that now."

"Right, well. It doesn't sound like our commander is asking for recommendations on this."

"I didn't take anything, this is mine." Lumina hadn't

said anything for several minutes. Now her words drew everyone's attention.

"Wait, the kid has one?"

Lumina dropped her hands and turned her head. Waters craned his neck to see. What he saw pulled his face into a map of concern and distaste. "Well, that's news. It doesn't look like a mushroom—er, a mushroom but not an Interface Implant Mushroom."

"But it is. Grown from her exposure to Quin's inoculation when she took on Synesis." Drinian launched into a detailed explanation of what had happened to Lumina and all of their theories about the nature of her implant.

Quin listened to the rising notes of fear, indecision, and near-resignation weaving through the room. She scratched an itch on her mushroom's leathery-soft snout. They were shutting down the project without trying any of the solutions she and the planetary ecologists on Earth had proposed. The commander had buried those without ever giving them a chance. This woman, once a friend, would send people to take her implant out.

Sixteen years, an unprecedented sixteen years spent sharing her body with this mushroom and it could end any minute, any hour. Shift travel was fast. They could be here at any time. That was what she couldn't tell. How long . . . ? Losing her implant would mean the project was dead, and the trees would go with it. She would fade with them if that happened, that is if she didn't go the moment they severed her connection to Synesis.

She closed her eyes and felt for the edges between herself and the mushroom. Distinct thoughts that were just hers. Ones that were Synesis. There were none. All throughout her body where nerve impulses traveled, she felt the trace of her mushroom—her friend. A drowsy response greeted her, thoughts touching thoughts like hands embracing. She was inhabited, entangled just as Lumina and her symbiont were. Would it look the same under Drinian's microscope? Did it matter? She wouldn't survive the separation.

She wet her lips and focused in on the room, the people in it. They were still talking. The conversation had stagnated in the same place or circled back.

"They can't take them if we aren't here when they come." All eyes turned her way. Her words had cut through everything else. Her heart pounded. Synesis didn't intervene. Didn't soothe or slow her.

"What—Where will we be?" It was Drinian, grasping at ideas in the air again with those large, brown eyes on her.

"We won't be here when they come. We'll be— somewhere else. But they can't shut down the project as long as we have our implants. And they can't take them if we leave now."

Lumina sat up on her knees bouncing in place as if she had reversed several years and was a small child again. "Somewhere with trees! That's where we're going. I know that's where we're going."

Chase turned away, covered her face with one shaking hand. But her posture was a straight line, the silhouette of a rigid pine in a gale-force wind. Lumina wouldn't be going anywhere if Chase opposed it. Would she do that? Hide the child here while the forests died off and they subsisted on potted plants?

Quin's voice came out a whisper. "Oui, Chéri, somewhere with trees."

THE OTHERS WERE PACKING. Quin had nothing to pack. She owned nothing. There was the uniform on her back, the gloves she wore. Her mushroom. Emergency food and nutrient supplements for Synesis filled her leather utility belt, crammed in pouches each time Drinian saw her. She traveled light and that meant she should have been ready. But the object of her attention made leaving a much slower process.

"Chase, Chéri Mwen, Lumina has to come with me. You do not."

But Chase wasn't bending. She sat perched on the arm of an antique sofa, Earth-made, of wood and leather, a thing of the past like everything else in Chase's villa. Her legs were crossed and her arms the same. She wouldn't meet Quin's eyes. "The ERF doesn't know Lumina has anything they could confiscate. She can hide it until they're gone. I can hide her here or—or I can come with you."

Quin took a breath; rushing this wouldn't end

well, but they did not have time. More precisely they didn't *know* if they had time or not. "You think that here is as safe as somewhere they cannot know to look?"

"No–Yes? It's close enough because they don't know to check her. They're coming for *you,* not her. But you're ignoring the second option. I could come. Why don't you want me to?"

Quin opened her mouth to answer but failed to find words she could say. *Because I would have to choose again . . . Because you already did.* Was that the wedge that had grown into a chasm between them? She'd awoken from the coma-like fugue state of advanced separation sickness and found Chase gone—gone and with a new passion—A colony to build. She had discarded all of their hopes to stop the decline together. Chase had moved on when *she* couldn't. Now she wanted to help. How long would that last? It was a valid question wasn't it? But the bitter taste coating those thoughts meant there was something deeper she didn't want to look at—or couldn't.

Her resolve solidified. Instead of addressing the question, Quin's answer sounded like nonsense to her own ears but it *felt* right. And it distracted Chase. "You think they won't look for me with you and Lumi? You are my listed family. If I died you would be sent my remains."

"Do you have to say it that way?"

"Yes, because this is that serious."

"You said you wouldn't take her from me."

"Yes, but you also said I could, that I shouldn't make that promise . . . that she is ours."

Chase's eyes flashed with anger. "But you made the promise."

Quin crossed the gap between them, lifted Chase's hand. "Are you not letting Lumina decide? Because she has already said what she wants? And she's frightened to stay. She's packing."

"I can help keep her safe, but for some reason you'd rather take her than have me come along. What is that?" She didn't pull her hand away, but Quin knew she wanted to. She considered dropping her hand, stepping away. The warmth that should have been in the gesture was cut off but she held on anyway.

"And the trees that she is connected to now? Will you keep them safe as you once promised, or have you given up on that completely? Because you are standing in the way of their well-being when you say you should keep her here."

"That's not fair."

Quin could see the wounding in her eyes, but it was necessary. She pressed on. "You know that my implant will die if I don't cure whatever in me is sickening the trees, and you know that I was the only one holding back the decline. I could recite back to you the letters I wrote to you about this? Does none of that matter?"

"I read them. But do you think a letter is the same as hearing it from you directly, or from the trees themselves? Whatever you say this message is, how am I supposed to see it the way you do or believe it's something we can fix, if I haven't heard what you've heard? Or felt it?"

Quin's hand shook. That dark place in her where everything went cold, shifted and grew with Chase's doubts. It catalyzed her own. No wonder she couldn't convince the ERF to keep trying, or teach her apprentices, or her fledgling trees if she couldn't even make Chase understand. She hadn't for all of these years, if Chase needed proof to believe her. "I'm sorry that you couldn't feel it from my words."

Chase grit her teeth and growled in frustration. "Then show me. All of it. I have the experience to handle it. You know that!"

"Chéri, you do not have an implant and I cannot—"

"I still have an active port. It could work the way it did with Drinian and Lumina. We've done like it before."

Chase gripped both of her hands now, the pressure an urgent demand through the layer of glove leather. "I don't want to feel separate from this anymore. I want to know."

Quin's face flushed with heat and she pulled away. She couldn't do this. Not now. "We've been over this. Every tree I connect with dies. If it did work, I could make you sick and if it didn't . . . I don't think–well I haven't–"

"You haven't what?"

Quin extricated her gloved hands and stood, stepped back from the couch. "I have not succeeded in sharing the whole message with anyone else. The apprentices cannot take in more than a fraction and they cannot process much of it." She had to pause, to breathe before she let the rest come out. "The ones who have tried for more, ended up in the infirmary, and the trees can only hold it a short while. They cannot repeat it all back. It hasn't been working for a long time."

"You don't know it won't work with me. I'm tired of feeling like it's something between us. Show me and Lumina can go. I won't get in the way."

"So you are holding her hostage? Because I won't experiment on you?"

Chase turned away, stared at the door. It was shut, but Quin imagined it opening. The commander would come through it and grasp her mushroom by its body. She felt the pulling sensation, the soft tearing sound of mycelium ripping away from her implantation site, and she shuddered.

No one came through the door but every moment they waited it was closer to reality. Urgency warred with a building malaise. She had been here so many times before, that look of hurt in Chase's expressive eyes, the impending death of the part of her that mattered most. Even this new threat to Lumina was familiar because she was wholly responsible for it. Now Lumina had no choice. But Chase did, and she wasn't choosing the fight against the decline. She was choosing Lumina and that made her a liability.

"I'm asking you to help me understand." The tremble in Chase's voice was another seed of guilt. She was a constant reminder of Quin's inadequacies.

"I can't do that for you—but—come with us. You can come with us and help Lumina. You're right. If you come, you won't have to worry about her."

Chase had frozen where she sat with her knees pulled to her chest in profile, her hair obscuring half of her face. Her back was ramrod straight but Quin could see a softening at her jawline, a slight tremble.

"Just come. Please. Just come."

"THERE'S no one else to go through. You want a ship then this is who we get it from, but Quin—" Waters was leaning in close, whispering for her ears only. "I asked her and she wants to speak to you."

"Limatha?—What is her reason? Because I—"

"Because you went out? Yes, I know about that. But no, I don't think that's it or she'd have already kicked us out on our asses."

Her face heated with embarrassment, and she groaned, muttering obscenities under her breath. She pictured that office, the glaring, suffocating noise of clashing colors and incoherent shapes, and the woman herself with a politician's mannerisms and speech patterns. It made her tired, the whole thing made her tired. The ERF was coming at some unknown time and she could feel the little spikes of adrenaline that resulted from that knowledge. They didn't move her fast enough.

The urgency from General Waters's announcement

was getting lost at each road block, Chase's demand to come along, this governor's request to speak to her as if she had any answers or any assurance that she wasn't taking them into inevitable failure. The rush of thoughts froze her in place. They made her doubt.

If she just sat still long enough, she wouldn't have to choose anymore. She wouldn't have to keep fighting, because they were choosing for her, no more trees, no more mushrooms. That thought brought a larger thrill of fear that lit up her insides. It should have brought a reaction from Synesis but she was largely still. Calm? Perhaps; these thoughts that her mind was toying with were not worth a reaction? Synesis made no argument.

"Quin?" The general's voice startled her.

"Yes?"

"I asked if you're going to do this." His eyes showed concern but more than that an urgency that she was supposed to be feeling herself. What was this lassitude, almost fatalism that froze her, even as surges of fear electrified her?

You know what it is though . . .

She listened for more than that sudden feeling, but it didn't come. She wasn't sure if it was her own thought or Synesis, or something else. An echo of Tree implanted in her head from one of many downloads?

"Just call her, yes." Did she look as distracted as she felt?

"It's already set up." And then he leaned in to whisper again. "What's *wrong* with you?"

"I don't know."

She had to get them all out of here before she got worse. Before she sank into defeated lethargy . . . The ship. She needed that ship—She took the VR comm headset he was holding out. She couldn't not take it as he was shoving it into her hands. "Put a call in to the governor, please." He was leaning close to the headset in her hands and directing the system to initiate the call for her.

The headset slid over her eyes and she was aware of a quiet sense of knowing. She *knew* what was slowing her, and to say otherwise was a lie. That aching paralysis that seeped from her thoughts and into her limbs . . .

It came when she'd visited the Pain Trees and it stayed with her.

The thought made her insides flip. Remembering it made her feel it—self-doubt—an avalanche of advancing cold as if there was no source of warmth in the whole of the cosmos.

The governor's image came through the lenses along with her voice, as a subdued, less detailed VR rendering. It was better than being in that office, but as soon as the Governor appeared in the VR setting Quin found she couldn't hold her tongue. "Your protection didn't last very long."

"Neither did your promise to stay in the villa." She raised a brow, gave a terse nod, and took a gulp of her drink. "No, it didn't. But I didn't know she was bringing you up on charges. I can only do what I can." There was genuine remorse in her eyes.

Quin had a sharp eye for dissembling. "And you can't do what you offered to do?"

"I can't go against the ERF's jurisdiction over you."

When she didn't respond, the governor filled the empty air. "But you didn't call me for this did you?"

"I called because Waters told me you needed me to ask you for the ship. But I can't think why, unless it's for you to tell me no or to extract a price."

"A price?" She seemed on the verge of laughter. "The price is you asking me, so I can tell you yes."

Quin's eyes widened and the words she was preparing dried up in her mouth, replaced by questions. "Why?"

"Well, it isn't because we're friends. We aren't, are we?"

Quin thought a moment and then shook her head.

"Do you have friends, Sgt. Fleury? In the ERF, back on Earth?"

Quin narrowed her eyes. It was an odd question, not what this call was about. But people flashed through her mind. Waters. He was a friend, wasn't he? He had been her superior, a complex intermingling of shared goals, and obligations. But were they friends? Would he call them friends? Earth . . . Inaya, they were acquaintances, antagonistic, but with shared goals, and Inaya had invited her to collaborate—She hadn't answered. She'd opened the letter, read it, but never replied. Her apprentices? Could friendship exist with an imbalance of power? And Chase . . . could Chase be called a friend?

But the governor was continuing her monologue, with questions that seemed to be rhetorical.

"Because I'm not loaning the ship to Waters. He's a good friend but there are limits to favors between friends. I'm loaning the ship to you." Her eyes took on a bright glint as she continued. "Why do you think I'd do that? I don't have to, you know. And I'm sure it'll piss some people off."

Quin shook her head. There was no reason for it she could find. She had nothing to offer this woman, nothing to offer that most people would value. Words, she had plenty of those. Failures? She had enough of those to share.

"I'm giving you my ship because I need you to succeed. I need to see forests on Genti-6. I need there to be trees on Earth if—when—I come to visit. Maybe I won't ever, but I need to know they're there. You're the only one I know that's still trying to make sure that happens."

The more the Governor spoke the more still Quin grew. There was an ache in her throat, a tightness that blocked any words she might have said. There weren't many friends left—not friends for her—though that was true as well. The trees had fewer.

"Take my ship. Waters knows the one. Don't bring it back until you've solved this. That's my price. We might not be friends, Quin, not yet anyway—I don't have the foliage for that, but we can be allies."

CHAPTER 16

STAND OF SAPLINGS

This ship was twice the size of common shift drives. It would be a waste of resources to make room for more than seats and emergency supplies. With shift travel, there was no need for anything more, but this ship was made for building colonies, transporting people and enough cargo to rebuild on a foreign planet.

Quin stared at the controls, pulse pounding, and in her periphery the side docking arm of the space station, and below the space elevator that carried them out of Genti-6 atmosphere. She knew where she was going. It was the only place Lumina could learn and be safe for now, even if she herself could have no relief. But a thought kept her from action. Lumina could be safe there. What of her apprentices?

She could feel Waters's eyes on her. He was waiting for her to plot a course, and he would expect a trip to the Pain Trees or a search for one of the seeded planets, because the Forest of Giants was a forbidden place, in need of protection from the decline—from her. Perhaps they could find another world where the haphazard seeding from the annals of Earth history had been successful. Too many uncertainties. But first, there was something she had to do.

Quin turned in her seat. The other passengers were buckled in. Lumina and Drinian were in the back with three rows of seats between them and the rest of the passengers. They spoke in low voices, unintelligible from this far away. Lumina's fungal growth had doubled in size, showing around her face in a chaotic formless pattern that would doubtless result in an unpredictable final shape.

Chase was nearby, in the first row of seats, too quiet. Even the absence of her voice caught Quin's attention.

Waters was on her right, staring as if he was more anxious than she to avoid being caught by the ERF. If she hesitated much longer and another ship approached the station, they could be tracked, or their shift could be disrupted.

She opened her mouth, but the words stuck in her throat. She knew where they needed to go, not as a final destination but a first stop and it would be a risk. Her hands slid across the control system and she set the coordinates for Earth. It might be the last time she'd set foot there if this didn't go well but it had to be done. It wasn't up for debate. Her apprentices deserved better.

She cleared her throat and pushed the words out,

projected her voice for Lumina and Drinian to hear in the back. "We need to make an extra trip. For a pick-up."

"There's a lot of places that won't let us dock when they know you're on board."

Quin threw an amused glance to Waters. "Hqan? Ou Panse Ca?—Because I need reminded of that? But we're not going to any of those places. We have a pick-up on Earth."

"Uhhh—" She could hear Drinian's concern in that one drawn out syllable.

"Isn't that exactly what we're avoiding? Like, getting anywhere near to people who're trying to arrest you?" Chase's words were quieter, spoken mostly for her.

She grabbed the multi-point harness and began fastening and tightening until they clicked into place and felt snug around her. The course was set, the bed of exposed nerves in her gut gave a feeling of hyper-alertness, a clarity of mind much sharper than anything she'd felt since visiting the Pain Trees after Genti-6. Deciding felt good. "If that was our only goal I'd agree with you. But my apprentices didn't deserve what happened to them and I'm going to give them more options. Does anyone object?"

Waters was rubbing at his jaw, talking to himself. "You want to show up there when they might already be on the way here? Maybe could work. Use a private docking station and elevator. You aren't going down though. I could do that. I dunno, seems like a fool's errand but I'm not going to be the one to say no. It's your neck on the line—" He winced before the words were all out. It was too close to describing what would happen to her if they were caught.

"D'accord." Quin reached for the switch that would separate them from the docking arm and begin their slower flight outside of the planet's and the docking station's immediate vicinity so they could shift.

It felt too slow, like space was parting before them at the pace of a spoon through cold taffy. Before they reached the threshold for a safe shift, the darkness in front of them wavered, a dizzying ripple in the star-pricked fabric of space. A much smaller ship than their own appeared, the usual pod-like shape, a small luminous egg of blue and green and brown like a stretched representation of Earth, the letters ERF etched in the side.

Thrusters emerged from the sides of the ERF ship and it slowed, turned. Quin flicked her eyes back to the controls, assessed the distance between their own ship and the station behind them. The governor's unexpected support might not last if they destroyed Genti-6's space elevator and docking station by shifting too close, but waiting a second too late could mean this other ship would lock onto their course and follow.

She watched the numbers, the distance between them and the station increasing slowly, too slowly. "Engaging . . . now."

Space twisted and wavered around them, obscuring the ship that had come for them. With their proximity, it could follow them through but that would be a risk on their part. They couldn't know who was on board. For all they knew she and Waters, and Drinian were on the planet surface, and this was a weekend away from the colony for bored teenagers. Somehow Quin thought they knew better but she could hope that indecision slowed their thinking and they'd dock and check the planet first.

The shift turned her stomach inside out and dizzied her senses. She made a mental note to thank General Élysée for the warning, even if he and the others hadn't the courage to fight their commander. She wanted to hope. Would he do more if she could rebuild the ERF herself, start over? The governor of Genti-6 gave her a ship, but more than that, she'd tasked her with continuing this mission. How much support could she expect?

And what of Inaya? She had invited Quin back to Earth. The homeworlders didn't have the ability to protect fugitives, even if they were so inclined. She wanted to believe that each of these contacts would form a new support for stopping the decline. She'd believed that before, with Waters, the commander of the ERF, with Chase. Hoping for that again was more than she could do.

CHASE COULDN'T LOOK AWAY, even as her eyes watered in the glare of the planet below. The blue and brown shape, dotted in swirls of white and green was as she remembered it but brighter, as if the mental images from her dreams had faded over the intervening years like photographs left out in the sun. She knew what she would find on the surface, a stifling feeling, and something like absence, something like visiting a cemetery, or your father's hospital room. Like watching as one body system fails at a time, breath growing shallow and rapid, color steadily more dusky. The Earth felt like that to her now. The less time spent there, the better.

The elevator was slow, agonizingly snail-paced while she looked at the deceptively beautiful, blue marble painted in still-life. It was a lie; she'd feel it when she set foot on that overused ground.

Waters cleared his throat across from her. She tore her eyes from the window. Anything was better than the seductive view of Earth, the planet she'd left to build a new one.

Was he uncomfortable? Readying himself to say something, to fill the air between them. Gravity was settling around them layer by heavy-cloaked layer. The blue of Earth filled all of the elevator car's windows.

"So Genti-6, huh? You've done a lot out there."

"Yeah." She could tell it wasn't what he wanted to

say, this was polite chatter and it grated on her. It wasn't as if they didn't have a past. He was a sergeant then and she an eager recruit like Quin. When things had gone wrong and the project was paused, she'd moved on and that was the end of their history. Still, there were two years of training between them—and now sixteen years of zero contact. The awkwardness was understandable, but getting past it would be better if it would make him ask his questions.

"I remember what Genti-6 looked like in the colonist requests, when it was first put on the list." He continued in the same way, rubbing his hands together as if the wait was gnawing at him as well.

She groaned internally. "It's something about Quin, right? You could just ask me."

He cleared his throat again, looking even more uncomfortable than before. He squinted one blue eye and then spread his hands. "You and she—"

"I know I said ask but I don't think this is your business." Her heart rate rushed ahead of her in a race against her tongue making the words dry up.

"Sure, but she's my friend. She's my friend but there are—limits. She'll only talk so much and it's gotten less since she brought those trees to Genti-6 and saw you. People, you know, lean on friends. Open up when things happen."

"Quin's not like that."

"I know. But she talks to you. She can sit in a room with me and write letters to you even when there aren't any letters coming back."

She felt an ache in her throat and a heaviness growing in her chest. "She talks to me, yes. It's a sharing, purging sort of thing but—" She couldn't find the right words, didn't know why she felt compelled to find any for this man. Sergeant—General Waters was just another person now, not a superior and he was practically a stranger to her. But he was a friend to Quin. Maybe that was why. "She talks in a way that doesn't leave room for her to ask me for anything. Except the listening. Which I do."

"Something's wrong there."

"It's just Quin."

"No, no. I was there when she brought you Lumina and she was breaking up in here after leaving. I thought she was gonna get back out and stay, but then she just talked and we left and she writes and writes."

"Yes. Like I said, that's Quin. She's made her decisions."

The elevator car came to a stop and she unfastened her straps. Waters stared at her and then after several moments shook his head, unclipped his straps and stood. He bowed his head, grabbed the overhead support straps for balance. His face had grown ashen and he was breathing through his mouth. "I think she needs you to, I don't know, help her figure her shit out." He was pushing to adjust to the gravity too fast.

She closed her eyes and gripped the supports on her side. She leaned her head back as the world swirled around her. It wasn't as bad as it would be with a fast entry, but gravity was a bitch and she'd stood up too quickly. "Quin will ask me if she needs my help."

She wasn't sure if it was true. It felt like smoke and mirrors. The years of distance between them stood out in sharp relief. Quin didn't ask for things, didn't need things. There was an understanding between them, and it meant no demands, no sacrifices, no restrictions on reaching for their own goals. Quin wasn't on Genti-6 because she needed things elsewhere and Chase, well she was there because that's what met her own needs. That was the narrative that had played in her head for years. What about now? She'd tried, more than once to reach out for more and Quin had pushed back.

She opened her eyes to find Waters staring at her, his color back to normal. "Okay?"

"Okay. So we collect Quin's apprentices somewhere?" She stood without support now, tied her hair back in two short braids.

Waters's face darkened. "You know where we need to get them from. They haven't been without their implants long enough to be out of the infirmary. We just have to hope they're all on their feet and coherent enough."

She looked him dead in the eye. "You're saying it's going to take both of us? Just say that. Because the implant infirmary isn't somewhere I want to see again."

Waters winced. "Right. It's going to take both of us. Sorry."

The air getting onto the bullet train was more humid than Chase expected, more humid than Genti-6 and it made all of her movements feel slow, dreamlike. The treeless landscape rushed by in a blur of browns, drab greens, and yellows. When it stopped, she found her stomach needed to catch up.

Waters was no longer watching or questioning her. His eyes were on his handheld device, tracking and sending messages. He'd done the same before they exited the elevator car. She'd assumed he was coordinating with the mysterious ambassador friend that owned this more distant elevator.

There was no one there to greet them when they stepped out, no security or technicians demanding to know who they were and whether or not they belonged there. Last count, Earth had half a dozen space elevators, all built during the first wave of enthusiasm for space colonization. Now that interest in Earth had dwindled and her attention was on Genti-6, she had no clue who owned each of the elevators or how many were still functional. This one at least, and the one operated by the ERF.

The feeling of isolation intensified as they switched from bullet-train to fully automated drone car. No other passengers, no driver. Instead of being a relief, she found the graveyard feel of their trip unsettling. This felt like venturing into the unknown. It left room for flights of the imagination, wherein the first actual person they met was armed and carrying orders to bring them straight to the commander of the ERF. They'd be forced to give up Quin and Lumina from the ship at the top of the elevator.

The crowd outside of the ERF's security station was unexpected. She recognized them as homeworlders by their old-fashioned climate-control suits and the braids they favored, elaborate patterns along their heads and down their backs. There were so many of them, more than she'd ever seen at a protest, on Earth or off it.

The tone of their clamoring shouts was different as well. She felt her stomach twist, at the slogans. Instead of the usual banners demanding the ERF concede to their natural jurisdiction over Earth's rehabilitation, these ones were exhorting the ERF not to leave. Wasn't that what they wanted, the planet to themselves, to rehabilitate in their own ways?

Dishonorable discharge . . .

Jumping Planet is for Quitters . . .

EAF not ERF = Earth Abandonment Force.

Rehabilitation takes W.O.R.K.

She couldn't read them all at the speed they passed the station. The train only slowed for a moving scan and then passed through the checkpoint. A green light flashed in front of them and the steel gates around the ERF opened up.

"They're just letting us through?"

Waters didn't look up from his device. "Yes, for now."

Her eyes widened. She didn't ask what that meant. She knew well enough what it *would* mean if this odd pattern didn't hold. There could be hundreds of ERF personnel ready to detain them, or there could be next to none. It all depended on how close to dissolution this last outpost was.

No one stopped them in the drone hangar, but it wasn't empty. Waters kept his head down and Chase copied him. She had to lengthen her stride to keep up. Her pulse in her ears was louder than the collective sounds of mechanics, drones, and drone mechanics going about the business of repairs and maintenance. The poorly ventilated space smelled of synthetic lubricants and burnt wires.

"General Waters!"

She froze inside, checked Waters for direction. He was slowing, turning, lifting a hand to return a salute to the much younger woman who had flagged him down. "Sgt. Madris. Hey!"

His enthusiasm seemed genuine, but there was tension in the lines of his face. He didn't stop but gave a quick nod, walked backwards and kept moving.

"You're too late to reactivate. They're shutting us down."

Waters laughed, a polite chuckle that Chase knew was forced. He gestured ahead of them. She could see sweat collecting around his collar. "Retirement party, and I'm late as usual!"

The Sergeant gave another salute and turned back to a tall mechanic drone making repairs on a land-ship's flight systems.

Waters picked up pace and Chase jogged to catch up. He leaned down to whisper. "And now we're on the clock. My name's in the security cameras, could be, and anyone in here could know to report to a higher up that I'm here. If I've been flagged that is—probably have been."

"And then what?"

"Then we send Quin a message to leave us before they send someone up there."

"Shit."

"Shit is right."

The infirmary was a large, sprawling building, the original white stucco peaked through the rust colored streaks of dust that stuck in the humidity. Even with the ERF shutting down and emptying out, the infirmary couldn't be as empty as the rest of the base. Where there were people there was illness.

Waters veered past the pathway that would lead to the front entrance and slowed his steps, he paused and waited for a cluster of young privates to pass. He made certain to look in another direction. If he made eye contact, they might recognize him. Unlikely out of uniform, but possible. As soon as they moved on he made a sudden turn into a covered pathway that circled the back of the infirmary. There were so many entrances she didn't know. She'd only used two that she could remember. It was that front entry that would make her heart race if she saw it again. But they were at the back of the infirmary now, standing in front of a door, waiting. Waters was on his device again.

"What are you doing now? You said the clock is ticking."

"Right."

The door hissed as it slid open to reveal a short, thickly built man in his fifties. The obvious aging signs of pre-longevity treatments were visible around his eyes and mouth. He wore the coffee-colored uniform of a general, adorned with more gleaming pins on the breast than she could count. His mouth was pulled into a tight line. Her heart stopped and she froze in place. His narrow eyes, almost black and shining with a nimble intelligence, smiled as he reached for Waters's hand.

"Who do you think has been clearing the path for us? Chase, Meet General James Élysée."

James pulled them both through the door then wrapped Waters in a warm embrace.

The security light came on behind them as the door locked. No one would come in after them.

Waters kept his voice low. His collar was damp with sweat. "Are they going to be ready to go?"

James's brow creased and he almost laughed. "No, no they aren't. They don't know up from under the bed. You just send that message to them all now. Wait long enough for the ones who can read to read it and then you haul ass to pick them up. I already authorized their release to you so if they can't talk and they can't fight back, you take them and answer questions later. The drone car you came in is going to be at this exit in twenty minutes. "Did anyone see you?"

Waters grimaced. "One Sergeant in the drone hangar."

The General seemed to be calculating in his head, and then he shook Waters's hand again. "Not too bad."

He grinned, the smile lighting his eyes in a way that looked reckless. Somewhere he was lighting explosives on a bridge and jumping off. "I have a retirement party to get to!" He turned on his heel and his footsteps echoed down a hallway to their right.

"There's actually a retirement party?"

Waters gave a sheepish grin. "Sure. It might be flimsy cover, but it's what we had on short notice. A surprise retirement party for the commander. James is giving a big speech in her honor while we get the hell out of here. She's gonna love it."

THEY WERE PACKED IN TIGHT. The ground blurred behind them, the security station far behind before Chase relaxed. She couldn't stop staring at the three who were unconscious. They were strapped to AI life-support systems that kept their vital signs stabilized. Their minds raced through hard landscapes.

There were monsters in there, with teeth like needles inoculating them with despair, self-doubt, hopelessness. The pathways out of the dead forests in their minds were unlit, the way out long and arduous. They'd grown accustomed to guides they were now cut off from.

Until they found a way up one of the paths on their own they were stuck, and even then there would be nightmares, while sleeping and waking, night sweats, the all-consuming feeling that they had had something more real than the waking world and now it was gone. If they stayed in the dead forest looking for what was missing, they would never wake up.

She wrapped her arms around herself in a tight hug, shifted her neck where that familiar ache was building to a buzzing nerve-itch she couldn't scratch. She'd been here before. Felt it herself but also watched others suffer through. Her own separation sickness had ended quickly. When the sickness had faded, she was quick to fill in the gaping hole with a new project, a whole new planet to make her forget and keep living.

Quin was like these other ones. Worse—she'd been the one to start it all. An exciting interface opportunity, in their early training turned nightmare when Quin seized up and couldn't break contact with the tree. She bit her tongue. Pink froth covered her mouth and still she gripped the trunk of the old, fading cypress as if it were a lifeline instead of the thing killing her. Waters panicked, ripped off her mushroom, and Quin had dropped like a sandbag. Orders came in to halt training, extract each of their symbionts. Quin slept through all of it, tossing and speaking gibberish in her sleep.

There were ten of them in the car, some sleeping but not unconscious. She'd spoken to them, helped Waters explain what was happening in no more words than necessary to get them moving. The best of them were disoriented. One who could speak identified herself as Ithaca. She was a study in warm shades of brown from her skin to her disheveled, illness-tangled hair. Her round eyes flashed silent fury. Questions bubbled up from that anger, questions about Quin. Where was she? Where were their implants?

Waters had turned, his expression softer than the situation called for. His tension had grown as moments ticked by but he didn't snap.

"Yes, Private Khan, Sgt. Fleury is waiting up in the shift drive, with all the—explanations, and options, If you'll just buckle up."

The girl's disorientation slowed her, as if the bridge between thought and action were blocked with too many impulses. Her eyes eventually cleared and she strode into the elevator and sat down. It was taking too long. More followed her until the elevator was full. They all recognized Waters and responded as if they trusted him, small favors.

They had to move faster. She had to move faster. She directed a cot with its flashing lights and beeps of data towards the elevator, steered a second that was malfunctioning. But the work didn't still the flow of memories. The image of Quin in the infirmary was emblazoned inside of her skull and with it the bleak absence of color to the world as her own mushroom died. No tree contact, no mushrooms. Quin had struggled and she had watched.

Until one day the paperwork was complete and the transport to Genti-6 was waiting outside. They said Quin wouldn't wake up and she believed them.

The girl on the malfunctioning cot moaned, turned her face. A trailing tattoo of delicate leaves decorated her jawline. She pulled against the straps on the transport harness and then her eyes opened. Quin was supposed to wake up like that. Chase placed both hands on the sides of the girl's flushed face. She couldn't help but smile as if she knew her. She knew, at least, what she'd been through. "You're awake."

The girl's eyes, large and blue, widened in her face. She leaned forward and vomited between her feet. "Then . . . Why the hell am I still moving." She pushed out the words between panting breaths.

Chase hurried to unfasten the straps so she could move then scrubbed at her own eyes and found them wet, her cheeks were too. "Because we're taking you to Quin. And she's going to get you new implants if that's what you want."

The girl folded at the waist looking like she might throw-up again but instead she held up a shaky hand and then she leaned up halfway. "Say that again?"

The elevator was made to hold ten at a time. They'd have to hope that it would carry fifteen. Waters loaded them in one at a time, lifted the ones still comatose off of their cots and wrapped their dead weight into seats as the sweat collected on his brow.

"I can help move them." She grabbed hold of his sleeve as he passed.

"You can watch the doors because time is up."

"They'll load in faster with more help."

He was struggling with the largest of the comatose apprentices, a young man that was several inches taller and wider than him despite his youth. "This is the last. The others are strapping themselves, shit–" He juggled the boy's weight and Chase stepped in, shouldering as much as she could so that between them they moved faster and with less chance of a fall.

The last straps clicked before they heard rapid footsteps from behind. Two guards had their feet blocking the door open, and the commander stood with two more, one held James Élysée's restrained arms. Bruises bloomed over his right eye. It was swollen shut, and the left side of his face was misshapen from a dislocated jaw. He was still smiling.

The commander took a step closer, then stopped. Waters had his handheld device up to the control screen for the elevator. "I'll override the doors if I have to, Ma'am. This thing's going up."

"To Sergeant Fleury?" She sneered when she said it and he could see a sheen of wild anticipation in her eyes.

"You think I'd bring her back where you could put your hands on her? No. I'm just collecting these kids for medical care and compensation, since you don't seem worried about the safety of your recruits." He faked a laugh and Chase tried to keep her face blank.

The woman's gaze grew cold, stiff. "They were being rehabilitated. They'll be honorably discharged."

"Oh, and their families thanked for their sacrifices, I guess, if those three don't wake up."

"Of course."

Waters moved faster than Chase would have thought he could. He was old, longevity treatments notwithstanding, and had always moved with a languid laziness that spoke of early retirement. Now he was at the door of the Elevator car before the two guards could react. He ducked down and shoved with his shoulder with the full force of his weight behind it. The guard went sprawling on the tile floors, the back of his head bouncing off the hard surface with a concussive impact. He was back up quickly, a reaction born of training but he staggered, disoriented by the blow.

Chase didn't waste time watching. She reached into her belt and retrieved her utility knife. Instead of rushing in, she slipped to the side and pressed the tip of her blade against the second guard's back until she felt the skin give underneath the fabric. The guard froze in place. The woman didn't cry out, but she did reach behind her. Chase ducked the blow and shoved the knife harder, felt the fabric tear. Her voice came out just above a whisper. "Get out of our way or I keep pushing."

The guard broke away and Chase let her retreat across the room, the doorway unblocked. The commander surged forward with her other guards. They drew weapons, but the door was half-closed before they had them out. Chase held her knife out, the skin of her knuckles blanched white against the all-purpose tool turned weapon.

If the ERF carried larger weapons or had walked in a minute sooner, they'd have all had their arms tied behind their backs with General Élysée. Chase shoved the knife into the sheath and then strapped herself into her seat for the ride up. If she vomited into the vacuum tube next to her seat, she could blame any number of things. The slow removal of gravity in seeping layers, the adrenaline crashing through her body, it was picturing Quin and Lumina down there, with their mushrooms peeled off and discarded like medical waste, that finally did it.

LUMINA unstrapped and pushed herself towards the front of the ship. She glided through the microgravity environment as if in slow-motion, one hand pushed harder creating torque and sending her into a spin. It was better than swimming, this time without the hindrance of gravity, but it was making her sick to her stomach, nauseous, and her feet were tingling with pins and needles the longer they were docked here. Still, she couldn't help but grin back at Drinian as the spin turned her midair.

It was a short flight to the front seat of the ship where Quin rested in her own seat, head tilted to the left to accommodate her mushroom and the new fruiting bodies growing from its back. Her hands cradled the back of her head, a relaxed posture, but her eyes were alert.

Lumina came to a stop using the hand grips on the side of the ship and the backs of the seats. She pulled herself into a front row seat then strapped in. They were alone except for Drinian. Which didn't count.

"Quin?"

"Hmm?" Quin's brow creased.

"I need to know about you and Chase. I asked you once—"

Now the politely quizzical expression shifted to concern tinged with irritation. "And my answers did not satisfy then?"

Lumina pressed ahead despite the thump thumping of her pulse in her ears. "Why do you keep writing to her when she doesn't answer? Why doesn't she? Why won't she talk about the time before I was born and why—"

"You kept reading them then. Letters that are not yours?"

It was an inevitable question. Lumina knew it would come if she pressed to know more. "Yes I—I read them all. I found them and I read them all and then I read them again and I still don't understand it. Sometimes I think you love her but she doesn't love you back. There are so many letters. And then she answers and I think maybe she does and it's you who doesn't, because you never come. I know she wants you there with us, at least—"

"At least what?" Quin's voice was low, barely audible.

"At least when she isn't in the caves, or the next quadrant they're seeding, or enriching, or whatever else."

"Hmm . . . perhaps you have answered all of your own questions, chéri. Or perhaps you are not supposed to be reading letters that are not yours and not meant for you to understand." The anger was clear and sharp in her eyes and then gone as quickly as it had flared up.

Lumina's cheeks felt hot and her ears burned with shame—the slow burn of rejection. "I'm—sorry."

Quin was silent and then her words came out softer, gentler. "So this is what the questions have been about, the looks, the curiosity. You want Chase and I to be something more than we are, because you read old words, old feelings, and now they are burning a hole in your belly like they do mine."

Quin stared purposefully towards the back of the ship. Lumina followed her gaze to where Drinian sat fidgeting with the implant equipment from his bags. He was tapping the side of an implant syringe looking close at it through a magnifying loop. Lumina couldn't help but smile.

Quin turned Lumina's face with a hand on her cheek. "Chase and I bonded over mycelial networks, speaking through plants we touched for two years of training. We linked mycelium directly using our implants, spending time in each other's heads, something like what you and Drinian have done. It is a bond, yes, a little like the familiarity of children growing up together, shared experiences, sometimes as strong as an addiction."

Was that all it was? Lumina looked back at Drinian. Familiarity wasn't what it felt like when he took her hand at just the moment she'd thought how empty her own felt—addiction? Was that what it was? The warm fluttering of heated anxiety that catching his eyes on her engendered. The thought weighed her down, compressed her lungs as if gravity had descended on her internal organs. "Is that why you write all those letters? Familiarity? Addiction? Which is it?"

Quin shrugged and looked out the star-filled window that faced away from the bright blue of Earth. "Rubama—perhaps, Lumi-Chér—it is both things. I am addicted to the familiarity of her."

The heaviness in her chest deepened into an ache that Lumina recognized. It pushed to the surface, unearthed itself like hidden bodies. "And me? Am I familiar? Something you made to fill an obligation. Just to end an addiction or feed it?" Her voice wasn't her own. She heard a tremor marking her words, and a brittleness. If she said anything else it would break.

"That is . . . that is not what I was saying." Quin pressed a hand at the back of her neck where the implant stage started and then she raised it higher to stroke the restless mushroom. It waved and twitched as if it might climb off of the stage and duck through its harness. It was suffering like Quin was, isolated by the gloves.

"Okay, fine. You were saying it's not love. You told me yourself to be careful of whatever this thing with Drinian is, because we were mind-linked and so it isn't real. It's a trick, just patterns and hormones and whatever—and now you're saying that's what happened with you and my mother and well—oh look here I am! So yeah, whatever you *think* you're saying, that's what you said and I get it." Lumina struggled with the straps, pulled at them until her hands remembered the way. She got up before Quin could say anything else.

There had to be somewhere to go, somewhere far enough away. Drinian was the farthest. He would know what she was feeling, some of it anyway, he would touch her hand and she'd feel that flutter of warmth and then she'd hate herself for it. It was fake. Addiction . . . familiarity.

She was frozen in the middle of the ship, unstrapped but holding onto the seat grips when the airlock hissed. Someone was coming through. If she'd felt sick before, this was worse. A spike of adrenaline froze her in place.

"Shhh . . . They found my apprentices. That's all it is." But Lumina heard the fear in Quin's voice, and her sigh of relief as the airlock opened. It was Chase in the doorway. Quin had that look on her face, the one Lumina recognized as she'd gotten old enough to really see it. She gave it new names now, the ones Quin used —familiarity, addiction. It felt hollow, inadequate, but then the look was gone, replaced by relief, and concern.

Waters pushed past Chase with the first of the apprentices who couldn't walk on their own. A tangle-haired brunette he called Ithaca. He snapped fingers in front of her eyes and mumbled to Chase. "She was better before."

"They'll go in and out like this for a while."

The girl was limp, only half-conscious. Her eyes wandered the ship as they brought her in, her lips slack.

"Please, everyone strap themselves in, help the ones who can't. We need to move and we need to get to where we are going. Quin . . . Do we have a course? There's no more time to think about it."

"Yes. I know where we're going. I've known it for a long time." Quin took Ithaca from Waters and strapped her into a seat. She whispered something Lumina couldn't hear, comforted the girl's sudden flood of tears. Then she pulled herself to the exit to help with the next one. "There's only one place we can go. A place with trees, the only one with grown, healthy ones."

CHAPTER 17

THE FOREST OF GIANTS

Quin walked ahead, the footsteps of Chase, Lumina, and Drinian close behind, muffled by the spongy layers of grass and decaying leaf litter. The resinous scent of redwood and Douglas fir, mingled with musty black oak rose from the imprints their feet made on the unmarred forest floor. Red-capped Amanita muscaria made trails through the undergrowth, their red-and-white dappled heads protruding through willing soil. Golden Chanterelles sported wavy caps and exposed gills like the fibrous baleen of whales and colorful Turkey Tails made fairy-sized steps up the bark of fallen Ponderosa pines. Mycelium spread so thick under the brittle, puzzle-piece bark and the mattes of loamy soil that it clung and held like spider-silk under their feet.

The trees were calling hard. That cool presence spreading out from their trunks like a symphony of conversation diffusing into the air. They had things to say to her and she was desperate to listen. Her skull throbbed with the urge. It was the thirst of the dying. The very fibers of her nerves were parched. It was a hunger that gnawed the tissues of her own muscles and bone making desperate repast of her body.

This wasn't a place she could risk an interface. Not as she was. The forest of giants was for Lumina, and the other young ones once they were ready, not for her.

The soft bristles of a cedar sapling brushed her jacket as she passed. She couldn't help but extend a gloved hand. The numb, touch-blind sensation of needles on leather intensified the hungry ache in her nerves. It wasn't Synesis who prodded her to reach out a hand. That was how it should have been, those subtle urges and tastes of neuro-chemical motivators to push and encourage her to bridge the gap, to press her hands into the damp soil of the rhizosphere around the roots of giants or lean her face against their rough trunks and make the connection. It wasn't Synesis, no. Her mushroom was quieter with each passing moment. The trees were all around them and she couldn't touch them.

Too long. It had been too long.

Tracks of fear skipped through her like a stone skipping across water, then sank to the bottom. That was where heavy things came to rest, to be buried in silt and forgotten until something came along to dredge it up. Synesis was too small in her mind, still there but not speaking to her, not asserting her own needs and interests. She was beginning to decline, like the trees they'd killed. To not respond to such a large arboreal presence could mean nothing else.

She put up a hand to halt their caravan. The meadow ended here. There were clusters of saplings at the drip-line of the mother trees—and she had to know. Verdant, palmate-leaved lupines pawed at her like grasping fog-damp hands. The plants had gone to seed but the pods were still green and fresh. They dwarfed her, nearly four feet tall and thick as the saplings she approached with purpose. But these smaller trees might not be enough to revive her mushroom. She bypassed the cluster of saplings for the first of the larger trees.

The oxygen was dense, heady and dizzying but not enough to make her sick.

The tree she approached wasn't as large as the ones they'd find in the center of the forest, maybe a hundred feet tall and twenty feet in diameter, a young sequoia that was clearly large enough to be one of the primary nodes of the forest. The uppermost portion of the trunk was broken off and scorched from a lightning strike, the remains of it decaying in the clearing they'd crossed.

She inched closer, reached out a hand. She could feel the barest tickle of its voice in the air—or was it memory from the first and only time she'd come here, her first communication with the mother trees? The all-encompassing flow of knowledge that had come close to drowning her, echoed in her memory. She could feel that again, hold it in her mind if she pressed on.

The dark red bark looked damp from a thick

morning fog the last of which crept at the bases of the trees as a spectral mist. Droplets of water fell from the canopy, brushed her cheeks and shoulders. That bark would be cool and soft against her palm. It would revive Synesis—and it might kill the tree, spread her sickness into its roots and contaminate this place. . . .

She pulled back, balled the shaking hand into a fist at her side, put on her glove and stepped back. How had her resolve slipped so far so fast?

Chase came up next to her. Worry lit her eyes and pulled her brows into an expression that made the shuddering ache in Quin's gut sharper.

"Quin? You're going to have to soon, aren't you?"

She flinched away from the question. The concern in Chase's voice brought her own words back to taunt her. Familiarity . . . addiction. Was that the root of their connection? Could it be boiled down to such narrow words when there were so many within the universe of language? But that was only what Lumina had heard, what she'd let her think, not the whole of what she'd said—and the truth was that she didn't know what she felt anymore, or what she wanted.

She turned away from the tree, still not meeting Chase's gaze. "It is that or I let her die. Synesis or this . . . the woods, the last one because I could not build another. They told me how, and I could not." The words felt hollow. There was no language for this.

"Okay. Okay. I'm not arguing with you, but you thought we should come here for some reason, yes?"

Chase didn't force herself into her line of sight. But her words pierced the veil anyway.

"A place to hide. And a place for Lumina and the apprentices. They will learn how. So long as we start them slow, on the saplings—J'espere—I hope it will work."

"And for you?"

"It was never going to be a solution for me."

"What? That isn't an answer. It's not even an option."

Quin shrugged. The gesture was an understatement, and she wondered if Chase felt it. It was taking everything she had not to shout, not to take her by the shoulders, and then what? Tell her everything that was eating her from the inside like a colony of termites? Her control was slipping. Bitterness building into anger, into fury. It was so close to the surface now that a single scratch could set it loose.

"What are you going to do? What can I do?" Chase dropped her voice to a whisper. "Either answer my question or tell me what's wrong so I can figure it out, because it isn't just these obstacles. You aren't yourself, haven't been yourself."

The rest of the group had scattered around the edge of the clearing, some had entered the shade under the canopy of mature sequoias. Waters was in discussion with Drinian, who was nodding without looking up at him as if digesting and planning as he listened.

Chase didn't let up. "You brought us here for a reason. I refuse to believe we can't help you here!"

"I did, but I shouldn't have! Not for myself." It was more of an outburst than Quin meant to allow herself. She winced and then pulled in a slow shaky breath to regroup. It was more than Synesis should have allowed her. Synesis did nothing, said nothing, no surge of soothing neuro-chemicals to still her trembling or clear her thoughts. That acknowledgement of fact brought on a storm of shivers. She crossed her arms. "I . . . brought us here because . . . the trees here thrive, succeed, for more than two centuries they have."

Her voice shook along with the rest of her body. She couldn't stop it.

Chase wrapped her arms around her. *She couldn't do that*—Quin recoiled, wrenched herself from Chase's grip as if the touch had burned her. She couldn't be touched, couldn't be held.

Hurt and confusion bloomed in Chase's eyes. "Whatever this is, we can fix it. None of us are quitting, see?" Chase gestured at the scattered remnants of the project, some of them still unconscious, others just unresponsive and Quin felt the urge to laugh or cry, maybe both at the same time.

She held back. Did it matter what she did now that the end was so close?

But Chase didn't stop. She encroached again, spoke quieter as if maybe Quin was afraid the others would hear their conversation. "I think you need to contact one of the trees, a quick download for Synesis. You're getting sicker."

The tree she had almost touched stood tall as if

mocking her. She didn't bother to hide the fear-cloaked bitterness that colored her voice. "And if it kills them? The whole forest? For myself? I would rather keep these gloves on and try to wait out the sickness, or let the death take me with it."

Chase flinched from her words and she felt a stab of regret.

Chase's next reply was gentle, carefully measured. "I think this is where I'm usually the one throwing out dramatic proclamations and you stand there like a tree to ground me. So considering the tables have flipped— this is the part where I tell you that you're looking at this from upside down, seeing the wrong side of things."

"I don't want to kill anything else ..."

"Okay, well, from what I remember of your stories, these trees are a lot stronger than anything you've been able to kill, stronger than anything else that you or the rest of us have ever linked up with."

"I didn't think you'd read those ones."

"What? I read all of them. I told you that. I just—"

Quin finished for her, the words boiling up from a place of resentment she couldn't admit was there. "— Don't always answer." Of course she'd felt moments, twinges, but those were weakness, weren't they, self-doubt, loneliness—and she'd always talked herself through them.

"Yeah."

Chase tilted an uncomfortable smile up at her, warm and genuine. Her eyes were greener under a canopy of trees. Quin couldn't find her own smile to offer up. She was searching for the next step, the next words.

On one path she admitted to upsetting Lumina, to misrepresenting her feelings, on another she vomited up the aching fears that had lodged deep in her head sometime after she'd planted the sapling orchard on Genti-6 and Lumina had accused her of not wanting her. Shadow conversations, none of them things she could say to Chase without hurting them both. All paths looked like bramble patches full of ankle-grabbing briars that would draw blood if they caught skin. It wasn't the time for these conversations.

It was never the time.

She pressed her fingers into her temples and rubbed. Broke away from Chase's eyes and looked for Waters and Drinian.

"They're waking them up—" She strode to the circle of reclining apprentices. They were spread out on the leaf litter of the forest floor and Drinian was making his way around the circle administering inoculations of mushroom culture into their Implant stages. Waters was assisting. He watched the small portable monitors on their wrists for imbalances in their vital signs. Lumina was nowhere in the small gathering and Quin's heart rate ticked up.

Fear prodded her. She turned this way and that, ducked her head under sapling boughs until she saw her. The fear wasn't unfounded. Lumina was reaching a hand towards a massive sequoia, close to touching. "Arrete! You're not ready, Chér."

The sudden shout startled the girl and she froze. Her hand hovered a foot from the bark of the tree. "Chase, can you please collect our child? Bring her to the circle if you have to drag her—tell her we need her help."

Chase passed her, squeezed her hand and moved to collect Lumina. But there was no time to watch her go. Jordan shook with the violent tremors of what looked like a seizure. She fought Waters's hands, where he held her down. She would hurt herself if he didn't. Her eyes were rolled in her face, blank and unseeing.

Quin was on her knees by her side faster than anyone else could get there. Drinian turned worry-wide eyes in their direction. He couldn't help. His hands were busy as he injected another batch of inoculant into another port, this one Ronin's.

Quin held up black-glove covered hands. Frustration, adrenaline and the beginnings of separation sickness made her shake, though less than the girl jerking on the forest floor. "Merde!! She'll reject the implant. I can't help her through like this!—"

A hand on her shoulder. Lumina was at her side. "But I could. I've been through it, or something like it anyway. I have practice."

This wasn't how it was supposed to be, putting these things on Lumi. Quin scowled but then she looked at Jordan's pale face, the clammy look of her sweating forehead. Chase stood next to Lumina, blanched of color, and she nodded.

"Do it!"

Waters provided the physical link, the tubing and mycelial graft to connect them through Jordan's implant stage and the hyphae of Lumina's free-growing mushroom. Lumina's eyes fluttered closed, a frown of concentration creasing her brow. Jordan's eyes followed as if by example and she stilled. Her heart rate slowed and the shaking subsided.

Drinian made his way around the circle. The implants were beginning to grow in, too small to see above the margins of their implant stages. A bright, fruit-yeast scent of growth filled the clearing. The recipients looked to be sleeping, but Quin knew better. The subtle smiles and twitching eyelids . . . they were in communication with their newborn symbionts.

She wrapped her arms around her legs and let half a sigh escape. There was a choice to be made here and there wasn't much time to do it if Synesis was declining. There was a moment back there, surrounded by soaring conifers, when she'd almost been willing to risk the forest for Synesis—for herself. If not that, what was she willing to sacrifice? There were Lumina's trees in the ship, and they might be enough for a few days, even weeks, but they would die at her hand and then what? She could not live as a parasite.

She was surrounded by new implant bearers, and they were all no better than children. Who would teach them when she was gone? And would they fare better than she when the last of the trees went the way of Earth? This place might remain if she left without harming it, a single sanctuary in the cosmos.

She caressed the velvety back of her mushroom with trembling hands. Too warm. The small body was feverish and gave little response. A shiver, a subtle purr. It was imperceptible enough to be a combination of imagination and wishful thinking. Synesis was the only mature implant and she was slipping into silence. She had to hold out a little longer. For the apprentices to be settled, for Lumi to be ready to learn from the elders, and for her to think.

IT WAS a siren song at full volume, weaving through Lumina like wild chords played into the gaps between her cells. The trees wanted to speak to her, to tell her everything, and she ached to listen. Her mushroom sang along with them, coaxing her, pressing her, and making certain she knew that it would feel very good to link with trees this old, just a little taste of dopamine, another step closer, fingers reaching out towards red sequoia bark and she would have all of it, the answers and the reward.

But they were watching her close, another step and they would call her back to the circle where the apprentices were sleeping off their new implants while their mushrooms grew in. She could still taste Jordan's thoughts but they were fading already, faster than they had with Drinian; their connection had been much longer. This time it was just enough to pull Jordan out of the panic she was caught in—so Drinian said—from the sudden shift from unconsciousness to a link with a new implant. She'd been lost in her own mind, grieving, and coming back into her body was too much.

That seemed right. It matched with what Lumina had felt in Jordan's mind, panic, confusion—she couldn't seem to decide what was real and what was delusion and so she fought with the implant as it tried to connect. But now she was still and resting with the others. Lumina felt her way around the bits of the girl that were still embedded in her after the connection was broken: a teasing sense of humor that could be cutting, something else that was even stronger, a protectiveness for her own that came before anything else—friends, family, the trees—And then there was the blurred and shifting self-image that clung in her mind more than anything else, a flashing smile, hair that changed in length and color and a body that was neither woman, nor man, sometimes both. Lumina knew where all of Jordan's tattoos were, and it made her blush hot under the tree that was still whispering that cool breeze of a beckoning song.

She leaned back and gazed at thick twisting branches wide enough to be trees themselves. Was this what Quin meant about the connection building familiarity, addiction? She'd have Jordan in her head now and feel like there were feelings between them that weren't built of anything real? Just implant mediated mimics . . . chemical signals and the memories burnt in deeper than they normally would be.

The ground under her was pillow-soft with

deciduous and conifer loam. Hummocks of moss and fern grew in thick patches. She could dig her fingers into the soil as she had seen Quin do in the little sapling orchard before she'd gotten sick and started wearing gloves. Would they notice, and would it be the same as touching the tree itself? She knew about mycelial networks, but she couldn't *know*. She hadn't tasted them. If these mother trees were connected to all of the younger trees, all the way down to the seedlings —would tapping into the mycelium be like talking to the mother trees or to the saplings. Would it matter where she tapped in? Right next to the base of this large one, or she could sink her fingers in between the tiny seedlings growing at the edge of the larger tree's dripline.

Where were Chase and Quin now? Gathered with the apprentices, with Drinian tending to the new symbionts. She brushed away the top layer of leaves, toyed with the damper layers with her fingertips. An electric tingling teased her fingertips like touching the tip of her tongue to a battery, more like static. If she pushed her fingers deeper into the rhizosphere it would come clear, but then what? Could she download from the mother tree that way? A ripple of fear mixed with the feeling of electric whispers from the ground. Quin thought it would be too much, and she'd drown in it. But that was before; she had a mushroom now.

A smile pulled at her lips at the thought, warm and full, and echoed by that bright presence in her mind that grew more lush as the hours passed. With soil covered fingers she prodded the many branched growth that had sprouted from the back of her neck. The tissue was soft and spongy, a light down covering the creature. It was nothing like Quin's but still very much alive, evidenced by how it swayed and purred at the attention. "What do you think? Should we talk to them?" She eyed the nearest large tree with longing—close enough to touch. "Or should I wait?"

The answer was immediate and emphatic, completely wordless but easier to understand than the clearest speech.

Yes! Talk to them now.

But the thud of footsteps made Lumina pull her fingertips out of the topsoil and brush them off on her overalls.

"You ah . . . okay?" Drinian stood over her, hands in his pockets, a quizzical glint in his eyes that shifted from her face to the mushroom on her neck, to the loosened soil that was scattered onto her clothes. He wore a smile that was uncertain as his shifting gaze.

She pressed her lips together and looked away. There was an ache when she did. If they were still connected, he would hear her thoughts and he wouldn't have to ask. Or was that why he was here, because he still noticed when she was feeling off, scared, conflicted. There was no other reason to ask. But with the distance between them, he wouldn't feel her answer and she could lie to him if it she wanted. "Yeah. Just bored I guess."

He tilted his head and shifted his feet, rubbed his

fingers across his lips as if tasting her answer for accuracy. He nodded, but the smile was gone. He crouched next to her.

Lumina's breath caught and she felt her whole body warm. She wasn't sure if it was embarrassment or alarm or something else. He was supposed to go back to the group, satisfied with her answer, not zero in.

"So, um. You brought Jordan out of that fast. She's good now, waking every few minutes and she knows who she is and where she is."

"Oh . . . good then, right?"

Drinian chuckled. "Yeah, really good. But are *you* good? Or you feeling the rip-aways?"

The word he used for it sent another little twinge or unease through her belly that spread into a wave of nausea, the physical manifestation of a feeling she wanted to ignore. It tasted like loss. "The what?"

"Rip-aways. I wanted a better word for separation sickness, you know. Cut the link and sometimes you get the rip-aways. The look on your face says yes."

She shrugged and looked away. He picked up her hand, turned it over and brushed bits of pine-needle and soil out of the creases in her palm. She pulled it away and tucked both hands under her knees where he couldn't find them.

"Oh, oh well—you have it worse this time, or maybe —maybe I've done something?"

She felt like curling in tighter, like a fern frond growing in reverse and reverting to its smallest, tightest furl, instead she opened her eyes and caught his with an unwavering stare. "Drinian, I can't tell what's . . . what's from a mushroom link and what's from me, what's you and what's just familiar, or easy, or comfortable. Now I have Jordan mixed up in there too and I can't feel where my edges end and others begin."

"Okay, well, it's um—it's been awhile since we had our—our link up. For me, what's left is a knowing and a caring. There's nothing fake or simulated about that."

Lumina felt his words like a sudden inrush of wind that only added to the tumult. Still, her cheeks flushed with heat. She forced a heavy sigh. "But it is, isn't it?! The neurochemical transmitters that the mushroom uses to ease, or soothe, or motivate, all that. It isn't just us. It's like an addiction, isn't it?"

Drinian's lips pulled into a half smile. The corners of his mouth tipped up then down as the smile shifted with the staccato flow of thought and emotion. "Well ah . . . love is, all emotion is—neurotransmitters working on the mind. If the source matters to you and you have this ah—symbiont then maybe you'll, well you'll be . . . unable to trust any feeling or, any want— that's going to be difficult." He searched for her hand with his eyes before remembering she'd hidden it away. Resignation colored his expression and he dropped his hands into his lap.

She closed her eyes and spoke into the darkness behind her eyelids. Closing off, denying that she wanted to grab his hand and lean into him felt wrong. "Guess so."

A SMALL FIRE, built of dead wood and forest debris flickered in a circle of scavenged rocks. The wavering firelight at their backs hid Drinian's startled expression and turned his gangly shape into a silhouette. It couldn't hide his shift in body-language or the way he wrung his hands and then tried to hide the motion in crossed arms.

Chase pulled at Quin, took her farther from the shared campsite under the high canopy of the old-growth forest.

Quin was never angry like this. But now curses were flowing from her lips in more languages than Chase could translate. She could guess at their meaning. She knew the cause. Drinian had jumped at the idea of inoculating Chase—her own idea—He was anxious and ready, and Quin was furious.

Her black gloved hands pressed against her eyes and then dropped to her sides. It had to be terror that fueled an anger so hot, Chase knew that much, she just didn't know what Quin was so afraid of. "You need my help. Lumina needs my help. And I was a linguist once."

"Yes, and you gave it up. You still suffer from the separation—I see it in your face, the flashbacks, the way you grip your neck or freeze up from the pain. You want that again? More of it, maybe you won't wake up. Maybe you won't be able to take a second implant at all. Then what?!"

Chase didn't flinch from the sharp stare that was usually so gentle but now roiled with emotion. "Then we see. We figure it out as we go. Like a mycelial network. We withdraw, reroute. You tried again when Waters approached you. You'd almost died and you did it again anyway. You put yourself right back into it and now you're acting like I've lost my mind."

"It's not like you to do this. Genti-6, Lumina, those are your worlds."

She bit back a sharper response. She had to remember that this wasn't Quin, not entirely. "And it isn't like you to make decisions for me. You never have. In fact you've asked so little of me I've—Well, I've sometimes wished you'd ask more."

"Le afhem."

"No, you don't understand. It's fine. But this isn't your choice, and you and Drinian made this same decision for your apprentices without being able to get their full consent. You can't tell me not to help you. Not this time."

She watched Quin's expression shift, the wounding in her eyes at the surfacing of the same memory that pulsed in her own. The day that Quin had attempted a download from a dying tree, brought in from a forest populated by the corpses of trees—victims of a climate that could no longer sustain them in the places they were rooted. If both of us try we don't have someone to get help—*let me do it myself* . . . Those were Quin's words, and Chase had listened. She had held back. And Quin had to be wrenched away from the tree, frothing and kicking and screaming gibberish, then silent, comatose.

Quin threw up her hands. Her already shadowed eyes darkened with this fresh wound. She stopped pacing. "Go then. Tell Drinian to inoculate you too. But you are not an island—an individual—not a tree paved into solitude. If you suffer, Lumina suffers and I—" The words cut off, and Chase watched her close her eyes before turning away.

"And you? Is this you protecting us? Protecting yourself? Or is our bond a vestigial thing you want to cut off . . . past Quin and Chase. Because you're pushing me out."

Quin looked frozen in the dim of oncoming twilight this far from the flickering of the fire that warmed and lit their campsite. She took another step and then locked in place a second time. Chase's breath caught in her chest.

"I don't think you need to ask me that, Chéri Mwen . . . But you have a thing to do. Allons-y—Be on with it, if I cannot stop you."

"I wouldn't ask if I didn't have to." But the distance between Quin's retreating back now wreathed in shadow, and Chase's smaller form, bare arms wrapped around her chest and covered in goose-flesh, took her words.

Drinian sat by the fire waiting, ready with the inoculation, but his eyes flicked back to the shadowy edge of the campsite, Quin's path out of the circle of light into the near-dark of the forest. "Is she um—?"

"Going to flay you alive if you do this?"

"Yeah—well—you of course are your own completely autonomous, um being, but—"

She laughed softly, the sound of it lightening the space between them. "Yeah, I am. And she knows that, but she isn't well, and that's all the more reason to do this." She straddled the rough bark of the make-shift seat, a broken chunk of decaying log pulled in closer to the fire along with several others to make a ring around the center of their camp. She turned her back to him and bent her head forward, then braced herself for the placement of a new implant stage and the inoculation.

Her bare arms trembled, welted and itching from insect bites. She pulled in a slow breath. The smoke from the fire stung her eyes but the smell of burning pine, and cedar formed a cloak to drape her nerves. She imagined it seeping into her through her pores and into her mind to pave the way for the deeper changes to come.

No going back. She shivered again, and then settled as Drinian's hands worked. He secured the pliable hardware of the implant stage.

"My hands are cold, sorry." He mumbled as he worked, blew on his hands at regular intervals.

"It's fine." She searched the ring of seats around the fire, the bodies there, mostly sleeping but some in quiet conversation. Waters and two of the apprentices were telling stories, watching the stars. Lumina wasn't there.

She cleared her throat, waited for the quiet chime of Drinian's testing equipment as another signal came through the stage and back to his device. "Do you know where Lumina is?"

"Mm-hmm . . ." There was no delay to his response but his voice had that far away, distracted quality of a split-focus. "She is—walking in the woods with ah—Jordan, who I might add—happily has ah, woken from her implant fever as good as new it seems. Success rates with this strain—Quin-Lumina's implant strain—are quite good."

"Oh. And you're worried about that—the new connection she's made?"

Drinian laughed. "Ah . . . you are perceptive, you are, but no, no. I feel her, conflicted—*she's* conflicted and that, that worries me for her."

Chase closed her eyes, held still as a mother tree while he inserted the tip of the syringe for the inoculation.

"She's going to figure it out . . . I think . . . but maybe not . . . alone—" Her train of thought continued past the ability to form words, or the need to. Speech evaded her as her body grew more still, and her mind expanded to welcome the new presence.

The spread of hyphae between her neurons was a tingling, awakening sensation. Where there was only Chase before, now there was another. Connections left dormant since the death of her first mushroom, connections that ached like many billion severed limbs reached out to the new occupant. The tension in her shoulders melted away and her jaw unclenched. The whole of her released as absence filled with presence.

This one tasted—or felt—of cinnamon and sun-ripened fruit, a steady sort, whispering affirmation and encouragement to the ebb and flow of Chase's slideshow of thoughts on display for a friend who'd been absent.

This was the introduction phase, the slow bonding of symbiotic partners that was deepest, most focused in the early moments but would continue in the background for the first several days as her mushroom grew in.

She opened her eyes what could have been hours later. The flames of the fire were still high and Drinian watched her expectantly from the same position as before. It was minutes then, not long at all, and she already felt they had been joined for a lifetime. A tremor of anxiety thrilled through her nerves and traversed their connection. Quin wasn't wrong; losing a second mushroom would be even harder. Her new friend placed a mental hand, a tendril of comfort where the fear had blossomed and she sighed.

This moment is the only one we can count on . . .

She saw the campsite with new eyes. Her people were still missing, scattered, and she felt the attenuation of that distance as an ache that her mushroom echoed, and questioned with a gentle prodding curiosity. Lumina was wandering still, and Quin distancing herself.

She explored the creature in the saddle with tentative hands, still new, its body much smaller than Quin's mature one. The skin was smoother, even more pliable, with none of the fruiting bodies that Quin's had. It was familiar and new all at once, unique from her first, the soft skin of its back rumpled with wrinkles of redundant skin. The layer of down that adorned a mushroom's back was long enough to be fur on this one. Even the free appendages, just long enough to reach her neck, had tufts of silken fur. Her touch lingered, exploring what was acutely other even as it was a part of her, then her thoughts moved. Her hand grew absent-minded even as she pet the creature, a thinking motion. It was time to bring Quin and Lumina back.

TIME WAS UP. Her head pounded, a throbbing multi-sensory assault that pushed Quin farther—faster— through the trees in a desperate stumbling sprint over moss-covered fallen logs and whipping bracken. The dense understory grasped and yanked at her clothing as if speaking to her.

Slow down.

The outer shirt of her uniform was suffocating, holding in the fever-heat that burned her. She tossed it aside. She wanted to shed the gloves as well, but she fought temptation. If it was Synesis pushing her to do it she couldn't tell; the thread between them was too distorted, too tenuous—and how was *that* even possible with sixteen years of mycelial growth inside of her nervous system? They were one ... they were *supposed* to be one. But Synesis's voice wasn't there, and the void of her absence ached. Was she empty now? It was silent in her head and yet, so *loud*. Her own thoughts were deafening. If Synesis *were* still there, cut off from her, she wouldn't hear it through this tumult.

So she ran, faster, harder, until she could no longer hear Chase and Lumina calling for her. The other voices had joined in by the time she could hear them again, clear but distant. Sounds echoed in odd ways through the forest. The trees caught hold of calling voices and moved them away from their source.

She stumbled, caught herself, and allowed her legs to run out beneath her to right her balance. The ground was brackish here and no longer held solid. She fell hard, with a splash of thick mud and decaying leaf-litter. It clung to her. She brushed at the mess painting her skin, breath coming in jagged gusts as she stared into the gloom.

The voices of her friends chased her, so distant, and just ahead was the thing she was running towards. It wasn't in her head when she'd started out, no. She had heard Chase calling and couldn't make herself answer. Tension in her throbbing mind had built until all she could do was run. She wasn't running anywhere. She was just running.

To what end? What purpose did she flee? Or was she running from?

Chase. She ran from Chase and this choice she had made. For so long Chase had stayed distant from the ERF and the forest's decline, only empathizing from a distance. Now, she had forced her way into the line of fire, so to speak. For what? So that she too could suffer the inevitable end? Could Chase not see that Quin was failing? And her mission a dying cause? Questions in her mind beat with a panicked fury. She wanted to scream them, but the forest wasn't an empty space for her to fill with this pain. It was alive with holy presence, the last cathedral of the wild.

Her breath burned chapped lips and stung a throat raw from the force of her respirations. She couldn't stop it—the entanglement that threatened to strangle her loves. She couldn't keep them out of harm's way. Lumina was a mycelial network as much as a girl, and now Chase had joined in this martyrdom. To die with the forest ... she had pictured that end for herself, should she fail the trees. Her stomach lurched with the magnitude of her realizations. It could not be the end for Lumina, and not for Chase. Which meant she could not let Synesis and herself go quietly.

The gloves itched and sweat crept and pooled against her skin. A tall cedar loomed in her path, reality resolving from the dark. She slowed, crumpled at the base of it, pressed her face to the carpet of needles then traced the svelte body of the tree to the sky with her eyes. Wind rustled in those high branches, the lush greenery like a curtain of hair falling over soft shoulders. The gloves would stay on here. She could not be a death sentence for this place. If there was a hope left, she would find it elsewhere.

The ship was ahead. The firelight of the camp sent a

ruddy glow through the trees at her back. There was one place she could take her gloves off without poisoning anyone else, without killing, a last chance if she could be strong enough this time. And maybe, if she did that, Synesis would wake the hell up.

CHAPTER 18

DEEPER, DARKER, FARTHER

"But you aren't like an apprentice the same way that the rest of us are." Jordan held Lumina's hand, those sharp blue eyes, so often hard and cynical, now earnest and awe-filled. "I'd deny it if you told anyone—but you already know I have a case of fungus envy over it. You got a head-start, right? Born with it?" She shook her head and then tilted a smile at Lumina.

Lumina inched their hands closer to the mother tree they crouched in front of, but then she pulled hers away and bit her lips. "You think Quin is wrong? That I could do it now?"

Jordan's wide mouth pulled into a grin. "Better than I could." She trailed her fingers across the top layers of humus, disrupted where their bare knees pressed into it. "I have, what, two years training? Little conversations with baby trees. Ha! Confused baby trees, and then they took my implant and I feel like I have to learn it all over again with this new one." She patted the tiny mushroom symbiont on her neck. It was so pale it glowed. Lumina couldn't decide if the faint glow reflecting on Jordan's skin was more green or blue. It looked like it would luminesce in the dark given the chance.

Jordan's attention was on the ancient tree, her own hand hovering inches away before she pulled back and brushed messy strands of sun-blond hair out of her eyes and back behind her ears. She sighed and Lumina felt herself flinch from her proximity— the smell of her breath was so familiar, the brush of it against her cheeks somehow intimate. "I think, Lumi—that you were made for this."

Lumina felt herself blushing and hated it, the heat spreading through her body and rising to her cheeks. It felt like flattery—too much when they'd known each other so little—but Jordan had been in her head and she in Jordan's, so she couldn't really say that, could she? Not when she'd felt Jordan's heartbeat rushing between them in the shared mind space of a mycelial connection and experienced Jordan's reaction to her firsthand. There was no room for doubting what she knew. And the older girl knew Lumina's own thoughts and impressions of the burning spark of confidence and cynical realism that made Jordan seem like a caricature of strength. She was a study of contradictions and it made Lumina feel like a wide-eyed child.

"I think . . . I think I was an accident. It was an

accident and it scares them—because we don't know enough. Not even Drinian, and he's trying to."

Jordan glanced away. "You talk about Drinian a lot."

Lumina pressed her lips together and lifted her fingers to follow the irregular flowery contours of the creature that had budded at the back of her neck. It was larger still, rumpled and layered like fleshy flower petals or turkey-tail mushrooms, without the expected mammalian body of the implants that Quin and the others had, all of them, smooth creatures with discernible heads, bodies, and multiple stalks that grew into the implant stage where their hyphae found their way into their host's bodies. Her mushroom did have many twisting stalks, some of them growing from her skin, the others waving and growing into more petals. She sighed. It was easy to distract herself with what was happening to her, this transformation that made everyone around her stare—among the uncommon she was now an oddity—but mention of Drinian made her skin heat up again. Her fingers brushed the modified implant stage that he had tailored for her, to help support her less conventional mushroom.

"Do I?" She smiled, followed the many thought paths in her mind that lit up with talk of Drinian. Most were hers and others her mushroom's, a web of memory and positive sensory feedback built not just through their time in the hospital but in the weeks after. He was embedded, entrenched like a symbiont.

Jordan brushed soil off of both of their knees and looked askance at her. "I'm not complaining—he's cool and I feel like—like I know him through you. When you were pulling me out it was like—"

"Like a group effort?"

"Yes! Like that!"

Lumina smiled, that warm-all-over feeling was less frightening now. "Well, he helped me out of the same thing, almost the same."

"You were trapped with the All-Question—piece of it. Fire . . . "

She nodded, wishing now that they were still linked, just as she often did with Drinian—She felt content, less afraid and she wanted Jordan to feel that, and Drinian. Not letting him touch her anymore, hold her hand, or lean against her—it was stupid. The warmth of the moment changed, shifted into an ache so sharp that her breath caught and she held it against the pain. Was this missing Drinian? Was it a tree-missing thing like before?

She had to get Drinian, tell him. Jordan could go, but then she would be alone with the mother tree. Was it her mushroom guiding her hands? One reached for the bark of the mature tree while the other wound her fingers deep into the layers of leafy rhizosphere. She hadn't decided to do it, hadn't committed before it was done.

Thoughts rushed ahead of her into the connection her hands forged with the tree. It was as if she were being drawn out through a syringe plunged deep into her mind. Quin wasn't here. She'd taken the ship somewhere and wasn't answering Waters's attempts to contact her. But she was here—and Chase, and Drinian, and Jordan, all of the apprentices starving for Tree contact with no word of how to go about it safely. *Not the mother trees—it's too much, trè danjere.* There were seedlings here, something they were all more familiar with, but Quin hadn't said whether they could make a connection with them without tapping into the whole forest.

It didn't matter now. She would answer the question for all of them.

The connection shifted from inadvertent upload of her surface thoughts and recent memories, to download. It reversed flow. Now she was the sink instead of the source and everything the mother tree—centuries old—had to share poured into her. Jordan shook her. Lumina sensed her standing, felt the vibrations in the ground as she ran.

Speech escaped Lumina. She was locked in. Her whole body shivered, then vibrated with the intensity of the flow. Her sense of self grew distant, an island, until her last clinging grasp on that too ripped away in a rising tide of unfathomable magnitude.

THE LAST TIME Quin stood in front of the Pain Trees she thought she could force them to learn. Now, she shifted her feet, crouched in front of the gnarled and twisted trees that should have been elders of their species, cypress with their red aromatic bark and thick branching needles.

The Pain Trees weren't the first cypress she'd met. The ancient tree they'd brought to ERF headquarters to study had been a cypress, languishing and uprooted so that she and the others might learn from its final days of life. She had never told anyone what the old cypress had said or tried to explain how it broke her for so long.

Now that she was here with the Pain Trees again, she couldn't keep it out of her head. As soon as her hands had touched bark, the saw blades and axes of countless generations broke her flesh, many small moments of callous destruction became a culmination of war against her kind—*Tree-kind*. The tastes of intimate minglings under the soil had dwindled until she was cut off and blinded. The voices of her people screamed warnings into the twilight of arboreal history. Severed limbs, trunks cut to bleeding stumps until the world turned upside down and her crown was bundled next to the roots of her brethren. Bear, and boar, and bird disappeared. Now the seedlings of her enemies asked why the trees were dying? *Quin* had asked it. The Cypress had answered, and the pain of Earth's obliteration of the forests, the weight of that responsibility and regret, even as humanity sought to back-track, became her own.

These trees before her had a different story, but their suffering was familiar. The idea of teaching them, helping them, was still there in the back of her mind but she kept it tucked away, discarded. Whatever it was these trees needed, she didn't have it. She needed something from them.

Her hands shook as she lifted both towards the stained bark. They should have died as saplings, but they had struggled, pushed forward and persevered. They were still here to answer Quin's questions if she could make them—to connect with Synesis, to revive her if it wasn't too late. She hoped the contact couldn't sicken what was already ill.

What question could these ones answer? What would she ask? She realized there was only one thing that she needed to know. It was the same she would have asked the mother trees on Ross-128B if she could.

"Why isn't it enough?" She whispered the first question as she pressed her bare hands into the bark. The feel of the rusty, sap-soaked flesh didn't repulse her any more than the tree's appearance did, it was just sap, blood was blood. All bodily fluids were the same, a lubricant for the stuff of life. She leaned her forehead against the tree and then wrapped her arms around its girth in a full embrace. *Why isn't it enough?*

A series of images came to her, slow as the seep of sap in winter. It took a moment to understand the difference in how it felt, like listening to garbled speech, or seeing through murky water. These messages weren't being translated by Synesis, instead deciphered by the parts of her brain that already knew. Tree was a language, chemically transferred yes, but it was comprehensible after repeated exposure and translatable only if you knew it like she did. These were messages she'd felt before, things the Pain Trees had always repeated as if stuck in a never-ending loop, not the grand repeating cycles of the All-Question and its answer but tight truncated spirals that fractured, splintered and then repeated. *Pain embedding hyphae of honey-fungus—decay is the new symbiont . . . carving pathways in bark grown spongy, neglected . . . isolation is inevitable . . .*

She didn't argue with their message. That would bring pain. She was here for Synesis to drink in what she needed. Her mind created imagery of the message. Crumbling rot, a fetid soup of dissolution, and Synesis stirred, her presence thickening in Quin's mind like a cool fog in the forest of giants. The mushroom joined the tree's message, doubling and tripling the significance until it was an all-encompassing full-sensory experience.

Quin's skull, hollowed out with white-teeth clacking, became host for symbiotic fungus turned parasite, never giving, only taking. Her skin thickened into bark, sloughed and peeled with black-rot and beetle infestation. She was too tired to argue. She listened, watched, repeated the message back. Her hands grew slick against the tree bark. The sweat of a seeping unease, and an accompanying fever coated her body.

She tried to think past the message, to mind-whisper to Synesis. *Ask them . . . please ask them!* But Synesis didn't answer, and her own inner monologue grew chaotic. *Ask them . . . Ask them what? The questions!*

So you can pull it out of them—the last they have to offer? A dying gasp and you think it should go to you? Where are the children?!!!

It sounded like a scream in her head. Tangled voices, merging and echoing until she couldn't separate them or make sense of whose voices they were. Her own thoughts should have been clear. They weren't. Any clarity she had was eroding under the force of the tree's presence.

Go back and find them!!! She sucked in a breath and forced her eyes open. The questions were lost somewhere in this mental polyphony. If there had been an answer she didn't know it. There were only more questions in her head. Tears seeped from the corners of her eyes down her frozen cheeks, mouth slack and unable to scream even as the many voices screamed inside her. Could she let go, push away from the tree and crawl away? Maybe. But whether she could grab hold again, that was less certain. Light was fading above the horizon and a dense fog came up from the ground to surround the bodies of the Pain Trees. It softened their sharp edges, gentled their shapes.

What—What . . . is . . . missing?! There it was. The question she had come to ask.

A response, at least she felt it as a response, was almost immediate, those first images like slides locking into place in front of a light—PAIN! . . . No, there has to be something else. She shook against the tree and her mind recoiled. *They don't know. This is all they know. You've told them more but you haven't shown them more. GO*

BACK AND FIND THEM! What was Tree and what was Quin? What was Synesis? Anything? She couldn't tell.

She pushed off from the tree's sticky bark and fell back hard. Her skull made a sharp impact with a fallen branch and it drew blood, but worse than that she felt the internal reverberations of fruiting bodies forced off of her mushroom as she landed on her back. The voice of those painful exclamations was the same as the insistent thought, that demanded she run for the ship and make the shift back to the forest. It had sounded like the Pain Trees, or even her own thought in the link but that wasn't right. It was her mushroom—Synesis was awake, wide awake, and she was making it very hard not to run back to the ship. *Go back.*

Okay, I'm listening.

Quin flexed stiff fingers and rubbed at the indentations made by the tree bark. She searched the ground for her gloves. In the mist and gloom they were hard to find; it had to be done by feel and all the while an urgency more insistent than any bodily need built inside her. She abandoned the search. *I don't need them?*

"J'espere . . . mais–"

YOU DON'T NEED THEM.

The message was so large inside of her it felt like suffocating. The gloves had been choking her, sickening her where they clung to her skin as if she needed those pores in her hands to breathe, to eat, to survive.

It was Synesis! Alive! Very alive and awake, and there was no ignoring these demands.

She faced the ship and saw the gloves discarded

beside a granite boulder that jutted out of the fetid soil. They must have slid off of it when she'd tossed them aside. She bent, picked them up, almost discarded them but then shoved them into a pocket.

A sense of urgency propelled her towards the ship—go back and find them—It was definitely coming from Synesis, but the message was foreign, singular, so much more specific than, 'reach out, speak with this tree or that one, rest, no more . . .' These were things she had come to expect her mushroom to compel, nothing so complex as to go somewhere that wasn't within their immediate sight. And the ambiguity of that last part—*find them* . . . It could mean find any of the others she'd been traveling with, Waters, Chase, Drinian, or maybe her apprentices. It could mean the trees. That felt closer, except that she knew it was something else. Something highly specific, something urgent. Wondering what Synesis meant was pointless. She could find nothing in this place.

CHAPTER 19

CHILDREN OF THE FOREST

Despite the speed of shift travel, some places were distant enough to take days, others only hours. Three hours wasn't a high price to pay for travel from one star system to another, but this one felt like an eternity. Any measurable length of time has landmarks and recurring cycles, the rising and setting of a star, waking and sleeping cycles, the taking of meals. There were none of these for Quin, just the increasing urgency of that single imperative, arising for some unknown reason from Synesis and sending a cascade of chemical signals through her whole body. Run, climb, fight, search—*find them*—but she could do none of these things and so she closed her eyes, counted breaths, ran her ungloved hand down the marred but still velveteen back of her companion symbiont until she arrived at her destination with a subtle brush of nausea and vertigo.

Before she could orient herself, she saw the ships,

three of them, descending into the thick atmosphere of the forest planet ahead of her own. The thrumming command that beat inside of her like drums across a great expanse became a roar. There was no going faster, no overtaking them. All she could do was master herself and wait.

They might burn up in the planet's atmosphere like tiny fragments of debris, those small ships carrying the intent to thwart, to dominate, to harm. She flinched at the violence of the fleeting wish.

The fiery glow of friction against their hulls as they descended ahead of her only enhanced the adrenalized beating of her pulse. She unfastened her straps as soon as her own ship set down, pushed past the roar of redistributing blood flow that came with the settling of gravity around her.

"Merde!"

The ships were open. Obvious footprints from several pairs of booted feet led from the capsule shaped vessels into the forest. She ran back to her own ship, stumbled but caught herself with the rail on the side of the short ramp. They might be out-numbered, if not they were figuratively out-gunned. This unit wasn't armed, and hadn't been for decades, but even peace-forces were trained in inflicting violence when necessary. And Mara—Commander Lariat— wouldn't be here if she didn't think violence was necessary. Quin grabbed the radio from the control console and took it with her. Messages flashed on the record.

She played them now, unable to run full speed once

the waves of nausea and vertigo descended in earnest— even a few hours in space and reentering a planet's atmosphere meant surrendering to the blanket of stabilizing gravity and the redistribution of blood and lymph in her body.

"I don't know where the hell you've gone but Lumina has contacted one of the mother trees. She's— not making much sense. So maybe get back here. We need you *here*." It was Chase's voice, passion cloaked in careful tones. But as the second message started, that caution, holding back to shield the listener, gave way to sharpness, urgency that just didn't have space for gentleness. "I don't know how long she can do this— how long you stayed in conversation with these trees when you made her, but I won't let her do it alone anymore. You need to come back and finish what you started, Quin."

Quin stumbled again, put out a hand out to catch herself and felt the bark of a young tree catch her. She bent double and vomited whatever was left of the rations from the last time she ate, hours ago, days ago? She couldn't be sure, but it tasted of bile and nothing else as it burned her throat and coated her tongue. She sputtered, gagged again, but she didn't feel it this time. The tree had things to say to her and her hand was bare, ungloved as her mushroom had insisted they be. The voice was quiet, distant compared to a communication with the mother trees, but it was coherent, a pulsing cycle of understanding and there were echos of something familiar.

Lumina . . . Chase . . . She could feel them. Their thoughts were seeping into the mycorrhizal network of the forest. They were still connected, not damaged or deprived of their symbionts. She had to move, to get closer.

The nausea was gone, and lightheaded or not, she could move faster now. She ran, side-stepping and vaulting over fallen branches and logs encrusted in moss and fungus. The nerves in her bare hands tingled with the whispers of everything she touched in her path, but she couldn't stop to listen or to translate. There were voices in the forest, raised voices shouting, and she could hear the discord in their exchange rising, culminating in something—screams.

The clearing was just ahead. She wanted to be faster, needed to be faster. She was going as fast as her body could be pushed with no space for thought or choice, but there was space for self-judgement. A single core thought broke open her mind and leaked blame into her already overloaded amygdala.

I shouldn't have left! I shouldn't have—

Someone was screaming, a sharp persistent shriek of pain, or panic—like a rabbit caught in the talons of a falcon.

The largest trees were ahead, the understory sparse around the most massive tree and around it, bodies in conflict. ERF peacekeepers, seven of them in their foliage patterned uniforms grabbed hold of her apprentices. Waters fought them off. Jordan had one pinned against a tree, but Lumina was screaming. They had hold of her by the waist, another pried at her fingers to wrench her from contact with the mother tree and the commander was standing by, giving orders.

Quin saw red, all of the pain of self-blame shifting to be hurled at a new target. The commander didn't have time to turn before she had her grappled from behind. Quin, taller and with greater reach, swept the woman's legs from beneath her. She shoved her forward and pinned her beneath her wiry frame. "Di yo sispann— Call them off." The words came out a growl in the commander's ears. The woman struggled, spit leaves where her face pressed into them.

"You'll break my—ah . . . my neck—get off!"

"That's right. Das ist gut, das du verstehst. I will." Quin could feel it in her forearms, in the tightness of her jaw, that heated burning in her skull and the pulse of blood in her veins that called for an end to this. She could kill this woman, spill her blood into the loamy soil to fertilize the trees that her presence threatened. Something small and distant cautioned her. Killing would cross a line she couldn't recross, but she couldn't hold back or loosen her grip or the commander—Mara would feel it.

Lumina was still screaming, and they had Chase's arms strapped behind her back, a cut bleeding into one of her eyes. "Make them stop or I press harder."

The pain was enough to make the commander shake.

Quin thought she felt a click in the commander's mind, a pause, a shifting of gears and then the other woman, sputtered, choked out a command and the soldiers released their hold on Lumina and Chase. They stepped away from the others they were fighting to subdue and they pulled in, formed a circle with their backs to each other. Quin rose onto hands and knees with a grunt. She lifted the commander with her until they were both kneeling, her arm held around the bruised throat but looser. The commander was panting. Sweat made her throat slick. "You've stolen property, kidnapped recruits—"

"Discharged recruits—you discharged them, crippled them."

Mara's voice was low, a husky threat. "Their families have been informed of their kidnapping."

Quin's arm tightened reflexively. *Is this what we want?* She shook her head, eyes widening as she took in the sharp smell of sweat and fear on Mara. She dropped her arm and backed away and then crossed in front of the other woman to face her. "Tell their families that every one of my apprentices is here consensually, and we've healed them from the harm you caused."

Mara backed away a step. A sneer curled her lips as she rubbed at her reddened throat.

Quin held up her hands in peacemaking. "You came here to confront us, to force us. But that isn't what's going to happen."

"Why can't you admit when it's over?"

"Because it isn't. *You* might be done—and I think you shouldn't be—but I have sixteen people here who want to keep fighting the decline."

A sputtering laugh erupted from Mara's lips and she looked from one person to another, including Quin's group of renegades and her own peacekeepers. "Thirty years of the Interface project—fifteen straight with her working on it—and now she says with this little collection of trainees she'll keep it going single-handed. Is that the kind of logic that's keeping you all believing in your false prophet?"

Quin took a step back. A cloud of doubt swept through her with Mara's words, her scoffing tone. "No one calls me that but you."

"Because no one is ready to admit we're done. Earth, the trees you worship, it's all done."

Quin bit back a cutting response. There had to be something that would change the direction of their conversation, even if she wished the commander was still being kept silent by an arm at her throat. "Let me . . . show you at least. I've tried just explaining it, telling you what the trees say, but it's a paper cut-out comparison." Quin hesitated, doubts creeping in. Would it poison Mara? Could she be poisoned worse? Or was Synesis right that she no longer needed the gloves? It was all she had. "I could show you, with a partial link. Temporary, Drinian could fit you with a new implant stage—without a mushroom—and we could link."

Drinian was nodding from where he crouched next to Lumina, one hand on her slumped shoulder. She was still in communication with the mother tree. "Yes, that would be possible, simple, quick."

Something shifted in Mara's eyes, but it was fleeting. Temptation? Hope? It was no longer there when her eyes narrowed. Mara laughed again, more of a snort than a laugh and then she shook her head. "You think I'd let you make a puppet of me, for your fungus to marionette, the way you do to yourselves? No, thank you. And we'll be taking you all back with us for court-martialing."

Quin nodded. An opportunity had passed. If she was a puppet to her symbiont, then she was a willing one and there were things this woman would never know because of her bigotry. The commander had eyes on her peacekeepers again. She looked ready to signal and Quin could feel the tension baking off of them.

"You don't want to do that." She pulled the radio from one of her cargo pockets and held it up for all to see. "I've already sent a message to our friends on Genti-6 to be ready with news of our detainment for all of the colonies and what remains of Earth's officials. A peacekeeping and rehabilitation force turned militia."

Mara's eyes were wild, flicking from the scattered linguists to her own people and then back to Quin. She stabbed one finger at the air between them. "They don't interfere with our courts and discipline."

"They will if you do this—" Quin searched for more words, her palms were slick with tension and the phrasings of more languages than she could count were competing in her head. "You've shut yourself down. Put yourself into retirement and discharged us. What are you even doing here?"

Her last question hung in the air until Mara answered, her voice shrill. "Following through, tying up loose ends, because you can't just say you'll do something and then let it slide!"

There was a double meaning behind her words and they dug at Quin—*You haven't delivered on anything you promised*—But she could feel Mara's resolve slipping, hands shaky, eyes darting.

"Chér, you say that you are following through, finishing, but that is what you say you can't do. The interface project is what needs follow-through and you quit a long time ago—so just go and we'll finish it. Unless you *want me to show you*."

Quin stroked Synesis and smiled at the pseudopods waving like little arms next to her face. The commander shuddered, her face going pale.

"Then go." Quin took a step towards her and then another, closed the gap between them. The Commander stood firm. She shook with rage.

"Je suis désolé—for all of your losses—I'm sorry, your mother, this project, Earth . . . you can let go." Quin's voice was barely above a whisper, meant for Mara alone. She leaned in, her lips hovering above the commander's ear. "Go before there are more things to regret."

Mara turned on her heel and barked out several commands, to board the ships, set coordinates. The clearing emptied out. It would have been silent except for the shuffling of feet in the leaf litter and a soft keening that came from the base of the mother tree.

A wave of relief washed over Quin, her muscles tingling as some of the tension released. She searched for Waters and found him at the edge of the clearing. His eyes followed the departing soldiers through the underbrush.

"Follow them to the ships?"

He nodded, pressed a hand on her shoulder, and squeezed.

"See that they leave?"

He nodded again and then cracked a smile. "They don't have any other business here if they're done with us."

She placed her own hand over his and was startled by warm skin. She was still barehanded, no gloves between them. Synesis held her hand in place against her impulse to pull away, insisted again that the gloves were unnecessary. Waters patted her hand and then jogged after the peacekeepers.

Lumina was slumped against the tree, a humming vibration shaking her whole body. Chase was next to her, propped up between Drinian and Jordan. All of the other linguists crowded in, close enough to listen, to watch, but distant enough to avoid touching the mother tree. Lumina's seemingly permanent and intermittently painful demonstration must have sobered them and was serving as cautionary tale. Quin knelt down at Lumina's right shoulder and spoke softly. "Can you let go, Lumi?

Lumina's brows creased and she moaned something unintelligible. It sounded like something Quin had heard before, mind-babble trying to decipher and mimic Tree with words that couldn't do it.

"Lumina?"

"Ah, Quin there's um . . . well your friend—your—Chase. They pulled her off when she was in there with Lumi."

Quin's attention turned to Drinian, but it was a gradual transitioning. Lumina needed her attention, to feel for her level of distress, how much danger she might be in, but she hadn't forgotten Chase standing next to the mother tree, swaying, trance-like. "Mmmm. Well, Chase . . . Chase needs to go back in. She can bring Lumi out, and if she can't you can, like before."

Drinian shifted, cleared his throat. "Well ah—I tried already. You were gone a long time—day and a half? She's been like this the whole time, and I couldn't feel her through the Tree-speak because it was—"

"Chér—slow down. Breathe."

Drinian's sigh was a shuddering one. "Right, yeah—well." He rubbed water from the corners of his eyes. "Well, uh . . . I'm a bit of a broken record, but she's stuck in there—only said a couple things and I think—I think you need to—"

Quin squeezed her eyes shut and held up a hand, turned away from him. Sharp lights of fear in neon red and shadow were threading through her and twisting her gut into a tight knot. Jagged images of the Pain Trees with their repeating loop of imagery, broken off and decaying without new growth, flickered forth like slides on a projector sped up past a human's ability to process. It was hard to form words, to grab hold of them. She wasn't sure what would come out once she finally did.

"Where are the children?" She shook her head. That didn't make sense, something the Pain Trees had said, but it was disconnected from everything else and sounded like delirium. She tried a second time, pulling words from the center of calm that Synesis was weaving as quickly as possible. "Mwen—mwen pa kapab. Mwen pa—I can't." She opened her eyes and held out her gloveless hands. "Everything I touch is sickened. It came from the Pain Trees, I think, and I was just there again. If it gets into these trees . . . if it kills this forest, then I've done nothing—have nothing. There are small ones I touched on the way here. They will die like the others. But their connection was tenuous. The mother trees . . . I won't risk infecting them."

Drinian cleared his throat and looked around the circle of silent apprentices and then back at Quin. He set his jaw, pressed his lips together into a firm line. There was a shuddering seed of doubt in his eyes. "I'll ah—I'll try again, with her mother if you think we can, because well—I don't know Tree well yet. This mushroom and I have no practice."

He shrugged and gestured at his immature fungal symbiont, larger than the apprentices but smaller than hers. "I guess we've bypassed the learning, and the training wheels and—" His words trailed off into mumbles and he knelt down behind Lumina. His arms enfolded her as he reached for the mother tree. Her hands were scratched, bleeding from scrapes and cuts where she'd fought to keep hold. Drinian covered them with his own and wove their fingers together, against the bark of the sequoia. The change in him was almost immediate. His eyes rolled back, showing white. The lids fluttered half closed and his body slumped against Lumina.

Quin took Chase's limp hand from her side. Chase swayed back and forth to a rhythm only she could hear. Quin could guess what the song was, the All-Question and the answer, put into her head by the mother tree incomplete. She needed to see it finished. Quin moved her like a doll, brought her to her knees, then she kissed the back of her hand. She pressed the supple palm into the bark of the mother tree until she felt tension return to Chase's muscles and her hand gripped the bark on its own. The other hand came up to join the first and Chase shuddered. Her eyes, darker under the shade of the thick pine canopy, opened wide and flickered with awareness but not wakefulness. She was dreaming in Tree. Her back arched, and the dark waves of her tangled hair draped over the newborn mushroom on her back.

Quin backed away, crossed her arms over her chest.

"You're just going to let them do this? Just gonna come back when they called for help and put them back in there alone like they already were?" Jordan's voice was sharp with incredulity. Criticism was something she'd never been afraid of, especially with authority figures.

Quin covered her eyes with a weary hand and then turned to face her. "What, Chér, would you like me to do, eh? Poison the whole forest? Might as well cut it down while we're at it. One mother tree at a time and watch the saplings she is shepherding shrivel up and die next." She could feel something dangerous building inside of her with each word that erupted from her lips. She spit each of them, throat clenching, forehead hot and pulse throbbing. "If you know the way to do this maybe you can do it. Bury your hands in the soil, find roots—ask the forest why, ask why the trees are dying even still after I gave them the answers she gave me! Ask them and then listen long enough until you can barely catch breath—attende—careful not to drown in the answer, and then? Then you have to share it with the rest of the galaxy but without words, and in a language no one else speaks!"

Jordan's eyes narrowed but she took a step back.

"Go on! Ithhabi Chéri. And then you can tell me what I've done wrong."

"Quin? What are you doing?" The voice was distant, Waters coming back from seeing the commander off.

"Okay." Jordan blinked back tears, but her face was hard, her resolve harder as she pushed past Quin and grabbed hold of two other apprentices, Ithaca, and a tall, long-haired youth with a shell-shocked expression on their moon-shaped face—Ronin. "Come on, we know enough—crash course starts now."

She hovered her hands over the bark a few feet away from Lumina and with a head-tilt and quavering lips egged the other apprentices on. "Anyone not on this tree is a little chickenshit and not worth their implant. One . . . two . . . three . . ."

All of the apprentices were there by the end of her count. The numbers stopped as soon as her hands met the weathered red bark of the giant sequoia, but her slack lips kept moving, even as she slipped forward and pressed into the bark.

Waters cleared his throat. Her internal landscape, better since Synesis had woken from dormancy, was breaking apart in a cascade of chaotic half-thoughts and internal barbs of wordless self-flagellation. Even the act of taking a breath felt too treacherous to chance and so she sucked in air in short, measured gasps, heart pounding as her throat constricted tighter. What was this? Her vision was going dark—not spotty but inconsistent and she felt as if the rest would go at any moment.

Her mushroom was still there, but where were the soothing influxes of neurotransmitters? She should be swimming in endorphins, GABA, serotonin, something, anything. She put a hand out to steady herself but then pulled back and crouched instead. Trees, there were only trees to hold her up, and that couldn't happen.

"Are you sick?"

"I've been sick for a long time . . . still sick—I guess."

"Are you sick in the head? Damn—sorry Quin, but you just sent a bunch of children and one minimally experienced retiree into a download with a mother tree when you barely survived it sixteen years ago, well-trained. And well, you don't sound like yourself. The way you just tore into an apprentice—"

"Well, you haven't been yourself in years, Waters. You brought me in, pulled me back in and then you started quitting. You could have been commander, and you let her take it. And here we are."

A deep frown was pulling Waters' lips down, aging him. There was no fire in his eyes or his voice, just a firm resolve. "Thats right Quin. Here we are. Here I am. With you—and where were you a couple hours ago, if not running away? We could throw blame back and forth all night if that's what you need."

Quin's head was pounding, her vision swimming, and still no reprieve from Synesis came, instead there was that siren's call to reach her hands out, to dig under the leaves, to find roots. "No, I—don't want that but I—think I need to go again, somewhere I can't sicken anything."

Waters looked startled when she glanced up at him from the ground and tried to stand. "What? Where? The Pain Trees? That's where you were, wasn't it?"

She reached up for his hand but he wouldn't take it. Instead he crouched next to her. "I know that's where you go, and I know it's killing you. So you'll have to get there yourself if you're going."

The conflicting urges froze her in place—reach for a tree, any tree, or run for the ship. Shift to the Pain Trees and stay there this time. The thought put her back there in the swampy mire, bile threatening to come up her throat as the screaming trees forced their refrains of suffering into her. She would drown in it if she went back.

She shuddered and wrapped her arms around herself, rocked side to side unable to sit still with this feeling. Normally when she was feeling this way she would reach out. She would write to Chase and the act of writing soothed, even when Chase didn't answer. But eventually the silences grew longer, Chase's and her own, and the reaching was harder. *She's right there . . .* It wasn't a thought in so many words but a set of images forced into her awareness like a hand of cards, each of them things she'd shared with Synesis when she'd first grown in. There was the image she traced in the dark on the back of her eyelids before she slept, Chase under a birch sapling, her dark hair encrusted diamond strands in the rain that fell around them, and there was the brush of their hands against the tree's bark. There were more, but she didn't want to see them. She fought the stream of images.

Stop . . . please . . .

SHE'S RIGHT HERE.

I can't . . .

WHERE ARE THE CHILDREN?

We're waiting for you . . .

The last thought in her head was a startling one. It pushed her to her feet in search of a source as if seeing it could show her. It was not Synesis, but was coming from her. Quin strode to the mother tree and the circle of people who'd become silent extensions of it, crouching, kneeling, lying wrapped around the tree's base with their fingers locked to it. Silent extensions mostly, some were whimpering, others mumbling unintelligible things. It was Chase that drew her in with her whispers, too quiet to hear unless she leaned in. She had to come closer to hear it.

Chase's skin was blanched the way it did in the deepest sleep when her stillness made Quin want to feel for a pulse, but she wasn't still now. Her eyelids fluttered and her lips formed words.

"We're waiting for you. Please . . ."

"What?"

"It won't . . . won't stop until you come too."

There was a quaver in Chase's voice and deepening creases of pain around her eyes. She searched the rest of their faces, saw the toll this download was taking. Jordan's arms shook. Her head was tipped back in full surrender to whatever stream of knowledge the tree was imparting. Lumina's cry had softened, gone almost silent, what was left of it something between a repeating sigh and a pant.

"Merde! Merde—merde!" She looked up at Waters and shook her head. Doubts pooled where she'd erected a wall of determined certainty for so long. This forest was too important. She hadn't been able to prove she wouldn't damage it if she made contact, but everything was pointing towards one inevitable action—she could join or what—the forest would hold the rest of them hostage?

"Quin—"

"They're waiting—they need me to join in but what if it kills them all—makes them sick?"

He blinked back tears. "Well, then we reseed. We start over, start better, like you said in those, um proposals."

Quin tried to smile for him, but her face wouldn't obey, not with so many conflicting urges clamoring in her head. He read the proposals ... we could reseed—but thousands of years, hundreds at least, that's what it would take to have a forest of ancients like this. And their mushrooms, it could sicken them.

No. It will not. Reach them—dig. Death if you don't and pain—slow, fading, eating away—I'll grow into your bones.

The message came in flashes of vivid imagery. A threat or a warning. It pushed Quin over the edge of her endurance and she shoved her fingers into the soil at the base of the mother tree. She dug deep, scooped and gouged and pulled out handfuls of rich humus. There were truffles here, large tuberous fungal growths with thick webworks of hyphae growing from them and into the tree's roots. Quin wrapped the fingers of one hand around the hyphae and then reached over Chase's shoulder and pressed the palm of her other hand onto the tree's ruddy bark.

IT HAD BEEN SO LONG. There had been no intact consciousness she could speak with. The saplings she tended babbled like children, and spoke back what she taught them, a distilled, regurgitated version of what she'd learned from this very forest. And not even that since she'd sickened—after the Pain Trees. It was after— it was the Pain Trees, but it wasn't really. The realization was carried away as she descended deeper into the web of neural connections. It wasn't like it was before, that rushing outpouring of knowledge, of Tree-story. This was a careful, gentle flow and it wasn't permeating her headspace. It was dancing around her, whispering, massaging. She pulled away, not physically, mentally. She erected membranous barriers between herself and the mother tree.

I'm not well.

You're not well. Come . . .

It wasn't a command. It was a dialogue, an invitation. Quin felt her body shaking, full body trembling like a tuning fork struck hard against stone and she tensed against it. Too long. It had been too long. There was too much at stake.

She answered in Tree, in ancient imagery and allegory—fields of saplings overcome by fungal infections, others dropping all their leaves without explanation, all at her hand. Her body shook harder, but she pushed ahead—the forest needed to know and then maybe they'd let her leave to protect themselves.

The next images were harder to conjure. Her lips curled in distaste, a silent cry in her throat as she imagined and showed them Chase, Lumina, Jordan, the whole collective of her apprentices turning ashen grey with dry rot and crumpling into decay at the base of the mother tree. The sickness spread from their hands into the healthy layers of bark and cambium and it climbed the towering height of the tree's trunk high into canopy until she too crumpled. From there it infected the mycelial network into the whole of the forest. The final image was a jumble of jagged, tree skeletons sticking up from the ground like broken teeth. She finished the outpouring with a final shudder and then fell silent.

It was done. The story she told was vivid enough for her to believe it was now reality—that the telling of it made it manifest. She expected the silence that descended around her and she accepted it.

But the space cleared by the bulldozing effect of her story was silent and still enough for her to feel other presences. Each had their own thought-prints. Distant and dispersed in the forest, behind trees, with only their whispers reaching her.

Where are the children? It was the voice of the mother tree rising out of the stillness.

Yes, where are they? I'm only here so you'll let them out of this intact—it's too much.

It is so much—will you hear it now?

If you let them out—yes, I have heard it before.

You heard but you did not listen.

Quin's mind stuttered, stumbled over what felt like an accusation but also a realization, a pinprick of light on the ignorance she'd been fighting.

Tell them to go first.

The whispers grew louder and they had the feel of argument heard through closed doors. One voice rose in volume and then another. Someone waxed sarcastic. Silence again.

They are free to go. . . . They choose to remain and listen, to each other and to us.

Quin floundered. She couldn't force them out. Couldn't pry them away from the tree—but they might not be able to break away in self-preservation if it was too much. She hoped they could, but she couldn't know. Now that she was here she needed answers. It had to be enough.

Yes, fine. Just tell me what to do—tell us what to do.

It came on fast, not a drowning as before but a stripping away of the barriers she'd erected between her thoughts and the tree—trees—the whole forest, not just the trees, the mycelial network and the fungal consciousness it housed—It had a consciousness! Of course it did, the same as Synesis. If Quin was reacting with her body and not her mind, her eyes would have widened, blinked at the little effort it took for the forest to shatter her protective shell. And why not? They almost killed her with the flood of Tree-thought the first time she'd come here with Lumina still gestating in her AUC.

Lumina . . . A sequence of faces created of forest things, moss, lichens, twigs, and squirming crawling insects filled Quin's mind, they flashed in a repeating cycle, replaying, merging into each other, Lumina, Drinian, Jordan, Ithaca, Ronin . . . saplings from each orchard she'd grown and tended, interposed with the faces, her tame struggling trees, the flourishing ones in this forest growing at the drip line of their mother trees in mixed age clusters. Again, the cycles came faster, slowed, stopped. The Pain Trees flashed to life, stark against a setting sun, mature but stunted trees in unnatural fused clusters, forced by the capsules that held them prisoner for most of their growth. They were all the same approximate size and age, no seedlings, no saplings. Her own orchards again . . . all siblings of the same generation.

There was a pause and then the cycle started again, faster, slower.

Where are the children!

WHERE ARE THE ELDERS . . .

Quin was hot all over. Her skin must be suffused with circulation, sweat beading on her forehead but she could only imagine it. Physical sensation was distant now. It was another cycle. Like the All-Question and the answer, one and the same, the question and answer preceding each the other ad infinitum. It was the All Question! The Pain Trees, her seedlings in the orchards, and Lumina, these apprentices, all incomplete in isolation.

Oh . . . She couldn't breathe. That was familiar. Her body was there, at the base of the tree, but her mind was far, so far from it. Breathe, breathe.

Quin gasped, sucking in greedy breaths. Her skin tingled all over. Her face was wet with tears but now that she was breathing, conscious of it, she knew she already had been; it was only fear, an imprint from before. She could be mind and body all at once. Her eyelids fluttered and she pulled back from bodily sensation again. She kept hold of the thread of her breaths, in, out . . . repeat. She wasn't shaking anymore. She was listening.

She made a clumsy reply, stitching together the best phrasings for the concept she thought the forest was giving her. She mirrored it back like a small child parroting early language. *They, none of them have a continuation—a physical time-keeping—a 'where I came from', a 'where I'm going'.*

Yes.

Quin could feel pleasure, approval from the forest.

What isn't of a trunk, or a branch, or a root fades from notice . . . and in the forgetting they burn life. Ideas don't grow forest . . . blood and bone and flesh grows a forest. Young needs younger—in turn needs older.

They need saplings, seedlings, mature trees, ancients . . . all at once.

Yes, Present is blind of future—unless it sees through past. The thousand rings, the hundred rings, dozen rings . . .

D'accord, D'accord. But how do we give them this?

Quin flashed the denuded fields of Earth, long-since stripped of ancient trees but also their corpses and the mycorrhizal networks that linked them, and the colony planets had never had any of it. They were still trying to build biomes that could support trees.

There are none . . .

TAKE US! It was an imperative explained in detailed imagery. For every twenty take one, none together but scattered throughout the forest, old enough to carry the past and some that are older, declining. The dead can be taken whole or cut, the roots and soil around them and their seedlings, all together. *This was a blueprint, a plan she could follow.* The uprooted trees and soil would go to Earth, to Genti-6, and each planet that was ready for trees, ready enough . . .

But the ruthlessness of it turned her stomach, the graphic butchery like what caused the beginning of the decline on Earth—It was a risk and a sacrifice, but it wasn't the same as the clear-cutting, poisoning, and genocide of all but a few species—old Earth's legacy—it was the forest demanding this.

To spread . . . to continue . . . to help them . . .

I did try to teach them, to give them the question and the answers.

Had she forgotten too much, delivered it wrong maybe? The saplings had always forgotten after a while and yellowed more with each time they were taught and then grown forgetful, dropping leaves.

You tried to be the all-mother without roots in their ground or branches to shield, in the life of forest you are a blink, they can't see you.

I did what I thought you said—

But you alone? You were not alone before. You were many— we thought you were many but you have been just this one.

I was many?—Oh—I was many, Lumina . . . I had Lumina with me.

Where are your children?

Quin pulled up words to defend herself, it was what she did, there were always words to cloak herself in, in any language she needed. They didn't have the message to give the trees, Lumina was too small—she couldn't. None of them could.

Here they are.

And Quin felt them with her, no longer distant or whispering. They were attached, all of them, tiny nodes in the vast mycelial network. She felt their heartbeats quicken, relief. They felt relief. And laughter. They were laughing at her, no *with* her, because now that they were all here, sharing the message of a whole forest, a whole mycelial network, her reticence to let them do it, her terror of trying again herself seemed so small and so silly. They weren't curled up and strangled from the swift flow of Tree-speak. The all-consuming—eons spanning All-Question played in the background of their conversation like a sound-track and it hadn't flattened them or left them breathless or catatonic.

The forest felt Quin's question before she could formulate it—how was she so affected, barely able to take in what the children were so easily absorbing?

Before you were one and one. Now you are many . . . and one.

It felt unfinished to Quin, but the explanation stopped there as if it was enough—now you are many. A tree is always many, always connected and cooperating, of course that was enough answer. The answer she'd been fighting against for so long, afraid to need, afraid to reach out and find the offer of help an illusion, the connection forged too stifling, a poison, or her need becoming harm, a drain when she only wanted to give.

So she'd poisoned herself, become the poison. Quin walked the path of her slow decline, reliving it, sickening as the trees sickened, on a path of self-made isolation and instead of blame she felt . . . relief, the weight lifting now that she could see herself clearly in the link, a self that was separate enough for her to reach with mycelial hands and draw herself closer, bind herself to the others. Her breast heaved with tears, the internal storm too long withheld. It broke like the breaching of a dam.

"Quin?"

Chase was right there like a whisper against her cheek. She was a part of their collective. The others were just as close if she thought of them, but it didn't feel like being crowded or watched, it felt like encouragement, and shielding, as if their friends were holding cloaks around them to create a break from the wind.

"I am—here, Chéri mwen."

"Good." Chase didn't use words. Images were better —she could share decades worth in a matter of moments. They were young linguists together and Quin could see herself through Chase's eyes, perfect, quick-eyed and brave, but always gentle. Their experiments with connecting mycelium through their implants didn't cause obsession or a false sense of closeness. It was already there. Chase loved her—Their parting played in loss-tinted memories. Chase's feelings could not be mistaken in the link, the depth of her grief as palpable as that of the Pain Trees while Quin was in a coma—suffering, incoherent, then deathly silent.

Doubt took over, internal conflict, the decision to leave when it became certain Quin would die, or at least never wake. The news of her recovery was a flash of light like an exploding star and then the slow disappointment of expectations impossible to meet. Then Quin made Lumina, a gift of flesh and blood to love, a piece of Quin—and always letters, so many letters, each of them read more times than she kept count of. Replies, sometimes formulated and reformulated in her head and other times manifested and sent. Quin felt every word of those missing replies and with them the fears that kept Chase from sending, that she was a burden to her, that she would say too much or say it wrong, or that she would finally ask Quin to choose her instead—and they'd both regret it.

Lumina came closer in the link, her presence becoming a close, warm thing, shining into their collective awareness like a rising sun as soon as the thought of her arose. *Lumina.* Quin saw her clearly, without the distractions of their waking world and it shook her. It was an intensity of emotion that was too much to feel. It would obliterate her, like walking into the sun.

But it didn't. It was just Lumina, a child who had needed her, wanted her, had her–and still did–Chase's memories of Quin on Genti-6 replayed, holding a miniature Lumina, infant, then child. Quin's hand prying a lichen covered stone from a crevice for small hands to grasp, and letters full of Earth stories and old fables.

I forgot myself . . . addiction, familiarity . . . it was never those things. The words felt empty, hollow, falling away in the link like so much chaff in the wind.

You never said you didn't want me. Just things, changed. I needed you more.

Je suis ici . . . ich bin hier . . . mwen la . . . hineni . . . Here I am.

Lumina was smiling, glowing brighter under the attention and—the flow of story moved. Chase was leading them somewhere, pulling them forward until they saw new things, future things, a life intertwined instead of always passing, splitting, avoiding. Shared missions, compromises, partings, but always with the promise of reunion.

It felt—Quin couldn't help but smile—like after years of living and breathing the All-Question, dreaming it, writing it into her letters, struggling to hold onto and share it, Chase had grown roots and branches and become a tree herself and she was singing their own personal rendition. It was full and complete. It was more beautiful with each of the others there, all of them trees, nodes of the forest, feeling and embellishing their own parts of the story.

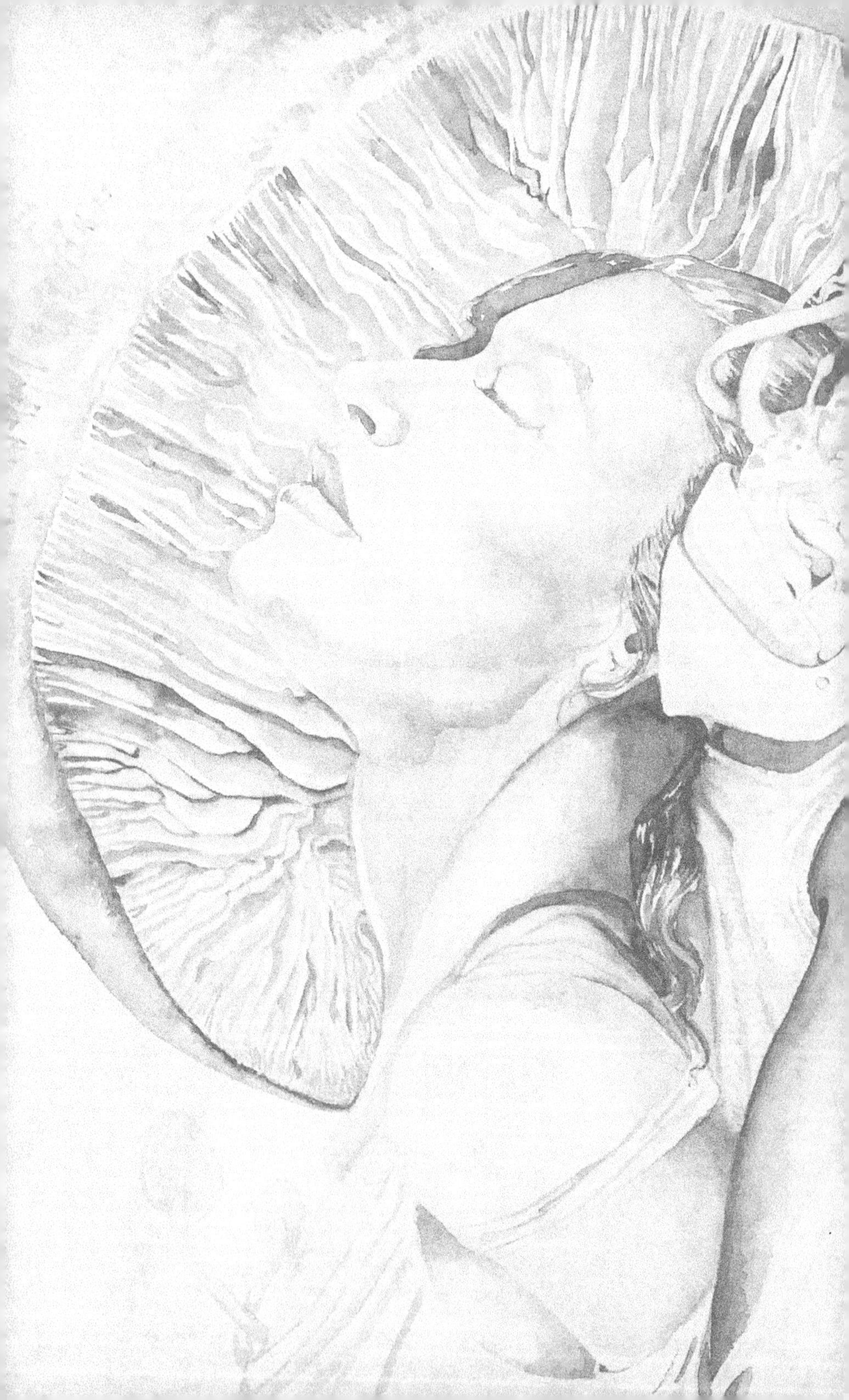

CHAPTER 20

HOMEWARD BOUND

They were close enough to Earth for a VR comm now. Quin could smell whatever it was that Inaya was cooking, but only because Inaya smelled it and the VR was picking up traces of those smells translated into electrical signals, something with cumin and turmeric, savory and filled with Old Earth nostalgia. Quin's mouth watered.

Inaya whispered to one of her children, there was a clink of serving dishes in the background and then the comm cleared, the room around them became sparse and tidy, old rugs well-beaten, restored to their original colors, shades of fuchsia, red, and indigo in shapes made of repeating petals, the tree of life . . . the seed of life . . . the fruit of life. Quin couldn't help but smile at the feeling of kismet, of cosmic connection and intentionality.

There were little fragments of the All-Question

everywhere she looked, now that she understood. Parts of the message had seeped into human consciousness long before the human race had come to a scientific consensus that trees and fungus had language, and knowledge that we might need. How long had the Earth been trying to tell them? If a handful of people, whole cultures, had been trying to share the All-Question since the beginning, how much longer would it take?

Inaya was waiting patiently, her arms crossed and eyes focused in that perpetually shrewd expression of a grassroots leader. Quin had come to expect that look from homeworlders.

"You did not call me to smell my curry and watch the children at lunch—or to tell me the ERF isn't done dipping its fingers into our business and telling lies. I know that much, so what is it? You want me to be more gentle in my refutations of their rumors?"

"None of those things. Lakin raihat al ta'am latheeth —khana bahut sugandhit hai—It smells delicious truly, but no, I have something for you—if I can use your old ships. We're close, Mars Base. I can take them and have them back for you today."

Inaya blinked twice, but otherwise her face was still. Whatever thoughts were in her head she was masking from the VR and Quin couldn't read her. Anxiety twisted in her gut but it was a fleeting, fragile thing in the face of the chemical ease Synesis shared with her in the afterglow of the forest. The anxiety faded but her attention held taut; this was the first step in a multi-term plan that would span ages. It was the first piece that needed to click into place. Quin regretted the tension between herself and the homeworlders. But regret was a waste, moving ahead differently was what they needed now.

Inaya looked up from beneath her brows and then tipped her head as if still deciding. "You can't be working with the ERF—they've denounced you, called for legal action against you. And the things they are saying . . ." She made a sound of disgust. "But the things you do—taking our resources to other worlds, spreading our seeds to these colony planets when the Earth needs all of that attention and more."

"On that we need to agree to disagree. I won't stop spreading trees, hopefully with more success now. But this time—this time I have resources for Earth."

Inaya's eyes widened and then narrowed again. "We need a full meeting, with other leaders present. What could you have for us?"

"More formal meetings, yes, collaboration, absolutely, before you decide on anything. But right now, I have what the forest thinks you need. Let me show you."

All it took was another nod.

Quin pulled the headset off to face the collection of linguists, her team, no longer apprentices after what they'd done together.

"Inaya was curious enough I think—to agree. She's still wary but willing. We need to head to Earth before she changes her mind."

Waters cleared his throat. "We'll need to do more

than VR comms and messages to make sure the governor on Genti-6 understands what's happening—I can do that."

"We're going with you, to Genti-6, I mean." Lumina and Drinian were sitting in a small cluster with, Jordan and Ithaca. She leaned forward. "It's my home still. I need to see to the trees if any are alive—and bring mother trees."

"Okay." Chase was nodding, a proud smile pulling at her lips.

Quin followed her gaze to Lumina, sitting tall and confident with her companions. Any visible uncertainty or confusion Quin had instilled about her burgeoning connections had vanished.

"Genti-6 then. Chase, you are going there as well?"

She shook her head. "We need to stay in groups, no one alone as long as there is any question of whether the commander will confront you again, or any of us. And I want to see Earth. I want to see it with trees. I want to see the start of it with you." Chase held her gaze and didn't drop it until a warm blush rose to Quin's cheeks.

Quin followed the look in those green eyes and leaned down to whisper. Her lips brushed Chase's cheek. "Kèlkeswa sa ou vle mwen pral ba ou."

Chase's blush deepened. "I'll remember that."

Haitian-creole was close enough to other languages, mostly French, but she couldn't remember Chase speaking her childhood language. Normally she had to translate when she spoke it to her, but the look in

Chase's eyes said she understood it well enough this time.

"Then Earth first, for larger ships, you three to Genti-6 and we'll follow with the trees after Earth has them. And Drinian?"

"Mm? Yes?"

"How quickly can you prepare more of Lumina's strain of mushroom?"

Drinian broke into a grin. "Oh, so fast—I could, well, it's actually already started, since the forest. I'm not so good at waiting."

Quin laughed. "I think we'll want as many as you can prepare."

"You're in trouble with that commander."

"What, ex-commander? She disbanded, sold out, shut down the whole she-bang." Paul Waters leaned back in a chair that he couldn't remember from previous visits to Gwen's office. It was awkward, the inventive design not quite fit for his bulk. He shifted, stood, and instead strode over to the couch Gwen was reclining on and sat on the edge, scooting her over just enough to fit.

She raised a brow as much at the liberty he took as at his words. "Not yet. She's trying to reinstate, claiming a galactic security threat posed by . . ." She smirked and patted him on the knee. "Radicals! And there are still groups that listen closely to the ERF and by proxy her—even with the ERF disbanding."

"Hm." It was more of a grunt than a word.

"I'm not exaggerating. She wants to clear-ground the homeworlders, ban them from interplanetary travel to stop their protests and she is building a case that you, Sgt. Fleury, and your band of zombie puppets—that's what she's calling them—are the next big threat. The decline is a done deal, she says. Fungal pollution is the new crisis."

"Well, she can damn-well shove her conspiracies and—"

"Tch-tch . . . Conspiracies or well-founded rumors?" She patted the cargo pocket of his pants. "What is this you've brought me again?"

He felt his skin heat and a scowl built an edifice of objection across his forehead. "An option, a safe and effective option for enhanced communication."

Gwen sat up and smoothed the tidy strands of silvery-grey at her temples, a leftover hallmark from before her longevity treatments were secured by a position in government. "Fungal implants, tethers, what did she call them? Puppet strings to these new trees you've brought in."

He growled in the back of his throat and stood. He rubbed a hand across his forehead and into the hairline that was reversing the years on his face as it filled out and darkened. "You know, I used to think that. Never took an implant all the years that I supervised the project and trained up the recruits but—"

"And now?"

"Now I'm taking one. Drinian has enough of these little vials for teams on every colony planet, a safer strain than the older ones, longer lived, and well . . ." He shoved both hands into his pockets, sat down next to her again. "No one's forcing it on you Gwen, but I think it's the right thing. The puppet strings are already there; maybe that's what makes us destructive. Throw an arm back, turn around, stumble, all the time knocking things over with those strings and we can't feel the fall-out until it's too late. Maybe the strings just need to be a little tighter." He pulled the vial out of his pocket and looked at the cloudy white contents in the light. He stood, ready to leave, and tucked the vial back in his pocket.

"You think I'm letting you leave with mine?"

He froze where he stood, eyes going wide in his face as a smile formed around questions. He waited. "Let me —leave, with yours?"

"A governor needs to be able to understand her constituents, and if I'm not mistaken, you've brought me a few new ones."

IT WAS A DISHEVELED, patched-together sort of forest, a Frankenstein's monster stitched from new seedlings, downy and full like green chicks with their feet in the soil, leafless orchard trees too thin for their age that were either dead or dormant and not much larger than the new seedlings, and interspersed among these youngsters no more than ten mature or nearly mature trees from the forest planet, tall enough to create a protective canopy along with the five ancients brought to serve as nodes of protection and learning. Massive chunks of decaying wood, logs and cut up stumps, some with their roots turned sideways and reaching across the forest floor like grasping, twisted fingers, turned the mismatched terrain into something that was far from the clean, orderly orchards and straight-lined forest replanting from Earth past or even the controlled groupings and tree-mixes of the more modern orchards that ecologists were beginning to create when the decline started.

They'd disturbed Genti-6's soil, pulled up and then mixed or covered it over with living microorganisms and specifically mycorrhizal fungus rich forest soil.

Lumina closed her eyes and dug her fingers into the soft rhizosphere at the base of the tallest of Genti-6's new mother trees. "Are you coming?" Her voice was impatient, already softening and growing distant as her mind merged with that of the tree. "I want to see if they're waking up the orchard trees that look dead."

She heard Drinian's footsteps crunch against the leaves and she felt him crouch next to her, felt the light rustling of leaves as he dropped the bag of spawning equipment he carried at her feet. But then his voice was closer than expected, facing her.

"How do I say, I'd like to kiss you in Tree."

"Ask this one I guess." The answer sounded silly

after it left her lips and she pulled back from the connection just enough, opened her eyes. "Oh."

Drinian was leaning back against the bark of the tree, facing her. "Ask the—ask the tree? I think that was just—"

"You weren't serious. It was like ah . . . a way to ask." She scrunched her nose and tilted her head, uncertain why they were still talking instead of kissing.

"Hmm . . . yes—yes, that one. An ice-breaker. But I could, well we could ask her." He looked up at the tree's prodigious height and squinted at the scattered sunbeams that caught him in the eyes.

"Sure." Lumina leaned forward and pressed her fingers deeper into the mesh of mycelium under the soil, she liked that closer connection. "Come on."

"Come on the kissing or—?"

"Come on let's ask, see what the trees say."

She closed her eyes and smiled as Drinian's hands joined hers under the layers of humus, tying around and in-between like roots themselves. He was there in her mind, standing under a forest canopy that covered the whole expanse of the sky, ancient trees all around them, bushy saplings tickling their arms and faces.

"I think—" Lumina traced his cheek with her fingertips testing the answering warmth, the odd sensation of wants, and questions, and answers leaping across the barriers of skin. That was the first answer. "I think the trees say it the same way—chemical messages, pheromones. Hey, I can feel the new growth! Mycelium is fast—"

"Fast, yes. I think in a few days, if they can wake them, we'll see new buds—"

Lumina felt for her physical body. Her chest rose and fell in sleep-like respiration and slowly, slowly, she leaned forward until Drinian's face was there. Now that she was in-touch with her physicality she could move without breaking the link.

She found Drinian's lips and kissed him. Slow surprise and pleasure spread into their connection through the tree's mycelium. Then he leaned into the kiss. It was soft and languorous at first, electric, as the heat blossomed and shifted across the mind link, a prismatic light show they could watch, and also feel in a multitiered feedback loop.

They felt each other's thoughts and emotions as they arose in the link, new colors in the figurative sky, images transposed over the feel of lips, mouths clinging and exploring, hands entangled and grasping still linked in the soil. Their touching was light on leaves.

"Lumi?"

"Mm?" She caught her breath and then caught another kiss, too quick to be anything but a breathy tease.

"This is . . . all ah—mediated by our symbionts, the trees, possibly the urge to uh—kiss triggered by dopamine, oxytocin, serotonin, released by the mushrooms instead of our own hypothalamuses."

She didn't pull away or recoil. She stayed close enough for their lips to touch between words. "Doesn't matter."

"Doesn't matter?"

"Doesn't matter. We're both . . . *all*. I get it now. It doesn't matter how I know you . . . like you. Just that I do." The concept was bigger than words and she stopped trying. Instead, she lapsed into Tree so that it came across as a whole concept that filled all of their senses, cells of like and other mingling, sharing, merging into colonies where each took on a role, protection, nurture, structure . . . colonies where the parts could only be explained by the systems they formed with others. Fungus and bacteria, tree and mycorrhizae, body and bacteria, ecosystem, star system. *It's lichen. It's all lichen.*

Drinian smiled against her lips as they took turns adding to the shifting imagery along with the tree. Their mushrooms added thought and meaning, bright notes of agreement.

"Mmm . . . biomes. And Jordan? You were worried about Jordan, confused."

"I like Jordan."

"Me too."

"I know, because she's a part of us." She sighed and pulled her hands out of the soil gently, detangling them from the mycelia and brushing away the chocolate cake crumbles of soil from her hands. She sat back, faced him and then looked up at the high branches of the mother tree against the wisps of high clouds moving in. It already felt fresher here under the trees. They were changing the microclimate. It would continue changing as the trees spread.

Earth

Homeworlder Headquarters

Back to back they could see the ships coming in on opposite sides of the horizon.

"It's like the sky's on fire."

Quin smiled but didn't turn. Their symbionts had reached across the small gap between them and were twisting hyphae together. The contact sent sparks of Chase across the tenuous connection. She leaned back, and felt Chase do the same, nestling into her until the curves of their backs fit together. Chase was happy, not restless, not thinking of being anywhere else. That much came across with clarity, and Quin marveled at how enmeshed their feelings were, like mirrors, or halves of the same fruit.

The ships were coming down on the landing pads now, great hulking things from a time long past, when humans traveled heavy, hoarding resources and possessions as if matter was finite in a galaxy. The universe had only just opened up to them through shift travel. Even the ships were resource hoards, the material used to make them, ten times what was actually needed for a quick shift across a few astronomical units. But these were serving their purpose now, or their final retirement if it worked. There were whole forests on board.

Quin tried not to disturb the delicate hyphae webbing between them when she turned. She settled next to Chase, but the height difference wasn't helping.

Chase snorted at her and settled into the crook of her arm, pressed into one side. "What are you doing? We're going to trip each other."

"You object?" It was a genuine question. Their closeness felt as new as it did ancient, and it was still shifting, still evolving since they'd left the forest.

"We'll see if I object to spitting dirt when I fall, but this?" She snuggled in closer and wrapped one arm around Quin's waist. "No, this is good."

"You won't trip because I'll catch you, with just this one hand, see?"

Quin lifted her against her side with one arm, just enough to walk two steps carrying both their weights and then released her, laughing, stumbling but catching them.

They could hear the grind and thrum of heavy parts moving, the bulk of the ships shifting as the cargo doors creaked open. A crowd had formed and by the time Quin and Chase arrived, a veritable swarm of bodies surged at the fences around the landing pads. Their clothes marked them as homeworlders. There weren't many others left on Earth, and these ships were coming down in one of the homeworlder metropolises, or what would be one with more resources and support —with the cargo they were carrying on these ships. For now, the place was a rural ruin-scape of stripped buildings, hollowed out of all precious resources, some knocked down for more thorough harvesting. What they were building—planning to build—would put Old Earth to shame, dwellings that would tower and merge with a canopy of trees and suspended walkways that left the ground free for forest to reclaim, all of it grown from dense fibered fungus programmed with structural plans. It was a stretch without funding, but Quin could see it happening if the forest regrowth worked.

The homeworlder city plans were at least two-thirds of what had Chase excited and willing to leave Genti-6 in other colonist's hands—for now.

The doors opened downward and the air around them changed. First came the smell that gusted out over the crowd, humid and oxygen rich. It was the smell of growing things, the sharp tang of conifer needles crushed between curious fingers. There was a fungal scent like freshly unearthed tubers, decomposing leaves and earthworm-turned soil, all of it melding together into something that had left human memory a few generations before but remained in story. It smelled like forest.

Inaya was several yards away and heading towards them through the crowds of excited onlookers. Her sari flashed gold and blue around her ankles.

"You did this? Took them from the seeded planet?!"

Quin nodded slowly, puzzled at her reaction. "Yes . . ."

"And will they live, or is this a side show, like handing us cut flowers?"

"The plan is for them to live. Most of them. Some were already dying, and they'll impart their knowledge and their nutrients to seedlings here."

"Arrogant! To plan and take and think you know." She looked into the gaping maw of an open cargo bay at the shadowy shapes of towering mother trees.

Quin cleared her throat and then ducked her head towards the trees. She shook her head at Chase who looked furious and on the verge of tears. "Inaya, This isn't my plan. This is the forest's plan."

"Because you say it is?!"

"No. Not just me. There were many of us there listening. The mother trees asked us to do this, so they could reseed Earth. They want to spread, to go on, to help us."

Inaya's eyes softened but they still held an edge of shrewd caution.

"You could hear it for yourself." Quin pulled out a vial and pressed it into Inaya's hand. "Ask them yourself. My technician can set you up with a translator, we can teach you, or the trees can."

Inaya stared at the unexpected vial a moment longer and then tucked it into a fold of her clothing. "We have scientists here on Earth, our scientists. You're giving me this? Because my people could replicate it, and the ERF—"

"Is no friend of ours."

Inaya's eyes widened and then she smiled. She

turned to the crowd, lifted an arm over her head and gave the signal Quin recognized from homeworlders who were being forced to clear a protest.

"Find your teams. We need to get these trees into the ground!"

Chase found Quin's hand and squeezed it. "You just gave that to them? What about, I don't know, all the tests and protocols, compatibility."

Quin shrugged. "They'll let us know if they want help. The more people who can understand the better. We've had trouble seeing eye to eye, and I think we need a mediator. The forest can do that."

The End

ACKNOWLEDGMENTS

More Than One is a story of learning to share the burden and to trust, and it is a story of found family, something I couldn't write without my growing collective of loved ones, some born to me and some found and adopted.

This story started as a dream wherein two friends estranged by distance, but not in their hearts, chose to create a special child of their combined genetics. From there the story merged with another that was brewing in my mind about learning the language of trees and using what they taught us to stop the gradual destruction of our forests.

I could not have written More Than One without the inspiration of my friend Piper Lovemore and her philosophy of being the change and the love that the world needs.

My mentors are the old growth forests, the mother trees, the great nodes of connection that share their resources with us younger trees, the saplings and seedlings. My father John Fors and my mother-in-law Patricia Hankins. My mentors, Kevin J Anderson, Gwyneth Gibby, Allyson Longueria, James A Owen, Mark Leslie Lefebvre, Mia Kleve, who all helped me with either publishing, marketing, editing, or cover critique.

The forest needs every generation of growth equally, and so I am equally grateful to my ARC readers Carrie Christopher, Wayland Smith, Amanda Lyons, Ian Strandberg, Magnolia Peggy Bushnell, Carmen Mason, and Beowulf Newman. My words would fall into dry soil if not for my readers. And so I must thank the eighty-eight special individuals who backed my Kickstarter. Your belief in me made this project more epic than it could ever have been without you.

My family of Fantastic Fors(and Newmans and Crawfords) are my circle of strength. They are the canopy that shields me and the trunks and boughs that support my growth just as I am theirs. Jason P Crawford, Aaron Fors, Angelique Gunnels, Jentina Grey, Alexis Fors, AnnElena Fors. Thank you, my loves. And the youngest of my family, the saplings, Ishmael , Beowulf, Odysseus, and Lilith Newman, you are the future.

ABOUT THE AUTHOR/ILLUSTRATOR

An artist of multiple mediums, CL Fors is a modern day renaissance author, illustrator, publisher, artisan dragon who creates to defend and uplift a world of hope and infinite possibility for all.

Cherrie is currently working on her first graphic novel, a science-fiction tale of a genetically engineered bat-piglet who escapes the lab and discovers the meaning of found-family.

You can find her work at her websites, socials, and her Patreon all listed below. You can subscribe to her newsletter for sneak peaks and freebies.

Newsletter: tiny.cc/clforstaproot

Website: www.clforsillustrator.com

Website: www.clforsauthor.com

facebook.com/CLForsauthor

instagram.com/c.l.forsauthor

bsky.app/profile/clfors.bsky.social

patreon.com/OrionsFlight

ALSO BY C L FORS

THE PRIMOGENITOR SERIES

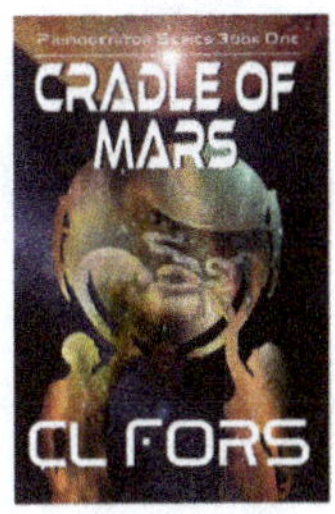

Cradle of Mars

Breach of Mars

Crowning of Mars

Futures of Mars

SHORT FICTION

Leeches (The Vampire Survival Guide: An Anthology for
Cautious Immortals)

Out of The Woods (Weird Wilderness: A Cryptid Bestiary)

ALSO BY EPITOME PRESS

 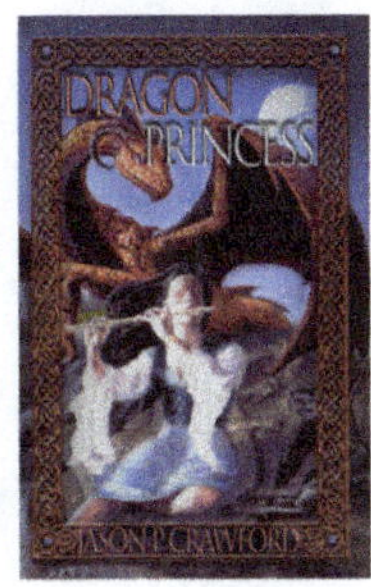 

Chains of Prophecy

Dragon Princess

The Drifter